HIS HELL GIRL

VERONICA LANCET

PREFACE

ARC VERSION

Dear brave reader,

You must be truly courageous to open the pages of this book.

THIS BOOK IS DARK. And by that I mean, it's super dark (but it's also cute and romantic). There is gore, lots of gore, some questionable romantic cannibalism, obsessive love interests and **VERY** disturbing scenes.

This book isn't your regular dark romance either. It has sci-fi and PNR influences and treads the line between contemporary and speculative fiction. So you must be able to suspend your disbelief at times. (Not when it comes to the love story, though, because who doesn't want a sickeningly sweet love story like Vlad and Sisi's?)

SO KIDS, DON'T TRY ANY OF THESE SCENARIOS AT HOME, ALL RIGHT?

This is your warning to turn back, or you will not be able to unread the things you read next. You will be grossed out. You will probably have nightmares. Not worth it if you ask me. So close the book and save yourself the trauma.

But if those warnings only made you more curious, then welcome to the dark side, friend.

Enjoy the mayhem!

FULL TRIGGER WARNINGS

animal abuse

blood (gore)

blood play

cannibalism

consensual non-consent

death

derogatory terms

descriptive CSA

descriptive rape

drugs

guns

human experiments

extreme graphic violence

extreme graphic sexual situations

extreme depictions of torture

grooming

kidnapping

knife play

miscarriage

murder

non-con/dubcon

primal play

self-harm

substance abuse
suicide
uncomfortable religious situations

1

SISI

AGE EIGHT

I swallow hard. My throat is sore, my breathing too harsh, but I can't stop now. I run to the best of my ability, knowing exactly what awaits me if I'm caught.

The buildings of the convent close in on me, and I wildly look around, searching for an exit. When I see none, I do the only thing I can think of… I enter the church.

Heavy steps resound behind me, a sign that they're not far behind.

I zone in on the confessional booth, and I swiftly open the door, cramming myself inside. One hand goes to my mouth and I try to regulate my breathing, so that no one can hear me.

My pulse is through the roof as fear overwhelms me, especially as I hear the screechy noise of the church door being opened.

They're here!

I hear their footsteps as they search the aisles, their voices loud, the echo reverberating in the building.

"I saw her enter here. She must be hiding somewhere," one of them mutters, annoyance dripping from her tone.

"Assisi! Come out! The more time we waste searching for you, the angrier I will get, and you won't like me angry," Cressida, my personal nightmare, yells.

A few years older than me, Cressida has always had something against me. It's rare that I get a day without someone saying or doing something to me. And usually Cressida is the mastermind behind all of my misfortune. I don't know what I've done to her to hate me so badly.

Although I've been at Sacre Coeur since birth, Cressida only came here a couple of years ago. She'd been abandoned by her mother on the convent's doorstep.

I know very well what it's like to be abandoned, since my own family left me in the care of nuns when I was mere days old, a fact which has been drilled into my head by the older nuns from the beginning.

God forbid I forgot just how unwanted I'd been.

Even so, I'd never taken out my anger on others. Not like Cressida.

Since she'd arrived at the convent, she'd become some kind of leader for the older girls, and they enjoyed nothing more than picking on others.

Because I was already ostracized by the older nuns, I'd been the perfect target for their taunts and punishments.

It's not enough that I have to withstand everyone's whispers that I'm the devil's child, or the fact that no one would willingly associate with me, since I bring bad luck. No, Cressida and her gang of mean girls had to resort to corporal punishments to make sure that my life *is* a living hell. After all, it's a fitting fate for the devil's child.

"Check the back, I'll check the front," Cressida orders them, and then I hear shuffling.

Their steps are coming increasingly closer to my hiding place, and my body is already quivering with fear. What they will do to me when they find me… I don't even want to think about that.

This week, one of my chores had included working in the kitchen, so I've been helping some of the other nuns with the preparation of the food. I thought it would be easy enough, since I could chop vegetables and peel potatoes without interacting with anyone. That's always my perfect type of chore, since no one will be able to pick on me in any way.

This time, however, it hadn't worked in my favor.

Somehow, Cressida had gotten sick from yesterday's lunch. Somehow she'd found out that I'd helped with the food, and in her mind, I was already guilty. I'd contaminated the food with my filthy hands and for that I needed to pay.

Following Cressida's mysterious sickness, a few other girls had fallen ill, and so I'd become the center of everyone's scorn—again.

More noise alerts me to their movements and they seem to ransack every part of the church.

Please don't find me… Please…

I still have the scars from my last encounter with Cressida. My knees had been so badly busted, I'd limped for two weeks. And that had been merely for meeting her eyes. She'd called me impertinent and proceeded to show me *my place.*

I don't want to imagine what she'll do to me now that she thinks I did something to her food.

"Do you really think you can hide?" Cressida's snide voice resounds right before the door of the confessional rattles under the force of her kick.

I scoot further back until I hit the wall, the old wood of the confessional creaking.

"Got her." Cressida smirks in amusement as she wrenches the door open to look at me with malice in her eyes.

A breath catches in my throat as her hand goes straight to the collar of my uniform, tugging me forcefully out of the booth and thrusting me to the ground.

My limbs are trembling as I see the other girls assemble around me. I try in vain to scramble back and find some way to escape them, but as they form a closed circle, I realize I can't do anything but suffer whatever they have in store for me.

"Look at her," one of them snickers, her foot making contact with my arm. I immediately wince in pain, trying to move out of her reach.

"Don't," Cressida's arm shoots forward to stop her. "Remember what we discussed. We won't solve anything if we beat her."

My eyes widen at her words, and I'm about to sigh in relief, but then she continues, and her words make me shiver in horror.

"We need to cleanse the sin from her." She smiles insidiously as she looks at me, and the other girls immediately agree.

It's not as if I haven't heard that before, since Mother Superior herself takes me weekly for a private prayer session to cleanse the sin from me. Since I was born with a red mark on my forehead—the Devil's mark—it seems I am bound to be sinful. But while I'd agreed to follow Mother Superior's advice to rid myself from evil, thinking it would make people accept me, I'd never truly agreed to her method.

Because I don't think there's anything wrong with me…

Now, staring into Cressida's eyes, I am terrified of what will happen to me.

"No, please," I whimper, but the girls are already on me, one on each side, grabbing one arm and one leg, taking me toward the altar. Cressida is trailing behind us, barking the instructions.

Removing all the Holy items from the table, they place me on it, quickly securing my limbs with some rope. I try to kick at them, but their nails dig painfully in my skin, and I find that I'm no match for them.

Not when I'm outnumbered.

When I'm mobilized to the table, the girls take a step back, letting Cressida pass as she comes by my side.

"I don't know why they would keep someone like you here. It's clear that you spoil everything you touch," she says, the corner of her mouth curling slightly.

She takes the Bible from a corner, opening it and reading a verse. One girl brings a container full with water and at Cressida's nod she pours it all over my face.

I blink twice, shocked at their actions. They keep pouring water over my face until I'm choking and sputtering.

"Deliver her from evil." I briefly hear Cressida's voice boom in the church, but my focus is on moving my head around to avoid the water getting in my mouth or nose. But the rhythm at which they are emptying the container on my face makes it hard not to swallow some.

"Stop," Cressida says, narrowing her eyes at my wet face. "This isn't working. I can still feel the evil radiating off her." She feigns consternation as she looks at my terrified expression.

"We need to make sure her entire body is sanctified." She instructs the girls, and they are quick to obey, stripping the clothes off my body until I'm left almost naked and shivering on the altar table.

Cressida keeps laughing, my torment seemingly feeding her mirth.

They keep on throwing water on me, and soon my teeth start clattering from the cold.

"Poor Assisi, she must be freezing," one of the girls comments, and they all start laughing.

Coming around the table, her hand grabs at my hair, tearing my updo, so that the strands are spilling down.

"Hmm," Cressida starts, her eyes sparkling with interest. My eyes widen as she comes closer, her gaze on my hair.

Please, no…

Although I know I'll never be pretty with my tainted face, my hair is the only thing remotely appealing about me. It's also the only thing I've taken great care of, making sure it's always combed and clean. And I've been growing it for years now.

As I look at Cressida assessing my hair, I already know what to expect. And it's killing me.

"Please, anything but my hair," I whisper, hoping to appeal to some humane side of her. But as she rummages the altar for a knife, I realize there's none.

"Pretty thing," she notes, "for someone like you."

She wraps her hands around the length of my hair, tugging it downwards until my scalp burns in pain.

"Don't worry," she whispers in my ear, "I'll give you what you deserve."

Holding tightly onto my hair, she uses the blade to cut through it.

I try to struggle against my holds, tears at the corner of my eyes as I will everything to be nothing but a bad dream.

But it's not. And as I feel the blade increasingly closer to my head, I know that the battle is already lost.

I still, my eyes blank, my tears spent.

Why? Why me?

There's no one to answer my questions, or even my deepest wish to be left alone.

No, the torment continues when Cressida gets up, smugly holding on to my long hair in one hand and waving it in front of me.

I stare bleakly at my most prized possession, now not mine anymore.

And to continue the disrespect, she flings it to the ground as if it were trash.

A sob catches in my throat as I look at my precious hair now lying on the cold floor, and suddenly I'm resigned. What can be worse than that?

What can they do that will hurt me more than having my only thing of value viciously ripped from me?

But as I watch Cressida move around with her band of girls, I realize I may have gotten ahead of myself.

It's late afternoon, already dark outside, and the church's

only source of light are the candles placed around the altar and down the aisles.

Each girl grabs a candle, and they surround me again, whispering some sort of prayer in tandem.

I'm confused as I watch them, but soon it's clear what Cressida has in mind.

"There's one way to make sure the devil stays away from your body." She smiles down at me, tilting one candle until the hot wax makes contact with my skin.

The other girls do the same thing, and they drop hot wax all over my body. Each time the wax touches my skin, I feel a burning sensation until it cools down and hardens. But time after time, the pain becomes increasingly unbearable.

"Now, girls," Cressida finally speaks, lifting a silver cross necklace and holding it by the chain, "let's make sure her body is properly cleansed of evil," she continues, the evil she so speaks of staring me right in the face.

My head hurts from prolonged exposure to pain, but as I see all the girls holding their candles under the cross, the fire heating the metal, I start shaking my head, willing my limbs to move.

Cressida's grin intensifies, and she moves the little cross up my chest until it's over my heart.

"Please don't," I beseech her, imploring her with my eyes. She just laughs.

Smugly, she presses the cross to my skin, the burning sensation unlike the one from before. My mouth opens on a low moan, my eyes tearing up from the intense pain.

She pushes the cross into my skin until it melts, giving way to the design to be forever embedded in my flesh.

I'm shivering, on the verge of fainting as she keeps on applying pressure, the hot metal wrecking me.

I don't even realize when she takes it off. I don't even feel when the bounds on my legs and wrists are unfastened.

I sit there, naked, in pain and alone.

The girls are long gone, but I barely find it in myself to stand up and pull my clothes over my aching body. It's like time stops. I don't know how long it takes me to get my bearings, or how I exit the church to head to my room. I hold tightly to what's left of my hair and I hide it in my pouch.

Then, I try to limp back to my dorm.

It's purely by chance that I see sister Celeste on my way back, and for the first time, I open my mouth.

"Sister Celeste," I start, my lips quivering until I start bawling, telling her everything that happened to me. "Why? What did I do to deserve this?" I ask her, hiccupping from too much crying.

Raising my eyes at her, I'm met with a disapproving gaze. Not at all the understanding one I was hoping for.

"Assisi," she starts, her tone stern, "I can't believe you would make up such strange stories about your sisters." She shakes her head at me, tapping her foot anxiously. "You're always getting in trouble, one way or another."

Me? I'm always trying to avoid trouble. How is it my fault that everyone hates me?

I open my mouth to say just that, but Sister Celeste speaks first.

"I don't want to do this, but you need a lesson. You can't go around accusing your peers of such heinous things. This is exactly why everyone doesn't like you."

I look at her in confusion, and it slowly dawns on me that *I'm* the guilty one.

"Come," Sister Celeste pats me on the back, steering me toward the west wing.

"But that's not my dorm," I whisper, almost wincing when she makes contact with my tender skin.

"You won't be sleeping in your room tonight," she says, and I frown.

I don't get to ask more questions as she leads me to a building I've never been to before. It looks older than the rest, and I get this strange feeling as we step inside. Goosebumps appear all over my skin, from the chilly air, or because I'm scared, I don't know.

Leading me down a narrow path, she unlocks a door with a key and pushes me inside. The room is bare save for a table next to the window.

"It's not the first time I've heard about you causing trouble, Assisi." She looks down at me accusingly.

"I've done no such thing." I try to defend myself, but before I know it her palm connects with my cheek and I fall to the ground, my eyes blinking rapidly the tears from the stinging slap.

"Sister Celeste..." I whisper, shocked at the turn of events. Isn't she supposed to be someone I can turn to?

But as I look at her, so smug, I see Cressida's expression in her and I know that she's just another bully.

And I'm the most hated person at Sacre Coeur.

Dragging me toward the window, she flings me about while she gets some items from the table.

I scramble back, scared of what she means to do to me.

"Assisi," she starts, and I freeze as I see what she has in her hand.

Soap.

"You must learn not to speak ill of your sisters," she repeats, kneeling down in front of me, the soap in her hand staring at me threateningly.

It's not the first time this has happened to me, and likely won't be the last.

But as she forces me to open my mouth, brushing the soap over my lips and making me suck on a small bit, I don't know what's worse—my blistering wound, the bubbles in my mouth, or the chemical taste that won't go away for hours.

She watches in delight as my face contorts, half in pain, half in disgust, continuing to force more soap on me.

More and more until I'm heaving on the floor. I spit and spit but the taste won't go away.

"Ungrateful brat," she says, her words biting. Standing up, she throws the soap on the table, giving me one last look.

"I hope after this you'll learn." She awaits for my answer, and I can only give her what she wants.

"I won't speak against my sisters again," I whisper.

"What's that?" she asks me to clarify, and I do. My tears are already dried as I give her the words she so wants.

"Good," she gloats, "now to make sure you will remember this," she raises an eyebrow at me, "you'll spend the night here."

She doesn't wait for me to reply as she leaves the room, the sound of the door locking, letting me know there's no way out.

I crawl on my knees until I reach the soap, my face scrunching in disgust, the taste still on my tongue.

But I'd learned something in my years in Sacre Coeur. Wounds fester and they get infected. And the burned cross on my chest won't be any different. I'm not even sure if soap will help, but it cleans hands, right? It should sanitize wounds too.

I wrap my fingers around it and lowering my uniform, I bring it to my wound, slowly rubbing it on it.

"Ahhhhh," my voice comes out in painful spurts, the sensation searing through me and bringing me closer to my pain threshold. But I bear through it, knowing that if this gets infected no one will help me.

I grit my teeth and hold my tears in as I wash what I can of the wound.

By the time I'm done, I'm sapped of all my strength and I collapse onto the floor.

It's dark… so dark and cold.

My teeth clattering, I turn to my side, wrapping my hands around my knees and folding my body to conserve heat.

2

SISI

AGE TWELVE

"Don't worry about me, Lina." I smile at her, leaving the clean clothes on the bed. "Take your time. I know it's hard for you right now."

"Sisi…" She shakes her head, and I can see the disappointment on her face. I don't have it in me to upset her even more, so I just pat her hand lightly. "Please don't worry about me. I have my friends, remember?" I continue to smile, even though the lie burns on my lips.

She slowly nods, traces of uncertainty still on her features.

"I'm sorry," she mouths, right before I leave the room.

I don't think I can sit there any longer, knowing that I could burst into tears at any moment. Lina's been my saving grace in this godforsaken place, but even *she* doesn't know the extent of what happens when I leave our room. And I *don't* want her to know.

I'd been lucky enough that Lina had beseeched Mother Superior to let us room together. But raising a baby has not been easy for her, no matter how much she tries denying it.

Claudia had been a welcome addition to our small unit, but it had also meant that Lina's attention had become focused entirely on her little girl. In a way, it's easier for me to avoid the questions in her eyes when she sees the bruises on my arms and knees, or the scars that have permanently marred my skin.

And besides, I'd developed an affection for the little girl too, and I'd never try to take away her mother's love.

Regardless of how desperate I might be for it.

Especially now that Claudia's been ill for a few days. I've tried to make myself scarce and give Lina some space. Even though it breaks my heart that I'm alone again on *this* day.

Heading to the back of the church, I go to the one place I know I won't be disturbed—the old cemetery.

It's a small area enclosed by an old, crusty fence. There are a few mausoleums that house some of the more eminent figures of Sacre Coeur, although to my knowledge, no one has been buried in this cemetery in a long time.

I head to the white marble mausoleum far in the back. Using a few pieces of wire, I open the door and sneak inside.

Last year, I'd found this place by chance. Cressida and her acolytes had been chasing me around the convent, and I'd thought that maybe they wouldn't dare step inside the cemetery.

But they had, so I'd improvised something on the spot, managing to open the door to the mausoleum and sneaking inside.

Since then, it has become my haven.

Inside, a tall coffin resides in the center, with a few items on the side. The rest of the room is bare, and spacious enough for me to hang around. I've even caught a few naps now and then, but during winter it's harder to sleep, since the floors get very cold.

I sit down, resting my back on the coffin, and I take a deep breath, willing myself *not* to cry. Not today.

Blinking twice, I look around, spotting some used but unfinished candles.

Maybe…

The thought spurs me into action, and I assemble some of the candles, looking for something to light them.

When I'm about to give up, I spot a small box of matches right next to the coffin. Taking it in my hand, I quickly open it to see a couple of matches left.

Yes!

I make quick work of the candles and I lay them in front of me, drawing my knees to my chest and watching the flames dance around.

"Happy birthday to me," I whisper, my eyes getting increasingly moist.

Using the end of my sleeve, I dab at the tears, telling myself it's not worth it.

It happens every year. Why should this time be more painful than all the others?

All the other girls get some type of birthday celebration. All but me that is.

Since the nuns say I'm the devil's child, they believe that the day of my birth wasn't a joyous event, but a cursed one. Why would they celebrate a cursed day?

So I've had to watch from the sidelines, year after year, how everyone gets their little day when they are the most important person. And I'm just forgotten.

"Why does it still hurt?" I ask myself, unable to answer the question.

Maybe it's because I finally found some type of acceptance with Lina and Claudia. Or because, once in a while, my brother, Valentino, remembers to visit me. I'd even met my other brother, Marcello, once, years ago. He'd been kind, yet distant.

Like all the others.

Staring into the candlelight, I muster the courage to make a wish.

I wish for someone to love me above all.

I decide to be selfish and ask for everything I want, knowing it's unlikely I'll get it.

I want to be someone's everything… Someone's reason for being.

Closing my eyes and picturing the warmth of that love —my soul suffocating from too much love—I blow into the candles.

Maybe this time will work.

I sigh heavily, knowing deep down that it's all for nothing. I wonder how long it will take for my hope to die? I have long years ahead of me in this awful place. Enough to sap even the last drop of hope from my spirit.

I wish I could at least understand *why.* Why had my family abandoned me? Did they also think I'd bring bad luck? That I'm so contemptible?

They must.

Resting my head atop my knees, I tighten my arms around my body, huddling myself into a small ball to preserve the heat.

It's getting late, and the nights are chilly, especially given the all-marble building.

Lingering just a little longer, I decide to head back.

I creak the door of the mausoleum open and I come face to face with my nightmare—Cressida.

"Told you she was here," one of the other girls speaks, her expression smug.

Cressida watches me with malice in her gaze, and I instinctively take a step back.

"She thought she could run away from us," she says snidely, looking me up and down. Most probably she's searching for the bruises from last time.

I shake my head, and I try to put as much distance between us as I can. I walk backwards until I hit the cold metal of the coffin, my hands latching on to it for support.

"Please. Just let me go. It's almost curfew time," I add in a small voice, hoping the threat of Mother Superior's punishment for breaching curfew would deter them.

"Assisi, Assisi, when will you learn?" She comes closer to me, her hand going to my chin to tip my head up, bringing my eyes to hers. "No one cares about you here. Mother Superior would probably give me a prize for showing you your place. After all, trash belongs only in one place," she smirks down at me, her mouth hovering over my ear, "in the trash."

She pushes slightly at my shoulder, but I no longer have anywhere to go, so I try to bypass her.

"Why are you doing this to me? What did I ever do to you?" My lower lip trembles as I imagine all the things they could do to me—already anticipating the pain and the humiliation.

"Why?" She laughs, slapping me once across the face. I quickly turn my head to avoid it, but the tip of her fingers still make contact with my right cheek. Her other palm follows closely, catching my left cheek with resounding force.

I wince in pain, and I lower my head, hoping that my subservience will make her take pity on me.

"Because I can. You're so pathetic, it's just too much fun to watch the fear in your eyes." And just to drive the point across she continues to slap me.

I put my arms up, trying to deflect some of the blows, but they still graze my skin, leaving a stinging sensation behind.

"Leave me alone!" I yell, unable to take it anymore. "Just… leave me alone." I swallow a sob, everything converging to an unbearable level.

"Girls, come see. Assisi talked back."

The other girls start laughing, coming closer and forming a circle around me.

"You want me to leave you alone, *Sisi?*" she asks, mocking the nickname Lina had given me.

"Leave me alone," I repeat, although the confidence from before is all but gone. With five girls surrounding me, what can I do?

"What do you say? Should we leave her alone?" Cressida asks and the others chuckle.

"We should. It's almost curfew anyway," another answers, and the others seem in agreement.

Squeezing my eyes shut, relief starts to fill me when I realize that they don't have the time to do more to me.

"You're right," Cressida says before suddenly pushing me to the ground.

Falling down, I try to scramble away from them, but one

hand motion from Cressida and the rest of the girls are on me, holding me down.

"We can't miss curfew. But *Sisi* can." She smiles insidiously, nodding to her friend to help her.

I watch in horror as they unlatch the lock from the coffin, both pushing at the top until it gives way, an opening forming at the mouth.

Terrified, I can only shake my head as I try to wrestle my arms and legs free of their hold.

No… no!

When the top is halfway off, Cressida scrunches her face in disgust, "huh, that smell…" Her face then slowly morphs into satisfaction. "Perfect for Assisi."

The girls start moving me around, and while I try to kick at them, nothing works.

I'm soon dumped into the coffin, my back landing on something hard, the sound of bones crunching, resounding in the small space.

I'm trembling from head to toe, but I don't dare move, for fear of what I might see.

"Sweet dreams, dear *Sisi*." Cressida glares at me smugly.

Just as it had been taken off, the top is slowly sealed shut, and the entire world becomes drenched in darkness.

I hold myself still, waiting for them to leave. I'll try to get out after that.

But just as soon as that thought crosses my mind, I hear the rattle of the latch. My eyes widen in disbelief.

"It's not real. It's not real," I whisper to myself. But as I move just one inch to the right and I bump into a hard object, it's suddenly very real.

"Calm down. I need to calm down," I say out loud,

hoping the noise will help me focus on something other than fear.

I breathe in and out as I let my hand roam around. I'd barely seen what was inside when they threw me in, and maybe it's better that way.

The smell is as Cressida had described… putrid. It's old and musty, and there's just something that makes me want to hold my breath in disgust.

I move around and I feel some type of material, as well as what I imagine to be bone.

Human bone!

Out of all the things they've done to me over the years, this has to be the most extreme.

Panic takes hold of me as I start imagining being forever locked in this coffin.

What if they take their prank to the extreme? What if they think that no one is going to miss me, so they just… forget me here?

It wouldn't be the first time someone's just vanished from Sacre Coeur and no one had batted an eye. There was Delilah, who'd only been here a year, and there were also the twins, Kat and Kris, who'd both disappeared at the same time. And *no one* had brought them up ever again. It was like they never existed in the first place.

And soon that will be me too.

The more I think of my bleak future, the more I realize I'm not ready to die. Not now or anytime soon.

I haven't even lived.

Clenching my hands into fists, I press them against the top of the coffin, punching, scratching, hitting—everything while hoping the heavy thing might budge.

But it doesn't.

I kick at it with my feet, using all the strength I can muster.

Nothing.

Somehow, the thought that I'll die here, and on my birthday, nonetheless, makes me want to fight.

I may have nothing to fight for, but at least I have myself. And maybe no one else loves me, but I do.

And I want to live.

I want to keep on going, because maybe, one day, my wish will come true.

Knowing I can't give up, I continue to kick at the top until exhaustion claims me and I drop back, my limbs sapped of strength, but my resolve still made of steel.

Because I can.

She's been tormenting me for years because she could. She was right about that.

Because I let her.

Now, as I sit in the darkness of this enclosed space, some clarity makes its way into my mind. Beyond the fear, beyond the panic that I might never see sunlight again, and that I might die next to a pile of old bones, there's a sudden realization.

I let her walk all over me.

Time and time again she'd insulted, hit, and punished me. Just because she could.

And me? For all my avowal of innocence, I'd been a willing participant. Because I'd allowed everything to happen.

I'd let them curse me out, hit me until my skin scarred,

and torment me until the nightmares kept me awake at night.

How did I not see this before?

I'd been so busy feeling sorry for myself, and crying about my wretched state, that I hadn't stopped for a minute to wonder why I let it happen.

You didn't think you deserve more.

That's probably the most I'm willing to admit to myself, the truth opening me raw inside and making me glance at my own reflection.

I'd been so wrapped up in trying to be good, trying to go unnoticed by pleasing everyone, that I'd never once fought back.

And for the first time, I vow that if I make it out alive, I'm going to change.

I may not be able to control how others behave, but I can ensure that I'll never be seen as a weakling again.

Why be good when people are bad?

Why indeed.

All my life I'd tried to show people that I'm more than the mark on my face. That I'm not actually cursed. But no one's ever tried to see beyond my physical imperfections.

I'd been branded the devil's child from the very beginning, so I'd done my best to show everyone that I was *good*.

And for what?

Hours pass, and the coffin gets colder and colder. I try to ignore the thought that I'm sitting on top of someone's old bones, or the simple fact that I'm sharing a tiny place with a dead person.

I hone in on one thing—my growing resolve.

I'm done being everyone's punching bag, just like I'm done with being unwanted.

If they don't want me, then so be it. I won't want them either.

Abandon me once, shame on you. Abandon me twice… shame on me.

But next time, there won't be a *twice*.

If there is a next time.

~

A ROOSTER'S MORNING CALL ALERTS ME TO THE PASSAGE OF time. My teeth clattering, my limbs stiff with cold, I'm barely aware of how long I've been in here.

There are a few crevices within the coffin that allow for some light, and I soak it all up, foolishly thinking it might warm my body.

I'm in and out of conscience after some time. Hunger and thirst are gnawing at me and I already resigned myself to never making it out of here.

"I wish…" I try to wet my already chapped lips with my tongue, my only thought to keep myself awake. "I wish," I start again, thinking about my birthday wish.

Maybe in another life…

"She's coming to. We may need to keep her…"

"Keep her? Here? No! I'm taking her with me," a voice gets increasingly heated.

I move a little, finding it hard to get my limbs to react. I feel the muscles of my face, stiff and sore, and I try to open my eyes.

"Sisi," Lina rushes to my side. "Good Lord, what happened to you," she whispers, tears in her eyes.

Her hands are all over my face, my body, her touch tender and affectionate.

"Lina," I croak, finding it hard to speak.

"No, don't talk. I got you," she says, her warm hands caressing my hair.

"Catalina, I'm not sure…"

"Sister Maria, Sisi is my friend, and I can take care of her. She's coming back with me." Lina's voice has a confident quality to it I'd never heard before.

I try to raise myself up, but she's quickly back at my side, taking me in her arms and hugging me to her chest.

"Lord, Sisi, what happened?"

"I'm fine," I manage to get out, although I'm not sure how long I was in that coffin.

"How did you…" I trail off, my strength limited.

"The sisters on gardening duty heard you scream. I can't believe you were locked in there… Sisi." She shakes her head at me, worry in her gaze.

"I'm fine. It was just a game," I lie, because I've learned my lesson when it comes to telling on the other girls.

No. No one can help me but myself.

And that's exactly what I'm going to do.

"A game? But…"

"Can we go back?" I ask, hoping she'll drop the subject. I don't want her to know what has happened to me, just as much as I don't want her to know what I will do from now on.

I've tasted enough human cruelty to last me a lifetime.

It's time I gave some back.

3
SISI
AGE FIFTEEN

Tying the garland at the end, I use some of the flowers to hide the uneven formation. Turning to Claudia, I lower it over her head, watching with satisfaction as a smile spreads over her face. Her hands go up and she starts feeling for the flowers.

"Wow," she breathes out, her eyes wide in wonder.

"You like it?"

"Like? I love it! Thank you, Aunt Sisi!" She lunges at me, almost throwing me off balance. I open my arms to return her hug.

"See, I'm good at some things too," I add a little drily, and Claudia chuckles.

It's a running joke among Claudia, Lina and I that I never do anything right. Granted, I rarely put in the effort, but they are right to laugh at me when I fail at even the most basic things.

Why, recently I'd been assigned to my first baking duty. Before, I'd merely assisted the older Sisters, so it hadn't been too hard. This time, however, I'd been the only one in charge of making the Sunday pie, and by mistake I'd added salt instead of sugar.

How is it my fault when they looked the same? Even the containers were the same color.

But that small mistake had gotten me in a lot of trouble. No one could eat the pie, and so Mother Superior had taken it upon herself to make sure I learned which is sugar and which is salt—by cleaning and organizing the entire kitchen. Part of my punishment had also been that I'd been prohibited from eating *anything* until the kitchen was sparkly clean.

I was lucky Lina had sneaked me some food, since that kitchen is enormous. I would have died of starvation before I was done cleaning it.

"You're good to me," she giggles, leaving my arms to go pick some more flowers.

I shift position, folding my legs under me, and I turn my attention back to my current punishment, picking up the hefty book and opening it on my lap.

This one isn't as bad as the kitchen one, but I still have to choose a passage from the Old Testament and write an entire essay on it. I guess that's what I get for accidentally falling asleep in class.

But really, how am I supposed to pay attention when everything is just so… uninteresting? I've been hearing the same stories of God creating the world, or Jesus sacrificing himself for our sakes, since I was a little girl. I probably know some passages by heart if I concentrate hard enough. It's always the same discussion about the same texts. Why would I be intrigued by that?

I know there's more to learn than the same old tales.

One time, I even managed to sneak into the library and I'd seen so many interesting texts... Still on the subject of God and religion, but they were exquisitely different from anything I'd read or heard before.

I'd managed to steal a copy of the Confessions of St Augustine, and I stashed that in my hiding place at the mausoleum. I've been reading it every chance I got, and while the moral of the story is that a religious life is better than a sinful one, I'd been able to read between the lines.

Life outside.

Sinful, immoral, seductive. It showed how *not* to behave, yet it only made me want to experience it even more. He'd even talked about carnal relations...

A blush envelops my entire face as I remember eating those words straight off the page, my curiosity about such an act only increasing the more secretive St Augustine was in his narration.

Why mention it at all if you're going to mince your words? For all his descriptions of his immoral existence before the church, I still don't know exactly what the act entails.

I sigh, the direction of my thoughts taking me further and further away from my assignment. Considering I have to turn it in tomorrow, I need to get my head in the game.

Hands to my temples, I give them a quick rub, squeezing my eyes shut and willing myself to focus.

"Claudia, don't go too far!" I call out to her when I see her running in the opposite direction.

Her shoulders slump when she hears my voice, and dejected, she comes back.

"You know your mother counts on me to make sure you're safe," I add as I pat her small back.

She gives me a tremulous smile and nods, taking a seat next to me and focusing on the flowers she'd already picked. She starts playing with them, trying to build another garland.

By chance, as she shifts positions and tries to get more comfortable, I get a closer look at her bare legs.

I frown as I survey a mass of brown and yellow bruises stretching from her shin to her knee.

"Claudia," I turn to her, "what happened?" I point to her bruises and her eyes widen. She folds her uniform over her legs, obstructing my view.

"Nothing," she mutters under her breath. "I fell."

"You fell? When? Does your mother know?" The words tumble out of my mouth, even though I can bet Lina doesn't know. She's so protective of Claudia that if she were aware of those bruises on her daughter's skin, she would have never let her hear the end of it—likely she wouldn't be allowed to play anymore either.

Lina is a little too much sometimes when it comes to Claudia's safety, but I can understand and appreciate her attention.

How I wish someone cared for me like that too…

"No," she lowers her face slightly, before coming closer to me. "Please don't tell her. You know how she's going to react," she says as she pleads with me with her big eyes.

I'm torn. On the one hand, I owe it to Lina to tell her, on the other, I don't want Claudia to lose her trust in me.

"Tell me what happened," I urge her, and she starts recounting how she'd tripped and fallen on the hard floor of the classroom. It had been only an accident, and she doesn't want Lina to make a big deal out of it.

"You're not lying to me, are you?" I narrow my eyes at her, and she promptly shakes her head. "If… someone was doing this to you, you'd tell me right?" I add for good measure, knowing just how easy it is to get picked on.

I'd sported my fair share of bruises growing up, and things had only changed in the last few years when I'd simply refused to play the bullies' game. Instead of showing them fear like I'd done in the past, I didn't bother with them at all. My indifference seems to have worked since after some time they simply stopped bothering with me, unable to coax a response out of me.

After all, that brand of evil feeds on fear, shame and self-loathing — and I'd had buckets of all three.

"Nothing happened, Aunt Sisi," she reiterates, "I just tripped."

I hold her gaze a bit longer, wanting to make sure she's saying the truth.

"Fine," I sigh, "you can keep playing, but don't go out of my sight, okay?"

She readily agrees, taking off once more.

Mildly satisfied with her answers but still a little suspicious, I banish all thoughts from my head and start focusing on my assignment.

Here it goes.

I STUMBLE OUT OF THE CLASSROOM, MY PALMS ALMOST bleeding from the teacher's lesson. I'd done my assignment, and I'd laid out all my honest thoughts on paper, eschewing the standard interpretation in favor of my own.

Big mistake.

Sister Matilde, my teacher, had been scandalized when she'd read my essay and she'd asked me to sit in front of the whole classroom, while she taught me yet another lesson. She'd taken a wooden stick and slapped my open palms with it until the skin broke, blood almost reaching the surface.

I'd taken it all without showing any weakness. I could tell, just like Cressida and her gang, that Sister Matilde was waiting for my tears to flow, for my knees to buckle when I kneeled to ask for forgiveness.

I'd given her none of that.

I'd stood still, stoically enduring the pain and the jibes that my classmates were throwing at me. I'd taken all the pain without a sound, just waiting until Sister Matilde got tired of hitting me.

Taking a deep breath, I focus on not giving in to the pain. It's not like it's the first time this has happened. But it's certainly the one time Sister Matilde had not held anything back.

I walk slowly toward my room when I spot Claudia. Head down, shoulders slumped, she's following a group of girls her age toward the back of the cloisters.

Confused, since I've never heard Claudia mention any school friends, I follow closely.

The open area allows me to see exactly what's happening, and I gasp when Claudia's pushed to the ground.

The girls, forming a circle around her, start taunting her and calling her all sorts of ugly names. The situation is entirely too familiar as I watch Claudia take it all. Head bent low; she's not even trying to defend herself when one girl tries to hit her.

I jump out of my hiding place, running toward her and trying to disband this awful mob.

Lord, you'd think in a place of God people would be more… godly. But no. Taught from young that being *good* means you are above everyone else makes these girls think that because Claudia was born out of wedlock she deserves their contempt.

"Stop it!" I call out, worming my way inside their circle and taking Claudia in my arms. "What do you think you're doing?" I ask, shaking my head at them in reproach.

Some girls have the decency to look ashamed at being caught, but one in particular, the leader I'm guessing, still has a look of arrogance on her face.

"Are you okay?" I quickly ask Claudia and she nods, her eyes full of unshed tears.

"You can't go around abusing people." I turn to the others, their gazes now focused on the ground.

"How would you feel if someone did this to you, too?" I ask, but no one replies.

Shaking my head in disgust, I tug Claudia to her feet, drawing her closer to my side.

"Go now before I give you a taste of your own medicine," I say in my most adult voice, and watch as the girls scurry away. Their leader is the only one trailing behind, but even she leaves when she sees she's lost her support.

"Are you hurt?" I ask Claudia, worried she might have gotten new bruises. She shakes her head, but I'm not convinced. I start patting her down when I hear another familiar voice.

"Look who's grown a spine," Cressida snickers from behind. I turn sharply to see her and her clique, hands on hips, looking mightily smug as they sneer at us.

Instinctively, I tuck Claudia behind me, taking a defensive stance.

"Go away, Cressida," I say, my voice full of confidence. I'm not about to back down, not when Claudia is also with me.

"Go away, Cressida," she mimics my voice, making an ugly face, and the others start laughing. "Look at them both, rejects. Devil's spawn and you," she cranes her neck, seeking to get a better look at Claudia, "with your whore of a mother. Aren't you ashamed to even show your faces around here?"

"How original," I counter, "you're just saying the same old recycled stuff."

I tighten my grip on Claudia's hand and I slowly back away, not wanting a direct confrontation that might result in her getting harmed.

The corner of Cressida's mouth tugs upwards in a vicious half-smile as she slowly steps in front of us.

She's one of the bigger girls in our age group, and I know I don't stand a chance, especially if Claudia might be in danger.

"Go home," I whisper to Claudia, and her big eyes turn toward me in question.

"Go, I'll handle this."

She seems reluctant, but as I urge her with my eyes she seems to understand the gravity of the situation as she suddenly darts out of the cloisters and toward the dorm.

When she's out of sight, I release a sigh of relief and I

turn to face my worst enemy again. And this time, I'm not backing down.

"You think we can't catch that brat too? Annie's gang will make sure she gets her due," she says smugly.

"Leave Claudia out of this. Your issue is with me," I reply, meeting her gaze.

I'd never thought that my problems would influence how Claudia is treated too… And now that I'm faced with the possibility, I don't think I can let this slide.

People can hate me and try to tear me down as much as they want. But they can't go after my family.

A smile suddenly spreads over my face as I take a few steps forward until I'm toe to toe with her.

"Don't want to," she replies, her hand already up and ready to strike. This time, however, I'm ready for it, and I catch it midair, my fingers tightening around her wrist in a painful hold.

A small wince crosses her face and she's quick to use her other hand. I don't give her an opening as I bring my knee up and hit her in the stomach.

A sudden intake of air and she gasps, bending forward in pain. I don't stop as I bring my hand down to her face, placing all my strength into a slap that has her stumbling back. Her friends are on the sidelines, just watching with wide eyes as Cressida falls to the ground. I give them a quick glance and they shake their heads, not wanting to get involved.

"Even your friends abandon you when you're at your weakest," I tell her, watching her pitiful form. "This is the difference between us, Cressida. You have friends when you have the power to terrorize them, but look how they react when you're down." I smile at her. Her eyes are still full of malice as she tries to get herself together.

"I may be hated by everyone else, but at least I have my family," I enunciate each word, knowing that most of the girls around are orphans, and a family is what they crave the most. "When everyone leaves, who do *you* have?"

I bring my foot as if I'm about to hit her only to see her coil down, folding her body in such a pathetic movement that I can't bring myself to stoop to her level.

Taking a step back, I shake my head at her before I leave.

When I reach the dorm, Claudia is waiting for me outside, her eyes red from crying.

"Aunt Sisi," she cries out, launching herself at me and letting her tears flow.

"Shh, it's okay. Nothing happened," I caress her hair, holding her close.

"But they… they," she hiccups, her words swallowed by the intensity of her sobs.

Taking her by the shoulders, I lower myself so that I'm on eye level with her.

"Claudia, what happened today is *not* okay," I start, "you should never suffer alone. If they hurt you, tell someone."

"I can't…. *Mamma* has enough on her plate," she whimpers, and I feel my own eyes misting. Catalina's always tried to take care of us, sometimes even disregarding her own health. Besides, in order to get some extra things for Claudia, she sometimes takes on double the chore load.

"Then tell me," I say, "I'll always be there to help you, okay? Don't hold it in. These people." I shake my head, my own emotions coming to the surface, "They think we're less because of our circumstances. But we're not. *You're* not, you hear me?"

I don't even know how to express everything I've held within myself for so long. How do I give someone else advice about this when I'm barely surviving myself?

"Yes, Aunt Sisi." Claudia whispers, and I use the pads of my thumbs to wipe the tears from her face.

"Don't let others tell you your worth. You're the only one who can determine that. No matter how cruel people are," I add, both for her and for me, "they can only hurt you if you let them."

She nods at me, her tiny hands clenched in fists. She nods before coming closer and hugging me.

"Thank you," she says against my chest. "Thank you."

We hold on to each other for a while, going back inside only when the tears have dried, and we've returned to our cheerful selves, for Catalina's sake.

"Sisi," Lina calls out to me one afternoon. Confused, I raise my eyebrows in question, but she just waves me over.

"Come," she whispers when I reach her side, "I have something for you."

Going inside our accommodation, she lifts the mattress up to reveal a few stacks of books. Taking a few out, she places them in my arms.

"I asked my brother to sneak some books in," she starts, pointing at the titles, "I told him something more romantic but classic," she blushes as she talks.

My eyes go down to the books and I see most of them are by someone named William Shakespeare.

"They're for you," she adds when she sees me staring at them in wonder.

"For me?" I repeat, almost numbly.

She nods. "I know your birthday passed but." She looks down, almost ashamed. "I've seen you hide around with that book of yours, and I know you're trying to read something... different."

"It's for me," I repeat in wonder, blinking rapidly to chase the tears away.

It's the first time someone's given me something... for me.

"For you," she confirms, giving me one of her kind smiles. I deposit the books on the bed and I give her a big hug.

"Thank you," I start, trying to keep my voice steady, "this means a lot to me." So much she can't possibly imagine.

"I'm glad you like it." She pats my back affectionately.

"I love it." I feel compelled to enforce it.

Drawing back, Lina purses her lips. "You'll have to be careful. If Mother Superior or any of the sisters catch you..."

"Don't worry. I'll be extremely careful," I assure her, immediately switching my attention to the books.

There are three of them, all skinny enough to fit inside my uniform. I quickly peruse the titles; *As you like it, Anthony and Cleopatra* and *Romeo and Juliet.*

I skim them quickly, frowning a little at the complicated language, but undeterred in enjoying this gift.

My first.

Thanking Lina once more, I head back to my sanctuary and I hide the books inside the coffin, knowing no one will look there.

For the next week, I try to squeeze some time daily to read, the content of the plays astounding me, making me gasp with excitement, and cry of outrage.

Soon, one play quickly becomes my favorite and as I read about Anthony and Cleopatra's struggles to be together as well as their devotion to one another, I can't help but want something like that for myself.

What would it be like… to have someone love me like that?

But even as I ask the question, I know it is a moot point. I'm destined for a life of loneliness, and even more cruelty. Once Lina and Claudia are gone… I don't even want to think about that.

I take a deep breath, trying *not* to think about that, knowing that if I dwell too much on it, I'm just going to get more depressed. And why should I ruin my mood when these books make me so happy?

The yearning between the two leads is so palpable on page that my own pulse starts racing as I imagine them in an illicit embrace.

But since my lord is Antony again, I will be Cleopatra.

So intertwined they were that one could not *be* without the other.

I sigh deeply, trying to picture a faceless man embracing me too, whispering words of love in my ear and peppering my face with kisses.

It might never come to pass, but at least I can dream about it.

Eyes closed; I'm lost in this conjured fantasy when my book is violently snatched from my hands.

Startled, I whip my head around and come face to face with Cressida, a smug look on her lips as she's looking at my book.

"Give it back." I jump up, my hand grasping for it. But since Cressida is taller than me, as she raises her hand in the air, I have no chance of reaching it.

"After you embarrassed me in front of everyone?" She spits the words out, and for a second I'm rooted to the spot as I realize that for the first time, pure malice is dripping from her entire countenance.

"You brought that on to yourself," I add, jumping up to get the book.

Seeing me so desperate for my book, she starts moving it from hand to hand, enjoying my futile efforts to retrieve it.

With a disappointed sigh, I stop.

"Aren't you sick of this? Why do you always have to pick on me?" I try to appeal to her rational side, if she has one.

She just shrugs. "You're there. It's easy."

Not unlike what she'd said years ago, surprisingly, her words have no effect on me. I'd had enough time to think on everything and I'd realized that how she treats me is not a reflection of who I am, rather of who she is.

I'm not the problem.

"Then how about I make it harder," I say right before I jump again, taking advantage of her diverted attention to snatch the book.

She reacts a second too late, but as my hand moves with

the book, her fingers catch half of it, pulling backwards until I hear a big rip.

We both stumble back, each holding half of the book.

Her expression is one of satisfaction, while mine is one of desolation.

My book…

I don't react for a good second. Not until Cressida continues her vile game by taking her half and ripping it further into shreds, the words I'd worshiped until a moment ago falling on the ground.

I feel a knot forming in my throat as I helplessly watch her stomp all over my prized possession.

Suddenly, all the years of torment, both mental and physical, flash themselves before my eyes. I remember how she'd pushed me around, hit me and cut my hair. How I still bear the scars of everything she's done to me and how I'd almost died at our last confrontation in this very place.

And suddenly, I'm done.

The torn half of the book in my hand falls to the floor with a thud. Not caring about anything anymore, I just pounce on her, my hands balled into fists as I take her unawares.

Her mouth forms an o just as my punch lands in her stomach, and she stumbles slightly backward. A harsh intake of breath and she's throwing punches of her own, aiming for my face.

It hurts when she lands a hit, but I don't mind it. I just continue, pushing her to the floor as we tangle on the cold marble, hands in each other's hair.

We roll around until I'm on top of her, my fists aiming for her face.

"No more!" I rasp, a rage unlike any other coming over me. "I won't be your punching bag anymore," I say as I continue to pummel at her.

Ironic that I'm treating her as my *own* punching bag, but after everything she's done to me, it's the least I can do.

Tears are falling down my face as I keep on hitting, her gasps of pain only fueling my rage.

One second of delay, though, and she has me flipped around, hitting me as well.

I close my eyes, wincing at the pain but struggling to get her off me. Mustering all the strength I can, I focus all of it in my legs. Bending them toward me, I take a deep breath and I push with all my might, shoving her to the side.

She's off me, her back hitting the hard coffin, her head banging on a corner.

I breathe heavily as I take a moment to get myself together, the strain from the fight getting to me.

But a second passes, then two, and I realize Cressida is not moving at all.

I turn my head around, and I'm greeted by Cressida's face, her unblinking eyes wide open. Blood is pooling at the side of her head where she'd made contact with the coffin.

"What..." I whisper to myself as I scramble to my feet, my entire body aching with pain.

I take a step forward, letting my hand move across her body, looking for some sign of life.

Searching for her pulse line, I find none.

She's... dead.

Open-mouthed, I stare at Cressida's dead body. A girl I'd killed. I look in wonder at her unmoving self and I feel... nothing.

No sadness, no regret, no remorse.

Just a deep sense of relief.

She's gone.

But what does that say about me?

I killed someone. Granted, it was someone who's tortured me my entire life, but I couldn't muster any type of regret.

What's wrong with me?

But as I stare at her, more and more, laughter starts bubbling inside of me. It starts slow. My lips curl up in a smirk as I look at her lifeless body, and then it erupts from deep within me. I can't even stop as I hold on to my stomach, still hurting from her punches. I just laugh.

She's dead.

Finally.

I take a while to compose myself, all the glee at seeing the person I'd hated for *years* get what she deserved spilling over. But as I calm down from my outburst, I realize I need to make sure she's not found.

For a second, my thoughts turn to what might happen should her body be discovered. I'd probably be sent to prison.

Is jail that different from this place?

For once, I don't care about the consequences of my actions. Either she's found, and I go to prison, or she's not found and the world will simply *not* miss her.

I certainly will not.

My resolve is firm, I only need to get rid of her body… As my eyes rove around the room, I have just the place.

After all, hadn't she wanted for me to die locked inside a

cold coffin? Fitting that she'd be the one spending an eternity in that exact place.

My lips twitch as the irony sinks in. Maybe it's a twisted game of fate, but at least there's some type of justice in the world.

And I know I will sleep better at night knowing she's forever out of my life.

Getting to work, I prop the lid of the coffin open, the exertion already enough to make me sweat. After, I use my hands to drag her body into an upright position, finding it difficult to maneuver her because of her size. It takes me three tries to get her on level with the coffin, and I manage to hold her long enough to push her into the confined space, smearing blood from her head wound all over the floor and the outside of the coffin.

She drops inside with a thud, and I take a deep breath as I look upon her breathless body—those eyes that are still wide open.

It should be abnormal... staring into the face of death so directly and so casually. But I find that after my own brushes with death, I'm unnaturally immune to it.

Assured that Cressida's body fits in the enclosed space, I get to cleaning the floor. Since I don't have anything else to wipe the blood off with, I reluctantly settle on the torn pages of my book.

But it's just my luck that instead of cleaning the blood, they are only smearing it more. I roll my eyes, annoyed, until another idea pops into my head.

Moving back to the coffin, I reach inside and feel for any material. First, I check the previous occupant of the coffin, but since the material of the habit is so old and brittle, I fear

I may make an even bigger mess. With a sigh, I turn to Cressida's body, tearing some cloth from her uniform.

Then, I crouch once more on the floor and start wiping. The material is a good absorbent, and soon the white marble floor is squeaky clean. I turn to the outside of the coffin, and I wipe the walls too, ensuring no trace of blood is left *anywhere*.

When I'm finally done with that, I move to the other side to push the lid of the coffin shut.

"Drat it," I mutter as I fix my feet on the floor, the slippery marble not helping with my exertion. I move around a little so my heels are against the wall, my hands on the lid. Then, pushing with all my strength, I eventually see it moving.

When that is done, I lift my hand up, swiping some sweat off my brow and thinking how to proceed next.

I check the latch on the coffin, ensuring everything is locked in place.

This is it… I guess.

My stomach is still paining me as I go back to the dorm, choosing to stealthily head to the shower area and wash some of the blood spatters off my uniform.

Claudia is still in class, so there's only Lina inside the room, her brows pinched together as she focuses on sewing an old dress.

"Oh, Sisi." She looks up, surprised to see me. I give her a quick smile and dash out of the room before she can ask more questions.

The bathroom is made up of communal showers that everyone on the floor shares. Heading inside, I deposit my clean clothes on the sink and get in the shower.

Quickly tugging my uniform dress off my body, I place it directly under the water stream. Taking a piece of soap, I rub at the stained areas, relieved to see that the red turns into a yellowy color. The more I rub, the more that fades, too.

When my clothes are done, I move under the shower, hoping the warm water would help the continuing stomach pains.

Holding on to my midriff, I take a deep breath, willing myself to calm down. But as I continue to wash my body, my hand moving between my legs, I can't help but gasp out loud at the sight of blood.

So much blood.

And it's pouring out of me.

"Good Lord," I mutter, staring intently at the red coating my hand, convinced this is a sign. "I'm cursed… that must be it," I say out loud.

For the first time, panic starts taking hold of me. Because no matter how much I wash myself, blood keeps pouring out of me.

This is it… the physical evidence of my sin.

There can be no other explanation. I'm being punished for taking another life, and nothing is more fitting than blood slowly coming out of my own body—until I'm bled dry.

My legs buckle and I drop to the ground, my back against the wall, water still falling on top of me. As it washes over my body, it turns a muddy color, mingling with my blood in a fitting combination.

Everything I touch is cursed.

The words I'd heard so many times from the nuns and other sisters are finally starting to make sense.

"Sisi?" Catalina's voice interrupts my musings, and I'm suddenly afraid she's going to find out what I've done.

I may not care about other people, but I do care about her opinion. I don't want *her* to be disappointed in me.

Before I can make something up for her to leave me alone, she opens the door to the stall, finding me huddled in a corner, bloodied water pooling at my feet.

"Sisi," she exclaims, horror in her voice. "What happened?"

I look up, into her eyes, and I say the only thing that I can think of.

"It won't stop… the blood."

Lina takes one good look at me and sighs, "Sisi…"

Helping me up and out of the shower, she leaves the bathroom briefly, returning with a pad. After I'm dressed and my uniform's been hung out to dry, she takes me back to our room to have a talk.

"It's normal." She explains that nothing is wrong, that I just got my period.

"Period?" I repeat, confused.

Lina purses her lips. "When a woman matures, she starts her monthly bleeding. It's a sign that you're now…" She trails off, a blush appearing on her face, "Ready to have children."

"I am?" My eyes widen, suddenly afraid. But Lina is quick to assuage my worries, doing her best to explain to me how children are made and that I have nothing to worry about.

"It will just be slightly uncomfortable when you get your

menstrual cramps. And you'll need to change your pad every so often," she continues, going over every detail.

I just nod numbly, half relieved and half in shock.

How ironic, that I should reach my maturity by spilling blood, when I've *just* spilled blood. Sick laughter forms in my throat until I can't hold it in anymore. Lina looks at me askance, but I just shrug it off as nothing.

Because at the end, an unexpected calm settles over me.

I'm already going to Hell. Might as well enjoy the journey.

4
VLAD

"*S*he's home,*"* Maxim tells me on the phone, and I let out a deep breath.

She's safe.

As safe as she can be. And as far away from me as possible.

"You really did it this time," Vanya quips from a corner, swinging her legs up and down on a chair.

"Go away, Vanya," I tell her, not in the mood for anything.

"She's going to hate you, you know," she continues, and I feel my ire rising.

"GO AWAY!" I yell at her, my eyes widening at my own outburst.

Vanya's expression mirrors my own as tears gather in the corners of her eyes. And just like that, she's gone.

I slump in my chair, wishing I could erase the day from my mind. Hell, wishing I could forget everything.

Sisi.

The moment I'd opened my eyes and seen her... Seen the magnitude of what I'd caused, a bottomless pit had formed inside of my stomach, making me unable to process anything else.

I could only see the prints of my palms around her neck, the gaping wound at her shoulder, bleeding and bleeding...

And then...

I close my eyes, the image too much. Her naked body had been riddled with bruises, fingerprints and red marks I'd caused on her skin. I'd seen them on her thighs, her hips... her breasts.

"Lord," I groan out loud, the ugly bite mark on her breast threatening to make me sick.

But then there had been the worst of all. The blood between her legs. The same blood staining my cock and letting me know exactly what I'd done.

I could have killed her.

Bleakness overtakes me as I realize this is truly the end. I'd allowed myself to believe I could be saved, and in the process I'd damned her too.

Fuck, but the sight of her so battered, so broken had killed something within me. For all my claims of unfeelingness, seeing her like that had shattered me.

I pick up the blood streaked hair I'd salvaged from the floor, my fingers tightening around the strands as I bring them to my nose, inhaling.

"Sisi..." I whisper, wishing for the first time that things were different, that I were normal and deserving of her.

The thought of never seeing her again causes such a deep agony within me that I don't know how I'll manage. It feels constricting to breathe just imagining a day without her, but a future?

Slowly rising from my chair, I go to the bathroom, carefully washing the hair and placing it in a safe space so it can dry.

The last thing I'll ever touch of hers...

But I can't regret my decision. Not when I'd almost killed her. Certainly, I'd defiled her in the worst manner possible, the vision of her bloody thighs, or the gaping wound at her throat threatening to make me ill.

And then there's her expression when I'd lied through my teeth, hurting her where I knew she would hurt. Because I knew that my brave, beautiful Sisi would never leave me unless I left her first. She would staunchly withstand everything until I actually killed her.

And I can't have that.

For the first time in my life I value a human life, and I find that in order to preserve it, I'd do *anything*.

"Stupid," I whisper to myself, slowly bringing my head against the wall, the impact barely tickling the surface of my skin. "Stupid," I repeat, pushing my head even harder into the wall, wanting the pain—needing the pain.

But it doesn't come. Not even when my skin breaks and blood pools down my forehead.

There's simply no outward pain, not as there is inward, my chest constricting with a foreign feeling.

So I just bang my head against the wall, the knowledge of the pain I'd caused her my main impetus.

"Why?" I rasp, bringing my fists forward. "Why can't I be normal?" I cry out, tired of this existence... tired of everything around me.

"Why can't she be mine?" The words tumble from my mouth as I fall to the floor.

I'd never wanted something for myself, never craved anything like I did her. She was the one person who welcomed me with open arms, the only one to ever see *me*. The one person who made me feel human.

And I almost killed her.

My eyes feel damp, from blood or tears I have no clue. Not when all I can think about is my barren future without her.

"Why can't she be mine?" I throw the question to the universe, already knowing the answer.

You don't deserve her. You never have.

And yet I had her. For a few brief moments, she was mine and I was hers.

I'm still hers, but she'll never be mine again.

I'd never wanted to hurt her. Hell, I'd treated her with kid gloves, afraid that my brutish nature would scare her away and make her realize just how *not* normal I was. And I'd been so careful.

Damn, but I'd been so careful. I'd denied myself countless times when all I wanted was to slide inside her slick heat, get lost in that luscious body of hers… finally make her mine.

But I'd refrained, because it would have caused her pain.

And I *never* wanted to cause her pain.

I can't help as the images of her battered body flood my mind, the fact that I'd taken her like an animal making me want to end my own wretched existence. Flashbacks dance before my eyes. Small snippets of me thrusting into her like a beast, her cries of pain as she'd tried to stop me, her small hands pushing at my shoulders when I'd been too rough.

"Sisi," I groan, fear, desperation, and desolation brewing inside of me, growing to such a crescendo that I start trembling uncontrollably. My entire body starts shaking, my vision blurry as everything comes crashing down.

I failed her. I failed her. I failed her.

"Fuck," I curse out, feeling myself slip, voices crowding my head, my pulse skyrocketing as more and more foreign thoughts seek to drive me insane.

I don't know how I stumble out of the bathroom, heading straight for my secret cabinet and taking out a sedative, injecting it in my veins.

Her face is the last thing I see. Her beautiful, beautiful face. The most beautiful I've ever seen, really. Her outline starts to take shape in front of me. My eyes droopy, I can only watch her in rapture.

"Hell girl," I reach out, clear air greeting me. "I'm sorry." I finally say the words she deserves to hear.

"I wish I were normal," I mumble, my body slowly shutting down. "Then I'd be able to love you too."

And then there's only blackness.

"HOW MUCH TIME ARE YOU GOING TO SPEND MOPING around?" Vanya asks as I drag one of the bodies to the back for Maxim to deal with.

"I'm not moping," I mutter under my breath.

"You are. This week alone you killed what ten people? Twenty?"

"More like fifty," I mumble, and she raises an eyebrow at me.

"They all deserved it," I tell her, "they've been coming after me for revenge one after another. What am I supposed to do? Welcome them with open arms?"

"Maybe." She shrugs, coming to my side to study the results of my latest episode. "Since you clearly have a death wish. You know very well that now you're *everyone's* target. Yet you stopped carrying a weapon around. If that's not suicidal, then I don't know what is."

"What can I say? My skills defy any weapons," I say smugly, but she jabs her elbow in my side, pointing to my new wound.

"Sure, then what is *that*?"

"I don't remember. Someone must have stabbed me during the last fight." I shrug, tugging my shirt up to reveal a nasty looking cut under my ribs. Almost like a ticklish sensation, I can barely feel it.

"One of these days you're just going to bleed out." She shakes her head at me, dragging me to the first aid kit.

"Wouldn't that be a mercy?" I whisper softly.

It's been three weeks since the warehouse incident, and all I've done has been courting death, but with no real result. After all, my self-preservation instinct flares up every time, and even if I want to, I *can't* go down.

"You need to take care of yourself, brother," Vanya says, worry shining in her eyes. "Remember your promise," she reminds me, and I close my eyes, sighing.

All I've been doing in the last weeks has *been* forgetting my promise. I'd been so bent on doing everything possible to escape the confinement of my own body that I'd completely disregarded my promise of revenge.

"You're right, Vanya," I concede. "I need to get my head back in the game."

"One might say you need to get your head out of the game. Stop killing people for a second and interrogate them. Remember what Oleg said?"

Her question gives me pause, and I replay the events of the day, wincing as I do because those memories contain her… But Vanya's right. Oleg had intimated that I'd upset some important people.

"You think they have something to do with Project Humanitas?"

"Maybe." Vanya shrugs, urging me to pick up a bandage. "But it's worth looking into it."

"You're right," I agree.

Taking some of the gauze, I start wiping the blood from the wound, noting it's not as shallow as I'd previously thought. I clean and disinfect it, but I'll likely need stitches.

"Call Sasha," Vanya tells me, but I just shake my head.

"I got this," I answer, taking a surgical needle and thread. I pull the needle through my skin, stitching the two sides together. My stitches may not be as clean as Sasha's, but they work. After all, who cares if my body becomes even more disfigured than it already is? I'd only cared what one person thought of it and…

I close my eyes, taking a deep breath.

I'd tried so hard not to think of her during this time, but the downsides of having a close to perfect memory is that I can recall in detail all our interactions… the way her skin felt on mine, or how her simple presence calmed me.

This isn't working.

I jab the needle harder into my skin, wishing I could hurt the same way I hurt her. But still nothing. The most I feel is a light caress.

"Vlad?" Vanya calls out to me, and it takes me a moment to react. "Vlad!"

"Yes," I mumble, raising my head to look at her.

"What's wrong with you?" she asks, narrowing her eyes at me.

"I don't know what you mean." I say, quickly finishing up sewing myself back together and putting everything back into its place. Turning my back to Vanya, I concentrate my attention on the pile of bodies at the end of the room.

"You're different," she notes, "there's something different about you."

"V, come on," I feign a chuckle, "I'm the same maniac bastard I was before," I joke, but she doesn't reply. She's just watching me closely, the scrutiny in her gaze a little unnerving.

"I should probably burn the bodies," I say out loud, steering the discussion into comfortable territory.

"It's her, isn't it?" Vanya shrewdly points out, coming to my side and forcing me to answer.

"I don't know what you're talking about."

"It *is* her," she affirms. But just then Maxim enters the room with a cart. He starts piling the bodies inside before going to the furnace to burn them.

"You're not getting rid of me." Vanya follows me around to my room.

"Don't I know that?" I mutter, the irony oddly amusing.

"It's her. That's why you're different."

"Let it go, V. I don't want to talk about it." My voice is weary, and as I open my drawer to take out the sedative, all I can think of is forgetting.

Jabbing the needle in my veins, I can hear Vanya saying more things, calling me out for my behavior, yet as I slowly succumb to peace, *her* face starts appearing in front of me.

And I finally feel light again.

5
VLAD

"Thank you Seth," I tell him as he brings me the latest batch of pictures of Sisi.

I'd asked him to watch over her since no matter how much I'd wanted to step away, I just couldn't. I need to know she's safe more than I need my next breath. And the pictures he's been taking for me have been the only thing keeping me going.

I never would have thought I'd become so obsessed with anyone, least of all a female. But Sisi isn't just anyone.

She's everything.

Picking up the pictures, I swipe my finger over her features. She's wearing a scarf over her neck, and I feel a pang in my chest at the thought that I might have scarred her skin forever.

She hasn't been out of the house much, and all the pictures are taken of her in the garden. She's so achingly beautiful that I cannot even find words to describe her. Even with her hair only reaching her shoulders, she's simply exquisite.

Out of pure instinct, I reach into my pocket, taking out the handkerchief she'd embroidered for me. I'd placed some of her hair inside, tying it at the ends to have it with me always.

Spreading out the material on my table, I take out some strands of hair, bringing them to my nose and inhaling—trying to get a whiff of her scent. But the more time passes, the more her scent becomes muted.

Eventually it will be all but gone.

"Why don't you just admit that you love her?" Vanya appears out of nowhere, pacing around in front of me. Not for the first time she starts interrogating me about Sisi. After all, she's the sole reason for my slight change in behavior.

Vanya's been the first one to note that I'd become more withdrawn and one hundred percent more reckless, so she'd started cornering me at every turn, demanding I do something about it.

And after my last incident with opiates, I can see why she'd become increasingly mad at me. After all, I'd been the one to criticize Bianca when she'd become addicted to coke, and here I was, slowly following in her footsteps.

Safe to say, though, I learned my lesson when I almost OD'd. Apparently my body is fully capable of overdosing, it just can't react that well to pain.

Of any kind.

"You know I can't love," I answer with a sigh. We've been over this before. I'm broken from birth and it's not like anything could magically fix it.

If I could, Sisi would be the first… no, the only one to whom I'd offer my love.

"You can't love yet you love her." She raises an eyebrow, her arms crossed over her chest as she stops in front of me.

"It's not love!" I groan out loud. "It's just my selfish desire to have her with me at all times. To feel her with me… to have her in my arms…" I drift off, the pain in my chest expanding. Why does it feel like I can't breathe? Like the entire room is getting smaller and smaller.

I close my eyes, taking a deep breath. I still remember seeing her with the evidence of what I'd done. The fact that I could have easily killed her had nearly destroyed me. For the first time in my life, I'd known real fear at the prospect of her gone. It had been like the worst hit to the chest, my mind fogging, my entire being racked with the worst pain I'd ever felt.

My fingers tighten over her hair as I hold it near, the only thing that seems to calm me these days.

"You selfishly don't love her, but you unselfishly let her go to protect her, even though it's killing you inside," Vanya says, shaking her head at me. "If that's not love…" She trails off and I lift my eyes to look at her.

"You, my brother, are a moron," she states, exasperated. "You're putting her welfare above your own! That's the very definition of love!"

"And how would you know?" I ask, rather peeved.

"Because that's what you did for me too!" she screams at me.

I look at her dumbfounded, wholly shocked at her outburst.

"You love her, you just don't know how to love. There's a difference," she points out.

"But how can I love if I don't know how?" I ask brokenly.

I just want her... I've only ever wanted her.

"You just do what other people do. Take care of her, shower her with attention, show her she is the only one for you."

"But she is!" I blurt out.

"Brother mine, sometimes I wonder how we're related. You're an idiot of the biggest proportions. You have to show her! Hell, she probably hates you right now for the last time. For abandoning her so ruthlessly."

"But I had to..." I say weakly, images of her poor battered body still haunting my mind.

"You didn't have to! You just ran at the first sight that things were getting slightly more complicated. You never even thought of getting help instead of throwing her away."

"I did... and look where it got me. I killed the damned psychiatrist." I look away, the flashbacks I'd recovered from that session still a sore subject. Especially as I look at my sister...

"And only because of her!" Vanya throws her hands up, exasperated. "You tried once and you gave up. Come on, Vlad. There have to be more ways," she tells me. "I don't understand how you can be so smart when it comes to everyone else, but so dumb when it comes to your own damned self," she says angrily, and I purse my lips, her words not unwarranted.

"What more can I do, V? I'm afraid to even place myself in the same ten mile radius of her, knowing that if she's even remotely close then I'll rush over to her and..." My breath hitches. "I'll hurt her again."

It's why I'm sending Seth to check up on her. I'd never be able to stop myself from going to her if I knew she was near.

"You need to do something about your episodes. That's the only way," she tells me.

I'm quiet for a moment, the mere prospect of having Sisi in my life again filling me with something akin to happiness. Not that I know what happiness is, but I expect it's something like what her presence does to me.

But before I can do that I *need* to get myself under control.

Try harder.

Damn, but I'd do anything as long as I could ensure I'm not a danger to her. I'm just out of ideas.

"Fine," I agree. "You may be right. But how do I fix it? She seemed so desolate when I told her…" Even if I do manage to get my episodes under control, I doubt she'd forgive me so easily. I don't even want to remember the words I'd spewed at her, the lies I'd purposefully told her to hurt her.

I'd wanted to drive her as far away from me as possible, and I'd succeeded.

"You go to her and you beg for forgiveness. You'll be lucky if she gives it to you." Vanya raises an eyebrow at me, and I can tell she's on Sisi's side.

As much as I'd like to argue with her, she's right.

I got scared and I threw everything away. I should have fought harder, tried harder. After all, Sisi is the one person in this world who would not have reviled me for my episode.

But in my defense, I'd never felt such fear as I did when I saw what I'd done to her. Hell, I'd never felt fear before *at all*. I'd been ready to ask her to fucking put me out of my misery. I'd been fucking terrified of doing more… of killing her. Because a world without Sisi is not a world I want to live in.

"You're right." I take a deep breath, finally ready to face my demons. "I have to. Because I think I do love her," I admit, my lips trembling as I utter the word *love*.

Vanya's deductions are perfectly logical. I wouldn't have reacted like this if I hadn't *loved* her. Hell, I pride myself on my selfishness, yet with her I'd been uncharacteristically *un*selfish. Maybe it's not the love regular people feel, but it's the nearest thing to it *I* can feel. And I'll take it. Because then I might have something to offer her.

Something other than destruction.

"Finally!" Vanya rolls her eyes. "My idiotic brother, you have your work cut out for you."

"Don't I know it?" I mutter.

One thing is for sure. When one is desperate, one resorts to desperate measures.

I'd thought that reaching out to a psychiatrist had been the height of folly given my own rather resolute beliefs regarding its scientific validity.

But what I'm about to do now defies every law of logic.

I watch as the plane dips toward the make-shift landing strip, already seeing the vast expanse of forest stretching all around the horizon line.

One of my contacts from Peru, Joaquin, is waiting for me when I land, the itinerary ready for this last attempt at regaining my sanity.

"Good to see you, Vlad," he adds drily when I set my luggage in the waiting cart.

"Joaquin, dear, if anyone heard you they'd think you aren't happy to see me," I joke, even though I know our acquaintance is strained at best. Still, he owed me a favor and I'm cashing in.

"I can't say I expected to see you here, Vlad. Ever again," he mutters, "not after you almost caused a civil war here."

"That I stopped too." I smile.

Since I'd taken over the Bratva, I'd also continued with its favorite pastime—drugs. I mean, it *is* a lucrative business, and over the years it has lined my pockets with gold, but it's also messy.

I'd continued my father's business associations with certain *organizations from* South America, and Peru has proved to be the best avenue for resourcing coca leaves and turning them into a people's favorite—not coca cola sadly.

This area in particular had not seen much competition from cartels or other organizations, so I'd focused my resources here.

Well, the moment I'd set my sights on this place, so had other people. And a small war had started in the region. While I can't say I *actually caused* the conflict, I definitely squashed it when I killed all those brave souls so ready to pick up a weapon and go against me.

"Did you make the arrangements?" I ask him as we head to the Jeep.

"After the mess you caused here, I can't say there are many people willing to work with you," he sighs. "Almost everyone knows your name by now, or has at least heard of *el Supay*."

"I didn't realize I gained such a reputation."

"*La gente habla*, Vlad. Rumors of your slaughter travelled all around the region. I wouldn't be surprised if people at the other side of the country speak about *el Supay con sus cuchillos*."

Leaning back in the car, I push my sunglasses up my nose. The heat is almost unbearable for someone used to New York winters, and I'm having a hard time concentrating on Joaquin's ramblings.

"I suppose it is to be expected that something unusual would make the superstitious talk." I allow, knowing that I hadn't made a good impression here.

"Unusual?" Joaquin scoffs, "They call you *el demonio*, Vlad. For them, you are the epitome of evil. No shaman will want to work with you," he says resolutely.

"And miss banishing *el demonio de mi*? I doubt there's not *one* shaman in this entire Amazonian basin that's not remotely curious about me," I fire back, a little too confidently. After all, I'd had an inkling that my reputation might prove to be an impediment. Still, these people pride themselves on their spiritual power, and wouldn't it be grand indeed if they could vanquish the very devil?

"I said it's hard. Not impossible. There is one..." he trails off.

"Great, there we go," I exclaim, ready to meet this person and be done with it.

I'm not necessarily sure anything will work at this point, but I can't say that until I've tried absolutely everything. It's a promise I made to myself. If I want to be worthy of Sisi, then I need to do everything in my power to save *myself*.

"A little problem." Joaquin coughs in his fist, looking a little guilty.

"What?"

"He's not... normal," he says sheepishly.

"Wonderful, since I'm not normal either."

"It's not that. It's just that... he's a recluse and rarely performs ceremonies for outsiders," he continues.

"Then we go to another one." I almost roll my eyes at him. Can't he see I'm in a hurry. The faster I see this shaman and I get my issues under control, the faster I can have Sisi back into my arms.

"Vlad," he sighs, exasperated. "There is no other. I told you. No one wants to work with you. *Todos creen que estás lleno de energía negativa. Nadie quiere trabajar contigo. Ni siquiera quieren acercarse a ti. Solo queda El Viejo*," he speaks fast, and I have to force myself to keep up with his Spanish.

"Fine. What do I need to do to convince this *viejo* to take me in?"

"He'll decide when he sees you. He's..." Joaquin shakes his head. "He may be a recluse, but that's because he's too powerful. He sees what others do not and it is too overwhelming for him."

"Let us go there, then. I told you on the phone. I'm in a hurry."

"*Estas cosas no se apuran*, Vlad," he chides, "El viejo will tell you more, and *he* will decide whether to take you on or not." His tone tells me arguing would be in vain. So I just nod and we continue to the hotel.

A change of clothes, a backpack well packed with

enough resources for a few days, and we are ready to start on the trip the following morning.

In the meantime I find more intriguing facts about this shaman that everyone calls *El viejo*. One of the most powerful shamans in Peru, he is one of the few ones reputed to be able to see both the human and the spirit dimensions.

Of course, I try my hardest not to snort every time Joaquin starts gushing about his prowess.

"He'll see right through your skepticism," he tells me as we begin our journey.

"You of all people should know I'm not doing this because I *believe* in it. It's simply my last resort."

"Then we might be making this journey in vain. *El viejo* will know. And this treatment is only for those who feel the calling." He grunts, clearly unimpressed with my lack of understanding for their tradition.

"You know I mean no disrespect, Joaquin," I address him in a playful tone, "but I'm a man of science. Surely you can see how these claims look from my end."

"And yet you're here, seeking to benefit from those claims."

"Trial and error, nothing else," I smile, "I'm merely testing the validity, even though the science behind it is flimsy at best."

"There are chemical agents in these plants that have been shown to help with disorders of the psychiatric realm," he replies.

"I agree. But there's a big difference between *some* benefits and life-changing moments, as some profess."

"Then you'll just have to see." He shrugs. "And judge for yourself whether it will be life-changing or not."

Starting from Manu, we have to venture off the beaten path deep into the rainforest. According to Joaquin, *El viejo's* dwelling is somewhere close to the border with Brazil.

The journey should take us a couple of days with a few stops in between.

The moisture in the air makes it hard to breathe, the direct heat from the sun messing with my senses. Joaquin is used to the weather, and to venturing into the rainforest, so for him it's a piece of cake.

We walk for close to ten hours, and Joaquin becomes increasingly more good natured as he starts interacting with the wildlife, telling me stories and facts about each animal.

I chose him well.

As expected, as a former ranger, he is very familiar with the area and with the dangers.

When the sun goes down, we finally take a break, making camp next to a huge kapok tree.

"Why now?" Joaquin asks as we sit around a small fire, roasting some meat we'd brought with us. "I've known you for years, Vlad, and you've never given any indication that you'd want to change."

"Different circumstances." I shrug.

Joaquin had been the first one to suggest seeking a shaman for my issues, citing a disconnect between my heart and my psyche as the main reason for my attacks. I'd disagreed, after all my heart is merely an organ that pumps blood. Nothing more, nothing less. Yes, it keeps me alive, but it does not dictate anything else.

I may have been wrong, though.

I'd never understood before the meaning of heartache, or heartbreak, or anything relating to the heart. Why would a perfectly healthy organ hurt? Biologically the only explanation would be an incoming heart attack, or a heart ailment of sorts.

But now…

I close my eyes and I see Sisi, her entire body covered in bruises and bite marks, blood pouring from her wounds. She'd looked beaten and on the verge of passing out.

And for the first time my heart had hurt.

Like a fissure slowly starting from one end and reaching the other, I'd felt a bolt of lightning go through that organ that's *only* supposed to pump blood. My chest had suddenly felt heavy, and I'd had a hard time breathing.

Heartache.

6

VLAD

It's taken me three decades to learn what heartache is.

And it fucking hurts!

Considering my pain receptors are ninety percent muted, that pain had resounded in my entire body. How I'd not succumbed under its weight I do *not* know.

"What could have changed for the mighty *Supay* to ask for help?" he jokes.

"Stop calling me that. I'm no demon," I fire back, a smile on my face.

"Debatable." He shrugs. "You still have not answered my question."

"I finally found something to live for," I say, avoiding more questions on the subject.

The night upon us, I try to not mind the mosquitos as they keep on attacking me. Vanya's been quiet all day, almost as if she's both excited and apprehensive at the same time.

"What if I disappear?" she asks, head on her hands as

she stares me in the eyes from her small makeshift bed in front of me.

"You weren't complaining with Sisi," I whisper, since she'd never said anything about how Sisi's presence seemed to undermine her own.

"But at least then I knew you had her. Now…" She trails off, looking tired and weary.

"Go to sleep, man!" Joaquin's voice rings out, and I sigh, watching as Vanya's form settles down into the ground, like fine dust, her eyes closed, her body gone in seconds.

And I'm finally able to sleep.

The next couple of days are spent wading through the jungle and avoiding close encounters with some dangerous animals.

"We should arrive there at sundown," Joaquin mentions when we stop for a snack.

Unaccustomed with too much sun, I'm getting more tired than usual, so that news is music to my ears.

"Perfect," I reply, popping a piece of fruit into my mouth.

Out of nowhere, a small monkey jumps on my shoulder, her tiny hands reaching for the food. Its brown-reddish fur glints in the light, its huge tail hanging over my back as it steals my food.

"Titi monkey," Joaquin points out, smiling at the monkey's antics. "The mate shouldn't be far off," he says and right on time, another monkey appears, carrying its young on its back.

"So cute," Vanya gushes, trying to wave her hand at the monkey currently residing on my back.

Joaquin nods. "They're one of the few monkey species

that are monogamous," he explains, going into detail about the monkey population of Peru.

"Vlad, look!" Vanya yells when the monkey jumps off my back, following its mate as they take their place on a tree. Their tails are hanging down, slowly moving toward each other until they become entwined.

"It's called tail twining," Joaquin notes, and Vanya can't stop running around, marveling at how cute the monkeys are. "It's an affectionate gesture for them," he explains, Vanya's eyes going wide.

"It's a sign, Vlad! It's a sign." She comes rushing back to me, her arms holding tightly onto me. "It's a sign," she continues, almost out of breath.

"What sign?" I ask, ignoring Joaquin's odd stare.

She opens her mouth to speak, but nothing comes out. In the blink of an eye she's gone, an unusual screech sounding in the forest.

"Shit!" Joaquin curse. "We need to move," he starts packing his stuff, urging me to do the same.

"Why?" I frown, confused at the hurry.

"We need to reach *El viejo* before sundown," he says cryptically.

Seeing to my own stuff, I place the backpack on my shoulders and I follow him.

We do in fact reach the designed spot just as the sun leaves the sky. A couple of connected cabins in the middle of nowhere, *El viejo*'s dwellings are nothing much — not that I expected much, anyway.

One step into the enclosure, and a man in a long robe exits one of the cabins, his eyes narrowed as he takes us in.

"*Abuelo*," Joaquin addresses him, lowering his head in a sign of respect.

The man barely pays him attention as he walks forward, his movements brisk for someone his age.

Stopping in front of me, he raises his head to look me in the eye.

"*Te estaba esperando,*" he states, looking me up and down before closing his eyes and breathing in the air around.

Moving around in a circle, he starts chanting something, his voice low.

"*Muévanse, siempre muévanse,*" he intones, the wind howling strongly as if reacting to his voice.

"Come," he eventually tells us, inviting us into his home.

"What are you seeking here, stranger?" El viejo turns to me, and for a moment I feel like his eyes can see right through me.

"What everyone else does." I smile. "To have my curiosity assuaged."

"Ah, a non-believer. I see." He nods to himself.

"I told him he wouldn't be well received because he doesn't believe," Joaquin interjects.

"He does not believe yet he is here. There is always a reason," he says, moving around the small space and offering us some freshly brewed tea.

"Tell me, stranger. What plagues you?"

He sits us on the floor, settling next to us and completing a circle of three.

"I have some episodes," I tentatively start, slowly recounting my issue. I may not believe in this, but the mere possibility that it might work, should it just be a fluke, pushes me forward.

I need her.

Sisi is my only impetus for moving forward, even when the entire process is so antithetic to my core beliefs.

"I see," *El viejo* responds, studying me, his shrewd eyes taking in everything.

"You're desperate," he continues, and Joaquin chuckles.

"The mere fact he's here means he's more than desperate. You've heard of him, *abuelo, el Supay*."

El viejo doesn't answer, still looking at me.

"You rule over death, when life is right in front of you," he says quietly. "I will help you, stranger. But not because you deserve it." He pins me down with his stare. "For you know you do not."

I nod at his words, the mere fact that I'd put my hand on Sisi making me the least worthy son of a bitch to ever exist.

"But because someone else deserves it. And through you, they will get what they deserve," he continues cryptically, and I frown.

"Don't." He puts a hand up when I'm about to speak. "We may have just met, stranger, but I know you." He pauses, the air swirling around, tension mounting. "You who profess no God and no religion but take science as your creed. But now there is no science and here you are." His words stilted, his phrases are mysterious at best as he continues to bare my entire identity.

"I know your problem." His hand comes up to touch my forehead. "It's here and." The hand moves lower until it hovers over my heart. "Your head rules everything, your heart six feet under. You cannot understand when you've never tried to listen."

"My episodes *must* be rooted in my absent memories," I

speak, looking him square in the eye. "And that is a matter of only this," I say as I point to my brain. "It's faulty, and I've heard that your potions may help with that."

El viejo stares at me for a second before he starts chuckling.

"Stranger," he smiles, "your problem is not a faulty mind. You cannot tell a dog to run while holding the leash," he responds, again his words haphazardly indirect. "Let go, and everything will go with it," he says, rising up.

"Go to sleep. All of you. Tomorrow we will start." He doesn't even spare us a glance as he leaves the cabin.

"He winked at me." Vanya comes closer to giddily whisper in my ear. I just roll my eyes at her.

But as I'm falling asleep, I can't help but continue contemplating his words, excitement simmering inside of me in spite of the way my logical brain is trying to pull the brakes on this.

The following day, cup in my hand, I see *El viejo* looking at me expectantly so I just chug it. We'd spent the entire day in preparation for this one moment — the consumption of the ayahuasca. El viejo had talked most of the day, trying to push me past my own biases and prejudices and to embrace the unknown.

Unfortunately, his words had gone on blind ears. And as I wait for the brew to take effect, I realize it's not working. Not one hour later, not even five. Not even the following day.

"You're not ready for the ayahuasca, stranger, and she does not deem to help you if you cannot help yourself."

"What do you mean?" I frown.

"Here." He pushes his finger toward my chest. "You're holding so tightly to your control, over your mind, over everything. You need to let it go," he says blankly.

"I can't," I reply honestly. I give up control when I lose my mind in my episodes, I'm not about to let that happen while I'm in control... while I can help it.

"But see, that's just your problem. You hold it all in so, so tightly. Things want to come out, and they do the only way they can. They seek cracks, and when they find them, they ambush them in order to get out. Your episodes are merely representation of that which you *don't* want out," he tells me, his words stunning me.

Because I don't want things to get out.

"How?" The words are out of my mouth before I can stop myself. How could I do this when I *know* that once I open the gates, Hell will come crashing down.

"Slowly," he grunts, telling me to follow him.

ALMOST TWO MONTHS LATER, DAYS FILLED WITH HARD LABOR and meditation, and *El viejo* finally deems me ready to try ayahuasca again.

For the first time I'd put my own prejudices aside and I'd allowed him to guide me, from telling me what I should gather from the jungle, to building things with my own hands, and finally to blanking my mind and letting myself go—even if just for a minute.

We'd started slow, and he's tried to target the rage I have within me. Breathing exercises on top of daily sessions of meditations seem to have done wonders to my mood, and for the first time I'm optimistic about the future.

Joaquin too, had been quite shocked by the effort I'd put in. He left me here after a couple of days and has only recently returned, curious of my progress.

"You've done a lot in this short time, stranger," *El viejo* tells me, handing me my cup of freshly brewed *ayahuasca*.

In the time I've been here, I'd also had the opportunity to learn more about the flora and fauna of the region, and especially what makes these plants so sought after. *El viejo* told me about his ancestors and how they used these plants to communicate with those *beyond*.

While I have not suddenly become a believer, I've certainly started to listen and analyze things from *their* perspective, figuring culture, geography and topography into how these plants are perceived and why some are even venerated.

I bring the cup to my lips, tasting the bitter liquid and giving a small thanks to mother nature for everything she'd given me these past few weeks. Closing my eyes, I will myself to relax, knowing that this time it will work.

"I am here, stranger. Let ayahuasca guide you on your journey," I hear *El viejo's* voice as the blackness of my closed lids starts shifting into colors and shapes, the entire space shifting with me until I feel myself shrinking down into the size of a particle.

My breath labored, I feel my heart beating strongly in my chest, my veins working hard to pump my blood. It's like every sound is magnified, or maybe in my small stature I'm just closer to these sounds.

I feel… everything. I hear the buzzing of the bees, and

crickets, and every other creature crawling on this earth. I open my eyes and I can almost touch the particles of light, so fine and separated in the ether as they greet my being.

Am I or am I not?

I don't even know what I am… or who I am, as I let myself fall and become one with the nature. The entirety of my history falls away as I take in the vastness of the sea, fear entirely absent as I let myself be carried by the waves, not even caring that they may drown my small self.

Water floods my senses, until I'm back on shore again.

I look around and there is not a soul in the vicinity, the expanse of land infinite for what my eyes can take it.

I walk around for what seems like an eternity before I spot something else.

A rabbit.

A small white rabbit hops toward me, stopping when he's a few steps away. His eyes are bloody red as he looks upon me.

It blinks. Then it runs.

I don't know why, but I follow, running after the tiny creature until I hit a brick wall, my entire body reeling from the impact.

"What…" I whisper, raising my head to regard the looming wall. Even as I look to the sky, I cannot seem to find its end point.

"Here," I hear a voice call to me, and without even thinking I follow. The voice gets increasingly louder, until I find myself in another room, this time filled with children.

I'm in the middle of the crowd as tens of children swarm around me, all of them screaming and yelling and protesting something.

Suddenly, they turn their eyes on me, noticing my presence for the first time. Their features draw up in anger and they give a shout before chasing me.

I don't even know how I evade them. I just run and run and run. My feet carry me to places I shouldn't be able to access. My body reacts first, and then my mind follows.

I watch how under my eyes, the background changes again, walls erecting around me, steel machinery appearing everywhere.

"That's it, my little miracle," I hear someone say, his breath next to my ear. "The aorta is the largest artery in the body. You've learned your lesson well," he praises, putting a silver tray with different instruments in front of me.

"Let's see how you put it into practice, too. Dissect the aorta from beginning to end, and you may earn a prize."

I nod, grabbing on to the instruments that I know by name by now. Every step, every technical term, it's embedded in my mind as I start the dissection, cutting into live flesh, the screams of my subject deafening, yet so familiar that I don't even mind them.

I am entirely focused on pleasing the man watching behind me, knowing that if I do, the reward will be good indeed — and not only for me.

I bring the scalpel down on his chest, removing all skin and flesh from bone, cutting into muscle until the sternum is visible. Then, I switch to different instruments to open his chest cavity to get access to his heart.

Blood comes out in spurts, my technique new and unpracticed. But I don't mind it as my sole goal is to bring this to an end and get my sister a new set of clothes.

Sister.

Where did that thought come from?

I have a sister?

I raise my head up from the opened up carcass in front of me, and I see *her*.

She's small, so excruciatingly small as she holds onto the rabbit I'd chased earlier. She notices me looking at her and she turns to me slowly, giving me a dazzling smile.

"You're back, brother," she whispers, warmth dripping from her tone.

"V…" I start, the name stuck on my tongue.

A light tremor goes through my surroundings, mounting until the very building I'm in starts shaking, the walls crumbling.

"V!" I yell to her, extending my hand out to her to get her to safety. But she just shakes her head, her arms tightening over the rabbit.

The entire structure collapses, and yet none of the debris touches me.

I blink and waves start crashing into me, the water so red you'd think it was blood.

"Run," I hear Vanya's voice in my head, so I do, the waves following me. One look back and like a tsunami, the waves are becoming taller and taller.

I open my mouth to reply to her, but everything happens at once. The water swallows me whole, inundating my senses. I taste the metallic hint of blood in my mouth, and as I try my best to fight against it, I can't do anything as I start choking on it.

"You shouldn't have come here, brother," my sister tells me as she slowly comes toward me. I'm still coughing up blood, the scenery changed again.

A sterile white room, devoid of anything but me and Vanya.

"V?" I ask, my voice ragged.

"You should have stayed back. You survived after all, and isn't life the best gift of all?" she asks, crouching down in front of me.

"V… what's happening?"

"There's a reason why you can't remember, Vlad. It was the only way to keep living," she tells me, her voice sad and rueful.

"I don't understand."

"Don't you? We've been together since birth. I know you best." She turns her gaze to me. "My twin, my very own flesh. My protector. But what happened to us there…" She takes a deep breath. "You won't be the same if you remember, Vlad." Her voice is gentle as her hand covers mine.

"I need to. I need to find Miles and make him pay and…" I trail off.

"I know what you want, brother mine. Your secrets have never been hidden. You want to be worthy of her love." She sighs, standing up and pacing the room. "But I fear you won't be able to handle the memories."

"I can," I reply, my voice resolute. "I can," I repeat with even more confidence.

"Maybe you are ready… maybe you've finally grown," she whispers, almost to herself.

Planting herself in front of me, she materializes a knife, handing it to me.

"Then do it. Finish off the one thing that stands between you and the past," she instructs as she closes my hand over the hilt of the knife.

"What… what do you mean?" I croak, my eyes wide.

"I've stood by your side all these years, brother mine. I've watched over you, steering you in what I thought was the right direction. But I see that I've failed you." She turns her head to the side, a lone tear falling down. "I've let you use me as a buffer, so you never had to face what really happened. But no more." She shakes her head, wiping at her eyes.

"V… I don't understand."

"You need to let me go, Vlad. Let me return where I belong so you too can return where you belong."

She orients the knife with the tip toward her heart, pushing it slightly.

"No… no… I can't," I suddenly say, the prospect of never seeing her again too scary to contemplate.

"She'll be there for you, brother. Lean on her as you leaned on me. Even more so." She smiles sadly. "But for that you have to let her in. No more secrets, no more omissions," she pauses. "Tell her about me." She pushes the knife a little deeper.

"No, V. I can't do this. You're…" I trail off, tears in my eyes.

"I'm part of you, Vlad. I've always been. But I'm also… more." Her mouth curls up. "And you need to let me go."

"V…" I shake my head, my heart beating loudly in my chest.

"You've suppressed everything, brother. But it's all in here." She touches her finger to my head. "You just have to let it all come back."

"Will it help the episodes?" I ask, ashamed to even contemplate this.

"Episodes," Vanya chuckles and I frown. "I'm afraid those are my fault. I tried so hard to seal the rift in your mind... banish all the bad memories, that I didn't expect they would fight me back. They should lessen once I'm gone, just as your memories should slowly come back."

"You mean..." I blink disoriented, her words strange and yet making sense.

"I've been your shield for too long, Vlad. I'm tired. Please let me go," she whispers, pushing the knife even deeper.

"V..."

"Please, brother." She turns her eyes to me, those black irises so similar to my own, and I realize I have a choice to make.

"Thank you, V. For keeping me company for so long. And I'm sorry," I whisper, finally pushing the knife into her heart.

A sad smile appears on her face, and as she closes her eyes, her form dissipates in the air.

And for the first time, I know it's forever.

"Goodbye, sister mine. I love you," I whisper, closing my eyes.

The next time I open my eyes I'm back in the hut, *El viejo* sitting next to me meditating.

"You're back," he says without looking at me.

"I am..." I respond, my eyes roving around the room, looking for her.

Swiftly getting up, I head outside, still searching for her with my eyes.

"She's gone, stranger," *El viejo* says. "It's for the best."

"How..." I'm about to ask him how he knows about

her in the first place, but one glance at his secretive expression and I realize some things are *not* meant to be understood.

"She said the episodes will lessen with time," I explain what Vanya had told me, *El viejo* nodding expectantly as if he'd been sure of the outcome from the beginning.

"You need to face your main trigger. Blood. Most likely it's one of the things that made you block your memories, but also the thing that will bring them back," he states, going over a few things that might help me.

"Thank you," I tell him honestly, my skepticism falling away for the first time.

There's a lightness inside of me that wasn't there before, as if I could spread nonexistent wings and fly.

"Don't thank me yet, stranger. There's much work to still be done," he says, going over another plan of meditations and ayahuasca treatments. "These should hasten the return of your memory."

I nod, ready to follow all of his instructions.

It's a couple days later when I head back into Manu to meet with Joaquin and get some resources from the village that my phone rings for the first time in months.

"Why, hi there, old pal," I joke when I see it's Marcello.

"Wow, you finally deign to answer your phone," he says drily. *"I've been trying to reach you for weeks."*

"Well, here I am. What's up?"

"I wanted to thank you for your help with Nicolo. And with every-thing." He takes a deep breath, and for the first time I'm stunned by something Marcello's said.

"You're welcome."

He coughs slightly. *"As a peace offering, I've been trying to reach you to invite you to the wedding. But you've been MIA for so long, it's already tomorrow,"* he chuckles.

"What wedding?"

Is he renewing his vows with Catalina? Somehow that's sweet.

"My sister, Assisi, is getting married to one of Benedicto's sons," he starts, but I stop listening after hearing Sisi's name. My entire body goes slack, and I find it hard to breathe.

"What did you say?" I ask brusquely.

"She's had the worst of luck," Marcello sighs. *"She realized she was pregnant earlier last month so we've tried to push the wedding so there wouldn't be a scandal,"* he continues, but I tune everything out.

My phone falls out of my hand, my feet barely holding me upright.

Sisi. Marriage. Pregnant.

I bring my fist to my chest, punching myself as hard as I can, feeling an incoming attack.

I wanted to do the right thing for once. Become a worthy man for her. But it seems I'm bound to be the villain anyway, because there's nothing in Hell or any infernal dimension stopping me from taking her back.

Even if she'll hate me even more.

My blood is pounding in my veins, and I feel myself slipping again.

Fuck, but just the thought of her with another man is enough to make me want to raze the village to the ground.

I need to get a grip on myself.

I know that if I let myself go, if I give in to this murderous rage inside of me, then I'm never going to make it in time for that fucking wedding.

And I'll lose her forever.

"Where are you, V? I need you," I whisper and for the first time, nothing answers back.

Even as I battle with my own self for control over my body, one thing is for certain. Nothing is more important than Sisi.

And for her, I'll prevail.

7
SISI

"Did you get it?" I usher Raf inside the house, already restless with anxiety.

Since Marcello is at his speech therapy today, I'd invited Raf to come over, asking him for a huge favor.

Blushing deeply, he nods slowly, handing me the bag.

"God, you're a sweetheart." I give him a big hug before I reach inside the bag to find the package.

"Are you sure?" he asks me as I all but drag him to my room.

"I don't know, Raf. I've been reading up on the internet about the symptoms and they fit. Besides," I add, dropping my head low, "it's not entirely improbable. He did…" I trail off when I see him blush even further. "Doesn't matter now. We'll see what the test says," I declare.

I unpack the test with hurried movements, almost afraid to find out.

For a few weeks now I've been feeling off. Weakness and nausea in the morning and just an overall state of tiredness that was inexplicable. It had all come crashing down when I'd realized that my period was late.

It was never late.

Since I'd first gotten my period, it had *always* come right on time, so I'd known when to expect it. When the day had come and passed and still no period, I'd started getting worried. And so I'd turned to the internet.

Pregnant.

The possibility that I might get pregnant hadn't even crossed my mind. After Maxim had dropped me off at home *that day*, I'd just shut down. Mentally *and* physically.

My body had taken the brunt of it, and I'd spent a week in bed just recuperating from the various injuries he'd inflicted on me. Two of them had even scarred pretty badly, the one on my neck and the one on my breast.

I don't even want to know what had happened down there because it had been excruciating to sit down, move around, or even go to the bathroom for the first few days.

Luckily, with Marcello in the hospital and Lina and Claudia gone, I didn't have to explain my sorry state to anyone. I'd put a scarf around my neck and some make-up on for Venezia's benefit, and she hadn't realized anything was wrong.

Slowly, my body had started to heal, but my mind was just lagging behind. There wasn't a moment where I wasn't thinking about him or trying to understand why he'd done that to me when I would have *never* left him.

Regardless of the damage to my body, I would have stuck by him. Because I knew it wasn't him. I knew he wasn't in control.

I would have forgiven him all the pain he'd caused my

body. But what I could *not* and will *never* forgive is the pain he'd caused my soul.

Unwanted…

Days on end I'd had nightmares, his words ringing in my ears, his mocking insults embedding themselves so deeply in my head I couldn't rid myself of them.

It had gotten so bad I could barely sleep, knowing that if I did close my eyes I'd see him sneering down at me.

And yet, despite shattering me inside out, I still couldn't shake the love I have for him.

I'm a fucking idiot.

I'd been so sure that with time I'd be able to put it all behind me, and while I'm still working on *not* loving him, the issue at hand complicates things. Because *if* I am pregnant, then I'll find myself with a pretty permanent issue.

Taking a deep breath, I head into the bathroom, following the instructions on the package and peeing on the stick. Then, I just wait.

"What are you going to do if you're pregnant?" Raf asks. He's sitting on my bed, watching me pace around like a lunatic.

"Can I not think about that for now?" My voice is low and a little trembly.

"Sisi…" he continues, and I know he means well. This isn't something to be taken lightly.

"I don't know," I admit. "I've never thought…" I've never even thought about having children. Me? A mother? What do I even know about being a mother, since I've never had one? "There has to be a solution," I say, although my voice lacks confidence.

"You could always get an abortion," Raf notes. "I could help you," he continues, but I quickly shake my head.

"No. That's out of the question," I tell him. He *should* know that I'd never do that, given my own history with being abandoned at Sacre Coeur. I'd never willingly do *anything* to harm a child of mine.

"I know," he sighs, "I threw it on the table just in case." He gives me a sad smile.

The phone rings to signal the time is up. My hands are sweaty, my entire body shaking as I pick up the test. Closing my eyes, I say a short prayer before opening them.

Pregnant.

"So?" Raf asks, and I sniffle a sob, my eyes already moist with tears. I hand him the test, going to sit on the bed.

Head in my hands, I massage my temples, trying to alleviate this feeling of doom that's settled over me.

A child.

My God, but how can I have a child? There's also Vlad and he… well, he cannot handle a child even more so. He's too unstable to even be near one.

Not that he'd want to.

Why is it that there are times when I forget he threw me aside? That I meant *nothing* to him? In his own words, he'd been bored and I'd been just an experiment. Someone to pass time with.

"Sisi." Raf sits down next to me, taking me in his arms. "It's going to be okay. We can think of something," he whispers into my hair.

Sobs rack my body as I expel everything I've been holding inside of me.

"Marcello will kill him. He'll kill me, he'll…" I can't even form proper words. "What do I even know about babies?" I cry out, my thoughts jumbled in my head, all my emotions coming to the surface. "I don't know what I'm going to do," I tell him sincerely.

I'm in so over my head.

"Marry me," he says suddenly, and I whip my head back, my eyes widening at his words.

"What?"

"Marry me, Sisi, and no one will have to know. Our families are already hoping we might become more."

"Raf…" I shake my head, speechless.

"We may not have known each other long, but you're my dearest friend, and the only one I feel safe enough to share my secret with. Maybe with time…" He trails off.

"I don't know what to say, Raf. This is so sudden. *Too* sudden."

I'd never thought of Raf as anything but a friend, and I don't think I'd *ever* see him in a different light.

Not after him.

"It would solve both our issues. My father wants me to marry soon anyway, and I could claim your baby as my own," he continues, surprising me even more.

"Raf… Thank you, but you know I don't feel that way about you," I admit. We'd been over this from the beginning. And while Vlad may be out of the picture now, that doesn't mean that he's not still in my heart.

"We don't have to be more then. We'll do just fine as friends," he starts, taking my hands in his. "I know you're not in love with me, just as I'm not in love with you. But we have what other people lack—trust. And I swear I would care for your baby just as I care for you," he says sincerely, and for a moment I'm lost in his light eyes. So full of kindness, and so fundamentally different from the pair I love.

"I'm scared," I whisper, taking a deep breath. "I never thought I'd find myself in this situation."

But what is the alternative, really? Give birth out of wedlock and be shunned like Lina had been? If Marcello doesn't kill me and Vlad first, that is. I've heard enough of our world to know that it's simply not done, and I've seen firsthand what Lina had had to endure because she'd been unmarried when she'd had Claudia.

I could withstand it. After all, I'm good at taking people's insults in stride. But what about my child? He's innocent and I *know* he will bear the brunt of it all.

"Okay," I whisper, "let's do it. You're right that it's the only way, and I promise that I'll be the best wife I can be. Just don't expect…" I drift off, and he catches my meaning.

"I know where your heart is, Sisi. You have nothing to worry about in that regard." He gives me a small smile.

"Thank you." I wrap my arms around him in a hug. "Thank you," I repeat.

ONCE THE INITIAL SHOCK OF THE PREGNANCY WEARS OFF, I start warming up to the idea. In fact, one might say I'm becoming too thrilled at the prospect of a baby.

I'll finally have someone *just* for me. Someone whom I'll love and will love me back. The fact that he's part of *him* is a plus, since this way I'll have something of him as well.

Marcello's been in and out of the house with his treatments, so I haven't found a good time to tell him the news about the marriage. But more than anything, I haven't been able to hear anything about *him*.

"God, I can't even say his name," I mutter to myself, annoyed.

He's become something of a *he who shall not be named* in my head, mostly because even thinking up his name causes me profound pain. That doesn't seem to have stopped me from being curious about him and wondering what he's been up to though.

Marcello's been tight-lipped and other than that, I simply have no other way of knowing about him.

"I wonder if you'll look like your father." I pat my belly, a smile on my face as I imagine a dark-haired, dark-eyed child —a carbon copy of *him*. All I know is that I'll lavish all my love on this child and he'll never have to doubt whether he is wanted or not.

"I love you, little one," I whisper, happiness already enveloping me as I imagine our future. *He* may not be in it, but I'll have the next best thing.

And that will make it bearable.

Raf's been nothing but a sweetheart as he'd inquired about my health almost daily. I know this marriage is advantageous for him too, since his father has been wanting a union with our family for a long time.

And when we'll be married, his father will finally leave him alone and everything will be in order for the inheritance succession. Raf may not want the power, but someone *will* have to take it, and better him than his awful being of a brother.

Even knowing that it benefits him too, I am eternally grateful to him for offering to help me.

Laying down in bed, I start reading a book about pregnancy that I'd gotten online, wanting to know as much as I can and be prepared when the time comes. Already, I have a feeling it's going to be a boy and I've started looking at names.

Immersed in my reading, I'm surprised when my phone starts ringing, Raf's name flashing on the screen.

"I'll be by the house in an hour," he says as soon as I answer.

"An hour? How come?" I frown, since we hadn't agreed on anything today.

"I've asked permission from your brother to take you out. With a chaperone, of course," he jokes and I release a small chuckle. Marcello's been very uptight about everything—especially about letting me unattended in the presence of any man.

If he only knew the things I'd gotten up to with Vlad…

A smile plays on my lips at the thought. He'd been so adamant about me being careful with men and especially Vlad, that I have no doubt he'd have an apoplexy if he knew I was already pregnant with his baby.

Shaking my head at the notion, I let Raf know I'll be ready for him. I slowly get out of bed, looking around for some clothes.

I take care to hide the scar on my neck with a scarf, not wanting anyone asking questions about what clearly looks like a bite mark. But as I take a seat at my vanity to put on some make-up, I can't help the way my eyes are drawn to the jewelry box and the necklace nestled inside.

I'd taken it off that night, and I hadn't put it back on since. Still, I had not been able to trash it. Maybe because the situation had not sunk in at the time, or maybe because I was still hoping that he would come back to me.

Would I have taken him back?

I don't know. If he'd come running back while I hadn't had the time to process everything, I might have still given him a chance. But as the days went on, I realized that if I ever gave in, I would just show him he could walk all over me at any time. That because of my feelings for him I would take it all in stride, ready to forgive him in exchange for a little attention.

Unwanted…

No, what's done is done. And I need to put everything behind me. A new chapter awaits me, and only by putting him out of my mind can I truly find some happiness.

Before I know what I'm doing, I palm the small box, taking it with me.

Raf is already downstairs, waiting for me. And after we leave the house, I throw the box in the first public trash can I see.

"Sisi." Raf shakes his head when he sees what I've done. I just shrug and keep walking.

"It's done," I say, feeling a massive loss inside my heart, but convinced it's just temporary, I shrug it off.

I'm not the first one to suffer from a broken heart and certainly not the last.

I will survive.

At least I hope I will. I don't know how in such a short period of time *he* had become such an integral part of my life. Even now, knowing he isn't near me almost makes me break out in chills, his proximity the only thing that could make me content.

Lord, I need to stop thinking about him. It will pass.

Eventually…

I hadn't told Raf all the particularities of our breakup, but he'd inferred enough to know how much Vlad had hurt me. And so he'd been a sweetheart, and he'd tried not to bring him up too much.

"So where are we going?" I ask as we stroll down the New York streets, his aunt a few steps behind us acting as chaperone.

"I thought you'd like to go to the hospital. For a checkup," he whispers.

"Raf." My mouth opens in shock at his thoughtfulness. "What about your aunt? Even now she's so vigilant," I note as the women narrows her eyes at us for being too close.

"I already booked the appointment. I can distract her for a while until you finish. Tell her you're getting your hair done or something," he suggests. "There's a salon right next to the clinic."

"Wow, you really planned this, didn't you?" I watch him in awe as a blush creeps up his neck. It's a stark contrast against his fair complexion and immediately visible.

"I've been reading about it. And it's good to have a consult early," he says shyly, and I take his hand in mine, giving it a big squeeze.

"You're a dear," I tell him with a smile.

Sometimes I can't believe how kind Raf is. Surely someone like him can't be real. And he continues to amaze me with his thoughtfulness.

"Thank you."

True to his plan, we make a trip to the salon, and while they make themselves comfortable in the waiting room, I exit through the back and head to the clinic.

I guess by now I have enough practice to sneak around,

so I'm not too worried. Especially since Raf's planned this to a T.

Inside the clinic I'm swiftly received by a nurse and after she has me fill in a questionnaire, she leads me to the consult room.

"Good afternoon, Miss Lastra," the doctor comes in, greeting me. I smile in return, even though I am a little nervous about what the checkup entails.

She tries her best to make me comfortable before starting on the pelvic exam. I try to ignore what's happening, or the fact that she's eye to eye with my lady bits.

"Everything looks good here," she finally says, and calls a nurse to wheel in a machine. "Let's do an ultrasound, shall we?"

I nod, and she pulls my shirt up, squirting some cool gel on my stomach. Removing a wand from the machine, she starts moving it on the surface of my belly, the gel making it slip around effortlessly.

"There it is." The doctor smiles, pointing to a small dot on the screen. "I'd say you're about seven to eight weeks along," she tells me, but I half-listen, my eyes glued to the screen.

"You can hear the heartbeat," she continues, and I close my eyes, honing in on the sound.

Good God, I'm going to be a mother.

I don't know why hearing that tiny heartbeat makes me tear up, but I can't contain my emotions as it finally dawns on me that I'm going to have a baby.

A human life.

Ironic how out of all that death and destruction we'd ended up creating a life.

The doctor prescribes me some vitamins and schedules my next appointment. After everything is set, I thank her and head back to the salon, a new optimism rising inside of me.

Things are going to change. This time I'll have someone to care for. A hand on my stomach and a smile on my face, I meet with Raf and his aunt again.

She doesn't seem suspicious in the least as she just gives me a nod, returning to one of her phone calls.

"I told you she wouldn't notice." Raf gives me a conspiratorial smile as we head back to the car waiting for us.

"Well, well, if it isn't my retarded brother," a malicious voice resounds from behind us.

Turning around, I note a man coming toward us, his arms around two girls as he looks down at Raf. He's wearing an all leather outfit emphasizing his lean frame.

Stopping in front of us, he pushes his sunglasses over his hair, the long, dark locks wavy and restless in the wind, his light eyes full of animosity.

There's a malice coming from him and I can't help the way my lip curls in disgust as he continues to insult Raf to his face.

"B-b-brother," Raf replies, almost hiding behind me, his shoulders slumped, his eyes stuck to the pavement.

"And what do we have here," he whistles, looking me up and down before chuckling. "Of course, the retard and the repulsive," he jokes, his eyes on my birthmark as the girls by his side start giggling. "The two Rs," he continues, seemingly very pleased with himself as the girls simply stare at him in awe as if he just quoted a Shakespeare sonnet.

"This must be your reprobate brother," I nod toward

him, not doing anything to hide my disgust, "three Rs." I give him a fake smile.

Raf had told me about his brother, Michele, and how strained their relationship was. In fact, strained might be an understatement since Michele is clearly a grade A asshole.

I'd heard all about the origin of their conflict and the fact that their father wanted Raf to inherit the capo title, and not Michele, even though the latter was the older one by a few months.

Raf hadn't been able to tell me why his father was so bent on doing that, even as his older son went off the rails. But the more Benedicto enforced the issue, the more Michele pushed back, doing all sorts of nasty things to get attention.

Of course, Raf had always been the target of his taunts, and one of the reasons why Raf's always tried *not* to draw attention.

"And you must be the nun my brother's marrying," he continues, coming closer and getting into my face, a smug smile on his lips as he no doubt thinks he can intimidate me. "Couldn't you have found another one? She probably doesn't even know what to do with a dick." He tries to pull another joke, and of course the girls by his side think he's said the funniest thing ever, their laughter irritatingly loud.

Not afraid of him, since I've met more than my fair share of bullies like him, I raise my chin slightly, meeting his gaze with mine.

Why, but he could be Cressida's male counterpart.

"Well," I start, a sweet look on my face as I slowly bat my lashes at him, "I certainly wouldn't know what to do with yours." I move ever so slightly toward him, my hands on his shoulders as I pat him lightly.

He frowns, not realizing what I mean, at least not until my knee makes contact with said dick. He winces in pain, bending forward, his eyes shooting daggers at me.

"Since you should probably buy a new one." I wink at him just as the girls by his side gasp, trying to help him.

One look at Raf and he nods, both of us getting in the car and calling out for his aunt to come along too.

I can already hear his curses and the way he calls me bitch as the car leaves the parking lot.

"Dear, was that your brother?" Raf's aunt asks, barely paying attention to us, "I should have said hello." She frowns for a moment before continuing her phone conversation, promptly forgetting us.

"I'm sorry," Raf apologizes as soon as the car is in motion, getting us as far away from that horrible human being.

"Don't. I understand now why you'd hate him. He's vile," I reply, my lips pursed. "A few minutes in his presence and I feel like scrubbing my skin clean. Ew," I stick out my tongue in disgust.

Raf chuckles, telling me that was a mild Michele, and that usually he's even worse.

I listen attentively, dreading the fact that he's soon going to be my brother-in-law. One thing is for sure. If Michele tries something, he's going to have a few surprises. I may be a *nun* but I guess he'll have a holy surprise when he sees I don't take anyone's shit.

8
SISI

"**W**hy?" I whimper in pain as I stare at his face.

So emotionless.

"This was just an experiment, Sisi. And it has failed," he shrugs, coming closer to me and gazing down at me with disgust.

"But I'm sure there are enough women out there to take your place, after all, you're nothing special."

I gasp at his cruelty, tears in the corner of my eyes.

"Please, don't say that," I whisper, wishing with my entire being that he would just laugh it off and say he is joking.

"Why?" He comes even closer to me, backing me into the wall. "Am I hurting your tender feelings?" he drawls as one finger moves down my face, the contact making me shiver. "Am I making you feel… unwanted?" he rasps in my ear, my entire body stilling at the words.

"Stop, please," I beg him, the words resounding in my ears, their echo unstoppable. "Stop."

But he doesn't.

Hands wrapped around my neck, he tightens his hold until I can barely breathe.

"Stop." *Even my voice becomes barely audible as I try to push him off me.*

But he doesn't budge.

He has an evil smile painted on his face, as if he couldn't wait to kill me faster.

One hand leaves my neck, the other still snuffing the life out of me. Hiking my skirt up, he's inside my body in one thrust, the pain making me blank.

"No!" I yell, shooting out of bed. I'm covered in sweat, my entire body hyperventilating.

It was a dream. It was just a dream.

I take a deep breath, trying to calm my nerves.

But as I glance down my body, my mouth opens on a silent scream as I see a pool of blood between my thighs, my sheets soaked in it.

I blink twice, trying to chase sleep away, convinced it's still a dream. But when I open my eyes again to see the blood still there, a new fear envelops me.

No… No… My baby.

And I scream. I scream to the top of my lungs, fear over-taking me and making me tremble uncontrollably.

Venezia is the first to burst through my door, her eyes widening as she takes in all the blood around me.

"Call an ambulance." I don't know how I find the strength to speak. Even more so in coherent sentences. But I do. And as it dawns on me that I need to act fast, I realize I can't succumb to fear, or desperation.

I need to fight.

Maybe it's not too late. I'd read about spotting. Maybe it's just that.

Even though looking at the amount of blood, *it's not that.*

I keep on holding myself together, even as they load me into the ambulance, and all the way to the hospital. I just close my eyes and imagine my dark-haired baby and how happy we'll be together. I hold on to that thought, and it's the only thing standing between me and a breakdown.

And then it happens.

"I'm sorry, Miss Lastra, but you've suffered a miscarriage," the doctor says, and I can't hear anything after that.

Just like that, *everything*'s been snatched away from me.

I can't even find it in me to cry anymore, or wail, or scream at the injustice. I can only stare at the walls that seem to share in my desolation—with their dark shadows filling up the light.

It's a while after that Marcello comes to see me, and I feel even worse for troubling him.

What if he sends me away? Again?

The thought is unbearable, so I do the only thing I can —I lie.

"We're getting married," I state as confidently as I can, trying to ignore the way my heart hurts as I lie about loving Raf, or about everything.

Like the overprotective brother he is, Marcello is contrite, trying to convince me that I don't have to marry Raf.

But he doesn't get it. He doesn't realize that I don't *have* to, but I *need* to.

Even now I feel myself succumbing deeper into myself, and I know that if I continue like this I'll only become worse.

I need someone who wants me, even if it's for all the wrong reasons. I just need somewhere to belong.

"We'll see," Marcello purses his lips, exiting the salon.

I promised Raf I'll marry him, and I will. Maybe in the process I'll find myself again too.

Lina and Venezia both visit me, shocking me with how much they've worried for me. It brings tears to my eyes to realize that there are some people who do care about me in this world.

But later, when the doctor discharges me home and I'm alone again, I can't help but reach for the small ultrasound picture I'd hidden in my drawer.

I hold it to my chest and I try to imagine again what it would have been like—the dark-haired boy I know I'll never meet.

And the tears start anew.

"Oh, God… why am I so cursed?" I ask out loud, only silence greeting me.

There's no other explanation for it. I *am* cursed.

And the worst thing is that… Life throws me the bait, giving me the illusion that I may find happiness, only to wrench it away from me at the worst moment—when I'm at my happiest.

It seems that it is my fate to be forever alone… and forever unwanted.

The days pass, but I barely notice whether it's day or night. The wedding arrangements are quickly dealt with, people coming and going from the house, Raf's family practically making camp here as they are getting increasingly excited for the wedding.

I just fake a smile and try to get through the motions, nothing really getting a reaction out of me.

Not even Raf with his sweet nature can make me snap out of my current state.

I'm simply surviving.

"Sisi," I hear Lina's voice as she knocks on my door the night before the wedding.

"Come in," I say, watching her enter the room, uncertainty all over her face.

"I wanted to talk to you before..." She trails off when she sees my blank face.

I nod, motioning her to the table by the window.

"I can't help but feel that you haven't been yourself," she starts, her hands fidgeting in her lap. I turn my head to her, my stare vacant—as it usually is—and I just shrug.

"I'll be fine," I respond, almost flippantly.

"I know losing a child can be extremely painful, but..." She starts talking, my ears already tuning everything out.

I'd lied that I hadn't known I was pregnant. That I was just as surprised as them. It made it easier to avoid their pitiful glances, and even easier for me to pretend that I'm fine.

But I'm not.

All I want to do is scream at the world that I'm *not* fine. That I want my baby back. That I want *him* back.

But it's never going to happen. No matter how much I tell myself that it isn't real — it is. And it hurts.

God, almost daily I have to battle with myself to even get out of bed. How I've managed to put on clothes, a pretty smile and nod at everyone's words is beside me.

I want to be left alone.

"You don't have to marry him, Sisi. If you don't want to." Lina's hand covers my own, the compassion reflected in her gaze almost moving me.

But how can you move something that does *not* exist anymore?

I've become increasingly certain that my heart must have died the same moment my baby did. Because that was the last time I felt something.

"It will be alright, Lina," I say stiffly. "It will all be alright."

The words sound fake to my ears too, so it's no wonder Lina frowns in concern, coming closer to me and taking me into her arms.

Once upon a time, that hug would have revitalized me. Now it feels just… bleak.

"I don't want you to feel forced into something just because you slept with him. Marcello isn't like my parents, Sisi. He's never going to push those outdated standards on you," she tells me, lightly stroking my short hair.

It's funny how no one's ever questioned my sudden change in behavior, my new hair, or the fact that I cannot exit the house without a scarf—during summer. For all their concern, do they *really* care?

"I want to," I reply, my gaze already fixed on the lawn outside, where my prince had once waited for me, to save me from my tower. "It's going to be fine," I repeat.

Lina doesn't seem convinced, but she leaves me alone at last.

And I can finally go back to sleep—the only time I can be together with my baby.

~

"You look so pretty, Sisi," Lina's voice makes me blink twice, and I try to pay attention to what she's saying.

Entwining the lace veil with a small diamond tiara, she places it over my coiffed hair.

"I can't believe you're getting married." I watch her through the mirror as she swipes a tear off her cheek. "You make such a pretty bride. The most beautiful." She leans in to kiss my forehead.

"Me neither," I murmur, forcing a smile.

Everyone around me is so happy, and given my atrocious lie, I can see why they'd be overjoyed for me. So I try to play into the illusion I've created, stretching my lips into a perpetual smile to ensure there's no doubt about my state of mind.

I am the bride, after all.

I stare at my reflection, unable to believe it's gotten to this point. How my life had degenerated in the span of one month. I'd never seen myself as particularly lucky, not given everything I've been through. But for one moment I'd thought that all the hardships would give way to happiness.

I'd left the convent that was the source of all my night-mares, and I'd finally found someone who understood me. Who saw *me* — with the good and the bad. I'd finally found myself after aimlessly wandering all my life.

But it hadn't lasted.

Now? Once again, I'm looking at a life of pretending.

Pretending I'm good.

Pretending I'm in love with my husband.

Pretending I'm not… more.

Recognizing the direction of my thoughts, I shake myself from my musings, turning back to Lina and smiling widely at her.

"It's going to be amazing," the lie just flows out of my mouth. "I never thanked you, Lina." I turn to her, the only truthful thing I'm willing to say today. "For everything that you've done for me at Sacre Coeur. I don't think I would have been here without you." I squeeze her hand.

Her eyes tear up again, and she can't help herself from sniffling, throwing her entire body toward me and wrapping her arms around me in a big hug.

"Oh, Sisi. You know how much I love you. You'll always be my sister. Never forget that," she whispers.

"Thank you. You and Claudia were the only two people keeping me sane there," I admit, returning her hug.

She may not know the extent of what happened to me at Sacre Coeur, but she's been my only source of comfort during those cold years. For that, there are no words that could do justice to how much I am thankful to her.

"You too Sisi. You were always the brave one, and you gave us a little courage each time." She smiles.

I wish I had that courage now, because even though my feet carry me toward Raf, my heart is already dead and buried.

The entire wedding entourage heads to the church, and Marcello and I are the last to arrive, prepared to walk arm in arm toward the altar.

"I'm proud of you, Sisi," Marcello tells me, kissing my cheeks right before making our entrance. It's the first time he's touched me for more than a second, and I soak in the contact. "But don't forget that you will always have a home with us," he continues and I nod, tears burning behind my eyes.

Following the musical cue, we walk slowly inside.

Raf is waiting for me at the altar, looking dashing in his black tux, his blond hair combed back, emphasizing his baby-blue eyes.

Ah, how I wish I could have loved him first. It would have saved me a world of heartache.

But even as those thoughts intrude in my mind, I know them to be wrong. Because although I am aware of my own heartbreak, I also know that there's only one man I could *ever* love. One man who seems to have been made just for me.

But it wasn't meant to be.

Maybe we were the right people at the wrong time. Or maybe he was just right for me, and I was wrong for him.

My feet feel heavy as I put one foot in front of the other, the distance shrinking by the second.

And suddenly I'm by Raf's side, the priest starting the ceremony, everyone looking extremely happy as they cheer us on from the sidelines.

A panic unlike any other takes hold of me, and I can barely stop myself from trembling.

"Will you..." the priest's words are a blur, my ears ringing with what I can only describe as a deafening sound.

I close my eyes, blinking rapidly. But then the entire room darkens, smoke infiltrating in the church.

For some reason, I don't know if this is real or if it's just something my sick mind is producing, rejecting the reality I find myself in and somehow creating a new one.

People are yelling, shots are fired. The noises become increasingly loud.

An arm sneaks around my waist, a hand on my mouth as I feel a hot breath on my neck.

"You're not getting rid of me, hell girl," he drawls, a dangerous sound that makes my already dead heart weep.

And then the world goes black.

9

SISI

A throbbing in my temples forces me to open my eyes, my lids are heavy, my entire body aching. It takes me a moment to regain my bearings and remember what had happened.

Pulling myself up, I note I am still in my wedding dress. But one glance around the room and I realize I'm in a foreign location.

I'm sitting on a huge king sized bed in the middle of an equally enormous room. I try to move my limbs, happy when I see that nothing is wrong with me.

But what happened?

I remember being so deep inside my head, trying to block the ceremony out and everything around me, that I hadn't realized when the whole church had filled with smoke. And then…

My eyes widen as I recall *his* words. In my ear. *His* arms. On my body.

"What in God's name happened?" I mutter aloud, more to myself.

The entire room is empty save for the bed. The almost ceiling high windows allow plenty of light to infiltrate the room, and I have to turn my gaze away, my eyes blinded by it.

I swing my legs off the bed, heading straight for the door.

If this is another one of Vlad's games, then he's going to be in for a small surprise, because I'm *not* about to allow him to embroil me in mood swings.

I can already foresee why he'd done this. He'd been too bored and had decided to mess with both me and Marcello.

A bitter smile escapes me as I realize I shouldn't think myself that important to him, after all hadn't he said the exact thing? That I wasn't the only woman in the world? He'd likely done it to toy with Marcello.

Regardless, I will not sit by and wait for him to make a fool of me again. No matter how much my heart still beats painfully in my chest knowing he's somewhere close. No. Our time has passed.

Wrapping my hand around the handle of the door, I pull down, not surprised to find the door locked.

Like the windows, the door is ceiling high as well. It's old too, the wood spoiled around the corners, the painting coming off in ugly stripes.

For a moment I'm saddened by what I'm about to do, since this is clearly a historic building. But he has left me no alternative.

Raising my foot, I balance myself on my other leg as I try to gain as much momentum as I can before kicking.

The sole of my foot connects with the wood, the sound reverberating in the room.

It's not budging.

The more I kick, the more I realize that for all its dilapidated appearance, the wood is strong — too strong for my puny kicks.

"Damn it," I mutter, using the back of my hand to wipe the sweat off my brow. It's hot, and this dress is weighing a ton.

A few deep breaths as I scan the room, and I decide I need to change strategies. Whatever happens, though, I'm not about to let Vlad get away with this. He may be bored, and looking for pawns to move around in his game of chess, but I won't be one.

It's only now that I realize what Marcello's been saying all along. Vlad doesn't know the meaning of friendship, or any relationship. He only knows how to use people to achieve his goals.

Like he did with me… until I proved to be useless to him.

Even now, he probably has some cameras installed somewhere, and he's watching from behind his wall full of screens, chuckling at my expense and at my poor attempts at escaping.

As soon as the thought forms in my head, I turn swiftly to the ceiling, finding the camera immediately.

Feeling my ire rising, I stomp until I'm standing right in front of it. I don't know if this has sound or not, but I have nothing to lose.

"You chose the wrong person to mess with, Vlad," I tell him, looking straight at the twitching lens. "You can't beat someone who has nothing to lose." I smirk, my hands going to my lengthy wedding dress as I grab onto the hem.

Without even thinking, I tear the lace up to my knees,

revealing the satin shift underneath. Using my teeth, I do the same until the lower part of the dress is completely gone.

With some breathing room, I'm immediately more at ease, air flowing around my legs and refreshing my body. My movements also feel less restricted.

And because I'm running on extremely low patience, I give him the middle finger too. Oh, how I wish I saw him react to *that*.

But I don't have time to think about that. Not when I need to get out of here.

Seeing that the door will not be a good option, I head to the windows, exhaling in relief when one of them opens.

At least I won't have to break this.

But my relief soon turns to fear as I gaze down and realize I'm nowhere near the ground. What is this? Second? Third floor?

"Good grief!" I get an overwhelming urge to cross myself, because even seeing how far the ground is from my position, I can't help but focus on it.

"It's not like I haven't done this before," I try to convince myself.

But it wasn't this high?!

"Okay, it's now or never," I whisper. The more I think about it, the more scared I'll be and I will never do it. Since I don't fancy remaining a prisoner, this is the only option.

"Fuck you, Vlad," I mutter, incensed that he'd put me in this situation in the first place.

Grabbing onto the frame of the window, I climb up on the sill, holding tight, my eyes half-closed.

"Why does it have to be so high?" I cry out in frustration.

But taking a deep breath, I still myself.

One. Two. Three.

And I jump.

Eyes still closed, I wait for the impending contact with the ground.

"Still dying to fall under me, I see," a voice says in my hair, strong hands holding on to me as they lower me to the ground.

Opening one eye, and then the other, I don't even know how to react to seeing *him* in the flesh.

I blink, my eyes on him as if I'm trying to figure out a puzzle.

He's still the same, even though it's been more than three months since we've last seen each other. But there's something different.

I can feel it.

His skin is tanned and there's a new stubble that wasn't there before. In all our time together, I'd never seen Vlad as anything but clean shaven.

The change is not only skin deep though. More than anything, there's something different about his energy.

Something warmer… something…

Stop!

I'm doing this again. Trying to understand him where there's absolutely nothing to understand. My lip curls up in disgust at my own self and my reaction to him, and I shove my hands forward, pushing him off of me.

"Damn, hell girl. Is that how you greet your future

husband?" he drawls, his voice still holding that alluring quality that always seemed to make me its captive.

I swallow, my own body betraying me as goosebumps form all over my skin.

"What did you just say?" I frown, taking a step back and putting some distance between us.

"Good on you to wake up," he says, his eyes looking up and down my body in a strange manner. "The minister is waiting."

He doesn't even let me reply as he wraps his fingers around my wrist, tugging me toward him and all but dragging me toward the entrance of the house.

My eyes widen as I realize where we are. Or rather, as I repeatedly blink, sure this must be a dream.

"You didn't..." I whisper as I take in the front of the house, once again proving my suspicions that he *did*.

"You brought me to New Orleans?" I ask in shock, staring at the most beautiful house I've seen in my life. I should know, since I've been stalking its social media page for a long time, simply mesmerized by the history and the architecture.

I should have realized that he *would* monitor my social media.

Damn!

"And your future home for the foreseeable future," he says, his fingers digging into my flesh as he leads me up the three steps in front of the entrance, only stopping when we reach the great hall where a man in a suit is waiting in front of an open book.

"Mr. Kuznetsov," he smiles, his eyes moving to me, "and the future Mrs. Kuznetsov I presume?" he asks.

"Kuznetsova, but yes. Now, why don't we get this done fast. I'm in a hurry," Vlad comments, his entire body tense.

I'm so shocked by the turn of events that I find my reaction delayed as I step back, wrenching my hand free from his grasp.

"What the hell is this, Vlad?" I turn my blazing eyes on to him. I can't believe the stunt he's pulled, especially since he's made it clear that he had no use of me before.

So what changed now?

"Sisi, keep your voice down." He comes closer to me, his scent inundating my senses. "You will agree to everything the officiant says, and you will sign your name on that piece of paper."

"You're crazy." That's all I can utter as I take in his features, the way his lip curls up slightly in an arrogant smirk, or the way his longer than usual hair falls on his forehead, making him look both younger and more dangerous at the same time.

"I'll do no such thing," I hiss at him, taking yet another step back.

He doesn't seem to understand that I don't want to be anywhere near him as he moves me into the wall, caging me.

"You will." He leans down, his breath brushing against my earlobe in a slow and sensuous caress. "You *will* say yes. You will smile and then you will sign your damned name on that piece of paper, or your God help me, you won't like what I'll do."

"What the hell is wrong with you?" I frown, his sudden outburst sending chills down my spine.

His hand comes up to cup my jaw, turning me so I'm looking into his eyes.

"Don't try my hand, Sisi. Not this time. I'm two seconds away from blowing up, and there will be a lot of bodies if you don't do what I say." He grits his teeth, his eyes unyielding as his fingers tighten over my flesh.

"I'm not marrying you, Vlad," I say, my voice softer. "Not now, not ever." I grab his hand and throw it aside, pushing my shoulder into his to evade him.

He's quick as he snakes one arm behind my waist, pulling me flush against him.

"I won't say this twice, hell girl," he rasps against me, and I feel the coiled energy in his body, the way his fingers play over the small of my back as if he might break me in two at any moment.

"You will smile." He raises his hand to my face, one finger dragging the corner of my mouth up, "and you will look happy like the bride you are today. You do that, and no one has to die," he pauses, his face closer until his mouth is but a breath away from mine, "for now."

I can't believe the gall of him. He's looking at me as if he's already won this game. As if he knows I'll obey him. Hell, I see the twitch in his cheek, a dimple threatening to form as he tries his hardest not to proclaim victory just yet.

A smile curves on my own lips as I play along for the briefest moment. Opening my mouth, I capture his finger and I bite.

Hard.

Well, as hard as I can.

And he's not even reacting.

"Sisi, Sisi," he chides, "my dear Sisi, I can see the wheels turning in your head, trying to find an exit. Trust me, there's none. Now, I didn't want to do this," he sighs dramatically, "but it seems I must."

I frown, his theatrics already tiring me out.

"You either marry me now, or I'll be forced to do something more… drastic. Like, say, detonate a bomb at your house. Why, your brother and his family as well as your sister must already be back there…"

My eyes widen just as his lips pull up into a smile.

"You wouldn't…"

"Oh, but I would," he replies, that faux charm dripping off his words.

And just like that, he's back to the Vlad I know. The unfeeling, I take what I want Vlad, that seems to have gotten it into his head that *he* will marry me.

And I know he will make true on his threat.

"So be it," I reply, schooling my own features into a mask of indifference.

Because he might threaten my family, and he might think this is just a game. But I don't plan on giving in to him —ever again. I might sign my name on that marriage certificate, but that's all he's getting from me.

I don't even wait for his reply as I extricate myself from his hold, going to the officiant and doing exactly what Vlad instructed—smile, say yes, and sign the damned paper.

"I wish you all the best, Mr. and Mrs. Kuznetsov," the man says as he leaves, distress written all over his features.

And then we're alone.

~

THERE'S MAYBE ONE FOOT OF DISTANCE BETWEEN THE TWO of us. We're both staring at the other, our breaths coming in short spurts.

He looks on the verge of an attack, and I have to force myself not to flee, the memory of his last episode still fresh in my mind—and on my body.

My gaze moves over him in what I'd call my first thorough perusal, since seeing him again. He's wearing a suit as always. Navy with white stripes, the molded material does nothing to distract from his thick thighs or his powerful arms. No, on the contrary, it only serves to emphasize his muscled limbs further, and for a moment I have to wonder if he hasn't indeed bulked up even more.

His neck is strained, veins protruding as he tries to regulate his breathing, his eyes set on me—unmoving.

He's seen his prey and he's ready to pounce. And just like that my feet are ready to carry me away from him too.

The tension is thick, the awareness even worse as I feel my body respond to his proximity. You'd think that after almost being ravished to death I'd have no desire to try my luck a second time, but as we seem to find a rhythm in our breaths, emulating one another, I find that my body doesn't like to listen.

It's already primed for more—for violence, for blood and destruction.

And I hate it.

I despise that he calls to that primal part of me that I'd tried my entire life to bury. I hate that even though my mind knows him to be facetious and a betrayer, my body fails to recognize the danger he presents to my entire being.

"Why did you bring me here, Vlad? What game are you playing now?" I ask, narrowing my eyes at him.

He's so tense I see the outline of his muscles through the material of his suit. His eyes don't leave mine as he takes a step forward. And another.

And so I take one back.

"Are you bored? Is that it?" I ask, backing further into the room.

I wish I wouldn't be so intimidated by him, but his mere presence dwarfs everything around him.

"Vlad!" I snap, raising my voice. "What the hell is wrong with you?"

"What the hell is wrong with me?" He's in front of me before I can even blink. "What do you think is wrong with me, Sisi?" He smirks at me, his hand reaching out to grab my hair, unraveling my updo until the strands fall down my shoulders.

"Don't touch me." I swat his hand aside.

"Oh, come on, hell girl, you can't tell me you haven't missed my touch," he drawls, his suave voice affecting me even as I try to remain stoic.

"No. I can't say I have," I reply drily, seeking to avoid his roving hands.

"Liar," he whispers, leaning closer to inhale my scent. "You don't fool me, Sisi. I can feel the way your body yearns for mine." His finger trails down the bodice of my dress, and while it might make me a *tiny* bit breathless, it doesn't erase the fact that I'm dealing with an android disguised as a human.

Catching his finger, I fling it off of my body.

"I said don't touch me, Vlad. I mean it. You may have threatened my family to get me to sign my name on that marriage certificate, but you lost your chance long ago," I tell him, my tone serious. "What happened? Got bored and decided to play with the poor nun again? Is that it?" I try my best to keep my voice under control, but his mere presence combined with his audacity make me want to get in his face.

"Sisi, you're breaking my heart," he jokes, taking my palm and fitting it over his chest. "See how it's beating for you?" he asks smoothly, a smile curving up.

For a moment—a *very* short yet embarrassing moment—I find myself feeling for his heart and trying to understand its beats. But it's just a moment before I recognize my own weakness and I push against him.

"You're insane." I shake my head, convinced he must have had some mental breakdown.

Why is he behaving like nothing happened? Like he didn't use and discard me just a while ago?

"Yes." He gathers me so close to him, our faces are barely apart. "I'm certifiably insane. And it's only because I've been without you for so long." He nuzzles his face in my hair, the gesture so incomprehensible I can only stay as still as a statue, trying to understand who this man is.

Because he's not the Vlad I know.

"Get off of me," I say through gritted teeth, the proximity killing me softly.

If this isn't the worst type of punishment, then I don't know what is… being taunted with the one thing you've ever wanted only for it to be wrenched away from you at the last moment.

I won't fall for the same trick twice, though.

"No," he answers matter-of-factly. His big hand splayed over my nape, he holds me close to him, his arm circling my back, so he has me flush against his body.

His mouth hovers over my face as he breathes me in, his eyes closed as if he's relishing the flavor.

"I'm never letting you go, hell girl," he rasps, his eyes open, dark and fearsome as they stare at me with unwavering conviction. "Never again," he says right before his mouth descends on mine, his kiss bruising as he tries to coax my lips open with his tongue.

Flexing my arms, I try to escape the cage he has me in, but he's too strong to even let me budge. No matter how much I struggle to get out of his grasp, it's in vain. If anything, his arms tighten even more around me as he forces me to return the kiss.

I keep my mouth shut, my lips firmly sealed as I deny him even the smallest opening.

"Open your mouth," he commands against my lips, but I just give a small shake of my head, my hands trapped between us as I keep pushing against his chest.

But when nothing works, I realize I need to change strategies. I let my body become slack against his. No more resistance, but no reaction either.

He continues to one-sidedly kiss my lips until he finally realizes the futility of it.

"Damn it, Sisi," he curses, letting me go.

Bringing the back of my hand to my mouth, I wipe him from my lips, my eyes on his so he can see the disgust in my expression.

"After everything you've done to me," I start, anger,

sadness and frustration mingling together and rising to the surface, "you have the gall to take me from *my* wedding, threaten me to sign my Goddamn name on a fucking piece of paper," I'm breathing harshly, "that by the way doesn't mean *anything* to me," my lip curls up in distaste, "and now you want me to just kiss you? As if the last three months didn't happen? As if you didn't crush my heart and leave me bleeding—literally and figuratively?"

He flinches, reacting to my words for the first time. But I can't stop. Not anymore. Tears of frustration threaten to make their way to the surface as I continue to speak.

"You *destroyed* me, Vlad. You have absolutely no right to strut back into my life as if nothing happened. Pretend nothing happened. And then expect *me* to behave like nothing happened. What the hell is wrong with you?" I scream at him, my entire body shaking.

"After everything I went through… you have no right," I tell him, closing my eyes and taking a deep breath.

I don't want to break down in front of him, no matter how mad he might make me. I don't ever want to show him my weakness, or the fact that *he* is my weakness.

He doesn't even reply. He just watches me, his expression closed off.

Not able to bear another moment in his presence, I make to leave.

"You were pregnant," he finally speaks, his words renewing my pain.

Were…

"Yes," I answer, willing my voice not to betray me. Of all the things he could have brought up, he had to go there. Is that why he's back in my life? To ask about the baby? Maybe offer some insincere apology?

But why would he even care?

"Was it mine?" he asks, his question shocking me to my core. I whip my head around, my eyes coming into contact with his.

And God... he really thinks...

Something breaks within me when I realize that in his mind I'd simply hop from one bed to another. Does he really think that little of my love?

But he does.

Laughter threatens to spill over as it dawns on me.

Unwanted... of course I'd fuck anyone for attention. Isn't that what he's been implying from the beginning?

My fists clench, and I have this sudden urge to hurt him —even though I doubt he'll care. I just want to wipe the grin off of his face once and for all. If I can't hurt his feelings, then I can at least hurt his pride.

So I answer his question.

"I don't know," I lie, holding my expression in check. I could have easily said no, but then he could have called my bluff. No, this should dig deeper into his ego and make him wonder just how long after him did I turn to another.

There's the slightest reaction in the way his jaw clenches, his eye twitching as he turns his deadly gaze on me.

"Did you fuck him?" The words are brusque, violence dripping from them as he takes a step toward me.

I don't back down. I raise my chin up, my eyes bravely meeting his as I show him that he doesn't scare me.

"Why do you care?" I throw the question out, trying to seem as nonchalant as I can.

"Did. You. Fuck. Him?" He grits his teeth, his body already crowding mine as he pushes me toward the wall.

"No," I answer, maintaining eye contact, enjoying the way relief floods his features before I continue, wanting to twist him up inside and make him hurt like I did, "I made love to him. Not that you would know what that means."

I give him a brilliant smile, playing his game. Leaning forward to whisper in his ear, I add, "He worshiped my body and made sweet love to me. He showed me it doesn't have to hurt. And when it does, it hurts good."

I don't know where this is all coming from, but I *want* to be petty. I want to cause him at least one percent of the hurt he's caused upon me.

"You're lying," he spits out, narrowing his eyes at me.

Ah, but it seems to be working.

Already, I can see his body slowly shaking, his jaw locked tight in place as he regards me. He might not have feelings, but he does have his pride. And I think I just injured it.

It takes everything in me not to gloat at the fact, and not bait him even further. But for him to truly believe me, I can't stoop *too* low.

The opposite of love isn't hate—it's apathy.

And he's been the best teacher in showing me just how much indifference hurts. So I return the favor.

"Think what you will, Vlad. Frankly, I don't care." I shrug, looking unbothered. "You threw me away, and he was there to pick up the pieces. Can you blame me?" I raise an eyebrow, waiting for his logical mind to process everything.

His expression morphs before my eyes, his eyes widening in horror and I have my confirmation that he *believes* me. Stepping back, there's a slight shake of his head as he looks at me in dismay, the muscles in his arms protruding as he clenches and unclenches his fists.

I'm not sure what type of reaction I was expecting, but certainly not this.

Turning his back to me, he punches the table, breaking it in the middle. I move to the side, his outburst taking me by surprise.

"Sisi," he calls my name, his voice ragged.

Still not facing me, he continues to punch the table, effectively destroying it. And when there's nothing more to hit, he falls to his knees, bleeding hands to his temples as he starts hitting himself.

A low and anguished moan escapes him—something akin to pain.

But it can't be…

"Sisi," he continues to say my name, his voice increasingly lower, raspier, and filled with… hurt.

I shake my head, unable to comprehend this display in front of me.

"Vlad, what's wrong?" I move toward him, my worry for him trumping my disdain.

"No," he puts a hand up, "all my fault," he mumbles something, his breathing punctured and heavy.

"Vlad…"

"Stay back," he wheezes, bending over in pain.

"I…" I trail off, watching him heave, his entire face strained, his eyes closed.

"Run," he says, the words are barely audible.

"Vlad." I take a step closer, concerned.

"Run!" he screams at me, and one glimpse at his features has my feet moving of their own accord. "Basement… Lock yourself…" He doesn't get to finish the sentence as another pained whimper escapes him. He seems to be battling with himself for control.

I know I should take this chance and just run away, but the sight of him crouched on the floor and in pain is etched in my mind, not letting me do anything but head to the basement and wait.

10
SISI

It's hours later that I reemerge from the basement. I'd been extremely surprised to see a panic room in the lower level, the steel door ensuring nothing can come through. It makes me wonder if it came with the house or it's a new addition.

Specifically built for him.

When I reach the ground floor of the house I come face to face with a freshly showered Vlad, a towel wrapped around his waist.

"I was just coming to get you," he says.

"Glad to see you're doing better," I nod my head at him, this time having a better grasp on my indifference. "Now, if you can take me back, that would be great," I add, crossing my arms over my chest.

I need to be as far away from him as possible. Only then I'll be able to get myself under control. Even now, seeing the signs of weariness on his face has me worried, one foot forward, my body prepared to go to him to make sure he's okay.

And I can't have that.

I'd come to grips with the fact that he has a certain *unnatural* effect on me a long time ago. But knowing that my *natural* inclination is to reach for him, means I'm also able to control myself.

"That's not happening," he answers casually, using a towel to dry his hair. "Your room is unlocked. I left some things for you there so go make yourself comfortable," he says, walking past me.

"What do you mean? You can't keep me here." I frown, turning to follow him up the stairs and into a room not unlike the one I'd woken up into.

"Oh, but I can, Sisi," he gives me a devilish smile, "you're officially my wife. That means your place is with me." He picks up his watch from a table, placing it on his wrist.

"Against my will. Really, Vlad, what's the point of this?" I sigh, done with everything. "Why can't you let me be?"

"Because I told you," he speaks slowly, enunciating each word. "I'm never letting you go. Where I go you go. And where you go…"

"I go alone." I don't let him finish his words, already getting mad at him again.

"I follow." He comes closer. So close I can still see some drops of water clinging to his skin, the ink drawing my attention. But as I notice that my eyes go lower and lower, I immediately whip my head up.

Too late.

He's regarding me with an amused expression, one eyebrow raised.

"Like what you see?" he asks, his voice arrogantly bold as he positions himself in front of me.

"I've seen better," I lie, shrugging and moving past him to sit on his bed. "We need to have a serious conversation, so drop those," I wave my hand toward his body, "seductive moves you're trying to pull on me. It's not going to work." But even as I say the words, I can't help the way my eyes try to drink him in again.

And then I see it.

I frown as I look better, realizing his tattoos look different. There's…

"That wasn't there before." I speak before I can help myself, pointing toward the triangle drawn over the evil spirits, almost as if it's caging them in.

"Perceptive." He smirks. "You're right. It's a new addition," he says, but doesn't elaborate.

I feign a cough to clear my throat.

I need to get a grip on myself.

"Right, so," I straighten my back, "I need to get back to New York. Marcello must be worried by now."

"I left a note." He shrugs, moving around the bed and toward a big walk-in wardrobe. Seeing that he's trying his best to avoid this conversation, I just follow him.

"So he knows I'm with you?" I ask, surprised he would have been so direct.

"Something along the lines," he says, amused, before dropping his towel.

It's so sudden, I barely have the time to react. My eyes widen, my mouth forming a small O as I simply take in his body.

Definitely bulked up.

I can't help but feel the heat creep up my neck as I see his ass, so insanely well sculpted. Even covered entirely in ink, the way his muscles flex when he moves is unmistakable.

And then I move my gaze up and I see him watching me with a smug expression on his face, so I immediately turn around, embarrassed to be caught staring.

"I didn't hear anything about your fiancé. Won't he miss you too?" he asks, and to my everlasting shame, it takes me a while to get my errant heart under control in order to answer him.

"Of course. Raf too. He's probably frantic with worry," I say absentmindedly, images of his naked flesh still playing in front of my eyes.

Damn it!

I was right the first time. *I am cursed.* And my curse is being saddled with him.

"Too bad you're already married, wouldn't you say so?" His breath is suddenly on my throat.

Moving my hair aside, he trails his lips over the back of my neck, settling over my scar. It's the ghost of a touch, but enough to make me shiver from head to toe.

"Vlad," I say his name, my nails digging into my palms as I force myself to remain motionless. "Drop the game."

His tongue sneaks out, and I feel him slowly move against my skin. My breath hitches, but as I realize he's getting the reaction he wanted out of me, I quickly turn around, pushing him off of me.

"Stop for one moment. Please." I'm breathing hard.

From arousal or from anger, I don't know. His pupils are dilated as he gazes at me, and I don't even have to look down to know he must be hard. "And put some clothes on," I say flippantly, keeping my eyes on his face.

"Go to your room, Sisi," he rasps, threading his fingers through his hair. "Unless you want something else to happen, you'd better go to your room and lock the door."

"Vlad," I groan, exasperated. "We need to talk and sort this mess out. I really don't understand why you're doing this, but I need to get back home and you need to mind your own business," I say confidently, pleased at myself for getting so many words out and so smoothly. And with how he's looking at me, it's a wonder I'm not already hiccupping, or worse, panting.

Panting… Good Lord, but I'd be screwed. Literally.

"If you're going to stay here we can talk, yes," he starts, and a smile of satisfaction pulls at my lips. "But it's not going to be the type of talk you're thinking about." He smirks. "So unless…" he continues, the innuendo clear as he's coming closer to me.

"Go to hell, Vlad." I turn around, already out the door. His chuckle echoes behind me, almost goading me to react.

Damn him, and damn this and damn everything!

After wandering about the house for a while, I finally found my way to the room, locking myself inside.

There has to be a way to get in touch with Marcello.

I can't just stay here, waiting for Vlad to get bored with me again. Because I know how this game is going to end. With me heartbroken—again.

"Damn," I whisper to myself, my eyes damp with tears.

I take off the wedding dress, remaining only in the satin shift underneath. Tired and frustrated, I climb into the bed and wait for sleep to come to me.

Damn you, Vlad. Why do you have to keep on hurting me?

Couldn't he have disappeared from my life forever? At least then the pain would have faded over time. Now the pain is raw again, my wounds opening up and bleeding anew.

After a good night of sleep, my resolve is strengthened. I just need to find a phone, call Marcello to come get me and everything else should be solved, too.

Eventually.

Getting out of bed, I notice that Vlad hadn't lied when he'd said he'd deposited some things in the room. There are a couple of dresses like the ones I used to wear, as well as shoes, toiletries and even under things.

Damn him.

I have to begrudgingly appreciate he'd supplied me with everything I needed, but that doesn't make me any less of a prisoner.

Getting ready for the day, I open the door, intent on seeking him out for another bout of discussions. I don't get to take one step outside of my room, though, as the entire hallway is filled with toys.

There are teddy bears in all shapes, and sizes, all scattered across the hallway and blocking my path.

What the… There must be hundreds of them.

"Vlad!" I yell out his name, sighing deeply as I realize another argument is forthcoming.

"Yes," he replies, coming out from the end of the hallway.

He's wearing a black shirt and a pair of gray sweatpants, and I have to say, I don't think I've ever seen him dressed so casually before.

"What's this?" I ask, waving my hand toward the army of teddy bears that seem to have laid siege at my door.

"Well," he starts, looking a little uncomfortable. He brings his hand up, scratching the back of his head as he all but avoids my gaze.

"Why is there an army of teddy bears here?" I ask, tapping my foot impatiently.

"For you," he eventually says, his voice going down a notch.

"For me?" I repeat, incredulous.

Closing the door to my room, I wade my way through the *many* teddy bears, trying to ignore the way they are so soft and oh so cute. But this is neither the place nor the time to gush over stuffed animals.

"Did you rob an entire teddy bear store?" I cross my arms over my chest, narrowing my eyes at him. "Unless…" my eyes widen. "Did you put something in them? Bombs? Listening devices?" I'm quick to grab into the nearest bear—a tiny blue one that is so soft I want to just pet him—and I pull, ripping it at the seams.

There's no way Vlad would do this without a reason. What is his purpose? Get me to lower my guard?

Speaking about trojan horses…

"Sisi," he groans, trying to take the bear from me, "there's nothing inside the bears."

"I don't believe you," I counter, tossing the first bear and taking another one, repeating the procedure and feeling it up for hidden wires or any other devices Vlad might have placed inside them.

"I knew you were a scoundrel, but I didn't realize you'd stoop so low to use *teddy bears*. What's wrong with you, Vlad?" I shake my head at him, sad that I'm destroying such cute toys.

"Sisi." His hands cover my own, stopping me from continuing to tear into the bears. "They were a present. Nothing else. I promise," he says solemnly, but I just push his hands aside.

"As if your promises count for anything," I mumble, not looking at him.

"I'm serious. I just wanted to give them to you."

"Why?" I fire back immediately.

"So that you're not... lonely," he admits, lowering his head.

I frown, unable to get a read on him. What's his angle this time?

"So that I'm not lonely?" I repeat, my eyebrows shooting up at his explanation before I simply burst out into laughter.

"I gather you didn't like them," he says quietly, staring at what's left of the little bear on the floor.

Before I get a chance to reply, though, he's gone, taking the broken teddy bear with him.

I knew it.

It must have something inside that I didn't notice, so he's taking it with him to hide the evidence.

Shaking my head at him, I decide that the sooner I get

out of here, the better. Who knows what other tricks he has up his sleeve.

To my surprise, I don't see Vlad the rest of the day. It's only the next morning that I note his presence again, and this time with an over the top gesture too.

"Seriously?" I roll my eyes at him, lifting up the hem of my dress, so that it doesn't get dirty. Then I try my hardest to bypass him and head downstairs for breakfast.

11

VLAD

"**V**anya, where are you when I need you?" I sigh, resting my head in my hands. She would have known what to do in this situation.

I don't know what I expected from seeing her again. I certainly hadn't thought about it much. I'd just acted on the spur of the moment, knowing that I could never let her marry anyone but me. And so I'd ensured—rather forcefully—that *no one* will ever be able to wed her. By marrying her myself.

But everything seems to have backfired.

What would Vanya say?

"Of course it backfired, you idiot! You threatened to kill her entire family." I attempt to imitate my sister.

Well, when you put it like that…

I'd been so desperate that nothing seemed off limits in the moment. I would have done *anything* to tie her to me forever. Hell, I *would* have killed her family.

There's absolutely *nothing* I wouldn't do for her, and that includes mass murder. And genocide. And even nuclear war.

Is there something worse than nuclear war?

Probably stealing candy from a child. And I would have done that too!

But now she hates me...

Not that I blame her, since she has every right to hate me. But I don't know how to fix it. I don't know how to make her see that I am sincere, and that I'm not playing any games. I don't know how to show her that I've changed—at least slightly—and that I'm ready to do whatever it takes to win back her love and her trust.

"I screwed up," I mutter to myself, my behavior from yesterday having been nothing short of atrocious.

But how could I have reacted any other way when she managed to break my heart with just a few words?

He worshiped my body and made sweet love to me. He showed me it doesn't have to hurt. And when it does, it hurts good.

I bring my fist up, banging it against my heart in hopes it may lessen the ache. Since she uttered them, those words have kept on replaying in my head, torturing me with the knowledge that she's no longer mine.

That she...

Not only can I not imagine someone else seeing her naked, or touching her. But another man inside her? Bringing her pleasure? Taking my place?

"Fuck." I punch myself even harder.

Why does it seem like there's a dearth of oxygen in the room? Or is it that my lungs can no longer process it? Because the more I think of Sisi—*my Sisi*—even in the same room as another man, I want to go crazy. But to think of her fucking someone else?

The pain is so unbearable, I can't even stand upright. My feet barely carry me to the bed as I collapse, face down on the mattress.

"It's all my fault," I whisper, knowing I have no one to blame but myself.

I pushed her away.

I pushed her into his arms.

She's right. Can I blame her when all I did was hurt her —both physically and emotionally?

Now I can only hope she'll one day forgive me. Even if I have to do penance every day for the rest of my life, I'll do it as long as she's with me.

She's my one hope in this fucked up world, the only star that shines brightly just for me. And no matter what, I'll regain her trust.

But where to start?

I also need to do it fast, since I'm sure Marcello will eventually figure out it was me who stole her from the church, and he'll come after me—guns blazing.

It's the reason I'd chosen this location, since it's far enough from New York to not give him any ideas, but it's also a place I know Sisi's been in love with for a long time.

Admittedly, I only know this piece of information because I've been monitoring her entire internet presence from day one, often shadowing her movements on the web to understand her better—her likes and dislikes.

When I'd seen that she'd saved multiple pictures of this location, including some of the city, I'd immediately put an offer for the place, intending to surprise her.

Alas, the surprise seems to have fallen rather flat, and she wasn't that impressed with me.

At least all my snooping has ensured I have all the knowledge to court her properly this time. She might be upset with me, but I'll do everything in my power to show her I am in earnest.

I've made extensive lists of items that she might enjoy, and with the help of some very insightful articles on the internet on how to court a woman, I'd designed the perfect plan to woo her.

Surely, at least *some* of the surprises I have planned should chip away at her distrust.

But even that makes me a little apprehensive, since the first one had already gone so badly.

I turn to look at the desolate gaze of the broken teddy bear and my hope crashes even more in my chest.

And I still have the gigantic bear I'd gotten for her birthday…

She'd not reacted as I expected her to. I thought that since she likes teddy bears so much, an entire legion of them would make her extra happy.

It only made her extra mad.

I should have realized she wouldn't trust my intentions, since I haven't given her much to go off of. From the moment she stepped into this house I just threatened and taunted her, because going on the defensive was so much easier than opening myself to a hell lot of hurt.

But it's not a good strategy.

No, according to online articles, I should try to show her my vulnerable side, not my barbaric one. Of course, all in addition to gifts, compliments, and attention.

I certainly have my work cut out for me if I'm to believe

these online gurus. But since I don't plan to give up—not until she forgives me—I have an entire list of things to do that should put her in a more forgiving mood.

Finishing my rather short wallowing session — since I can't afford to lose any precious wooing time — I take a shower and choose my clothing carefully.

One article had specified that I should put effort in my appearance, so I'd spent the entire night online shopping trendy outfits.

Since I'd ventured into the crazy world of online shopping, I'd also ended up getting her many things that women apparently like — perfume, jewelry, handbags and shoes. And because I'd never realized how pricey these things are, I'd had to have a few words with my bank repeatedly throughout the night.

I guess that's what happens when you spend thousands of dollars on clothes.

And while I'm still waiting for those to be delivered, I have another surprise planned for today.

Freshly showered and with a new attire—a fashionable one—I head to the front of the house to receive the custom order I'd placed for chocolate.

After all, every single article mentioned chocolate and that women love it. I also know for sure that Sisi loves sweets, so it should definitely earn me bonus points.

Signing my name on the form, I tug inside the cart full of chocolate treats, including one rather large chocolate fountain.

I quickly install everything in front of her room—an offering to my goddess—and then I wait.

I stare at my watch anxiously, waiting for her to open

her bedroom door and see the sea of chocolate I'd laid there.

Right on the dot, she swings the door open, her eyes widening as she takes in my surprise. I watch her expression carefully, hoping to see a positive reaction.

"Seriously?" she asks, rolling her eyes at me and raising her skirt to bypass the chocolate.

I watch stupefied as she leaves the hallway, making her way downstairs.

She didn't even bat an eye.

Not one to give up, I quickly follow her.

"You like chocolate," I say when I find her in the kitchen, looking around the various empty cabinets.

She pauses, turning toward me to raise an eyebrow.

"What are you trying to do this time, Vlad? Poison me? Give me some type of potion so I succumb to your wiles?" She shakes her head at me, turning her attention back to the kitchen.

"I didn't put anything in it. Look," I tell her, showing her a big box of chocolate and the fact that it's sealed shut. I open it and pop a few pieces in my mouth, wanting her to see there's no poison or any type of potion.

She watches me through narrowed eyes, almost as if she doesn't want to believe me. All the while I can't help myself and stare at her, her beauty never failing to make me speechless.

Even with her short hair, she's simply stunning, and those full lips... I have a hard time swallowing as I get lost in her features, her honey-colored eyes keeping me captive.

Damn, but she makes me forget myself.

"It's really good. Have some," I take a few steps so I'm closer to her, thrusting the box of chocolates in her face.

She looks down at them for a second before shaking her head.

"I'm hungry. So unless you plan to feed me some actual food, I don't care for chocolates now," she says, and my eyes widen.

Of course! Why didn't I think of this?

"Perfect." I smile at her, placing the box on the table and grabbing her hands to lead her to a chair. "Sit down and I'll make you something to eat," I say, a little too enthusiastically for someone who doesn't know how to cook.

But how hard can it be?

"No poison," she mutters with half a smile, and I can't help the happiness that blooms in my chest when I see that. Even if it's half—it's halfway there.

"Of course. I'll make you the *best* breakfast," I declare.

Leaving her at the table, I ransack the kitchen for some food, realizing that I hadn't gotten much.

There are just a few eggs in the fridge. Nothing else.

Shit!

Looking back, I see her watching me expectantly, and I know this is something that I *cannot* fail.

Taking the eggs out, I try to remember if I've ever read how they are cooked, and then follow the steps from memory.

Identifying an omelet recipe, I find a bowl, and crack the eggs, then I start whisking them.

"I didn't know you could cook," Sisi notes from behind, still watching me intently.

I didn't know either.

"Piece of cake." I beam at her, even though inside I'm sweating at the thought of doing this all wrong.

It's just eggs! How hard can it be?

When the mixture seems to be homogenous enough, I heat a pan and pour it inside.

Wholly focused on getting it right, I'm surprised when I feel Sisi behind me, draping herself on my back, her hands coping a feel of my shoulders.

"You've been working out," she notes, her hands going lower and distracting me from my task.

"Yes." I give her a strained answer, breathing in her presence, her fresh scent invading my nostrils and hypnotizing me.

"Everywhere," she whispers, her fingers trailing down my back and to my ass…

My eyes widen as I realize exactly what she's doing.

The spoon drops from my hand as I swiftly turn around, caging her in against the counter. As expected, my phone is in her hand, as she's giving me the sweetest look on earth.

"You're sly, hell girl," I drawl, enjoying the way she's batting her lashes at me as if I didn't just catch her trying to steal my phone. "What's next? Call your big bro?" I raise an eyebrow at her.

She doesn't back down as she pushes her chin up, bravely looking me in the eye.

"Yes, in fact, I will," she tells me, and a smile plays on my lips.

Marcello was bound to find out at some point, so I'm not concerned about him *that* much. He'll definitely cause me to change my plans a little, but I've already decided that nothing and *no one* will ever take me away from Sisi again—including myself.

"Go ahead," I dare her. I wonder what she'll do when she realizes that Marcello won't be able to help. Not now, not ever.

She narrows her eyes at me, doubting my intentions. I just shrug, even pressing my finger down to unlock the phone. "Do it," I challenge her again.

It should be a good thing too, since I'll officially announce to the world that she's taken.

A suspicious frown on her face, she quickly goes through my contact list, dialing her brother.

"Marcello?" she asks when he answers, and I tug her hand toward me, ensuring the phone is on speaker. She gives me a deadly stare that I just return with one of my charming smiles.

"Sisi, God! Are you okay? Where are you?" Marcello goes off, firing question after question.

"Don't worry, I'm fine. For now," she adds, raising her eyes to meet mine.

"Where are you? I'll come get you!" he continues, but I only let her say New Orleans before I take over.

"Marcello, dear friend, or I should call you brother-in-law now," I add, ignoring the way Sisi's eyes are shooting daggers at me.

"Vlad," Marcello says tersely. *"What the fuck are you doing?"*

"No warm welcome to the family? Sad…"

"Vlad, why is Sisi with you? What the hell is happening?"

"I thought my note made it clear enough," I speak, pushing my finger against Sisi's lips to shush her, "I just retrieved my property. You know, I tried lost and found first, but imagine my surprise when they directed me to a church," I feign a shudder, "you know how I hate those places." Sisi rolls her eyes at me, but I just continue, already hearing Marcello blow off in the background. "But now that I've found her, I'm never letting go," I add, "just a friendly warning."

"Vlad," I can hear the tension in his voice. *"What the hell is your game? And what the hell is your business with my sisters. Sisi, are you okay?"*

"Why does *everyone* think I'm playing a game," I groan, pushing my fingers against Sisi's lips when I see she's trying to speak. The little minx gives me a challenging look before opening her mouth, sucking on my finger.

"Fuck," I involuntarily mutter.

"Vlad? I swear if you so much as harm a hair on…"

"Bro in law, calm down. I'm not going to harm your sister. As a matter of fact, she's quite busy sucking on my…" I don't get to finish as Sisi's hand grabs the phone, pushing me off her.

"Vlad!" Marcello yells into the phone.

"I'm fine, Marcello." Sisi finally takes over, giving me a look that says *stay put.* "He's not going to hurt me, but he is quite adamant about marrying me."

"Already did," I add sneakily.

"I'm going to fucking kill him," Marcello keeps on cursing me out for a while, and even Sisi is getting bored of his tirade.

"I'll come get you, don't worry. I'm not going to let him get away with this," Marcello continues, and I realize it's time to put an end to the game.

Swiping the phone from Sisi's hands, I take over the conversation, making sure Marcello heeds my warning.

"Stay out of this Marcello. I let her call you out of courtesy, but make no mistake, you're never taking her from me. This extends to *everyone*, including that skinny little kid that thought to marry her. I will say this only once. *She is mine.* And trust me, I'll forget all our history in a second if it comes to it," I tell him, my voice serious.

"You're insane," he replies.

"Maybe. But remember, I'm the type of insane that would level an entire country to the ground if it came to it. So do yourself and everyone else a favor and stay the fuck out of it."

"You're fucking dead, Vlad." I try not to roll my eyes at his threats, but it seems he just doesn't get it.

"No, Marcello. Anyone who tries to take Sisi away from me is fucking dead. You included." I grit my teeth. If I am forced, then I'll just show everyone why they called me berserker in the first place.

And *no one* will escape with their lives intact. "She's safe, and I won't harm her. That, you have my promise," I say, swinging my gaze back to her. "But she is *mine*," I repeat before hanging up and flinging the phone on the ground.

"What..." Sisi's eyes widen. "You destroyed it..." she mutters as she stares at the broken screen.

"That was a warning for your brother, but also for you, hell girl." I tug her to me, forcing her to look me in the eye. "No one will ever take you from me."

"Until you get bored," she whispers.

"I won't ever get bored." I swipe my finger over her lips,

her pupils dilating as I bring my head lower. "Now let's eat," I speak against her lips.

Unfortunately, we'd both forgotten about the eggs while on the phone, and so I managed to burn the only available food in the house.

"I'm ordering some, don't worry." I try to placate her a while later while I hurry for my laptop, suddenly afraid she'll be cranky if she gets too hungry, and that certainly won't get me any extra points.

It takes a while for the food to arrive, but once it's all spread on the table and we're both digging in, silence descends.

Her gaze swings back to me curiously every now and then, and even as I lose myself in her beauty, I try to remember some of the advice I'd read.

"You're very pretty when you eat," I compliment her, a small smile tugging at my lips.

Her hand stills midair as she's about to bite into a chicken wing.

"Not that you're not pretty every day. In fact, you're pretty *every* moment," I continue, afraid I somehow blundered it.

She tilts her head to the side, still watching me.

"Beautiful, not pretty," I amend.

Damn it, I forgot that women care about particularities.

"Is that so?" she asks, unconvinced, her hand brushing against her bangs and revealing the birth mark on her face.

"Of course. Even that splotchy thing on your face is charming," I add for good measure, since there's no part of her that I *don't* love.

She blinks twice, slowly. Her mouth opens and closes a

few times before she suddenly gets up, taking the entire bucket of chicken wings and dumps it over my head.

"You're a cad," she mutters, stomping out of the kitchen.

And I'm left frowning, unable to understand what I'd said that was so wrong.

Fuck, but why am I such a big idiot?

Something I said must have upset her, and now I'm back to zero. Or is it minus?

I sigh, standing up and watching more tiny chicken wings fall out of my hair.

Why are women so difficult?

12
VLAD

Being completely ignored by her makes me believe I have to change strategies. At least slightly. The clothes, shoes and bags had all arrived, but she hasn't even acknowledged them. She'd once again rolled her eyes at me and moved on.

Luckily, this time I stocked up the kitchen so she had ingredients to make something to eat.

For all her annoyance with me, she did make enough food for two, and gave me a plate too. I have to admit I might have stared at it a little too much, that she almost took it away from me.

"Are you even eating?" she'd asked, her voice telling me I shouldn't upset her further.

But it wasn't that I did *not* want to eat. Rather, I didn't want for it to be gone so fast. After all, it was something she'd made with her hands—for me.

Well, not *for* me, but still, it felt like it was for me and I wanted to keep it for a little longer.

"Of course," I'd immediately answered, taking my fork and digging in.

Ah, but it had been so good.

I don't think I've eaten food that good in my entire life, and I was sure to point it out to her. But even *that* compliment had gone on deaf ears. She'd just nodded and then left for her room after she'd finished, instructing me to wash the dishes.

The cold treatment continues for over a week. I try to bring her gifts to show her that I'm in earnest, but she just ignores them, looking me dead in the eye and scowling at me, as if I were the scum of the earth.

In a way I am, because I *know* what I did to her was unforgivable. I *know* I hurt her too much for her to ever give me another chance.

But I can't stop trying. Not when the alternative is a slow suffocating death. Because without her I'm *definitely* headed for an early grave.

There's a little comfort in knowing she's near and *no one* else can get to her. But how does that even help me when she's scorned every single attempt I'd made at showing her how much I'm repenting for my behavior?

The time passes, and while she doesn't seem to actively go against me anymore, probably already resigned that there's no way out, her behavior toward me doesn't thaw.

When another week goes by and I've still not made *any* headway, I know it's time to change strategies.

And so I find myself with a conundrum. What can I do to pacify her? To make her see that my attempts are genuine, and that my compliments are from my heart too?

Maybe I should just give her my heart on a platter.

But that won't work. As much as I'd love to do that, I would like to be present to see her reaction to it, and I wouldn't be able to do it dead.

What if...

I pause, an idea taking root in my mind. And just to be sure I'm not making any more mistakes, since I wouldn't like to upset her again, I open my laptop and I start surfing the FBI's most wanted list.

Then I just work my magic to find someone in the city.

A little more time consuming than I would have liked, since now I'll miss a morning of gifts. But maybe she'll appreciate the extra creativity.

Armed and with a well-devised plan, I make sure to lock the entire house before I leave for the night.

Michael Garrett.

The one man who'd ended up in the vicinity happened to be the most wanted pedophile in five states. While Maxim gets me a weekly supply of prisoners for my therapeutic process, this needs to be more personal, since I'm doing it for Sisi.

And so I go to one of the locations I'd pulled from his cell phone—a suburban bar—and then I just carefully lay out the trap, making sure he's drugged up before I take him back to the house.

Michael doesn't seem like such a bright chap, although he's been evading the feds for a while now. But then again, I shouldn't be too surprised that state organizations are floundering. After all, *I* am the one benefitting from their incompetence.

Once his body is loaded in the car and I'm on my way

back home, I have to be extra careful, so that the surprise isn't ruined for Sisi.

Going to the basement, I access a part that's separated from the rest. I hadn't wanted for Sisi to see it and get scared of me—again.

And so when I reach my blood room, I lay Michael on a table, quickly getting to work.

The easy part is cutting him open and getting the heart out. In fact, it takes me less than half an hour to cut through skin, open up his thoracic cavity and get the heart out. And because it's not my first rodeo, I even manage to do it without making a mess.

As soon as I have the heart removed, I drain it of blood and cauterize the arteries so they don't leak even more liquid later on.

Then, I take a scalpel and get to work, carving a special dedication to Sisi.

Compared to the harvesting part, getting my strokes right is much harder, since the muscle has striations and is overall uneven.

It takes me a few hours of concentration to make sure everything is perfect. When I'm done, it's already close to dawn, so I know I can't waste any time.

Getting a silver platter and scattering some rose petals around, I'm finally pleased with the overall appearance.

If I can't give her my own heart, I'll just give her the next best thing.

But what if she asks for mine?

What if she's not satisfied with a substitute? I mean, I'm sure I could get a heart transplant... Yes, that would work. I'd be alive to see her reaction, and she'd still get my heart.

Win-win.

Just to make sure I have everything covered, I call Maxim and ask him to book me up for a heart consultation.

Maybe then she'll see just how honest my intentions are.

Still, I hope this will be enough since a transplant would put me out of commission for a while, and there's too much to be done to waste any time.

I already missed a day of gifts, so right before she opens her door, I'm there, waiting.

"What's this?" she asks as I come face to face with her.

"I made you a little something," I say, trying to sound confident even though I'm already scared I'll offend her yet again.

"Again?" She raises an eyebrow, arms crossed over her chest as she waits for me to remove the lid off the platter.

"Well, I put more work into this. I didn't just buy it." I give her my signature smile, my fingers on the lid as I lift it, carefully watching for her expression.

She squints her eyes at the heart, and for a few seconds she's quiet.

And then she laughs.

"Vlad," she starts, barely able to speak in between spurts of laughter, "what is this?"

"A heart," I answer, a little unsure of myself.

Damn, but I thought she'd like it.

"You brought me a heart?" She raises her gaze to meet mine and I nod.

"It's in place for my heart since I couldn't bring that and, you know, *actually* bring it," I try to explain, but she just keeps laughing.

"Vlad," she forces herself to keep a straight expression,

"you carved a heart on a heart?" She bursts into laughter again.

I turn the heart toward me, trying to see what's so funny. I'd carved her name with an arrowhead and a three next to it since that's what people use to indicate love online.

"I don't understand," I speak slowly, frowning in confusion.

"This," she points at the arrow head and the three, "is a heart. Carved on a heart," she giggles.

"You're not mad?" I ask, just to be sure. "I thought you'd like it." I put on a smile again, hoping to charm her.

"It's rather unusual," she replies, pursing her lips. "But I do like it," she notes, and I finally sigh in relief.

"Good, good. I thought you'd have wanted me to give you my own heart, but that would have been a little harder," I say and her eyebrows knit together in consternation, "not impossible," I amend, "just harder."

"You would have given me *your* heart?" she asks, blinking as if surprised.

"Of course. I can still do it, just not immediately. I asked Maxim to book me in for a transplant consultation, and after that you can have it." My lips pull up in a grin.

"Why?" her question throws me off.

"Why? *Why?* To make you see I am not playing any games," I take a deep breath, "I'm really trying," I confess.

"Where did you get a heart, though?" She changes the subject, not really acknowledging my statement.

"It wasn't an innocent person, I swear," I'm quick to defend myself, "it was a known pedophile, and I just got to him before the police," I say, quickly removing my new phone from my pocket and showing her his name on the FBI list.

"I see," she replies thoughtfully. "Is it clean?"

"Clean?" I repeat, confused. But then it dawns on me what she means. "Yes, it's very clean," I answer with a smile.

"Then come on, lover boy. I am famished and you caught breakfast. You should cook it." She winks at me, taking my hand and leading me to the kitchen.

Fuck, she's touching me! It worked!

I end up grilling the heart well while Sisi makes a sauce to go with it, and in no time we're both at the table, trying out the food. I also open a bottle of red wine on the side.

"You know," she starts, her mouth full, "I never thought I'd say this, but a pedophile's heart doesn't taste half bad," she comments, a mischievous grin on her face.

"Indeed." Is all I can say as I watch her give me a smile for the first time in forever. And just like that, I feel my own heart do some weird somersault in my chest.

"I'm sorry," I tell her sincerely, taking advantage of the one time she's not mad at me.

She frowns, placing her fork down to focus her attention on me.

"I never told you, but I'm sorry for what I did to you." I swallow, the images of that night still haunting me. "And for what I said. I want you to know I never meant any of it, I just needed you as far away from me."

"Why?" She regards me solemnly, her head tilted to the side.

"I didn't want to hurt you more than I already did. I…" I trail off, words failing me. Not that I've ever been great with them, as Sisi can attest.

"Why now? Why are you doing this now, Vlad? We had a clean break. *Three months* I didn't hear from you, and now you're suddenly here, in front of me, telling me that you're sorry?"

"I wasn't going to come into your life ever again, Sisi. I really thought that was it." My fists clench under the table, and I try my best to stay in control.

"Then what changed?" She frowns.

"I did." Her mouth parts slightly. "I realized that I couldn't do it. I couldn't *exist* without you. So I tried to get better. I *am* better."

"I don't understand," she replies, and I see this as my chance before she withdraws within herself again.

Pushing back my chair, I unbutton my shirt, taking it off and discarding it on the floor. Coming to her side, I take her hand and place it on my chest, right at the sharp angle of the triangle.

"This isn't just a triangle, Sisi," I tell her, using her own hands to trace its true shape. "It's an A."

"A…?" A frown mars her features as she leans closer to study the ink on my skin.

"The A that holds the monsters at bay," I continue, my hand on her hair as I lightly caress it. "I lied that night, Sisi. Fuck, I lied about everything. But the one thing you *need* to know is that you're not ordinary to me. You're one of a kind." I take a deep breath, pushing her chin up so she can see the sincerity in my eyes.

"*My* one of a kind."

"Vlad," she starts, and I can see tears glistening in her eyes.

"No, you don't have to say anything." I press one finger

to her lips, using my other hand to wipe some of the moisture in her lashes. "I'll wait for you. No matter how long it takes, I will wait for you. But I'm not letting you go. Not this time."

MY PLAN IS SLOWLY STARTING TO WORK. FOR A FEW DAYS now Sisi and I have developed a pleasant companionship and she no longer closes the door in my face. In fact, she even acknowledges my presence now, which is more than I would have hoped for.

But since it's not the best progress, I need to step up my game more. After perusing several articles, I've decided to heed their advice since they all seem to recommend the same thing—play hard to get.

I'm not entirely sure how this is the best approach since I just got her to talk to me, but if this is the key to making her more interested in me, then so be it.

As I look across multiple sites, I see that I need to be the one ignoring her now. All, of course, to make her reach out first.

"Damn it," I mutter to myself, a little reluctant to switch attitudes.

But if they say it will work...

For the next two days, I do just that. When I see her, I barely say a few words, more often than not showing myself unavailable to her.

I can see she's bothered by my sudden change in attitude, and it takes everything in me not to stop it immediately and apologize to her. But the more I look at the advice on the internet, the more they recommend the opposite.

On the third day, I don't even have to try, as I'm called away for the entire day. Maxim suddenly called me to ask for help in dealing with the police in the case of some missing prisoners. And since Maxim is not the best at diplomacy. I'd rather deal with it myself.

After an entire day of interviews, I come home ready to go to bed. Opening the door to my room, I don't even pay attention to my surroundings as I take off my blazer and my tie before loosening the buttons on my shirt.

"Fuck, you scared me." I jump up when the light turns on and I see Sisi sitting at my desk, hands on the table as she looks at me suspiciously.

"We need to talk," she says, getting up and plopping herself in front of me.

"We do?" I raise my eyebrows, a little confused.

"Yes." She nods, crossing her arms over her chest in a pose that tells me she means business.

Damn, I think I'm screwed.

Now I just have to see what I did wrong.

Again.

13
SISI

How does one go from promising to never let me go one day, to completely ignoring me the next?

I'm so frustrated I'm ready to throw my hands in the air. I'd prided myself on being able to read Vlad pretty well, and I'd even found myself believing his apology and his assurances about waiting for me.

But now? It's like he's done a complete one eighty.

A few days ago he was offering me his heart on a platter—literally. Admittedly, it was a very sweet gesture that had made me melt just the *tiniest* bit. But now he barely acknowledges my presence.

Truthfully, after his many displays of opulent gifts and surprises, I'd started to become a bit curious about what he'd do next. Well, consider me completely surprised when I'd opened my door to *nothing*.

Is that it?

Did he think that because we had one civil conversation he's already forgiven? Or that he doesn't have to make an effort anymore? If that is the case, then he is in for a surprise.

I might be softening toward him *just* a little, but that doesn't mean that all is forgiven. In fact, if he ever wants me to believe a word he says again, then he better put in the work to prove that he is trustworthy.

Granted, there's a special place in my soul just for him, and I can't deny the way he keeps on making my heart skip a beat just by being closer. Couple that with his sweet gestures and he'd managed to impress me.

I certainly would not have pegged him as the romantic type, but he's gone above and beyond to show me that he *can* be.

But the issue is not whether he can impress me with out-of-this-world gestures—though the heart had been a nice touch—but whether I can really trust his actions.

And seeing how quickly he's given up, I don't know if that is the case.

I've had enough time to ponder his behavior and his Jekyll and Hyde personality, and I've only come up with more questions.

Why now?

Was it his pride that took a hit at the thought of me marrying another man? Since we've long established that he cannot feel anything, then what is his motivation?

And that's my entire issue. If he could feel even a glimmer of the love I have for him, then I would not hesitate in giving him a second chance. But because I know him incapable of *any* type of feeling, I cannot risk my heart again. Not when his fickle mind might tell him to drop me again at any moment.

A couple of days of his bipolar behavior and I'm already sick of it. And so I find myself marching for his room, ready to demand an answer from him.

"Vlad," I call him when I see him exit his room in a hurry. He looks at me for a second before blinking and shaking his head.

"I'll see you later." Is all he says as he flies past me.

What?

And just like that he's gone, leaving me alone once again.

I'm speechless for a full minute as I stare at the space he's just vacated, unable to come up with an explanation for his confusing behavior.

"Damn you," I mutter, ready to turn back and waste even more time in my room by myself. By chance, though, I notice that he didn't lock his door, and the curiosity is already killing me as I catch a few glimpses of it.

I'd seen it before, but it had been rather bare. Now, in comparison, I can see it's teeming with stuff.

I don't even think twice as I enter the room, my gaze quickly appraising its contents.

There's his bed, and I avoid looking more than necessary lest I start imagining him sleeping there at night... no clothes... the sheets sliding over...

Damn!

I force myself to ignore the way my heart pounds in my chest at the thought.

Why is it that only he can make me feel like this?

In the last three months I'd had more freedom, thanks to Marcello's perpetual absence from home and Raf's companionship. We'd gone out a number of times, and I saw plenty of conventionally attractive men on the streets or at restaurants. Not once did I feel anything but boredom.

I'm convinced that there's something not quite ordinary about Vlad that calls to me like this—it's simply unnatural, the way my body simply *sings* in his presence, my entire being soaring, bathed in an unprecedented type of lightness. For all the heartache he's caused me, he should *not* make me feel like this—like I'm only whole when he is around.

It's like I was made for him, and him alone.

Shaking myself from my musings, I peruse the other contents of his room. There's a desk with a computer, a few black bags filled to the brim with things, and then there's his closet.

So many options.

Of course, knowing him, my first inclination is to go look at his computer, even while doubting it would be unlocked.

I pull the chair, making myself comfortable at the desk and I move my finger a little on the touchpad, bringing the screen back to life.

My eyes widen.

Unlocked.

Damn, but he'd been in such a hurry he'd even left his computer unlocked. It makes me wonder where he needed to go, and to whom.

Fists clenched, I take a deep breath as I make myself focus on the treasure in front of me. Maybe it's not *entirely* right for me to snoop, but since I'm technically his prisoner, I think we're past moral dilemmas at this point.

I look around his desktop, noting a multitude of apps all haphazardly scattered around.

Of course he would be messy.

Not recognizing any, I just pull up his browser. Immediately, tens of tabs appear on the screen.

"What?" I narrow my eyes at the various titles.

Women 101.

Ten ideas to court a woman.

Get her heart and keep it.

I keep clicking on tab after tab, all having somewhat the same content.

How to impress your crush.

The man's guide to women.

I can't even keep a straight face as I read through the articles, some of the ideas absolutely ludicrous. Like *play hard to get.*

Wait…

"Surely not." The corners of my mouth pull up as I realize exactly what Vlad's been doing. There are quite a few articles that suggest ignoring one's love interest to make them react and chase back. The more I read—including highlighted passages—the more I start chuckling, the irony superb.

"Damn, Vlad." I shake my head at the monitor.

I should have realized that someone with his limited social skills and nonexistent emotional intelligence would not be able to come up with *courting* strategies on his own. Why, he's been reading up guides on how to impress me.

"Why is this so cute?" I mutter, unable to wipe the grin off of my face.

He's been seriously researching this topic, and when I look further into his history, I see he's even gotten books on the subject.

Just out of curiosity, I open his eBook library, not surprised to find it full of books on dating and women psychology. Even more surprising, though, is how thorough he's been. There are notes to go with each book, and hundreds if not *thousands* of passages highlighted.

Including the so-called playing hard to get.

Suddenly, everything makes sense. He's been putting a *lot* of effort in this, misguided as it might be. And I can't help but be impressed and a little flattered.

My mood brightens, and I quickly close the computer, curious to see what else he's hiding in his room.

First, I check the big bags stashed in the corner of his room. Opening one, I note a multitude of boxes, one on top of the other.

Going through some of them, I realize it's gifts he never gave me—shoes and handbags.

Another black bag and I note more fashion items, from clothes, to perfume to everything you could possibly imagine.

"Does he really think these things can buy my forgiveness?" I mutter, shaking my head. While I don't really care for most of the things he's bought, I can't help but melt a little—just a little—at the effort he's put in.

When I've snooped in all the bags, I open his wardrobe, curious about what lies inside. A few more clothes than the last time I'd been in here, but other than that…

I still, blinking repeatedly as if I can't quite believe what I'm seeing. Taking a few steps, I reach the back of the wardrobe, coming face to face with a human-sized teddy bear. In fact, it's practically the same height I am.

It can't be…

Blue with a pink ribbon, the bear looks eerily like the one I'd seen months back, during my first visit at a shopping center. It had stayed with me because I'd never seen such a big toy before, and it was *blue*—my favorite color. The pink ribbon had only made it more endearing and I remember spending some time just admiring it, barely working up the courage to touch it.

It had reminded me of everything I'd ever wanted growing up, but never received—most of all, it had reminded me of comfort.

I don't know why. Maybe it was the hue of the blue, or the softness of the material, but for a brief moment I'd wanted it more than anything. Of course, I hadn't gone through with buying it, since why would a grown woman need a bear?

But to see it here…

My gaze strays even lower, and I recognize the teddy bear I'd ripped in front of Vlad the other day. This one, a different shade of blue, is only slightly bigger than my hand.

I frown, suddenly realizing something. *All* the bears had been blue, or at least a shade of blue.

Picking it up, I almost feel bad for committing bearicide, but as I pat him over, trying to locate the tear I'd caused, I realize there's none.

Instead, there's a black, ugly jagged line starting from the bottom of the bear and going up to its neck—holding the seams together.

He didn't…

I don't know why *this* of all things makes my eyes burn with unshed tears, but as I rummage more through the back of the closet, I find a small sewing kit.

He did.

And I'm suddenly more confused than ever.

Why would someone who has *no* feelings care about something as trite as this?

"What the..." I can't help but stare at the small bear, and the poor yet endearing attempt to put it back together.

Why would someone who kills people in cold blood care about a stupid teddy bear?

Numbly walking back into the room, I'm still holding on to the bear, my thoughts a big, jumbled mess.

Now, more than ever, I can't seem to get *any* proper read on Vlad.

There's so much contradicting information that I don't know what to believe anymore. He's putting too much effort into this for someone who supposedly doesn't care.

My treacherous heart hones in on that thought, and I cannot stop myself from hoping.

I need to get to the bottom of this... before I get my heart broken again.

My mind made up, I decide to wait and confront him. After all, it's the only thing I can do that will ensure I'm not simply building scenarios in my head.

Because I've learned already that misplaced hope hurts the most. And I don't want to fall prey to it again.

I decide to wait around until he comes home, alternating between snooping some more and rolling around in his big bed, unashamedly inhaling the scent off his sheets.

A small nap and a lot of boredom later, it's already night. I'm very close to giving up when the door to the room swings open, Vlad coming in.

He doesn't even notice me at first, intent on taking his clothes off.

"Fuck, you startled me," he says when I turn on the lamp on his desk, raising an eyebrow at him. Slowly getting up, I place myself in front of him, not willing to give him any opening to avoid me this time.

"We need to talk," I say.

"We do?" he asks, confused.

"Yes," I confirm, crossing my arms in front of me. "You need to stop avoiding me." I go straight to the chase.

"I'm not avoiding you," he immediately starts denying it, but I won't have it. Instead, I place my finger on his lips, enjoying the way his eyes widen—especially now that the roles are reversed for the first time.

"Yes, you are. And you need to stop taking advice from the internet. I doubt they know what they're saying," I continue.

"Wh…" He tries to speak, but I shake my head at him, not done.

"No more games, Vlad. Let's put our cards on the table for once and for all."

His hand comes up, capturing my wrist as he brings it to his lips, his tongue peeking out to lick the sensitive area. My pulse quickens, but I refuse to let myself be seduced.

"Vlad." I push my chin up, my eyes challenging him to take me seriously.

"You snooped." Is all he says, his eyes holding me captive with their intensity. There's no condemnation in his gaze, no hint that he's mad at my snooping. So I just nod.

"You're going about this all wrong," I tell him, wrenching my hand away and taking a seat on the bed.

"You don't need to try tricks like *playing hard to get*." I roll my eyes at him and he has the decency to look embarrassed at my words.

"We can just have a serious conversation. I'm all ears," I say, happy I've managed to remain so composed.

He looks at me for a few seconds before slowly nodding and coming to sit next to me.

<h1 style="text-align:center">14</h1>
<h2 style="text-align:center">SISI</h2>

He's not too close but not too far either. His position is awfully stiff too, his legs spread apart, his hands resting on his knees. Silence descends as neither of us starts talking.

It's now or never.

I don't know if I'm taking a huge risk, but I stretch my arm over to his side, my palm coming to rest on top of his hand.

He seems surprised by the touch, his body jerking up slightly before slowly becoming more relaxed. Still, there's a lot of tension underneath, and I can feel that he's trying to keep himself in check.

"Why did you fix the bear, Vlad?" I ask the question that had baffled me the most. Turning toward him, I watch him swallow hard, taking his time to reply as if he's choosing his words carefully.

"It was a gift. For you," he eventually says, his voice low and lacking his usual confidence.

"And?" I continue to probe. His shoulders angle up in a

careless shrug, his lips pursed as if he doesn't know the answer either.

"I felt bad for it," he eventually replies, and his words tug at my heart. "I wanted you to have it," he continues, and for the first time I note a raw vulnerability to him. "You like teddy bears. I know you do." His eyes meet mine, his gaze cloudy with confusion.

"Why are you doing all of this? What are you trying to gain?"

He takes a deep breath, sounding almost defeated.

"I know what I did to you doesn't deserve forgiveness. I know that," he pauses, his brows knit together in a frown. "But I can't do this without you, Sisi. I thought I could. I thought you'd be better off without me. Hell, you probably *are* better off without me. But I'm such a selfish bastard that I can't let you go," he says, his rough voice sending shivers down my back.

"What are you trying to say, Vlad? Help me understand you, because, honestly, all of your actions so far have done nothing more than confuse me," I tell him, my hand still on his.

"Sisi…" he groans, bending his head low.

"You know I'm not indifferent to you, Vlad. But at the same time, I don't know if I can trust you. You threw me aside once. Who's to say you won't do it again?" I voice out my utmost worry. "You approach everything from a logical angle. What if next time you *logically* decide I'm a liability again? I can't do this every single time. I can't just wait around for your moods to change."

"Sisi, nothing about you is logical. Nothing I've ever done when it comes to you is *ever* logical. I know I screwed up. Fuck, I know I've been the biggest ass, on top of physically hurting you too. But please, just give me one more chance to prove to you that I didn't mean what I said. That you really are the most important person for me." He turns his palm up, cupping mine and squeezing it.

"I'm not myself without you," he confesses, "I know it sounds strange. Hell, even to my ears it sounds ludicrous. I spent thirty years just fine without you, but now I realize I *wasn't* fine." he closes his eyes, taking a deep breath.

"It took me less than a day to realize that there's no more me without you," he leans forward, closing the distance between us, "no Vlad without Sisi," he whispers, his breath on my cheek, "but I was too damn terrified of my own self and what I could have done to you."

I'm lost in his eyes. His words have never been softer, or more imbued with emotion than now. Even knowing he *cannot* feel, there's so much feeling.

And I waver.

"Fuck, Sisi." He lowers his forehead, resting it on my shoulder.

I hold myself still, his ragged breaths only making my heart beat faster.

"I was so careful," he whispers, "I wanted to give you a perfect first time," he says, surprising me once more.

I just listen, knowing this is a rare moment for him.

"I was so careful to *not* cause you any pain. And what did I do?" He gives a bitter laugh. "I took your virginity like a fucking beast. I..." he trails off, a low sound escaping his lips. "I don't think I can ever forgive myself for the hurt I caused you."

"Vlad..." I trail off.

"Even knowing that, I can't help myself. I know it's a lot to ask, but I can only promise I'll spend the rest of my life trying to make amends. Just please, give me another chance."

I don't know how to answer. I'm simply speechless as I hold on to him, blinking away tears and trying to stop my feelings from clouding my judgement. Because the truth is that I still love him.

I never stopped.

And his words right now are like a balm to my battered heart.

But how much can I believe?

"I don't know how," I answer truthfully, my voice soft and even. "I don't know how, Vlad," I repeat, raising my hand to wipe a tear from my eye. "You know I grew up at Sacre Coeur," I start, trembling slightly as the memories come back.

He draws back a little, his eyes still on me as he waits for me to continue.

"It wasn't pleasant," I admit, *not* pleasant being an understatement. "I was an outcast, doing my best to survive. Honestly, I was just a child looking for someone to love me, but instead I only found hate."

I gather my hands in my lap, clenching them together as I recall the abuse I'd endured for years on end.

"But my time there made me who I am today. It gave me my fears *and* my dreams. And because of that, I don't know how to continue with this. I don't know *how* to forgive you," I whisper, wiping more tears from my eyes.

Without giving it a second thought, I stand up, my shaking hands on the fastening of my dress. His eyes look anguished as he gazes at me, his entire body stiff, as if he doesn't dare make a wrong move.

Before I lose the courage, I drop my dress to the floor, remaining only in my underwear. I need to show him the truth—make him understand *why*.

"I was five when I got this scar." I point to an ugly line running across my elbow. "I was running away from some kids who were calling me cursed and," I swallow, the memories still painful, "and the devil's spawn."

"Someone tripped me and I fell. My elbow was split open, and still, they didn't stop. I was lying on the ground, bleeding and crying in pain, and all they could do was laugh at me. Sneer that it was what I deserved because that's what cursed people deserve—pain. The nuns weren't any better. I should have gotten immediate help for my wound, but instead I was punished for running around." My breath hitches as I remember that particular punishment.

"I was locked in a dark room for two days. Two days that my elbow hurt like hell, and no one thought to help me, or even inquire about me. Eventually the wound closed by itself, but because it had never been cleaned, it closed with a few pebbles inside. I had multiple bouts of infection until Mother Superior decided that I should finally see a doctor. But even then, do you know what they did?" I ask Vlad's attention wholly on me.

"Mother Superior said I didn't need any anesthetic for when they cut into my skin to remove the pebbles, that they shouldn't waste precious resources on a naughty child."

"Sisi..."

"No, I need to say this." I stop him. "That was the first time I realized that *no one* cared if I lived or died. And things just got worse." I bring my hand up to my right breast, where they marked me with the cross. "This," I trace the outline of the scar, "was supposed to be an exorcism. They wanted to make sure the devil got out of me and *stayed* out of me," I explain, doing my best not to become overwhelmed by the past.

I continue to show him scar after scar. My knees that were busted one too many times, my palms full of abrasions from being hit with wooden sticks until I bled, the small indentations all over my stomach as I was kicked and kicked until I couldn't breathe anymore.

And then I reach for the newer ones.

"And you know how I got these," I say and he flinches, looking as if I'd just slapped him.

"But do you know what they all have in common? For every single scar, no matter how tiny, the inner pain was the same. For every single time my body yelped in pain, my soul wept for mercy. Do you know how many times I wished for death? How many times I'd wished I could just stop the pain for once and for all?"

My entire body is trembling at this point, my breath coming in painful spurts. "Because hurting here," I bring my fist against my chest, "makes every other type of pain pale in comparison."

"You have no idea how blessed you are that you cannot feel that pain, because that's the real hell."

He keeps staring at me, his eyes drinking me in like he's seeing me for the first time.

"And because of that, I promised myself I would *never* beg anyone for love or attention. You were right about me being unwanted," I say, and I note the way his jaw clenches, his fists gripped so tightly his knuckles are a stark white.

"But I swore to myself that I'd *never* go back to someone who would easily throw me away. It was the only way I could make peace with the hand I was dealt."

I bring my arms around my body, rubbing my skin, the air suddenly chilly.

"And that's why, Vlad, I don't know how to forgive you," I whisper, more tears falling down my cheeks. "Because forgiving you would mean betraying myself. And I don't know if I can live with that."

He blinks, his eyes unfocused. Slowly, he rises from the bed, coming toward me until we're face to face.

Still holding eye contact, he does something that completely floors me.

He drops to his knees.

Head bent low, he drops to his knees in front of me, his hands clenched by his side, his entire body quivering with unreleased tension.

This proud man is on his knees before me.

Eyes wide, I watch him do something I would have never associated with Vlad—he's bowing down at me.

Submission.

The mere fact that he's on his knees in front of me, a most humbling experience, tells me he *is* serious about this.

"Sisi," he starts, his voice grim yet laced with anguish, "I know I have no right," he breathes deeply, "but I am *begging* for your forgiveness," he whispers, his body wound tightly as if in physical pain.

"Vlad…" I shake my head, unable to believe what I'm seeing. "What… Why…?"

"I screwed up. But please believe me that I *never* meant what I said to you. I knew it was the only thing that would drive you away from me, and seeing what I'd done to you, I needed you as far away from me as possible."

"Vlad." I reach out, my hand palming his cheek as I turn his gaze toward me. "Does it really matter if you meant it or not?" I ask the question, not expecting an answer. "I told you my time there shaped my fears and dreams. My greatest dream has always been to find someone to love me above all. And I know that can't be you," I tell him gently, hoping he will understand why I can't give in to him.

Even if I forgive him for what happened, it doesn't erase the fact that he's not capable of the one thing I want the most.

His eyes look glossy as he raises them to meet mine, his mouth parted as if he can't quite believe what I've said.

"I want something that you're not capable of giving me," I whisper, my hand moving over his face in a light caress.

"What if I could?" he asks, catching my hand with his and bringing it to his lips.

I blink the tears away at his question, the pain in my chest expanding.

"You know you can't," I reply slowly, my own hope dying the moment I acknowledge it out loud.

"Sisi," he moves toward me on his knees, bringing his body in direct contact with mine, "I think I do love you," he says, and my heart skips at the sound of it.

But then I realize he's just trying to placate me. And it hurts even more.

"Please don't lie to me," I whimper.

"I'm not lying." He takes my hands into his before

placing them on his chest. "Please listen to me," he says brokenly, and even though I continue to shake my head in disbelief, I cannot *not* listen.

"I never even knew I was capable of love until you, Sisi," he starts, "I've always been a selfish, self-serving bastard. *Until you.* I never cared about human life, never gave a damn about who I killed. *Until you.* I've never cared about anyone's happiness before, mostly going out of my way to cause *un*happiness. *Until you.* And I certainly never cared about pleasing anyone before," he releases a harsh breath, "*until you.*"

He gives my hands a gentle squeeze.

"I don't know if this *is* love, since I have nothing to compare it to. But you *are* the most important person in my life, Sisi. You're the only reason I'm still somehow alive. The only reason I'm trying to get better… To maybe deserve you at some point in the future." His words ring in my ears, the sincerity behind them unmistakable.

"Vlad," I call out his name, overwhelmed by his declaration.

"I know I made a mockery of your love for me, when in truth, it warmed me where I didn't know I was cold. *You* made me warm, Sisi." He pushes my hands over his heart. "You made this Goddamn organ do something else besides barely keeping me alive. You made it *want* to be alive," he continues, his neck strained with tension.

"So please, Sisi, *please,* let me show you I *can* love you above all. Because I know I would take on the *entire* world for you."

My own knees buckle, and I fall beside him, my teary

eyes searching his features for confirmation that he is speaking the truth.

"You're my special, hell girl. The *only* one. And I don't know if that's how normal people feel love..." I stop him, pressing my finger against his lips.

"It is," I whisper, "because you're my special too," I say and watch in wonder how his expression changes right before my eyes. A face ravaged by pain suddenly becomes steeped in joy, his mouth pulling up in the most gorgeous smile I've ever seen.

"I love you, Sisi," he repeats, and those words alone have a way to move me beyond belief.

"I love you too, Vlad," I say the words back, moving closer to him and wrapping my arms around him, soaking in the feeling of finally being whole.

Because he completes me in an indescribable way.

"So much." His voice caresses my senses as he holds on to me.

And I do feel it.

I do feel his love, and retrospectively, I can see it in his every action.

He just didn't know it was love.

"Please forgive me," he whispers against my hair.

My hands tighten in his shirt as tears rack my body.

"I'll do better. I promise you I'll never hurt you again," he continues, slowly rocking with me, his arms tight around my waist, his face in the crook of my neck.

"Okay," I find myself saying. In spite of my rebelling mind, in spite of my entire history, I find myself giving in.

"I forgive you," I whisper, knowing the words to be true the moment I utter them.

I may have lost myself *that* night, but his words of love served as a beacon to bring me back to myself.

And because I do feel his love, in every conflicting action and in every misspoken word, I know I can never let go of him again.

"I'm entrusting you with my heart. Please don't crush it again," I tell him.

I don't know if it's the right decision. In fact, I'm not sure of anything else but the fact that I love him. And maybe for once I should let myself be led by my heart, not my mind.

We stay in silence like that, just holding on to one another.

"I'm sorry about the baby," he eventually speaks, and I feel a pang in my chest. "Even if it wasn't mine," he continues, and I feel his heavy breath on my neck. "I'm sorry you had to go through that."

I sniffle a sob, leaning back to look at him.

God, he really means it!

"It was yours," I admit, suddenly ashamed of my lie. "Nothing ever happened with Raf. I lied. I wanted to hurt you somehow…" I trail off.

But the look in his eyes has me blinking my tears away, a lightness appearing on his face, his shoulders sagging in relief.

"Sisi," he groans, his hands cupping my face. "You did hurt me," he says quietly, "I don't think I've ever known greater torment than imagining you with someone else. Pregnant with someone else." Closing his eyes, he sighs, as if a weight has been lifted off his chest.

"Never?" he asks again and I shake my head. He brings

my face to his, peppering me with kisses. "You have no idea what that means to me," he says between kisses, "you're mine... only mine..."

"I am," I admit, "you're the only man I've ever kissed, the only one I've ever touched, and you will be the only one I'll *ever* give myself to. You have my word. How could I even think of someone else when all I see is you? When my heart is so full of you? Even when I hated you I loved you," I confess.

And even when I hated him I could recognize that no one would be able to replace him.

"Sisi..."

"There's no me without you either." I nuzzle my face against his chest, realizing I've never spoken truer words. "No Sisi without Vlad." There's nothing logical about us, nothing remotely explicable about the way I feel about him. I just do. Even now, I feel him deep inside of me, his presence soothing me and calming my clamoring soul.

"And no Vlad without Sisi," he completes the sentence, laying his forehead on top of mine. "I'm yours. Wholly yours too, Sisi. I would *never* even look at a woman that's not you, let alone touch. You're the only one in the world for me," he rasps, and relief floods my senses.

I'd never even let my thoughts wander there, because I knew that the thought of him with someone else would drive me crazy. But hearing his confirmation does wonders to my mood.

We stare into each other's eyes, and I feel a peace settle over me.

"I'm sorry about the baby." He gives me a pained expression. "If you want, I'll give you ten. No, a hundred babies. Everything to make you happy, Sisi. *Everything*," he says with such staunch conviction that I can't help but cry even more.

"For now *you're* enough," I whisper, touched by his words, but unsure if I'm ready to go through another heartache again.

He nods, a small smile on his face as one finger traces my scars. His mouth quickly follows as he kisses his way across my entire body, covering each scar.

He lays me on the floor, spread for him, a look of pure adoration on his face as his eyes survey me.

"You're perfect, Sisi. And I love every scar of yours," he murmurs, lowering his head to trace the cross scar with his tongue. "They made you into who you are," he continues, speaking against my skin and making me shiver—the combination of his wet tongue and his warm breath fogging my senses. "And that makes them beautiful."

I press my hand to his cheek, taking in his heat, somewhat unable to believe any of this is real.

"Please don't hurt me again," I whisper, some residual fear still in the back of my mind.

"I'd rather die than cause you pain again, Sisi," He effortlessly gathers me in his arms, taking me to the bed. "I'll spend my entire life making it up to you for everything I did," he whispers, his breath fanning on my face.

His lips take mine in the sweetest kiss, and I can taste his desperation behind it, the way he's putting everything he has in this *one* kiss.

"Stay with me," he says, his arms tightening around my body. "Stay with me tonight."

I still for a moment, the pain from before still fresh in my mind.

"We don't have to do anything. I just want to hold you. Please, Sisi," he pleads, and I find myself nodding.

"I'm scared to…" I trail off, trying to find the proper words.

"I know," he replies, "and I can't blame you. I'm sorry," he apologizes again, and I don't think he's ever said sorry to someone before—let alone this many times.

"We'll move past it." I lightly caress his face. "Slowly."

"I'll go as slow and I'll be as gentle as you want me to, Sisi. I just need to know you're by my side. The rest doesn't matter."

He holds me close to his body, spooning me from behind as I tell him everything that happened in the past few months, as well as why I'd agreed to marry Raf. I can feel the tension in his body every time I mention his name, so I want to make it clear that Raf's never been anything but a good friend.

"I don't know what I would have done if you'd actually slept with him," he suddenly says, his voice somber. "Killed him? Hunted down his entire family and killed all his living relatives? Given you a lobotomy…" he trails off and an amused smile creeps on my face.

"You'd have given me a lobotomy?" I shift, turning so I can face him.

And he's definitely not joking.

"So that you'd forget ever being with him. So that I'm the only one for you. *Ever*," he continues, still as serious as before.

"Oh, Vlad." A small smile tugs at my lips while his expression remains stoic.

"I'm serious," he pouts, and I'm suddenly reminded how cute he can get in spite of his psychotic tendencies. But that's what I love about him. That duality and the fact that I *know* he's only cute with me.

I'm his one exception, just like he is mine.

"I love you," I whisper, laying my head on his chest, my entire being infused with happiness when he says the words back.

And I sleep peacefully for the first time in months.

15
VLAD

"**M**mm…" I bring her closer to me, my face in the crook of her neck. "Can we stay like this forever?" I ask sleepily, worried that once I open my eyes reality will come crashing down and everything will have been a dream.

The mere fact that she's next to me and letting me touch her is more than I could have ever hoped.

Hell, when she'd told me about her time at Sacre Coeur, I could only listen, mentally making a list of all the people I need to dispatch—and painfully, too.

To think of Sisi, my brave and beautiful Sisi, being put through so much suffering kills me. And I intend to make sure those people get what they deserve—a very drawn out death at the end of my knife.

I still can't believe what a lucky bastard I am, and that she'd actually forgiven me, even regaling me with those words again—love.

Shit! I'm so fucked.

Now that I heard her say the words, I'm never going to get tired of hearing them.

Even now, looking at her sleepy form, with the way her lips twitch, the corners lifting slightly, I get this insane urge to smother her with kisses.

Is this what love feels like?

Because I think I like it. No, scratch that, I fucking love it. And her. Always her.

I fucking love her.

Fucking Hades in the ninth circle of hell, but I'm in trouble. This time, though, it's the good kind.

Our conversation last night had given me a better glimpse into what makes Sisi into the magnificent woman she is—perseverance. Against all odds, she survived.

And I was the one who found her.

Now I'm going to keep her for the rest of my life and I'll do my very best to make her the happiest.

A little too happy at the prospect, I keep tightening my arms around her, wanting to never let go. To always have her near.

Maybe I should cuff her to me.

The moment the thought comes to mind, I still, my eyes slowly opening as I realize what a great idea it is. That way, I don't have to *ever* spend a moment without her.

"What's going through that mind of yours?" Her voice brings me back to reality, and I look down to see her gorgeous eyes sparkling with mischief as she watches me closely.

"That I'd like to cuff you to my side," I tell her seriously. "That way I don't have to miss you ever again."

"Not a bad idea," she whispers, leaning into me. She's

wearing only a bra and her underwear, but suddenly that's all my mind can process—and my cock.

Damn, I need to get myself under control.

I know she's not ready for anything physical, likely she won't be for a very long time. And I don't want her to think I'll pressure her in any way.

We're going at her pace, even if it kills me.

"I can't remember the last time I slept this well." She brings the back of her fingers to my cheek, slowly trailing them down. "Or was this happy."

I capture her hand, bringing it to my lips.

"Me too, hell girl. Me too. And because of that, I don't want to leave this bed." I smile, tugging her into me and cuddling her.

Her small size makes her fit right at home in my arms, and I listen to her small sounds, the way she seems to purr as I bring my hands down her arms in a light caress.

"Then let's not. We can always watch a movie in bed," she suggests and I quickly agree.

Anything to keep her close. The more time I spend by her side, the more I'll realize that it's not a dream and that she's actually mine.

We end up spending the entire day in bed, alternating between watching movies and pillow fighting, all of them ending with us in rather compromising positions that have my cock dying for relief.

Like now.

I stare into her eyes, her legs spread to accommodate my pelvis, my hands hovering above her head as I hold a pillow. We're both breathing harshly, and I don't know if it's from the exertion or the titivating contact.

Does she know how hard I am?

Her eyes slip lower, to the tent in my pants, and a blush creeps up her neck. I'm so fucking stunned by her beauty, that I just still, my pillow dropping from my hands, my eyes fixed on the pretty red on her cheeks, or the way she pulls at her lower lip, biting it in an entirely innocuous way, yet that alone has the blood all rushing down to my cock.

She raises an eyebrow at me, but she doesn't waste any time in switching our positions until she's the one above me, her pillow aimed at my head.

Giving me a sly smile, she brings it down over me, some feathers flying out of the pillowcase and causing her to giggle.

"I win," she whispers, only now realizing that although she's won this, her position means that she's sitting right on top of my dick.

"I can't help it, hell girl. You have that effect on me." I smirk at her.

She keeps playing with her lip, her teeth nibbling at it as if she isn't quite sure what to do next.

Moving slightly off of me, she keeps her eyes on me.

"Why don't you do something about it?" she asks, and I see the way her pupils expand, her chest rising and falling with every labored breath.

She's as turned on as I am.

But I know we can't do anything just yet.

"What do you want me to do, hell girl? I'm all yours," I tell her. Maybe it will help if she regains some type of control over this. I know the last incident scarred her, both mentally and physically, and I'll probably regret what I did to her for as long as I live.

And because of that, I'm willing to do whatever it takes until she's comfortable with me again. I'll go as slow as she wants me to, even when my instincts demand that I fuck her into oblivion.

I need to get a grip on myself!

"I want to watch you," she says breathlessly, her eyes lingering over my erection. "No touching. Just watching."

She doesn't have to tell me twice as I pull down on my pants, my cock springing free and slapping against my abdomen.

"I forgot how big you were," she whispers, her expression changing to one of apprehension.

I feel a pang in my chest, the thought of hurting her physically hurting *me*.

"It's only for your pleasure, hell girl. Never pain," I assure her, "unless you ask for it." I smirk at her, using my hand to grip the base of my cock, my fist tightening over my shaft.

Her mouth opens slightly as she watches me work my length up and down, her eyes following my every move.

Slowly, she removes her top, bringing her voluptuous tits into full view, her nipples tight and straining in the air.

I let out a groan at the sight, pre-cum generously oozing from the tip. I swipe my thumb over the head, using the moisture to coat my entire shaft.

"Fuck, hell girl, you're temptation personified," I rasp, watching her bring her hands up to play with her nipples.

"Did you touch yourself while I was gone?" I ask, the image already forming in my mind and making me even harder.

She blushes, slowly nodding.

"And what did you think of while you were petting your little clit?" I ask, tightening my grip at the same time as I hear her small gasp, her spine arching and thrusting her tits in the air.

"You," she says, her voice barely above a whisper. A flush spreads up her chest and to her cheeks, her tongue peeking out to lick her lips in between small whimpers.

"What was I doing?" I continue to probe, her little mews doing wonders to my cock, the bastard preening at the sounds, my balls almost drawn up in pain from being too full of cum. I have no idea what spell she's cast on me, the way my body reacts *only* to her, but I'm not complaining.

She fucking owns me!

"Fucking me," her eyes flutter closed, "fucking me like an animal," she continues, her voice becoming increasingly higher pitched and breathy. "Chasing me and taking me on all fours... like a beast," she says on a strangled moan and I can barely stave off my climax.

It seems that for all her fear about the pain, there's also a secret thrill in being chased and subdued. My dirty nun might be naughtier than I'd expected.

We might indulge in those fantasies in the future.

"Take off your panties." I issue the command without even thinking. "Let me see that pretty pussy," I say with a gruff voice.

She doesn't even hesitate, the minx. She slips her panties down her legs, positioning herself right in front of me before slowly opening her legs and letting me see the wonder nestled between.

She's wet and slick and glistening with need, and I'd like

nothing better than to dive in, taste her with my tongue and have her come all over my face.

But not now.

"Slide your fingers down your tight little pussy," I order her, all the while continuing to work my cock, imagining my hand is her pussy, gripping me tightly and sucking the fucking life out of me.

Oh, but I'd gladly die.

She does as instructed, two fingers descending between her pussy lips. They are almost immediately coated in her arousal and she uses it to smear it around, making me jealous of a Goddamn finger.

"Whose pussy is that, hell girl?" I demand, wanting her words.

"Yours, only yours," she cries out, eyes closed, her fingers circling her clit.

My own movements gain speed as I can practically smell her arousal from where I'm sitting, the scent intoxicating and so fucking delicious I'm one second away from jumping on her, ready to lap at her juices.

"Are you imagining it's me touching you?" I continue to ask, enjoying the way her cheeks flush, her mouth opening and closing with each stroke of her clit.

"Yes," she whimpers, "I'm imagining it's my God touching me," she says, the words taking me by surprise and making my balls contract, my orgasm imminent.

"Fuck me, hell girl," I groan. "How can I last when you say things like that?"

I squeeze my cock, my eyes almost rolling into the back of my head at the sensation.

"My not so saintly little nun likes to play dirty," I drawl, watching her own movements quicken, her mouth parted, her breath coming in spurts.

"Come for me, Sisi, let me see that pussy come for her God," I command her, and it doesn't take long before she's moaning my name, her legs quivering as she rides her climax, her pussy gushing out juices and drenching her fingers.

Fuck!

Her eyes snap open, her glazed pupils taking in my engorged cock and the way I'm pumping it like a mad man, the sight of her only fueling my own pleasure.

"Come on me," she says, moving on all fours and slowly coming toward me until her face is at eye level with my cock. "Come all over me," she repeats, and it's enough to make me bust, cum shooting out of my dick and all over her face.

She's like a goddess waiting for her offering, lips parted, tongue out, my cum hitting her mouth before settling nicely all over her face.

"Fuck," I groan, the sight of her covered in my seed undoing me.

Marked. She's marked.

She blinks, her eyes focusing on me before a seductive smile appears on her face, her fingers swiping at my cum and bringing it to her mouth.

"I fucking love you Sisi," I tell her, my hand on her nape as I bring her flush against me, holding her captive as I ravage her mouth with my own, tasting myself on her tongue.

Wrapping my hand around her wrist, I bring her fingers to my mouth, sucking them clean and finally tasting the nectar I'd been missing all these months.

And fuck if it doesn't make me hard again!

"I need to get on birth control," Sisi sighs, snuggling closer to me a while later, after we've both taken a shower.

"We're not in any hurry. I told you, we're going at your pace," I tell her, smoothing her hair with my hand, enjoying its silky texture.

"Just to be prepared. I don't want to get pregnant and go through that again."

"Was it that bad?" I ask. I'd read up online about miscarriages and I'd tried to understand as much as I could. Still, that was only the theoretical side, not the more personal one.

She nods, her small hand tightening in a fist.

"I'd already imagined him," she says, "he would have looked like you, with dark hair and black eyes." Her voice trembles, and I know this is hard for her.

I may not have that much experience with this feelings business, but anything that hurts Sisi hurts me too. So I just wrap my arms around her, holding her close and wishing I'd be able to take away some of her pain.

"Tell me about it," I prompt her, thinking that might help her get it off her chest.

And she does. She tells me all about the boy she'd imagined, and how she'd already loved him. Her tears fall softly down my chest as she finally releases everything she's held inside for so long.

Emotionally spent, it's not long before she falls asleep.

Still holding on to her, I close my eyes too, unaware that like everything else, happiness is ephemeral too.

The nightmare has just begun.

16

VLAD

My eyes snap open, my heart beating loudly in my chest. There are a few rays of sun filtering the bars of the only window of the room.

My sister is huddled by my side, her entire body shaking, her lips purple.

"V, wake up." I push at her shoulders, but only a few small noises escape her lips as she tries to open her eyes, her body coiled tightly to preserve heat.

I quickly shimmy out of my thin shirt, laying it on top of her. But as I try to cover her with it, my hand brushes across her forehead and I notice she's burning up.

"V…" I mutter, worried.

We've been here for a long time. I'm not even sure how much time has passed anymore. The only thing I know is that days turn into night and then into days again. Sometimes we are taken out of the room for a medical consultation, but other than that we're just left alone.

The only people we've interacted with have been the doctors, who aren't very talkative. They only record their measurements, and then we're taken back to our cages.

Because I can't call this room anything but a cage. Not when the bars mean that we're treated worse than animals.

And because of that we're now both one step away from going crazy, the isolation almost unbearable.

"V," I continue to get her to rouse.

"What…" she mumbles, her eyes sluggish as she tries to pry them open. "Here," I say, getting some water and forcing her to drink.

"You need to hold on, V," I tell her, stroking her hair.

She's been getting weaker and weaker for a while now, and the tests we have to undergo don't help much. Not when every single blood draw weakens even her more.

"I…" She shakes her head, some droplets of water falling down her chin. "I don't know how much longer…" she whispers.

"You need to, V. For me," I take her hand, hooking our pinkies together, "we're in this together. Always," I tell her, desperate to make her not give up hope.

"Always," she whispers, her lips tugging upwards slowly.

Truth is, I don't know how long I can keep this up either. I've been trying to be strong for her sake, but even I am losing hope.

Vanya eventually beats her fever, and color starts to climb up her cheeks. Her mood, though, doesn't improve.

One day, we're picked up by guards and taken to a new room, where two doctors we haven't seen before are waiting for us.

The tests are routine, and we're already used to the blood draws or the weird machines that they put on us. But this time, they also give us some questionnaires and some drawings to interpret.

I'm not exactly sure what this is, but apparently we both pass all the tests, as the doctors inform us that we'd be moved to another facility.

We're both confused at the whirlwind move, everything happening too fast.

Loaded in a black van, we're taken to the next location, but our living conditions don't improve. If anything, they are even worse than before.

The cell is dirty and the food is barely edible. The only difference is that we now have round the clock guards and even more tests.

The first week we're there though, we also get a present.

The first present we've ever been given here.

One of the guards comes and brings in a baby rabbit, telling us that we need to make sure we raise it appropriately.

I'm immediately skeptical, and my suspicion doesn't abate. But the rabbit's arrival makes Vanya break out of her shell and she starts to become more active. She now smiles more, and her mood has considerably improved.

Seeing the changes in her makes me thaw toward the rabbit, too.

"I named it Lulu." Vanya beams at me, holding the already two months old rabbit in her arms. It's definitely growing every day, and I can't believe that they saddled us with another mouth to feed when we barely get enough food as it is.

"That's nice, V." I try to return the smile.

"He likes it when I rub his belly. Look," she giggles, turning Lulu on his back and petting him on the stomach.

I don't know if Lulu is very keen on that, but it makes Vanya happy and that's enough. Though I am a little put off that Lulu's fur is clean and shiny while Vanya's clothes haven't been changed in months.

She's smiling happily in her tattered and dirty dress, a stark contrast to Lulu's pristine coat.

"I can't believe they let us keep it," she whispers, holding Lulu to her chest and cooing softly.

"I don't think we should get too attached, V. I don't have a good feeling about this," I tell her for the thousanth time.

"It's been so long, brother…" She shakes her head. *"If they had meant to do something, they would have done it already. It's been months and they've let us keep Lulu,"* she says, and while I have to agree with her reasoning, I still can't quite feel comfortable.

The door to the cell rattles, and two guards step inside the room.

"Your turn, brats," they yell, coming inside and grabbing us roughly. Vanya accidentally drops Lulu, her eyes immediately filling up with tears as he yelps in pain.

But we don't have any time to react as we're shoved outside the cell and taken down a dark corridor.

"Vlad," she whispers in a low voice, *"I'm scared."* She looks at me, her eyes wide with fear.

I am too, but I can't show it. Not when she needs my support.

"It's going to be okay. Just like the other consults." I try to be optimistic, but something about this feels awfully ominous.

Even the building looks worse than the one we'd been in before, so I don't have high hopes.

We make a right down a narrow staircase before we're ushered inside a huge room full with medical equipment.

Vanya and I are separated by the guards as we're pushed toward a pair of high beds. We barely have time to react as we're raised on the beds, our hands and feet strapped to the metal hinges.

When the guards are gone, it's not long before a man comes inside. He's wearing a white robe, like the other doctors. His height is like my father's, but he doesn't have the muscles to accompany it. With light-brown hair and dark-blue eyes, he doesn't look as menacing as the other doctors. He even has a small smile on his face as he comes toward us, picking up a pair of gloves on the way.

"What do we have here?" he exclaims, his gaze moving quickly over me before switching over to Vanya, his eyes lighting up with interest.

I swallow, unsure if I like that.

"And who is this little princess?" He heads to Vanya's side, picking up a strand of her hair and bringing it to his nose, inhaling.

"What's your name, darling?" he asks, a weird smile on his face.

"Vanya." My sister blinks, just as confused as me.

"Vanya, such a pretty name. For a pretty lady," he comments, going around his table full of utensils, his hands moving dramatically in the air as if he's contemplating which one to choose.

Eventually, he settles on a small set of needles, turning back to us, his smile even wider.

"I'm Miles," he says proudly, "and you're very lucky to be chosen. My criteria is very strict, and I have to say. We haven't had a full set of twins pass the tests in quite a while." He moves around, coming to sit next to Vanya's bed.

"And you, darling, are the first girl in a very long time," he sighs. "But such a pretty thing you are," he continues, his gloved hand trailing down her cheek.

I guess you could say Vanya's pretty. She's definitely the more good looking one of the two of us. With her frail frame, black hair and black eyes against pale skin, she looks like a porcelain doll. But I don't like the way he's saying it to her. It feels... predatory.

"Why, I'll have the best fun breaking you," he says excitedly, and I frown, not really understanding his meaning.

He heads to my side first, regarding me for a moment through narrowed eyes before choosing a fairly big needle.

"Now, let's see how this feels," he says, inserting the needle into my arm without any preliminaries.

I jerk away in pain, my eyes wide as I take in his smile.

"On a scale of one to ten, how much does it hurt?" he asks, his hand applying pressure on the needle and moving it around.

"Five," I answer, taking a deep breath and forcing my eyes not to tear up in pain.

Somehow I think he wouldn't appreciate that display.

"Wonderful," he replies, taking out the needle, blood gushing out of my skin before choosing another one and jabbing it again into the same spot. The tip is bigger, so it immediately enlarges the wound.

I stifle a moan of pain.

"Now?"

"Seven," I say, cursing myself right away for not going to a higher number. Because if this is seven…

His smile never falters as he takes an even bigger needle, repeating the procedure until I yell a painful ten.

When he's done with me, my arm is a bloody mess. I can't even see the original wound as multiple holes are centered around the same area, blood gushing out in spurts.

Unlike previous consults, he doesn't even bother to give me a gauze for my arm, or even clean some of the blood.

No, his attention is switched to Vanya, and his smile widens as he regards her pale face. My stomach is in knots as I know he'll do the same to her, but I can only helplessly watch as Vanya turns her eyes to me, her cries muted as he makes a mess of her flesh.

"My God," Miles breathes out, amazed at Vanya's perseverance. "You're a wonder, aren't you?" he exclaims in disbelief after he disposes of the tenth needle. He seems to be impressed that Vanya hadn't cried out even once.

What he doesn't know, though, is that my sister's already developed her own mechanism of dealing with outside stimuli. She finds her refuge in me. The moment our eyes met I knew she'd shut down, only waiting for Miles to be done.

Even as blood pours out of her wounds, there's barely any reaction.

"I think I have a winner," Miles adds, an expression of pure happiness on his face.

I don't get to dwell on it, as we're quickly taken away and put back in our cells. Vanya is back to herself the minute she sees Lulu, taking him in her arms and staining his white coat with her blood.

"V," I try to pry her hand away, using the end of my shirt to scrub some of the blood away.

"I'm fine." She shrugs, giving me a smile.

But it's not too long after that another guard comes to our cell. This time specifically for Vanya.

"But we're always together," I add as they try to pry her from my side. *"You can't take her."*

"Orders are orders, kid. He only wants her.*" He points toward Vanya. And when I try to physically put myself between him and my sister, he easily swats me aside, the back of his hand connecting to my cheek and sending me flying.*

"It's okay, Vlad. I'll be fine," Vanya adds with a sympathetic smile, and I can only watch as she's taken away from me.

I spend the next day and night without closing my eyes for a second.

Where is she?

My body simply can't relax as I'm picturing thousands of scenarios, all of them ending with my sister dead.

But the dreaded wait comes to an end when the cell door opens, and Vanya struts inside wearing a pink dress, her long hair braided in two pigtails.

"V?" I take a step toward her, surprised at her change in appearance. Even her wound had been taken care of.

Yet for all the clean clothes, there's a haunted look to her.

"V," I rush to her side, my hands on her shoulders. *"What*

happened? Are you okay?" I ask, patting her down. Her reaction is immediate as she pushes me away, recoiling at my touch.

She moves to a corner of the cell, lying down and drawing her knees to her chest.

"V," I ask tentatively, for the first time truly worried.

Whatever had happened to us, she'd never given me the silent treatment.

Never.

The exclusive visits continue and slowly, even Lulu fails to rouse Vanya's interest. She barely speaks to me, and when I try to comfort her she rejects away all of my touch.

"V, please talk to me," I beg her one day when she comes back wearing yet another new dress, but with tears falling down her cheeks. "What happened?"

"He said I was his special girl," she whimpers, her hands on her face as sobs slowly rack her body.

"V..." I trail off, not knowing how to help her.

"It hurts... but I have to pretend it doesn't," she whispers.

"What does? What hurts?" I immediately imagine Miles hurting her even more, trying to take her pain threshold to a different extreme every time. In my mind, I can't help but see her bloody and bruised, but there's barely a mark on her flesh.

"He likes it when I'm on my hands and knees," she starts, her voice small, "naked..." she drifts off and I frown.

Naked?

"There's something poking inside my body, and it hurts. Every time..." She takes a deep breath. "And you're not there to help me through it," she says the last words on a sob, tears flooding down her cheeks.

I move closer to her, slowly wrapping my arms around her body, and for the first time she allows my touch.

I don't understand what's happening to her at first. It takes me some time before I fully realize what's poking her body every time, and what Miles is doing to my sister.

And I only do when it happens to me too, during one of Vanya's absences when a guard sneaks inside our cell.

Pinned down, and stripped of everything, I can only hope it doesn't last. Almost triple my size, I don't stand a chance as he pushes his elbow into my nape, holding me in place as he fondles my butt.

No matter how much I try to move, or yell in protest, it's in vain as he shoves himself inside of me, my body screaming in pain as he tears me apart. As much as my body wants to reject him, the strength of his assault is no match for a child's body. I feel his nasty hardness buried inside me, the pain unbearable as he digs himself deeper before retreating.

At some point I just stop fighting, holding myself still as he thrusts in and out of me, the smell of his sweaty body on top of my own threatening to make me sick.

But even as I hear his grunts on top of me, all I can think is my sister. My baby sister who had to endure this violation time after time, withdrawing deeper into herself and rejecting even her brother's touch—blood of her blood.

It's only then that I truly understand what Vanya has to go through every time Miles calls on her, and I don't think I can bear it. I don't think I can live knowing that someone hurts my baby sister like this.

I need to do something about it.

It's the turning point as I realize I must save my sister somehow. Because she's all that matters. I can take anything.

Rape. Pain. Torture.

I'll bear everything as long as I can spare her.

Armed with staunch conviction, the method to get the attention off her comes to me during our consults.

Each time he cuts into my skin, asking my pain level, I close my eyes, willing my body to obey me, and I say the lowest number I can. I continue to grit my teeth even as his experiments grow in size, when he's no longer satisfied with needles and now requires knives to cut into our flesh.

I bear it even when I see him peel the skin back of my arm, unveiling my veins and muscles.

In fact, this particular experiment finally gains me his attention.

"Maybe I was wrong," he notes, studying my reactions as he pokes and prods at my exposed arm.

After so much time around blood and knives, I'm already desensitized to even seeing my own naked flesh.

"We'll see," he comments, moving back to Vanya.

This is her time to put on a show. I'd asked her—begged her—to cry and wail the moment he'd cut into her flesh. To not hold it in and not take refuge in me. To simply let it out.

One questioning gaze in my direction and I nod. The moment the knife touches her arm, she starts screaming in pain. Miles' eyes widen in horror as if he can't believe what's happening.

He keeps on cutting, but Vanya keeps on screaming.

Until he's done.

Removing his gloves, he throws them on the ground, stomping out of the room and letting one of his assistants come in and sew us back together.

And I know I finally have his attention.

And just like that, Vanya's special visits stop.

By now I've realized what Miles seems to be looking for—the test subject who performs best on his experiments.

And if that ensures that my sister will be left in peace, then I'll be the very best one.

No matter what I have to do.

I know my plan works when the following day I'm the one called to his office.

Stepping inside, it's nicer than anything I've ever seen. Everything is so shiny and new, and there are lots of devices everywhere.

As soon as I'm pushed inside by a guard, Miles rises from his chair, his smile wide as he takes in my small form.

"Vlad, wasn't it?" he asks, and there's a fake air around his entire demeanor. But knowing that this is the only way to spare Vanya even more pain, I nod, playing along.

"Yes, Sir," I answer, and he motions me to a chair next to him.

I sit down, trying to ignore the way my dirty clothes or my even dirtier body stains the shiny leather, or how Miles flares his nostrils when he catches a whiff of me.

After all, whose fault is it for my sorry state?

"I've been watching you, Vlad." Miles crosses his legs, bringing his arms forward and resting his chin on his hand. "And I think you've been hiding your potential from me."

"I don't know, Sir," I answer, trying to seem baffled at his question.

"Here," he says, grabbing my recently sutured arm roughly. I internally wince at the pain, but on the outside, I don't show it.

I just blink once, staring at Miles and showing him exactly what he wants to see—no reaction.

"I thought your sister was above average. But you my boy," he whistles, "you might just be my little miracle."

"What is this for, Sir?" I ask before I can help myself.

He narrows his eyes at me before chuckling.

"An inquisitive mind. I like it," he says, getting up from his chair and telling me to follow.

Pressing a few buttons on a keyboard, another door opens in the back of the office. As we step inside the room, I see computers and other machines, all surrounded by rows and rows of books.

"Interesting, but you're the first one to ask me for the purpose," he notes, and I can tell there's an underlying pleasure in his voice.

He stops in front of a huge blackboard, the entire surface scribbled in white signs.

"This." He pulls down on a paper, bringing it down and showing me an illustration. "Is the brain," he starts explaining. "And this," he points to a region in the center, "is the amygdala. To put it simply, it regulates some of the basic emotions in humans—particularly fear."

He walks around, chatting enthusiastically.

"You see, there are people out there, psychopaths, who do not have the full function of the amygdala, and as such they cannot feel what regular people feel. They don't know fear and they don't know remorse. But there's one catch. Psychopaths are unpredictable. Too unpredictable," he mutters under his breath.

He stops and I wait for him to continue, curious what the point of this was.

"But then there's also people like you. Intermediaries," he says, his mouth curving upwards. "Your amygdala is developed in such a way that while you're not as far gone as a psychopath, you're not completely normal either."

"You mean my emotions are not so strong," I comment.

"Right and… wrong. I've studied your kind for a long time." He smirks. "I'm older than I look," he sneaks in a joke. "And while not every specimen is the same, I've noticed a pattern. There isn't a lack of feeling per se, but there is a difference in what you can feel. Everyone is different." He shrugs. "Some people don't know love, some don't know hate, and others just don't know fear."

He turns fully toward me.

"Of course, I'm only interested in those that lack fear. You see, fear

is one of the worst human traits. Acceptable, from an evolutionary point of view. But not from a mercenary one." He taps his foot anxiously. "But for what I have in mind, it's the requisite trait to have."

"What do you mean?"

"Super soldiers." He smirks again. "The perfect human weapon that knows no fear, nor," he nods at my arm, "pain. A killing machine if you will."

"What about remorse? Don't some people have it while others don't?" I ask, his theory stirring something inside of me. For all my apathy toward the man for hurting my sister, I can't help but be intrigued by the way his mind works.

"Smart," his mouth draws up, "we just erase it out of you. One step at a time." He comes closer until he's sitting right in front of me. "And you, my little miracle, might just be my winning prize."

"Me?"

"You think I haven't observed you until now? Your intellectual attributes are perfect. But I've never been quite sold on your physical or emotional abilities," he says jovially, "until now."

He strokes his jaw pensively before adding, "And if your physical form is better than I'd hoped, then that only leaves one thing."

He stops, and I raise my head to look at him.

"Your emotions," he declares happily, giving me my first ever assignment.

"Show me how wrong I was about you, Vlad, and together we'll conquer the world," he tells me, after which I'm once more taken to my cell.

The first thing I see is Vanya petting Lulu, her features light for the first time in forever. And the dilemma in me grows.

Take away her happiness, or take away her pain?

But in that moment, I know there's only one correct answer.

I shut myself down as I stomp toward her, wrapping my fingers in

Lulu's coat and yanking it from her arms. Taking a few steps to the middle of the room to give the camera the best view, I raise my emotionless eyes to the red lens.

Lifting a struggling Lulu toward the camera with one hand, I use the other to feel for his neck. Finding a proper grip, I twist painfully until I hear a crack.

Lulu's motionless body falls to the ground, and I blank everything out.

Vanya's cries, her condemnation and most of all her small punches as they hit my skin.

I just block everything.

That day marks the birth of Miles' little miracle.

A killing machine.

17
VLAD

I jerk awake, sweat clinging to my skin as I replay the events from my dream in my mind.

Fuck, but it had been worse than I imagined. Way worse. And somehow I'm sure this is one of the tamer ones.

Ever since I've returned from Peru, my dreams have served as flashbacks, sometimes the memory is sharp like today, other times it's faded. Still, every piece of the puzzle is heading in one direction.

I was Miles' plaything. And Vanya must have paid the price for becoming a useless experiment.

My fists clench as I realize just what had happened to my sister, my mind clamoring with loud voices, my chest thumping with pain.

Shit.

I need to get out of here.

I look down at Sisi's sleeping form, even now her body searching for mine, a small sigh escaping her lips, and I'm reminded again of what I'm fighting for. I promised I'd never leave her and I'm not going to disappoint her again.

Even if I have to kill a part of myself to ensure that happens.

I already feel myself slipping, and my hands feel sticky with blood. Opening up my palms in front of me, it takes me a few tries before my eyes can see the reality and not another phantasm borne out of my sick mind. I blink, and empty hands become bloody, before they're back to normal and bloody again.

Damn it!

My sight becomes foggy, and even though I know what I'm seeing is false—a mirage—I can't help but doubt myself.

My hands are clammy, and the sweat clinging to my fingers resembles the oozing blood staining them after each kill.

Recognizing that I'm headed down the road of no return, I quickly leave the room, hoping Sisi won't notice my absence for a while.

I may not want to admit it, but I'm still a danger to her, and I would never do anything that might harm her again.

I've already caused her enough pain to last her a lifetime and it's a true wonder that she's forgiven me. I'm not about to jeopardize any of that.

Since I left Peru sooner than expected, I'd had to forgo some of the things *El Viejo* had prescribed. Instead, he'd given me a few guidelines on how to get my episodes under control.

"Understand the source and you will know the answer," he'd said cryptically.

But understanding the source is not that easy when one *cannot* remember it.

The dreams and flashbacks I've been having from my

time with Miles have given me some insight into what went on there. He was trying to make me into a perfect killing machine, and as such, I can only imagine the training, both mentally and physically, he'd subjected me to.

Surely, my scars show one side of the story, and given what I do remember now, I'm convinced most of them are from his attempts to desensitize me to pain.

I close my eyes, trying to push the memories away. Seeing myself pinned down under the weight of some slimy human had definitely not helped improve my mood. If anything, the flashback's only served to heighten my blood lust, the need to kill enveloping my senses.

I force one foot in front of the other as I make my way to the basement. I barely manage to call Maxim and ask him to ensure the room is ready for me. But with the way I'm teetering from wall to wall, my movements uncoordinated and sluggish as my sight betrays me, my mind slipping from me, he'll have enough time to get things in order.

To put *El Viejo*'s teachings to use, I'd had to improvise a little. Certainly, his advice to understand the origin of my trigger and to face it instead of trying to avoid it had given me quite the dilemma.

Since I'd seen what my episodes do to my surroundings I'd always sought to control them, avoiding looking at blood to the best of my ability — even if that has proven a bit difficult in my profession.

Still, I'd become inventive, using all sorts of torture techniques that ensured my prisoners spilled their secrets but *not* their blood. From venomous spiders, snakes, to bullet ants and flesh eating maggots, I'd found multiple ways to get what I wanted from a target without succumbing to an episode.

Still, staying away from my trigger hadn't been all that efficient, and I've noticed that in the last few years. Whereas before it would have taken quite a lot of blood to make me lose myself, nowadays I only have to see a couple of droplets and I'm gone.

The more I'd tried to suppress myself, the more I'd lost control. And it's become so bad that *no one* is safe around me.

Understand the source.

I can't understand the source if I have no recollection of it. So the safest course of action for now is to give in to my episodes. Fully embrace them as they come and let myself wreck everything around me — in a controlled environment of course.

So I'd resorted to building my own slaughter room. If my beast wants blood, then blood it shall have.

I finally make it to the basement, and punching in a code, I make my way inside the room.

Built in the style of a Roman bath, the room is made entirely out of white marble. Two columns are on each side of the room, holding together an arcade with a painted ceiling — scenes of warfare and bloodshed. In the middle, there is only a circular pool filled with fresh water from the Mississippi. The entire room has a draining system meant to collect all liquids in the pool.

And of course, like the pagan I am, I cannot commence my ritual without a sacrifice. As soon as I enter the room, I'm tackled by five burly men, all shouting and yelling obscenities at me — probably because Maxim had kidnapped and locked them in here.

As soon as I have a target in sight, though, I no longer hear or see anything, but a river of blood awaiting me, their corpses the ultimate offering.

And so I move.

My moves are pure instinct as I hit, duck and hit again, fluidly evading every punch as I land my own. Two men are quickly down, and the other three are just a matter of time. Dancing to the beat of their hearts, I apply all my strength in my fists as I nab one in his Adam's apple. Hearing his trachea break, the force of my punch kicking his bones to the back and cutting his air supply. With a strangled breath, he's down too.

The next two are a piece of cake as I aim for vital spots, their eyes rolling in the back of their heads as they succumb to the ground.

Panting, the fog clears only slightly, enough for me to notice the knife Maxim throws in the cage from a secret window in the ceiling.

I'm quick to grab the handle, dragging the bodies until they are aligned with the small drainage pipes, my blade cutting their throats and watching how the blood pools down until it slowly starts moving toward the pool.

I do the same with each body, positioning their slit throats, so that all the blood is collected in the pool. Now, all five drainage points are occupied by corpses leaking their life's essence into my pit.

In no time, the clean water becomes murky, the blood infusing color into it. And slowly, ever so slowly, a rusty color gives way to red.

More blood fills the pool and I close my eyes, the sight caressing my entire being.

Impatiently, I rip my clothes at the seams as I practically dive forward, the bloody water hitting my skin and making me sigh in pleasure. The metallic smell overwhelms my nostrils, and I can only try to inhale deeper.

Submerging myself in the water, I let the blood coat every inch of my skin, the texture—though diluted—feeding my inner beast. And though it asks for more—it always does—it's finally at peace.

I stay under water, losing myself in the sea of blood, the death that surrounds me, the all-encompassing red.

And I wait.

Not unlike the other times, being suffused in blood does calm me. And I find that my consciousness starts returning slowly.

I break the surface of the water, breathing hard, my eyes finally accommodating to the sight around me, clarity returning to my mind.

"Damn," I mutter as I take in the mangled appearances of the men I'd just sacrificed.

I'd certainly gone the extra mile to ensure they're really dead.

I'd spent a lot of time ruminating on *El Viejo's* advice and trying to apply it to my own situation. At last, I'd realized that there was only one solution—give in to the blood. Literally.

It had been a little trickier getting the resources for this, but I'd quickly found a way to steal some prisoners—people no one would miss—after ensuring that their blood tests are up to date, of course.

Maxim's been in charge of procuring healthy prisoners for me to kill and, well, bathe in their blood.

"It sounded better in my head," I say out loud, rolling my eyes at my own circumstances, somehow amused I'd had to resort to this. After all, I'm no Elizabeth Bathory. My own proclivities do not lean toward achieving eternal life. I'll be happy if I get to retain this one.

And it's been working. Surprisingly, my crises have become shorter, and once I'm submerged in blood for a couple of hours, they are as good as gone. Sure, I have to kill a few people for that. But I'll choose Sisi's safety over *anyone*.

This one practice has made me less volatile, and more likely to control myself even at the onset of a crisis. Whereas I would have usually blanked out immediately, now there's a sliver of conscience left even during the worst of the attack.

It makes me... hopeful.

Now, if only I could remember what the initial trigger was. All the flashbacks I'd had so far had featured a lot of blood, and more often than not it was my own. But so far I haven't felt anything other than outrage at my memories.

Nothing I'd seen had made me particularly receptive or angry. Of course, my compass is a little skewed, since I probably had to bear every insane thing one could imagine. From rape to mental and physical torture, to having my body opened up for Miles' perverted joy, I don't think there's much that can trump that.

I'm deep in my thoughts, my body still neck deep in blood, when I hear the creak of the door.

My head whips back, and I watch with horror as Sisi tentatively steps inside, her eyes widening as she takes in the carnage around. Her gaze finally settles on me, and she looks at me curiously, tilting her head to the side and studying me as if I were a curiosity.

"What are you doing here?" I ask, my voice brusque.

How did she get in here?

I'd taken every precaution to make sure she wouldn't find out about this. Now that I finally got her to give me another chance, I don't need her to see this and realize I'm still a monster.

The room is purposefully hidden from view and the door is password protected. How could she have found her way here and opened the door, too?

She doesn't answer, merely shrugging as she moves around the room, assessing the damage. Bending a little, she studies the corpse of one of the prisoners, her finger trailing over my straight cut. She does the same with all the bodies before stopping in front of me.

"Interesting," she notes, and I try my best to read her.

Is she mad? Disappointed in me? Is she going to leave me? She can't do that. No, of course I won't let her do that.

But is that a good *interesting* or a bad *interesting?*

Does she think I've been deceiving her?

Fucking Hades, but that will earn me minus points, and I barely got a few as it is. I can't lose her trust. Or her regard. Or her anything.

My heart starts beating wildly in my chest as I realize she's got me cornered. Rising out of the water, I start wading toward her, but she just stretches one arm toward me, her hand raised as she shakes one finger back and forth in a *don't you dare* type of movement.

Fuck… I'm fucked.

"I can explain," I immediately say, but she continues to move her fingers to her mouth in a shushing movement.

My mind is immediately in overdrive as I command my brain to think of all potential scenarios and what I can do to get out of this mess. I already have a list of gifts prepared, as well as more carved hearts since they seem to do the trick.

I prepare to exit the pool, but just as I take another step toward her, she stops me. One hand up, she shakes her head at me, motioning me to stay put.

18

VLAD

Her fingers are already on the buttons of her dress as she slowly unbuttons them. Her eyes are on me, as if she's daring me to look at her sensuous movements.

She doesn't have to tell me as I'm already enthralled by the flesh peeking from her collarbone… then her cleavage… Soon, the entire length of the dress has been unbuttoned, and she slides it off her body, dropping it to the ground.

"Fuck," I whisper as my eyes take in her form.

She's not wearing anything under.

I survey her from head to toe. Her golden olive skin glints in the lighting of the room, making her look like a goddess come down from heaven—responding to the offering of blood. Her tits are round and firm, the nipples already hard and pebbled.

My gaze goes lower, to her smooth stomach and defined waistline.

I swallow.

I don't think I'll ever get used to the sight of her. She is so exquisite that no words can describe her. Fuck, but even a dictionary would likely be speechless—or is it wordless?

See, even my brain malfunctions when it comes to her!

Her hips are curved and shapely, flaring slightly outwards in the perfect hourglass figure. I move lower, to the small patch of trimmed blonde hair nestled between her legs. That delectable place that's only mine, and will *only* ever be mine.

"Sisi," I hiss, my body already primed for hers, my cock straining to attention as my eyes bask in her glory.

I was made to worship this woman.

There's no doubt about it. Not when my knees tremble slightly, already seeking to kneel in front of her and give her the respect she deserves.

She's the only thing in the entire universe that could bring me to my knees, and oh, but I'd gladly fall. For a taste of her, I'd do more than that. I'd prostate myself at her feet.

She moves, her feet almost gliding on the marble floor, her long, toned legs flexing and emphasizing her shape even more.

Damn!

She dips her toes in the bloody water, her lips twitching when she approves of the temperature. Then, slowly, tantalizingly so, she starts descending, the bloody water greeting her skin and staining it.

I watch, hypnotized, as she submerges herself until her hair is drenched in blood, the light-blonde becoming a pinkish red.

Coming up for air, she raises an eyebrow at me as she

wades through the water to reach my side. Her entire face is now reddish, not unlike mine, and I feel the urge to grab her and bring her to me.

Simply devour her.

But first I need to see how mad she is at me.

"Sisi," I start, but she places her finger on my lips, coming to my side and nuzzling my throat, her nose moving up and down on the surface of my neck in a soft caress. I still, not knowing how to react.

"You've been naughty," she whispers in my ear, her teeth catching the lobe as she nibbles at my skin.

"Fuck, Sisi," I groan, "you can't go around saying things like that. Especially looking like *that*," I tell her, my voice strained.

"Like what?" she asks, leaning back to bat those pretty lashes at me, her eyes twinkling with hidden meaning and mischief.

The minx.

I snake my arm around her waist, bringing her flush against me. In two steps, I have her against the wall of the pool, her legs open as she wraps them around me, her pussy rubbing against my cock.

"You know very well, my little seductress," I tell her, my fingers digging into her cheeks as I raise her head to look me in the eye. "You're the epitome of sin." My breath on her lips, I trail my hand down her neck, collarbones, before brushing the tips of my fingers over her nipple.

She gasps, a quick intake of breath as her eyes turn to me.

"How did you get in here, Sisi?" I lean in until we're

mere breaths apart. She doesn't look away, holding my gaze defiantly.

"Through the door." She shrugs, a hint of a smile on her lips.

"Sisi." I raise an eyebrow. "That particular door is password protected," I say.

"And whose fault is it," she starts, coming even closer, her tongue peeking out and brushing over my lips as she skirts by my cheek to whisper in my ear, "that the password is my birthday?"

I can hear the amusement in her voice, and my own lips twitch up.

"Hmm, my bad," I drawl, bringing her back to face me, my thumb under her chin. "But how did you *find* the door? Only Maxim and I know about it."

"Your friend Maxim can be very talkative for the right incentive," she continues, trailing her nails over my chest.

Her touch is making me lose my mind, especially when I need to keep my head in the game. A breach of security is a breach of security, no matter who the intruder is. And since Maxim can barely speak a word of English, I'm even more curious how she got the information.

"What did you do, Sisi?" I ask, a grave expression on my face. Inside, though, I'm almost overflowing with pride.

She's one of a kind.

"I just detailed some procedure from an anatomy textbook." She smiles sheepishly. "You've corrupted me," she says seductively, her fingers splayed over my chest. And to show me just how much of a minx she is, she raises herself on her tip-toes to place a kiss onto my lips. "*On mne mnoga skazal. Vse tvai secreti,"* she whispers cheekily, my eyes widening at her words.

"Sisi!" I groan, closing my eyes, my ears basking in the sound of Russian on her lips.

"I learned. A little," she blushes slightly.

"For me?" I ask, incredibly surprised. I'd have never thought she would have made such an effort for me.

She nods. "I wanted to be able to tell you I love you in your language too, among other things," she continues, and my lips widen in a smile.

Knowing Sisi, among other things means she doesn't want to be kept out of the loop, her inherent curiosity unquenchable.

"And?" I prompt her, dying to hear the words.

She bats her eyelashes at me, licking her lips suggestively before saying. "I might tell you. After you tell me what this is all about." She motions to the blood room. Pursing her lips at me, she awaits an answer.

"It's… complicated," I reply, not knowing how much I should tell her. Because if she finds out everything… I don't know how she'll react to that.

"It's not." She shakes her head, her teeth peeking out as she bites her lower lip. "We're in this together," she says, a smile tugging at her lips. "You promised you'd trust me. No more secrets."

"Hell girl," I groan, knowing she's right. "I do trust you." I take a deep breath, my eyes searching hers. "But you might not see me the same when you find out some things about me."

Her hand tightens over mine as she brings it to her lips, laying a small kiss on my knuckles.

"Vlad," she says, her tone serious. "I've seen you at your worst, and I'm still here."

"This might be worse than that…" I trail off and her lips are set in a thin line as she raises an inquisitive eyebrow at me.

Fuck! It's now or never.

I know Sisi won't drop this. Whenever she gets something in her mind, she *always* sees it through. It's one of the things I love about her, but in this instance, I'm afraid it might cause a rift between us. Because there's no sugar coating my past. I just need to hope she won't see me differently.

"I told you about my sister, Vanya, and that I didn't remember what happened when we were taken." Taking a deep breath, I start. Sisi is listening attentively, and I force myself to tell her everything I've kept bottled up for so long.

"She was dead by the time we were found." I use one hand to tug a strand of her hair aside. "What I didn't tell you is that I didn't realize she was dead until years later."

"What do you mean?" She frowns.

"Something happened to me there," I purse my lips at the understatement, "and I never registered her death. To me she was still alive. Like you, I could touch her," I move my hand over her cheek, "talk to her, do everything with her."

"You're saying you were seeing your sister's ghost?" she asks, incredulous.

"Not a ghost. More like a figment of my mind. A phantasm borne out of my dependence on her." I sigh, knowing I'm about to peel all the layers and show myself bare before her.

"I was very lonely as a child. No one wanted to do anything with me. Vanya was the only one I could talk to… interact with. The only one by my side. Until I realized she wasn't real."

"When did you?"

"I was fifteen," I start, telling her the incident with the clothes and how my father had told me that Vanya had been dead for a long time. "That's when I had my first full-on episode," I explain, the thought of never seeing Vanya again having been so agonizingly maddening I'd just snapped.

And so I tell her everything from the beginning. How everyone had shunned me since Valentino had found me and how my morbid fascination with death had made people fear me, or deem me a *freak*. Vanya, or who I thought to be Vanya, had been the only one by my side, and the *only* thing keeping me remotely sane.

"And then you came along." I give her a smile. "From that first moment in the church, something happened."

"Vlad," Sisi says my name in a soft voice, and I see pain in her gaze. *For me.* Tears gathered at the corner of her eyes, her hand squeezes mine as I speak.

"For the first time, Vanya disappeared," I continue, and her brows knit in confusion.

"You mean…" Sisi trails off, and realization dawns on her as she draws back. "Is that why you sought me out?" she asks suddenly, her voice broken. A small shake of her head and I can feel her entire body trembling.

Damn! I'm making a mess of this.

"In the beginning. Yes. I wanted to figure out *why* you seemed to drive her away," I speak fast, trying to get everything out before she jumps to conclusions. "But one moment in your presence and everything fell away. I can promise you, Sisi, that Vanya's presence or absence was the last thing on my mind when I was with you."

She blinks fast, trying to process everything. For a second I'm afraid she's going to take this the wrong way, that I'm only with her because of that.

"Go on," she says hesitantly.

"She's gone now. For good," I assure her, recounting my trip to Peru, my one last attempt to get myself under control. Her eyes widen as I tell her what I'd been up to in the last few months, and how under *El Viejo*'s tutelage I'd managed to unlock a deep part of myself. I also share that my little blood ritual has been quite helpful in helping me overcome my crises.

When she doesn't speak, merely regarding me quietly, I feel compelled to placate her.

"Please don't think that I'm with you because of that. Is that why I sought you out initially? Yes," I admit, inwardly wincing at my own words, "but that's not why I stuck around. That's not why I'm here. I love you, hell girl, and before you, I never thought to get better. I was fine just living in between episodes."

Sisi nods thoughtfully.

"Why did you stop seeing her?" she eventually asks.

I close my eyes, dreading what comes next.

"Because I started to remember what happened during my time with Miles," I start, and I tell her everything I'd remembered so far—everything that had happened to Vanya and me, but also what I'd done in order to get into Miles' good graces.

The details are gruesome, and her face scrunches up in

horror as she listens to me. I don't sugarcoat anything as I tell her about the visits from the guards, or even Miles' own depraved proclivities.

"Good Lord," Sisi whispers, her hand coming up to cup my cheek. "Is this what you were afraid to tell me? God, Vlad. Why? Why would you think I'd judge you for something like that? My heart weeps for what you and your sister went through. And *none* of it was your fault." She lays her forehead on top of mine. "None," she repeats.

"I still don't know the whole extent of it. But I have a feeling something Miles did to me damaged me completely," I confess. "He was trying to build the perfect soldier. And in a way, he did succeed…"

"He didn't," she interrupts me. "He banked on you having no feelings, Vlad. Maybe you are fearless when it comes to death, and remorseless when it comes to killing. But he didn't take into account your capacity for love." She prompts me to look into her eyes, so clear and sparkling with warmth.

"Sisi… please don't make me into something I'm not," I tell her, knowing my own–rather unfortunate–limitations.

"No, you listen to me Vlad. I heard everything you told me. And you know what I see?" she asks, her tone serious and I shake my head, almost absentmindedly. "I see a loving brother who'd do *anything* for his sister. I see a loyal man who's dedicated his entire life to find and avenge his sisters. A lonely man who sought refuge in the memory of the one person who was dearest to him." She purses her lips. "And a fierce man who'd fight even himself to be with the one he loves."

She pauses, and I can hear her heartbeats, as well as

mine. The room is entirely silent except for those small *thump* sounds that seem to increase in speed with every passing second.

"I see a man with an unlimited capacity for love. Maybe you lack other feelings, Vlad. But I think you make up for it in other ways." Her hand settles over my heart. "Your ability to love is the type people write sonnets, myths and fairytales about. The all-encompassing type." Her lips tug up in a smile. "And I feel immensely blessed that *I'*m the one you chose to give your love to."

"Fuck Sisi. I…" She places a finger on my lips, silencing me.

"I see *you*, Vlad—with the good and the bad. I see the real you. The killer, the animal, the lover." Her hand drops to my chest, and she draws little circles over my heart. "And I love every one of your facets. For me you're just *you*." She takes a deep breath. "From now on, don't shut me out again for fear I might think less of you, because that will *never* happen."

"Damn, Sisi, what did I ever do to deserve you?" I wrap my arms around her shoulders, drawing her in my embrace. "You're one of a kind, hell girl. *My* one of a kind," I speak against her hair.

We stay like that for what seems like forever, wrapped in each other, blood clinging to our bodies, hearts beating in unison.

I should have realized that my Sisi would be nothing but understanding. And yet, I'd been scared to tell her everything, always thinking that she'd realize her mistake and decide to leave me. Yet somehow, with just a few words she's managed to quench all of that fear.

I need to trust her.

My brave Sisi has the strength of a thousand men. Of course she wouldn't balk at anything.

I tighten my grip around her body, my entire being suffused with love for her.

"I killed someone," Sisi suddenly speaks.

19
VLAD

Her voice is shaky as she takes a deep breath. "I didn't mean to, but I didn't regret it either," she continues, telling me about an older girl who'd terrorized her for years and how she'd gotten rid of her body. "You're not the only one with a stained past, Vlad," she says, leaning back to look at me.

"You could do no wrong in my eyes, Sisi," I tell her sincerely. "You could kill a million people and you'd still be my Sisi." If anything, I'm even prouder of her for standing up for herself and for taking a stand against those who wanted to hurt her. Because anyone who dares to mess with my Sisi deserves nothing but pain.

And I aim to see that done. Soon.

Bringing my hand up, I swipe some strands of hair off her forehead. "You're perfect to me."

"See? This is how I feel about you, too. You wouldn't be my Vlad without your flaws. And because of that you are perfect for me."

She raises herself up, and twinning her arms around my neck, she presses her lips to mine.

I relish the soft feel of her mouth against mine, the way her lips part slightly, her tongue meeting mine as they dance around each other.

I bring her flush against me, my hands on her lower back as I deepen the kiss. Her tits brushing against my chest, her stomach cushioning my hard cock, I already feel I'm about to combust.

How is it that one look at her and I get painfully hard, one touch of hers and I'm ready to spill myself?

As someone who's never been interested in the opposite sex, I'm simply baffled by the way my body reacts to hers. The epitome of femininity, she's uniquely attractive—made just for me. And I plan to worship her for as long as I live.

"No more secrets now," she whispers against my lips.

"No more secrets," I agree.

Her hands secured around my neck, I swoop her in my arms, exiting the pool. Red droplets of blood mixed with water cling to our skin as they make their way down, dripping onto the floor.

Sisi's watching me through hooded eyes, a comfortable sigh escaping her as she snuggles closer to me.

Taking her to the shower stalls, I turn on the water, letting it wash everything away from us.

Under the powerful jet of the shower, murky water falls down our bodies, washing the red away. I lower her to her feet, and grabbing a sponge, I lather it with soap as I start tracing my way down her body, cleaning every spot.

She doesn't speak as I move the sponge over her neck, and down her tits, only watching me closely, mouth half parted as she releases a small gasp every time my hand brushes over her nipples.

I move slowly as I clean her body, washing the blood away to reveal her pristine skin.

Dropping to my knees in front of her, I glide my hand over her stomach and lower, towards the patch of hair between her legs. Her breath hitches as I gently dab at the area.

"Vlad," she whispers, looking down at me. Her eyes are misty—from tears or water from the shower, I don't know.

The corner of my mouth curls up in a lopsided smile as I lean forward, placing a kiss on her belly. I lay my cheek to her skin, closing my eyes and simply enjoying the feel of her next to me.

She threads her hands through my hair, massaging shampoo into my scalp. Her touch is firm yet gentle, thoroughly cleaning my hair. A sigh of pleasure escapes me, my skin tingling as she trails her fingers down my face before she cups my cheek.

"We'll get through everything," she says. "Together. We're a team, remember?" She smiles at me and I feel my own lips twitch in response. I take her hand, kissing her open palm.

"Yes. We're a team, hell girl," I agree, rising to my feet. We stand for a moment under the strong jet of water, letting it rinse over our skin, before I carry her out, wrapping her in blankets and drying her.

I don't wait for her to say anything as I take her to my room, fully intent on showing her just how much she means to me.

The goddess of my heart.

She doesn't question where we're going, or what I'm doing as I lay her on my bed, stepping away to watch her in all her glory, Spread out on the bed, she's temptation personified, the epitome of warmth on a cold winter night.

Because she's the only thing that's made my frozen heart thaw, the ice slowly melting, the beats speeding up. And just like that, it beats *only* for her.

"What are you doing?" she asks, almost shyly as she sees me open one drawer, taking out a bottle of body oil.

Since I'd shopped for about *everything* a woman might require, I'm fully stocked to meet her every desire.

"Spoiling you." I smirk at her as I lower myself onto the mattress, my hand slowly brushing up her thigh. "I want to take care of you," I continue, my hand moving higher until it reaches the curve of her ass.

She purrs softly, turning on her stomach and pushing her ass in the air. Not unlike the first time I saw her, I find myself enthralled by her sinuous curves.

I trace the contour of her cheeks with my fingers, enjoying the way goosebumps appear all over her skin.

A faint shiver makes its way down her spine, a tiny mew escaping her lips as she closes her eyes, her entire body slack and relaxed as she lets me do whatever I want to her.

Not one to let an invitation go to waste, I'm quick to squirt some oil into my palms, laying them on her skin and spreading the moisture all around.

"That feels so good," she whimpers as I move higher, massaging the oil into her back.

Straddling her ass, my dick is resting between her ass cheeks as my hands move gently up her back, massaging her shoulders and her neck.

She doesn't realize, but there's an ever so slight thrust of her ass toward me, pushing my cock further into the valley of her ass, the action so innocent, yet so maddening I have the hardest time controlling myself.

I grit my teeth, continuing my ministrations and trying to ignore the way my cock seems to beg for mercy, the bastard twitching in search of her hole.

This is about her!

I repeat that in my head, trying to find some equilibrium. But the truth is that the moment I have Sisi naked in my bed all bets are off.

"I should ask you for a massage every day from now on," she says, "you're quite good at it."

"You'd be tempting fate, hell girl," I drawl, the thought of having her naked and under me *every day* without being able to do anything a pure torture. But if my girl wants a massage, then I can only indulge her.

She raises her head, looking back at me, her eyes dipping to my painfully hard cock. Her mouth opens on a small O, her eyes widening slightly. Immediately, her lips twitch up, and a mischievous smile appears on her face.

She scrambles back, disentangling her body from mine.

I look at her questioningly. The oil covering her skin glints in the light, making her look ethereal like a fairy, the glossiness of her skin only increasing her appeal and making my blood thump faster, all of it pooling lower, and making my arousal incredibly painful.

On all fours, she moves toward me, a sensuous glide of her limbs that stops my breath. Especially when she licks her lips, looking at me from beneath her lashes and tempting me to perdition.

Fucking Hades!

If I thought that I was gone before, then now I'm simply obliterated. The sight of her plump rosy mouth as she skims her teeth over the surface of her lower lip, nibbling so slightly, makes me physically ache.

It takes Herculean strength for me to stay still and not do something I might regret—like pin her to the bed and find my relief in her sweet little body.

"Fuck," I mutter under my breath, her hand on my cock as her tongue peeks out to lick the head. "Sisi," I groan, the wetness of her mouth too enticing for me to keep still.

My fist wrapped in her hair, I urge her forward as she opens her mouth to take more of me in. Her tongue caresses the underside, and my breath quickens as she tightens her grip, sucking me deep into her mouth.

She licks the entire length before placing a kiss on the head.

Moving up my body, she twines her arms around my neck, her eyes on mine as she says the words that make my heart stop in my chest.

"Please make love to me," she whispers.

My eyes widen at her request and I search her face for any clue that it's what she really wants. There's a small trace of apprehension as she continues biting her lip, her gaze a mix of fear and desire.

"You don't have to, Sisi. Certainly not to please me," I tell her, even though my balls draw up in protest.

"I want to." She nuzzles my cheek. "I want *you*. I want to feel as close to you as I can," she continues, her hands splayed over my back.

"Sisi..." I growl. She doesn't have to tell me twice. I shift her on her back, her legs open on either side of my body, her sweet pussy calling to me.

My hands circle her waist as I bring my mouth to her skin, skimming the underside of her breast before taking a nipple in my mouth. I feast on her tits like a starved man. Holding her in my arms for so long yet not daring to do anything other than hug her had been agonizing.

Now that she's finally given me the green light, I aim to worship her like the goddess she is.

Her legs are restless as she's trying to push me up her body, her hands reaching for my cock. One look at her and I can see the frustration in her features, the way she's breathing hard as if she could die if I don't get inside her the very next second.

"Not yet, my little sinner," I tell her, my tongue tracing the scar on the swell of her breast before moving to the small mark I'd left around her nipple, kissing it lightly. "You need to be ready to take me," I say as I move lower, sliding my tongue over her stomach before opening my lips and sucking on her skin, blood pooling to the surface and marking her as mine.

I continue to take my time kissing her entire torso and leaving small love bites everywhere, pride swelling in my chest as I see her covered in my marks.

"Please," she moans as I reach lower, my mouth hovering on top of her pussy. I inhale her scent, the musky flavor tickling my senses and intoxicating me.

"This is mine, Sisi." I speak against her mound, brushing my mouth against her small lips and blowing soft air against her glistening arousal.

"Yes," she replies with a breathy tone. Her eyes are

closed, her spine arched, as she opens her legs even more, inviting me to feast on her.

I trail my hands down her waist until my palms cup her hips, my thumbs pushing into the soft skin right above her hip bones as I bring her closer to my mouth.

"Say it," I rasp out, my mouth watering for a taste.

"Yours," she whimpers, trying to get me closer. "I'm all yours." She gives me the words that have the power to unman me.

I trail my nose up her pussy, prying her lips open and giving her a long lick, lapping up her juices. She's already dripping, her pussy gushing out nectar for me to get drunk on.

"I was made to worship your pussy, hell girl," I say as I drink her in. It's sweetness and sin mixed together in a deadly combination. Like ambrosia for a mere mortal, her essence has the power to make me invincible. Because with her by my side, I truly feel indestructible.

Her hands find their way into my hair as I settle my attention onto her clit, sucking it into my mouth and making her scream in pleasure, her legs quivering, her thighs clenching around my head as she tries to keep me locked in place.

Her breaths are uneven, and I don't let her get even one second of rest as I continue to tease her, eating her pussy up like it's the best meal I've had in my entire life. By now, we've explored each other's bodies enough to know exactly what the other likes, and I love using that knowledge to drive her crazy—time after time.

By the time I'm done with her, she's going to be so wet

and relaxed she's going to forget all about her fear, her pussy perfectly primed to swallow me all up.

Using my tongue, I swirl it around her entrance, pushing it inside just enough to tickle the outer wall, knowing it only takes a few strokes for her to come.

"Vlad!" she screams, her voice increasingly louder, her hands wreaking havoc on my scalp.

Still, I don't stop.

I feel the way her body's trembling as she's coming down from her climax, and I want her to ride her pleasure longer.

I push two fingers at her entrance, testing her tightness. She's still snug as a glove, and for a moment I fear it might be painful for her again. But as soon as that thought crosses my mind I realize that if she still feels pain, then I haven't done my job right.

My mouth on her clit, I start moving them in and out, feeling her walls clamp down on my fingers, her moans vibrating in the air. Adding a third finger, I try to stretch her even more.

"Vlad..." she whispers with an uncertain tone, her eyes wide open to stare at me.

"Shhh." I blow air over her clit, continuing to pump three fingers in and out of her. Although apprehensive in the beginning, she's starting to relax her muscles, her entrance stretched to allow for the extra girth.

I increase the speed, biting on her clit at the same time.

"Fuck! Vlad... I can't..." She tries to speak, but her entire body crashes as she starts trembling uncontrollably, her orgasm reverberating through every cell, and every corner of her being. Mouth agape, eyes rolled into the back of her head, she can only ride her pleasure before it starts to subside.

Seeing her undone like this alone is better than a thousand orgasms, her lips parted, her cheeks flushed.

I move up her body, still trailing kisses up her neck, sucking on her skin to place more visible marks on her body, wanting *everyone* to see who she belongs to.

"I love you," I whisper before I take her lips in a long kiss, using my hand to align my cock to her entrance.

I only get to nudge the head inside her warm heat before I feel her tense, her entire body stiffening up under me.

"Sisi," I raise my head to look at her and I see the unshed tears at the corner of her eyes. She's trembling slightly as she tries to hold herself still. "We can stop," I tell her, my hand caressing her cheek.

"No." She shakes her head. "I want this. I really do." She grips my shoulders, her legs tightening around my ass as she tries to bring me into her.

Her features are strained, her eyes immediately closing as she waits for pain to come. Somehow, that alone is enough to make me stop.

Placing my palms on her ass, I turn us around until my back hits the mattress, Sisi bouncing on top of me.

Her eyes widen as she sees the shift in positions. Her pussy is sitting right on top of the base of my cock, her wetness dripping over my balls and making me groan in frustration.

So close yet so far.

Her gaze settles on my cock, apprehension in her eyes as she brushes one hand over my length, her lips pursing as she is undoubtedly thinking about my size and what that will mean to her body.

"Sisi, look at me." I push her chin up. "This is all yours." I motion to my body. "You're in control, hell girl. So use me," I prompt her, hoping that by giving her the reins over this it seems less daunting.

It takes everything in me to stay still as she slowly starts rocking over my cock, her eyes still assessing it with mild trepidation.

But I just let her set her own pace, knowing she needs this to get over her fear.

She props her knees on the mattress as she pushes herself forward. Taking my cock in her hand, she raises herself over me, positioning the head at her entrance.

"You're in charge," I assure her once more.

Nodding at me, she lowers herself slightly, and I watch mesmerized how her folds engulf my cock. The feel of her wet, warm walls immediately hits me like a bullet to the chest, and it takes everything in me to control myself. Especially as she's still so wary, even now closing her eyes, her lower lip trembling as she accepts me into her body.

The moment I'm one inch inside she stops, a gasp escaping her lips. She braces her arms on my chest, holding herself still.

"Does it hurt?" I ask immediately, worried.

I'd tried my best to get her off as many times as possible to ensure she'd be slick and dripping, enough to take me in without issue. But I know my size, and even if she weren't still basically a virgin she'd have trouble fitting me inside of her.

I raise my hand to her face, caressing her cheek with my knuckles.

She bites her lip, her eyes on me as she slowly shakes her head.

"I feel you stretching me," she says, lowering herself another inch. Mouth parted, a moan makes it past her lips as her eyes flutter closed—this time in pleasure, not trepidation. "It feels so good," she whimpers, and I finally relax, leaning back and letting her go at her own pace.

"You're so thick and..." She trails off, her tongue peeking out to wet her lips as she seems to be at a loss of words. She looks so fucking sexy, like a wet dream come true, the sheen of perspiration on her body arousing me further as I can't help but imagine her entirely covered in my cum.

Her hands are resting on my abdomen, her arms making an inverted triangle that emphasizes her luscious tits, perky and full and tempting me worse than the devil.

Slowly, she pushes herself down another inch, my cock weeping with joy at being welcomed into heaven. I throw my head back, the feeling of being surrounded by her heat unlike any other. Since I don't remember a lot of my episode, this is the first time I'm experiencing this, the way my cock nestles right at home inside of her.

Her walls clamp down on me, squeezing me so tightly, I have to make a conscious effort not to come too fast.

"You feel like heaven, Sisi. Fuck..." I mutter incoherently, unable to verbalize just what she does to me.

I'd known from the moment I had first seen her that she was temptation incarnate, succeeding in making me feel things that no other had before her. I'd known how dangerous she was—to my senses, to my heart, to my fucking everything. Because one bat of those pretty lashes of hers in my direction, and I was fucking damned.

Damned to be her slave for an eternity.

The corners of her mouth quirk up as she watches me surrender to the ecstasy of being inside of her, and she seems to gain new confidence as she takes one deep breath before pushing herself all the way down my cock.

We both sigh in pleasure at the sensation, and for as long as I live I don't think I'll ever forget the sight of her on top of me, my cock so deep inside of her.

"God, Vlad," she says in a breathy tone. "I had no idea." She seems just as dazed as I am as she rocks herself slightly, her walls stroking my cock in a tantalizing caress that has me seeing stars.

Me neither.

"Can you feel that, hell girl?" I ask as I splay my hand over her stomach, feeling the place where we are joined, "We're one."

"Is that so?" she asks mischievously, her fingers drawing random figures on my chest. "Does that make you hell boy, then?" She gives me a wicked smile as she lifts herself ever so slightly before coming down again.

My mouth opens to answer, but no sound comes out, the pleasure so intense I fear I may be forever broken.

"As long as I'm your other half I'll be anything you want me to," I answer, my voice thick and husky. Anything to ensure that she's never leaving my side.

"Hmm…" She trails off, moving her hands up my chest until she's resting on my pecs, and using me to push herself up, this time until I'm halfway out before sliding down again, more forcefully.

"What if I decide to go take my vows and *actually* become a nun?" she continues to ask, and I see what she's trying to do. She wants to torture me, knowing that I could never last a day without her.

It becomes increasingly difficult to stave off my climax, the little minx enjoying tormenting me with her little movements.

"Then I'll follow you and become a priest and I'll try to defile you at every turn," I answer with a strangled moan.

"You're wicked." She swallows, her pupils eclipsing her irises as she turns her gaze on me, desire dripping from it and only inflaming mine more.

"I'm yours. However, and whoever you want me to be. I'm yours," I confess, my hands on her hips as I urge her to move—finally put me out of my misery.

"Good." She smirks at me, raising herself up until my cock slips free of her pussy, and agony hits me immediately as I feel bereft without her warmth. "But all I want is *you*."

Her small hand circles my length as she guides me back into her haven, easily lowering herself on me this time, her pussy so fucking soaking wet her juices are pouring down my shaft.

Now this is what heaven feels like.

20

SISI

I clench my thighs around him, pleasure shooting through me at the smallest movement.

God, but I didn't realize it would be like this! I'd build up all that fear in my mind, thinking it would be like last time. There had been only pain. But now… only pleasure.

I would have never thought that something as monstrously big as his dick would slide inside me so smoothly. Certainly not with the way it seemed to grow in size the more I stared at it. There had been a stretching sensation in the beginning, but even that had faded as I'd taken more of him into my body.

I sigh out loud as I feel his cock hit deep within my womb. I'm just so full of him I don't think I want to be *without* again.

"I didn't realize," I whisper as I brace myself over him, feeling his bulging muscles under my hands. "This feels so good I could pass out," I breathe out, the small rocking of his cock against my walls sending shivers down my back.

My eyes snap shut as I feel myself coming, just from that *tiny* thrust alone.

"I feel the same, Sisi," he rasps, raising himself on his elbows to come closer to me, "you make me feel things I never imagined before," he confesses, his words filling my entire being with warmth.

I wound my arms around his neck, bringing him flush against me. My nipples brush against the smooth surface of his chest, and I shiver at the feeling of being so close to him.

We're one.

His hands on my hips, he lifts me up and down on his length, each stroke of his cock making me want to die of pure pleasure.

"You have no idea," I barely manage the words out, "how much I love you," I say in between moans.

Flesh slapping against flesh, his arms are tight around my waist as he pushes his cock even deeper inside of me, the strength of his thrusts doubling my pleasure.

"I do, Sisi, I do," he speaks against my cheek, and I can feel the sweat clinging to his skin, "because I feel the same."

Grabbing my jaw with one hand, he turns my head around, his mouth on mine as he swallows my cries. He pushes his tongue into my mouth, kissing me with an intensity that has my entire body weeping with unimaginable bliss.

"Yes," I whimper when I feel him even deeper.

That's when I realize that I want *everything* he has to offer. Not just this gentle fucking. I want to feel his savagery in my bones, the way he pounds into me as if he might break me.

Just thinking about him taking me like a beast has my

pussy clench up in response, more juices flowing down his shaft.

Yes. I want *him*. The *real* him.

Leaning back, I urge him to switch positions so that he's on top. My back hits the mattress, my legs opening up to accommodate his pelvis.

His hands are on my waist as he keeps on thrusting into me—slow, measured thrusts that are meant for my comfort.

But I don't want that.

Now that my body realizes there's no pain, there's no more impediment to letting him take me as he wants.

Knowing he will need some coaxing, I take his hands in mine, moving them up my body until they reach my neck.

Wrapping them around my throat, I squeeze my legs shut, trapping him in place.

His hands are slack as he just looks at me, confusion mixed with desire in his eyes. But I also see something else.

Hope.

He wants this as much as I do. And when he sees the confirmation in my gaze, relief floods his features, his hands tightening over my neck, his thrusts taking a violent turn.

My mouth opens on a sound that never leaves my lips, my pussy opening up to meet each one of his maddening thrusts. I feel the way his cock reaches deep within before retreating, the base of his shaft slapping my pussy as it invades me even further. Long and thick, it manages to stimulate every sensitive spot inside of me.

He applies more pressure on the sides of my neck. Not enough to hurt me, but enough to make me lightheaded as he continues to push himself into my body, assaulting my senses with such intense pleasure, I fear I may actually black out.

He's already made me come so many times, and as I feel another orgasm near, I doubt I'll be able to take much more.

"Fucking hell, Sisi," he grits out, his fingers digging into my flesh, his hips pistoning in and out of me, "you're fucking amazing," he groans, a deep sound that reverberates in my very being. "*My* fucking amazing."

I hang on to him, my hands on his arms as I take everything he has to give.

Out of nowhere, he shifts me over, throwing me on my belly and spreading my legs before diving in again.

Braced on my elbows, I gasp as I realize he's much deeper than before.

How is this possible?

He drags my hips toward his, his fingers digging into my ass cheeks as he continues to impale me on his cock.

I can only push my ass into him, meeting him thrust for thrust as I focus on the feeling of finally being one with the man I love.

The only man I'll ever love.

"You're mine," he growls, his voice hoarse. His hand lands on one cheek in a resounding slap, the slight sting only enhancing the pleasure.

"More," I demand, knowing he has more to give me.

Savage. Unrestricted. Beastly.

I want all of him.

"My dirty little nun wants more," he chuckles, another slap landing on my ass. I whimper, clenching my walls around him in approval.

Then his fist is suddenly in my hair, his fingers digging

into my scalp as he pulls me toward him, my back to his front. He has my hair wrapped around his fingers as he twists my head to look at him.

There's a savagery in his gaze that wasn't there before. And hell if it doesn't make me hotter, my pussy spasming around him the more he pulls at my hair.

His mouth tugs up as he notices my reaction, an arrogant smirk enveloping his features as he lowers his mouth to my ear.

"You want me to wreck you, don't you hell girl?" His deep voice sends shivers down my back, the way his warm breath fans over my ear, my entire body primed to respond to his in *any* way.

"Yes," I reply, struggling to keep myself from moaning out the answer.

"Good. Because I own you," he says, and his words shouldn't make me so hot. God, they really shouldn't. But in this moment all I want is to be *owned* by him, to be at his mercy as he does whatever he wants to my body. "I own every hole in your body," he continues, bending me forward and slamming into me even harder, the hand on my ass moving slowly down until his thumb is caressing my rear entrance.

I feel him spitting on my ass, his thumb swirling the saliva around as he pushes it into my hole, the muscles resisting at first before slowly giving way.

I gasp, the sensation wholly new but not unpleasant.

He keeps thrusting into me, his thumb imitating the same movements, and my body unable to take the double stimulation.

"Your pussy's mine," he grits out, his cock slipping

almost completely out, the head teasing my entrance in a shallow thrust before fully surging inside and hitting my G spot. "Your ass is mine." His thumb slips deeper inside, and my muscles immediately tighten around him.

"Every inch of you is mine," he declares, wrenching sensations out of me I'd never thought possible.

"Yes," I moan, letting him do whatever he wants to my body. "And you're mine too," I continue, needing that confirmation.

"Yours?" he asks, almost offended. "There's no me without you, hell girl. You fucking own *every* piece of me," he grits out.

"My mind," *thrust*, "my heart," *thrust* "my fucking damned soul," *thrust*, "this cock," he says, pulling out all the way as he slaps his length against my clit before stroking it along the seam of my pussy lips, "that's never been inside another, that will *never* be inside another," he growls, "just like your pussy's only mine and will *only* ever be mine."

My heart skips a beat at his words, and I relish the way we have this unique connection.

Out of nowhere, he moves behind me. I look back to see him on his knees, his mouth on my pussy. His finger still in my ass, he continues to slowly move it in and out of me as his tongue laps at my wetness before pushing it against my entrance, twirling it around my opening as he ravenously drinks me in.

"No one," he speaks against my lips, his breath hot as he blows air over my clit, making me shiver. "No one's going to know how sweet your nectar tastes." He continues to lick me, a long swipe from my clit to my ass, the sensation shocking me as he suddenly replaces his thumb with his tongue, the tight ring of muscle relaxing and responding under his careful ministrations.

God, but I'd never dreamed about half of the things he's doing to me. It seems so dirty and forbidden and I love every single moment of it.

"Or how your tight little ass begs for my cock." He pushes his tongue inside and my eyes widen, mind-blowing pleasure shooting through me. "And you'll get it, just not now," he declares and anticipation builds inside of me.

Yes! I want everything he has to offer.

Before I can even reply he's back inside me, stroking me so deeply I want to weep.

"I love you," I cry out, both my heart and my body in alignment as an orgasm tears through me.

"I love you too, hell girl. I adore you. I fucking worship you. There's no one that compares to you," he grunts, his thrusts picking up speed. "No one that can hold a candle to you. My fucking goddess," he mutters almost incoherently.

My pussy tingles with awareness, his guttural sounds coupled with the way his cock is still forcefully slamming into me enough to make me violently come—again—my walls spasming all around his length.

"Yes, that's it, hell girl. Come for me," he commands in my ear.

His hand wrapped in my hair, he grips it tightly as he brings me against him, my back fully fitted to his front, his mouth on my neck as he licks my scar. His other hand slowly caresses the front of my body, from my breasts lower, to my stomach before eventually settling on my clit.

Already sensitive from the many orgasms he's wrought from me, it's almost painful to the touch.

"I can't…" I trail off, unable to come again.

"Yes, you can," he states, his voice serious as his fingers continue to stimulate my clit.

My body tries to jerk away from his, but he's holding me tightly in place, his touch igniting me again despite the initial promise of pain.

"Vlad," I whimper, on the edge of the precipice. So close, yet so far.

He lowers his mouth to my neck, sucking at the sensitive skin, his movements on my clit quickening as his cock continues to assault me.

And suddenly, the combined action has me screaming my climax, the force of it so powerful I'm literally seeing white in front of my eyes.

My entire body becomes slack as I fall face down onto the mattress.

"That's my good girl." I hear Vlad's satisfied voice as he pats my ass affectionately.

I can barely move, but I can still feel the ferocity of his thrusts as he chases his own pleasure.

His cock swells inside me even more, and I feel the warmth of his seed as it shoots straight to my womb. He holds my ass tightly to him as he empties himself inside of me, ensuring not one drop of his cum is wasted anywhere else.

Collapsing on top of me, he gathers me to his chest, his cock still inside me, his arms tight around my shoulders.

"Did I hurt you?" he asks, nuzzling his nose in the crook of my neck.

"No. It was perfect," I tell him, holding him close and snuggling into his embrace. "I love you."

"Love you too, Sisi. More than anything," he says and my chest expands with an overwhelming amount of happiness.

He is mine. And I am his.

Finally.

21

SISI

His mouth trails wet kisses down my cheek, his stubble tickling me as I shift in bed. My eyes open, my pupils accommodating to the light as I take him in—freshly showered and insanely attractive.

"You didn't shave," I whisper, my palm cupping his slight growth.

"I know you like me when I embrace my less than civil side." He smirks at me and my own lips pull up in a smile.

He's right. I do like when he leaves his gentlemanly ways at the door. Especially since losing his manners has never been sweeter.

"What time is it?" I ask groggily as I try to rouse myself.

"Time for a surprise," he says rather vigorously, gathering me in his arms and lifting me off the bed.

"What?" I'm suddenly alert, frowning in confusion. "What surprise? Where are we going?"

Though I am reluctant to admit, I'm a little sore from our activities last night.

"You'll see." His mouth quirks up as he carries me out of

the room and to the basement. "You probably noticed that the entire basement is custom made," he starts as he plugs in a password to yet another steel door. "And I made something for you too," he tells me, and I can tell he's entirely too excited about this.

Once the door is open, he takes me inside a rather sterile looking room, with only a chair and some tools in the middle.

"Are you going to torture me?" I ask, amused. The entire setting looks like a torture chamber, and knowing Vlad's affinity for torture, I wouldn't be surprised.

"There's only one type of torture I have reserved for you, hell girl," his voice is low and seductive as he blows hot air into my ear, "and it's the type you beg for," he continues, and without even turning to him I can feel his arrogant smirk.

I shake my head, unable to wipe the smile off my face.

"Stop this and tell me what we're doing here," I demand, a little too curious about his *surprise*.

He strides to the middle of the room in two steps, carefully placing me in the chair. Laying a quick kiss on my forehead, he drags a table with tools toward me, motioning with his hand at the various devices.

"I'm giving you a tattoo," he declares proudly, opening up the kit to reveal a tattoo gun and other tools.

"A tattoo," I frown, a little taken aback by it.

"Yes!" he exclaims, and his excitement seems to have doubled. "You asked me for one a while back," he continues, slowly unbuttoning my nightgown to reveal the scars on my chest.

After I'd found out that his many tattoos were to hide his

scars, I'd been overly enthusiastic about getting one too. But Vlad hadn't been too receptive at the time, saying he didn't want anything on my skin.

I wonder what changed his mind…

"Why now?" I narrow my eyes at him.

I'm only too happy to get a tattoo, but I also want to know what prompted his change of heart, since he was pretty adamant about no tattoos in the beginning.

"Because you want it," he starts, choosing his words carefully, "and because I don't want you to have bad memories from that place—ever again."

I stare at him dumbfounded for a moment before a stupid grin slowly appears on my face.

Grabbing his cheeks in my hands, I bring him closer for a kiss.

"Thank you," I whisper against his lips.

His eyes sparkle with joy and he looks like he's won the lotto as he starts preparing the equipment.

I watch him amused, once again surprised to see how little it takes to make him happy. And as I look at his carefree smile, it dawns on me that his happiness has always been contingent on making *me* happy.

Whenever he's done something to please me, he's been pleased with himself too, and the realization warms me even more.

I can't help myself as I reach out, fitting my palm to his cheek. He looks startled, but immediately gifts me a gorgeous smile as he places a kiss in the center of my palm.

"You're so good to me, Vlad." I tell him, fighting back tears.

There's something infinitely special about him and the way he treats me, his love boundless.

"No. You're good to me, Sisi," he replies, holding my hand close to his face. "You make me happiest," he simply says.

My heartbeats accelerate and I feel a tingle in my lower belly.

Butterflies. He makes me feel butterflies in my stomach.

His entire presence makes me so giddy, my body is no longer my own when he is around.

"I love that you thought about this," I add as I see him test the tattoo gun, "but do you know how to tattoo?"

His gesture may be sweet, but I have to wonder about his artistic prowess. In all the time we'd spent together, he'd never once mentioned a passion for it, or even better, a talent.

He stills, raising his eyes to look at me. Pursing his lips, he's quiet for a second, and I almost groan out loud.

"I don't *not* know how to tattoo," he answers, a sheepish smile on his face.

"Vlad!" My eyes widen at him and I swat him playfully. "You're not just thinking of doodling on my skin, are you?"

"Would that be so bad?" He shrugs, and my mouth hangs open in shock. I don't know whether to be scandalized or impressed by him. Sure, it's the thought that counts, but am I actually considering letting him do this?

"You're joking, right?"

"Relax," he catches my hand, holding it tight in his own. "I've had enough experience over the years with my own tattoos. Who do you think filled them in or continued some of the designs?" he more or less rips the shirt off his torso, pointing to several designs.

"See, I did this," he declares proudly.

I squint to make out the shapes, and I nod appreciatively.

"I didn't realize you had a knack for drawing," I comment as I trace the intricate forms on his chest. "Wait," I still, my finger on top of the triangle on his chest. "You added this?" I ask and he nods.

"I like to tweak the designs every now and then. But this was the first time I altered the meaning of the original ensemble."

"I love it," I tell him sincerely.

"Now let's see what you want." His enthusiasm is infectious as we start going over potential designs and concepts.

"I want one on the cross here," I point to the ugly scar on top of my breast, "and one here," I move my hand up to my neck, to the scar he'd given me months ago.

He blinks, his eyes focused on that spot as he swallows deeply.

"I'm sorry," he apologizes again, eyes closed, a look of pure agony on his face. "I don't think I'll ever be able to make it up to you for that... or anything." He sighs, his features forlorn as he looks anywhere but at me.

"Vlad," I tip his head up, "we need to move on. We're here now, and stronger together *because* of that incident. Please stop torturing yourself with it. I told you." I take a deep breath, wanting him to see the sincerity in my eyes. "I forgive you."

"Thank you," he says earnestly, and I gift him a smile.

"Here," I point to my neck, "I want a V."

His eyes immediately widen. Stupefied, he looks at me as if I'd grown a second head.

"You mean..." he trails off, dumbstruck, and for as long as I live I don't think I will forget the look on his face. The incredulity on his face reminds me of the time he'd deemed himself unworthy of my tears.

"I want one dagger here," I take his finger, the tip touching my skin as I show him what I have in mind, "and another line starting from the tip of the blade, here." I move his finger around in the shape of a V.

He doesn't speak, still looking at me reverently, his gaze fixed on the small scar at the base of my neck.

"And I want a red drop of blood falling from the blade," I continue, letting his finger trail down to my collarbone. "Because our relationship was forged in blood, tested in blood, and made stronger by blood," I remind him.

Our paths had crossed because of blood, and our relationship had been destroyed because of blood. But in blood we'd found each other again, and we'd shared every little piece of ourselves — every sin, and every transgression.

"Sisi..." he starts, shaking his head at me as if he still can't quite believe it.

"I want you with me. Always."

"Your wish is my command, Sisi," he replies, his voice thick with emotion.

Opening a tube of anesthetic cream, he applies it gently over my skin, his attention wholly focused on spreading it evenly.

After cleaning it, he makes a quick draft in pen, giving me a mirror to check the design.

"Wow," I whisper as I crane my neck to see the entire drawing. The scar is no longer visible under it.

He even added some intricate details to the dagger, making it seem like an ancient relic. The hilt is thicker than the blade, ending with a rounded corner that has an encrusted jewel.

"Ruby," he says when he sees me examine the jewel. "Red like blood. Precious like blood. And beautiful like you."

And just like that he's back to work, focused again on my neck. As if he didn't just melt my heart with a single sentence.

"Tell me if it hurts," he whispers as he brings the tattoo gun to my skin, tracing the sketch he'd made.

It doesn't hurt at all. Like a tickling sensation, I only feel him glide over my skin, his breath hot as it lands right on my ear lobe, making me squeeze my thighs in response.

How is it that he makes *every* mundane action so hot? I can't help myself even as I know that he needs to concentrate on my neck.

Instead, my eyes take in the great expanse of inked muscle, the flex of his arms, the defined pecs and…

I swallow as my gaze dips lower to his pebbled abdomen, the urge to touch him almost unbearable.

"Done," he says and I almost jerk in my chair. I hadn't been paying attention to anything *but* him. Although the tattoo isn't big, I'm surprised he's done so quickly.

He cleans the area before giving me the mirror again to survey the final product. The V is clearly defined even as the dagger takes the central stage, immediately drawing the eye to it.

For the blood and the ruby he'd chosen a deep red, and

as I see the drops fall from the ruby down the blade and toward my collarbone, I can't help but be impressed.

"This is amazing," I breathe out, turning to find him watching me with an inscrutable expression on his face. "What is it?" I frown.

"Hell girl… you have no idea what it's like to see my initials on your skin," he says, his hand hovering on top of the tattoo.

A crazy idea springs into my mind, and I blurt it out before I can think it through.

"Let me give you one, too. Matching tattoos. You can get an A. Here," I point toward his neck, one of the few areas on his body that's not covered in ink.

"You'd draw it on me?" he asks, almost as if he can't quite believe it. I nod, and a wide smile spreads all over his face.

"Do it!" He turns, giving me the side of his neck—the same area he'd done my design on—quickly going through the basics of tattooing.

Not a moment later and I have the tattoo gun in my hand, the tip touching his skin as I try my best to keep my fingers from trembling.

I can't believe he'd so readily agree to this, especially since I know he'd kept his neck clean of any ink so that it doesn't peek out from his clothing. With the initial I'm drawing, it's bound to show and let everyone know who he belongs to.

And that makes me feel fuzzy inside.

I focus on getting the letter right, doing a cursive A instead of a standard one. As I cross the middle of the letter, I add a drop of blood falling to the ground to emulate my own design. Although it's nowhere near his level of skill, the letter is clean and simple. After I add one last stroke, I lean back, surveying my work.

"I think it's nice," I tell him proudly.

He takes the mirror, inspecting it, and a reverent smile appears on his face.

"Thank you," he says, unable to take his eyes off it. "Now I can have you with me always too."

It takes a while before we can move on to the next tattoo, mostly because Vlad seems to be quite enamored of his new piece of ink, grabbing the mirror and staring at it every few minutes.

"Have you thought about what you want there?" he asks when he finally puts the mirror aside.

"Yes," I say.

I'd had a *long* time to think about what I'd like to take the place of the odious cross that reminds me of my worst nightmares.

In the beginning, I just wished it was gone. But with time, I realized that it's still a mark that proves I've been through fire and made it out alive.

Picking a pen and a paper, I start showing him how I'd like the cross to be changed into a different design.

Embedded deep in my skin, the scar is pretty gnarly, the edges a deep pink due to the fact that it had never healed properly. Just thinking of the pain it had caused me for months on end renews my anger towards Sacre Coeur and everything I'd had to endure there.

"That's amazing, hell girl," Vlad finally speaks when I'm done. "And it embodies everything you stand for."

I nod, pleased he gets it.

After we go over all the details, he begins by sketching the image on my skin. Soon, he's picking up the tattoo gun, starting to etch the permanent ink into my skin.

This one is more complicated, and it takes twice as long to get everything right.

"What do you think?" he asks, his tone hopeful as he puts the gun down, handing me the mirror.

Taking it, I start studying his work, immediately in awe by the level of precision.

"You're really good at this." I praise him, and I swear I note the smallest tinge of a blush on his cheeks.

Smiling to myself, I continue to look in the mirror. He'd perfectly depicted a woman being burned at the stake, the body of the cross serving as the wood holding the woman captive, her hands and feet tied, her mouth gagged. Small flames engulf the stake as the woman slowly succumbs to her death. Still, her eyes are unflinching as she's facing her execution with courage, knowing it's not her fault she's being punished. It's just the world she lives in that's unaccepting of those differences.

She bears the mark of the devil, and her entire life she's been shunned for it, everyone seeking to condemn her for something that was not her fault.

But in the end, even as she knew her life was going to end, she preferred dying for her principles and ideas, her chin raised high, her convictions unwavering. She never once considered changing to accommodate other people's beliefs—never taking the easy way out.

And just like that, I find myself in the drawing. My entire life I'd been conditioned to be a certain way, condemned the moment I didn't fit other people's mold.

But as I stare at the tattoo—the permanent drawing making its house on my skin—I can't help but be happy with all the choices I'd made.

Yes, I'd suffered for being different. But I hadn't conformed. I'd stayed true to myself, and I'd been rewarded for the entire ordeal.

Placing the mirror down, I direct my gaze toward him— my prize.

Because I would have never reached this point if I hadn't held on to my true self. I hadn't let those nuns beat obedience into me. I hadn't let the mean girls destroy my core. And because of that I am here.

With him.

Both with our idiosyncrasies, both matching and complementing the other. I know we were made for each other, our very beings vibing with one another.

"It's perfect," I whisper, tears already at the corner of my eyes.

He's managed to illustrate exactly what I'd been feeling for years.

"You're perfect, hell girl." He comes closer to me, his thumb under my chin as he prompts me to look into his eyes. "You're the bravest, most wonderful woman I've ever met. And because of that, I know how lucky I am that you forgave me," he says, his mouth coming down on my cheek, his tongue slipping out to lick one tear.

"I know how tightly you hold on to your principles. And I know what it must have cost you to forgive me." He contin- ues, moving to the other cheek and repeating the movement, swallowing up all my tears. "For that, I can't tell you how grateful I am."

I raise my eyes to his, noting the ravage on his features as he gazes at me with love, sorrow, and more love.

Adoration.

It might be more apt to call it adoration. The way I *know* he could never last without me. The way I know *I* could never last without him.

And suddenly I'm at peace with my past. All the resentment settles down in my heart as I realize everything happened *not* to tear me down, but to strengthen me.

Make me strong enough for him.

"Why, Vlad, you might actually sound like a romantic." I poke him playfully, a little overwhelmed by emotion.

"Of course." He smiles, the tension from his face gone. "I'm adopting romance as my new religion, with you as its goddess."

His glib tongue never fails to amaze me.

"Is that so?" I ask, trailing my finger down his chest, once again marveling at the hard wall of muscle that meets my touch.

"Yes," he rasps out, his voice full and husky. "I'll worship you," he starts, and my pulse picks up, "I'll kiss the ground you walk on." My breath catches in my throat, his words starting to affect me, the room suddenly too hot. "I'll be your servant, your whipping boy, whatever you want me to be," he continues and my eyes snap shut, his deep voice caressing my senses and making me shiver.

"Hmm," I murmur, feeling him so close, yet too far, "your arguments are pretty convincing," I manage to say, "I guess I *could* allow you by my side," I add cheekily, and he smirks. "But I thought you were *my* God." I raise an eyebrow at him.

"Still am." He winks at me, seductive arrogance dripping from his crooked smile, his dimple prominent and begging to be kissed. "But what's a God without his goddess? We rule together, hell girl." His hand comes up to my face, his thumb brushing against my lips as he backs me into the wall.

"Remember, there's no Vlad without Sisi." His intent gaze on me, I don't miss the way his pupils dilate, his entire body ready to ravish me.

One arm snaked around my waist, he effortlessly lifts me in his arms, my legs wrapping around his waist.

"And no Sisi without Vlad," I complete the sentence, his mouth claiming mine in a searing kiss that has my toes curling in excitement.

Holding on to him, I let him show me just how much we're one half of a whole—always needing the other to be complete.

22
SISI

"Tighter," he commands, his voice stern as he hovers behind me, his eyes sharply assessing the shape of my fist.

"Like this," he tsks, coming closer. His front fitted to my front, he wraps his hand over my fist, dwarfing it.

It's not the first time I've noticed that his giant hands seem to swallow mine.

He carefully organizes my fingers in a tighter fist, his feet knocking at mine as he arranges my stance, too.

I wobble slightly as he kicks my feet apart, my position now emulating his.

"When someone tries something," he whispers, his voice deep and grave, "you kick first, ask questions later. Or even better," I feel a smile pull at his lips, "kill first, ask questions… never," he chuckles, and my own lips twitch.

"Come on, you know I've gotten better," I complain slightly, half turning my head to bat my lashes at him. The action catches him by surprise, as I knew it would, his eyes zoning in on my poor attempts at flirtation.

Still, it's enough to have him wholly enthralled, his Adam's apple bobbing up and down as he swallows forcibly, his pupils dilating.

Taking advantage of the millisecond his guard is down, I grab on to his shirt, positioning my hands and legs the way he'd taught me in order to balance weight much greater than my own. My grip solid, I throw all my strength into moving him.

He's like a rock—heavy and unbudging. And even though my technique is flawless, I can see I'm not likely to gain the upper hand on him. Not even by using his weakness —batting my lashes at him.

There's a split second reaction as I note the corner of his mouth tugs up before he lets his body become slack. Barely realizing what I'm doing, I'm kicking him to the ground, his body falling effortlessly—suspiciously effortlessly.

Vlad even has the gall to complain about the pain as his back hits the hard floor.

I simply raise an eyebrow at him, knowing he just did it to please me.

"Again." I cross my arms in front of me, beckoning him to resume a fighting position.

Almost from the beginning he'd insisted on teaching me how to fight, saying he'd feel much at ease if he knew I could take care of myself.

We'd done some basic training in New York, but ever since we got here, he'd been more rigid with the training schedule, giving me lessons in shooting, knife fighting and fist fighting.

To my great surprise, he hadn't been kidding when he'd said the entire basement is custom made. There's a shooting range equipped with everything to ensure I become proficient in hitting my targets, but there are also a couple training rooms—one specifically designed for knives, and one resembling a gym.

I'd been dumbstruck about the size of the basement, but Vlad had recounted he'd expanded it under the gardens too, not only under the house. He's essentially imitating his own underground bunker from New York.

Sometimes this gives me pause, and it makes me wonder if this is all he knows—living underground and away from people.

Certainly, he seems more comfortable under a layer of cement.

"Stop treating me like I'm fragile," I tell him. No matter how much he wants to train me, he can't help himself from holding back.

"You're not fragile," he says as he gets back to his feet. "You're anything but fragile, Sisi." His hand cups my cheek as he brings me into him. "But I'm a brute, and I know my strength. So I can't *not* be careful with you."

I roll my eyes at him, a little annoyed that he's not trying harder, but understanding where he's coming from.

"Fine," I huff out, taking a step back and assuming a fighting stance again.

We do a few more rounds where he teaches me some parrying moves and how to evade capture before we focus strictly on building my strength through weightlifting.

"You're doing great," he praises when I finish one set, my arms already sore.

"You're not a bad teacher." I shrug, taking the towel he offers and wiping the sweat off my face and body.

Vlad had thought of everything, and he'd bought me an entire set of gym clothes, most of them involving yoga pants and a sports bra, which retrospectively hadn't been the best decision.

Not when he can barely take his eyes off my boobs when we're doing an exercise. Or the way I know he's staring at my ass when I squat.

I might have even gone out of my way to tease him a little, flexing my ass or bouncing my boobs when I know he's looking, but pretending not to.

The reaction is immediate and he's promptly caught. He's not the only one with betraying clothes, and his sweatpants do little to hide just how affected he is.

After hours of training, we finally finish for the day, quickly showering before going out in the city for dinner.

"Tomorrow we're doing knives," he speaks as the waiter brings us our food.

"Yes," I exclaim, bumping my fist in the air.

He'd made a strict schedule for me, with every day accounted for. Somehow, though, he'd decided that the focus should be on building my strength and learning hand to hand combat. So he'd only set up one day for knives and one day for shooting.

"A weapon can always be taken from you," he'd remark whenever I'd pout about it. He knows that I've developed an affinity for knives—probably because of him. Still, he hadn't budged in his conviction.

Vlad's lips pull up in a smile at my excitement and I cannot help but notice how handsome he is, freshly showered and wearing a dashing suit. Dressed all in black, it only serves to emphasize his striking features even more.

His hair is longer, refusing to cut it ever since I'd complimented him on it. And I do like it. It makes him seem younger, more carefree. Especially with the way it curls around the end, giving it a tousled appearance.

"You're the most beautiful thing I've ever seen," he suddenly says, taking me by surprise with the change in subject. His eyes are fixed on me and it's like he's devouring me with his gaze.

A blush creeps up my cheeks at his scrutiny.

When he'd told me he planned on taking me out on a dinner date, I'd tried to put some effort into my appearance.

Since I hadn't had a lot of practice with make-up and dressing up, I'd quickly searched the internet for some ideas. I'd managed to put on some eyeliner and mascara as well as a reddish lipstick to contrast with my pale hair.

I'd also chosen to go with a lacey off-white dress, not too long, but not too short either since Vlad had been very vehement in his refusal to let me leave the house if there was too much skin showing.

"You should have been a poet, not a killer," I retort, bringing my glass of lemonade closer and placing my lips around the straw.

"Can't I be both?" He raises one eyebrow. "Although imagine if I could kill people with my words," he says pensively, going in depth about the merits of personally killing someone personally versus via proxy.

"There's this manga, Death Note" he starts, explaining it's some Japanese comic book, "and the protagonist acquires a notebook in which once he writes someone's name, they promptly die."

"Don't tell me you'd like one of those too?" I ask, a little amused. Although, as he excitedly recounts the events from Death Note, I find myself invested in the story and its twists. Certainly, I can see the appeal to someone like Vlad, who might just be the nerd of nerds.

"I don't know. Depending on my goals," he adds after spending some time thinking about it. "If my aim was world domination, then a death note would definitely be more helpful than my bare hands. Especially when it comes to the evidence left behind, since forensic science is evolving and the tech is more sensitive than ever to the smallest amounts of trace evidence."

"But you don't want that," I say confidently, because I know him. He'd never opt for world domination because it would be too boring for him. Maybe he'd enjoy one day of it, but after that he'd want to return to his usual routine of murder and mayhem.

"Indeed," he drawls, his lips spread in a wide smile, his white teeth gleaming in the dimly lit restaurant and making him look like the predator he is.

"World domination is for the weak," he adds. "I prefer to do things my own way." He brings his arms on the table, cracking his knuckles.

My eyes are drawn to the veins bulging in his arms, the way his big hands could snuff the life out of a man without even trying.

"I may like to be in the loop, but I rarely interact."

"That's because for *you*, power isn't in numbers," I note, "but in knowledge."

"Exactly." He smirks. "You know me well, hell girl," he mentions, and I shrug.

"I've been studying you. After all." I lean forward,

pushing my boobs out as I do, his eyes immediately snapping to my cleavage. "The devil you know is better than the devil you don't."

"Is that what I am to you, hell girl? The devil you know?" He comes closer, and even though we're on opposite sides of the table, we're so close our faces are almost touching.

"Hmm," I murmur, letting him stew a little. "You're the *only* devil I want to know."

"Good," he breathes out, his eyes focused on me in a way that has goosebumps appear all over my skin. "Otherwise I might have had to change your mind," he rasps out, and for a moment I can only imagine what he has in mind. His gaze holds me captive as I see myself spread out on the table, and him working *hard* to change my mind.

"Are you enjoying your meal?" the waiter's voice brings me back to reality, my eyes widening at the way I'd lost track of everything.

Vlad is watching me amused, swirling his glass of red wine.

"It's wonderful. Thank you," he tells the waiter, pure charm dripping from his voice.

I don't even pay attention as the waiter mumbles something before taking his leave. I'm still focused on *him*, and the way my heart is beating insanely fast.

"You know," he starts, a wicked smile on his lips, "there *is* something else I'd love to dominate," he says suggestively, and I cross my legs, moisture already pooling between my thighs.

"Is that so?" I ask, almost breathlessly.

It dawns on me that we've barely touched our food.

Engrossed in the conversation, we'd simply forgotten it was there. And especially now, when he looks at me as if he'd eat *me*, I can't muster any appetite.

At least not for food.

"But I wouldn't need any notebook for that."

"Really?" Shaking off one shoe, I lift my leg toward him under the table, my foot touching his thigh before I move it slowly towards his crotch, feeling him hard and ready for me just as I am for him.

He stifles a groan just as I brush my toes across his length.

"I only need these," he raises his hands to show them to me before sneaking them under the table, catching my foot and stroking it gently.

My breath catches in my throat as he slowly massages my foot before taking it and placing it right on top of his cock.

"Vlad," I half-moan, impatience growing inside of me.

Snatching my foot from him, I quickly put on my shoe before standing up.

"I'm going to the bathroom," I say, a little too abruptly. But as I take two steps away from the table I turn to look at him, his eyes are on my ass.

A daring smile playing on my lips, I use one finger to give him a signal. Then, I just head to the restroom.

I barely get inside when he bursts in, closing the door and locking it.

One step and he has me backed against the sink, my back to his front as he quickly lowers the zipper of his pants. He roughly lifts the dress over my ass, bending me over the sink. One hand in my hair, the other on my hip, he enters me swiftly, a brutal thrust that has me almost coming on the spot.

"You can't help yourself," he grits, his movements gaining momentum, his cock moving in and out of me at lightning speed. "You have to tempt me *every* fucking second." He continues, savagely imprinting himself on my body. His hand moves from my hair to my throat, squeezing gently as he brings me closer to him, still.

"Look at you," he prompts me to look in the mirror, seeing us tangled together, our cheeks flushed, our hot breaths fogging the glass. My mouth parts on a moan, but he slips his thumb inside, blocking the sound.

"Look how you drive me so crazy..." he speaks, his breath on my cheek. "So out of control," he continues, each word accentuating his vicious thrusts, "completely insane."

I'm barely aware of anything else but his invasion, trying but failing to keep myself from screaming out his name as I'm coming, my walls closing in around him and causing him to shout my name as he fills me with his cum.

"My fucking temptress," he speaks against my cheek, sweat clinging to our skin from the brief albeit laborious act.

It's only when we're back at our table that we finally dig into our food, our appetites seemingly returned.

23
SISI

The knife slips easily from my hand, rotating in the air before reaching the middle of the target.

"Not bad." He nods at me.

He's leaning back against the wall as he watches me throw the knives, his shrewd eyes analyzing everything—from my posture to my breath and to how I'm holding the knife, he has indications for everything.

Vlad might sometimes be an overbearing ogre, but he is a wonderful teacher. The evidence being my insane progress in just a little time.

If before I had trouble even getting the knife to embed itself in a target with its sharp side forward, now I can effortlessly throw it and more or less hit the bullseye.

I know I have a long way to go. Certainly, I don't think there's anyone more proficient in this than him.

He strides to me, grabbing the bag next to him and throwing it at my feet.

"You're advancing fast, hell girl. Time to switch up the

blades," he jokes, opening up the bag to reveal even more knives, all different shapes and sizes.

"You've learned how to throw basic knives, but how about we try some daggers?" He plops himself on the floor, sorting through the bag.

Curious, I sit down too, watching closely as he removes the blades and organizes them on the floor, pointing at each one and telling me a little something about it.

"You know what my blades of choice are." he points to the shashkas, the curved blades that he's always using in combat. "They are for close combat only, the curve of the blade making it easy to control movement and slash some-one's throat," he explains, taking one shashkas and showing me how to wield it.

"Always aim for the throat and the battle is immediately over," he says, raising his eyes to mine. A mischievous glint and he has the blade against my throat before I can even blink.

Indeed, the concave part of it seems to fit perfectly against my neck, and he moves it slightly, showing me just how easy it is to pierce the skin if necessary.

"See, piece of cake." He grins, chucking the shashka away before moving to the next.

He introduces knives from all over the world, giving me a brief overview of each.

"I also like Japanese blades." He picks up a knife with a thick, triangular blade and a smaller hilt ending in a rounded hollow corner. "This is a kunai, and you might find this easier to handle." He places it in my hand, letting me become familiar with its shape and weight.

"This is more comfortable," I agree.

Not as long as the regular knives, the rounded end makes it easier to hold it.

"Watch this." He smirks, gathering five kunai. Holding one in his hand, the others are wrapped around his fingers.

Standing up, he barely focuses on the target as he throws them, one by one, with such speed and ease that I have to force myself *not* to blink so I don't miss it.

"Wow," I whisper when my gaze moves to the target. All five are gathered in the same place, their tips millimeters apart, almost as if they are fighting for supremacy.

"Practice makes best," he says as he helps me to my feet.

Gathering the knives back, he fixes my stance, wrapping my fingers carefully around the hilt of the kunai.

Still behind me, he whispers words of encouragement in my ear.

"Now!"

At his command, I put my strength into my arm, aiming the kunai at the target.

"You're a natural," he praises, inspecting the result. A bit off mark, it had still hit the target.

"I love this," I tell him sincerely.

There's a certain type of rush in wielding a powerful blade, and I can see why it's his favorite activity.

Backing up into him, I feel the contour of his body fitted to mine. Turning suddenly, I place the tip of my blade to his neck.

"Bloodthirsty?" he asks, not even batting an eye at the sharp edge currently lodged just below his Adam's apple.

"Just thirsty," I fire back suggestively, playfully moving the blade around his flesh. "Sometimes I wonder if you're even human," I murmur, danger rolling off him, a predator's eyes watching my every movement. "If you bleed like the rest of us…" I trail off, lowering the blade down his neck and around his collar bone.

He's wearing a black shirt that's completely molded to his muscles, the wide neckline giving me access to his skin.

"You think I'm not human, hell girl?" he asks, his hand on mine as he tightens it over the blade.

"You're… something," I reply.

There's a mythical quality to him, both in the way he presents himself to the world, but also in the way I know him intimately. There is a savageness deeply ingrained in his bones, a ferocity in his gaze as he lays it upon me. It makes me feel wanted in a primal, primordial way. As if there's no space, or time, or anything.

Just him.

It reminds me of the first time I saw him. How the pure danger emanating from his pores had turned me on, the way his promise of death had never been sweeter.

It's inexplicable.

Animal magnetism, primitive attraction, deadly seduction.

He embodies everything I should run away from, not toward.

My hand becomes slack in his, but he doesn't let go. His eyes still on mine, a sensuously wicked smile appears on his face as he digs the knife into his skin, just above the collar of his shirt.

I watch stupefied as the blade cuts through flesh, red drops bursting through the surface and coating the tip.

Eyes wide, I look at him questioningly.

"Tell me," he purrs, his tone smooth and alluring, "do I bleed?"

He doesn't let me answer, pushing the blade even deeper, more blood reaching the surface.

"I do bleed," he continues, low in his throat, "but only for you."

Lifting my other hand, I trace my finger over the small wound, swiping some of the blood and bringing it to my lips.

"Only for me?" I repeat, the metallic taste flooding my mouth.

"Hell girl," he groans as he watches me lick my fingers clean, "you're not playing fair."

"Fair?" I ask, amused. "How is this fair, then?" My lips pull in a mischievous smile as I move the blade into the other hand. He releases me, frowning as he watches me wield the weapon in the air.

Giving him a knowing smile, I set the blade to my own chest, pushing the tip ever so slightly. I feel a small pinch before the skin gives way, red liquid slowly gushing out.

His gaze is focused on my skin, and for a second I'm worried I might have poked the beast. He looks feral as he backs me into the wall, one hand grabbing both arms and raising them above my head.

"Not fair," he growls before lowering his mouth to my skin. I feel the suction as his lips wrap themselves around the small laceration, and he laps at the blood, taking it all in.

The slight sting of the cut coupled with his warm mouth make it increasingly harder for me to breathe, the hairs on my body standing to attention as I want to beg him to have his way with me.

But just as soon as he's on me, he's gone.

Head hung low, he takes a step back, not looking at me. There's blood residue around his lips, and as he starts pacing around restlessly I know I might have pushed him too far.

"I need to..." he drifts off, frowning as if he doesn't know what he needs to do, either.

"Go," I urge him. "I'll find you later."

He whips his head at me, regarding me for a moment before briskly nodding. His face is pale, his features taut and full of tension.

Without lingering, he leaves, heading straight for the blood room.

As I hear the door close behind him, I feel a little guilty about baiting him when I know blood is his main trigger. Still, there had been a moment where I'd wanted nothing more than to offer him mine in exchange for his.

Maybe it's crazy, but his trigger might just be my biggest turn on.

Shaking my head at that absurd train of thought, I continue practicing.

I push myself harder, and two hours later I'm still throwing knives at the targets. My breathing harsh, I stop for a moment, sitting on the floor and grabbing a bottle of water.

A little tired, I end up staring at the wall for a full minute, unable to get myself together.

Out of nowhere, though, a blasting sound erupts through the air, and my hands automatically go to my ears to shield them.

What?

Disoriented, I look around me until I locate the tablet in

the wall on the other side of the room, the screen a bright red. Standing up, I hurry to it, plugging in the password to get access to the main frame of the house.

The screen flares to life, and a warning message greets me, the entire area red. I click a few things, and multiple windows appear, each showing a different part of the house.

The live feed.

But as I look through each of them, I realize what triggered the alarm.

My eyes widen when I spot at least five armed men wading through the garden and assessing the perimeter. Another two are already in the house, on the ground floor, and more are going up the stairs.

Shit!

All are heavily armed and in full gear. Some look military, but I can't be sure. All I know at the moment is that I have to get to Vlad.

Refusing to lose my calm, I start collecting as many knives as I can, strapping them around my body. I need to be smart about this. The best I can do is get Vlad and go together to the panic room.

I already know I'm likely to find him naked and unarmed so that will *not* help against blazing guns.

Checking the feed again to ensure they're not yet at the basement, I steel myself and open the door, heading on to the corridor.

Damn, Vlad!

Why did he have to build this gigantic basement? It's the size of the entire property, probably even bigger than a football field, which means that even though the intruders are not here yet, they might get down any moment with the time it takes me to reach the blood room.

Holding tightly onto the knives in my hand, I hurry down the corridor, my senses sharp as I listen for any noise.

I'm halfway across when I hear gunshots. Instinctively, I duck, closing my eyes.

Fuck!

The shots are coming from upstairs, and from the sound of it they're shooting down.

The trap door!

My eyes widen as I whip my head around, looking at the trap door that leads to the basement from the living room. Part of the original construction of the house, it's made fully of wood.

And it's *not* bulletproof.

"I'm fucked," I whisper to myself, wildly looking around.

I can run across and hurry to the blood room, but they would undoubtedly make it downstairs before that and I'd be a direct target in an open field. They'd shoot before I could do anything.

No, that's not an option.

Turning around, I catalogue the various rooms around. Even the panic room is too far, but that's out of the question as long as Vlad's not with me. I could never save myself knowing he'd be a living target. No matter how proficient he is in *everything,* he is *not* immortal.

A little closer is the shooting range, and as I hear the latch of the wood give, I know I have the best shot of getting there, maybe even arming myself further.

I sprint as fast as I can, getting to the door just as the

trap door is smashed to pieces. Closing the door, I will myself not to despair. I just need to find guns and ammo.

Granted, I hadn't had as many shooting lessons as I'd like to feel comfortable with a gun, but I guess today is an exception. Opening up the gun cabinet, I try to remember Vlad's lessons. I need something that can hold the most rounds, since I know I'm slow at reloading and that's time I *cannot* waste.

Sorting through various handguns, I finally find a rifle. Checking the cartilage, I'm happy to see it's fully loaded so I won't have to spend time looking for that too.

Armed to my best ability, I head to the tablet on the wall, plugging in the password and accessing the feed from the hallway.

Three people are down, searching the basement, with the rest still upstairs.

Ok, three isn't that much. Three is doable.

But not for me.

Damn, but what am I doing? I'm not a warrior. I'm the furthest thing from one if one takes into account the fact that I've spent twenty years in a Goddamn convent. But conflict and death won't care if I'm a nun or a soldier, so I'd better put on my big girl panties and brave this through.

For now, I just need to make it to Vlad.

Releasing a breath, I nod to myself. But as I look at the screen again, I realize the men are already heading to the other side of the level.

To the blood room.

I don't know how they will find Vlad, and if he'll be in any capacity to fight. His moods are so fickle that I simply cannot risk it.

Pursing my lips, I say a small prayer before I open the door.

Rifle under my arm, my stance ready as he'd taught me, I get on my haunches and I aim.

The three men are in formation, one ahead, two behind. I have the advantage that they haven't realized my presence yet, so I focus on the one ahead, since I'm thinking he might be the leader. Since they are all dressed in uniform, likely with bulletproof equipment underneath, my *only* bet is the head.

Once I have a good aim, the rifle pointed at the back of his head, at the bare skin between his neck and his cap, I squeeze the trigger.

I reel backwards as the bullet flies towards its target, promptly embedding itself right where his skull meets the cervical vertebrae.

It's a split second where he falls to the ground, the other two men immediately on me as they bark some orders.

Blinking rapidly, I realize there's no time to lose. Not when they're also shooting at me. I barely have time to throw myself inside the room before bullets fly past the door.

Time is of essence as I have to quickly decide how to tackle this. The men will surely come to the room, and just like the hallway, it's an open field.

Trying to keep a handle on my panic, I realize that the only hiding place is… behind the door.

Closing my eyes, I take a deep breath, situating myself behind the door and waiting for them to burst through. If I can take one down, then I can handle just one person, right?

I better hope so.

A few more seconds and the men almost tear down the door.

"We need to get to Kuznetsov." One notes while the other grunts, using his fingers to signal something.

I wait until they are further into the room before I announce my presence. Holding tightly onto the rifle, I aim, managing to nab one of them in his cheek.

Blood spurts out as he falls to his knees, his gun dropping to the ground, his screams of pain worse than a woman's. I don't even have time to consider that as I see the other aim at me.

Before I realize what I'm doing, I pull the door toward me, using it as a shield.

Bullets hit the steel door, and I'm grateful that Vlad's had the entire level custom made. It certainly made the difference between life and death just now.

Debating what to do next, I take a risk and I drop the rifle.

At this point it's all about timing, and taking the time to get the target right might cost me precious seconds. Wrapping my fingers around the hilt of a knife, I wait until the bullets quiet before peeking inside the room, immediately throwing the knife at him.

Missed.

Out of bullets, he's abandoning his own weapon and picking up the one of his fallen friend.

Shit!

Already on automatic pilot, I reveal myself once more, my sight clear as I make eye contact with him. He has a smug expression on his face, as if he's already won this, even though his partner is sitting in a blood bath that *I* caused.

I let my lips spread in a smile before I move my shoulder back, preparing for the throw. He smirks as he takes in my knife, probably expecting me to miss again.

Ah, but I have a surprise for him.

After all, if there's anything I know how to do well, that's survival.

And so I keep my smile on, my fingers tight against the hilt of the kunai, and I throw.

His lips are stuck in a perpetual smile as the tip of my knife lands right in between his eyes. He falls to the floor with a thud, but I can't even gloat in my win.

Not when I have to get to Vlad as soon as possible.

I all but run out of the room, heading straight to the blood room. But just as I am two steps from opening the door, four more people appear in the hallway, all coming from the direction of the hatch.

My eyes widen in horror as I realize I'm truly caught.

Their weapons are pointed toward me as they slowly advance.

I could surrender, but that's simply out of the question. Not when I know what they're likely to do to me if they get me. I'd rather die than open myself up to that type of hell.

I take another knife from the back of my pants, ready to do whatever it takes.

"It's just a girl," one of them mentions as they get closer to me.

"Where's Kuznetsov? He told us he'd be here," another says and I frown.

Who told them?

"Doesn't matter, you know the drill. No witnesses," the third one chimes in, and I know my time's up.

Vlad…

But just as I'm about to either let them kill me, or do the honors myself, the door to the blood room swings open.

A naked Vlad entirely covered in blood struts out, his eyes immediately locking with mine. He looks me up and down, giving a small nod when he realizes I'm unharmed.

As he fully comes out from the room, I realize he's *not* unarmed. One rifle in one hand, one corpse in the other as he's dragging the body across the floor, he doesn't seem to be still in the throes of an episode.

If anything, he looks perfectly sane.

The men do a double take when they see him, the sight of him in a blood bodysuit seemingly making even seasoned soldiers sweat.

My own heart finally calms down as I know he's here, and that he's lucid. That means they don't stand a chance. And so I release a relieved breath.

"Duck," his voice is soft and I don't even question the command, throwing myself behind him and ducking at the entrance of the blood room.

The entire thing happens in slow motion as Vlad single handedly opens fire on the three men, bullets raining on them and penetrating every inch of their non-armored body. He's so fast they don't even get to point their weapons toward him.

When one makes a feeble attempt at shooting at Vlad, he simply lifts the corpse with one hand, using it as a human shield.

Once everyone's down, he dumps the corpse, hurrying towards me.

"My brave, brave, girl." He takes me into his arms,

rocking with me. "I'm sorry I wasn't there earlier," he says, holding me so tight I can barely breathe.

"It's okay," I say, even though my body is trembling slightly from the adrenaline residue. "We're fine. We're both fine." I lean back to look at him.

He shakes his head slightly, cupping my cheeks and laying kisses all over my face. "We need to get out of here," he mentions, tugging me to my feet.

"There are more people upstairs," I tell him what I'd seen on the camera, including the fact that someone must have told them his location.

"Fuck," he curses under his breath.

Passing by the dead men, he picks up their guns, handing me two and keeping two to himself.

"Stay next to me, hell girl. If anyone shoots, get behind me, okay?"

His features are stern, his voice grave as he more or less orders me to let him take any bullets meant for me.

I want to argue, tell him I'd never do something like that, but one look at him and I know he's not likely to be amenable. So I just nod.

"Good," he grunts, taking my hand as we go to the ground level. "We need to get to the car, and then we'll head straight to the airport," he explains, telling me the house is compromised now and he's not taking any risks with my safety.

We're in the service elevator, which luckily has a tablet too, so Vlad is able to monitor the activity in the house.

"You took three out, I took four..." he speaks, more to himself, doing the math as he counts a couple more people on the upper floor. "They fucking sent an entire unit."

A hint of a smile appears on his face, and I frown at him.

"Whoever told them about me gave them good instructions." He smirks, a sinister pull of his lips that promises bloodshed and death.

Even as I feel safest next to him, I can only rue the day those people decided to attack *him*. Because I don't think there's anyone more dangerous out there. If there's such a thing as a killer trophic chain, then he's on top.

And he proves my point as he leaves me in the elevator with a shrug and a kiss, striding in the middle of the living room in all his bloody naked glory, guns raised high as he shoots a few rounds in the air.

Thudding steps resound in the house as the remaining men all hurry downstairs. Locked in the elevator, I can only watch through the video feed as he baits them out in the open.

A total of five men ambush him, all seemingly flabbergasted at finding him naked and covered in blood.

"You dare," he says with a smile and I turn on the volume on the camera, not wanting to miss anything, "to come into *my* house, and threaten *my* woman?" His voice thunders in the room, yet the smile's still set in place.

The men are in position, but Vlad doesn't seem to care as he simply discards his weapons to the floor.

My eyes widen, and I can't quite believe what I'm seeing. Especially as he'd insisted on taking them from the dead men.

But as the others fix their guns on him, he does something that completely shocks me. He ducks low, throwing himself between two men.

The entire thing happens so fast it's as if someone applied special effects to the footage.

He raises himself up effortlessly right behind the two men. They don't even have time to react as Vlad takes hold of their protective caps, bringing them together and hitting their heads.

They struggle in his hold, but they're no match for him. Even with their army training, since they're clearly professionals, they look like children being scolded by an adult.

The other three men are ready to fire, but seem reluctant since Vlad is using the two men's bodies as shields.

"Not so brave now, are you?" he asks, banging the men's heads together once more, but this time, he undoes their caps, throwing them to the ground before hitting their heads again. The sound of bones cracking is unmistakable, and even the remaining men have a hard time believing what they are seeing.

Certainly, even for me it looks almost impossible, and I'm used to associating the word *impossible* with Vlad. His strength must be incredible if he's breaking their skulls with his bare hands. And it looks effortless, no visible strain on his face.

He continues the motion until the skin is broken, brain leaking out from the cranial vault. At this point, the men aren't even struggling anymore, their bodies slack, their weapons now at Vlad's disposal.

This is all a game for him. A show.

"What the…"

"He's not human… he can't be," one man curses out.

And as the others keep mumbling incoherent sentences,

I realize Vlad's real purpose for the spectacle—he wants their fear.

The panic is visible on their faces, their feet unconsciously taking a few steps back.

Vlad's smile is unwavering, but his gaze is deadly.

Still, I can't feel sorry for them, because they *did* come into our home intent on killing us. They brought it upon themselves.

Fingers molded to the gun, Vlad shoots.

Two men fall down, blood pouring out of their necks and flooding the floor. Only one is still alive, and it's on purpose as Vlad lets the corpses drop to his feet, advancing toward him.

The man doesn't even try to put up a fight as he falls to his ass, trying to crawl backwards, an expression of pure terror on his face.

"Who sent you?" Vlad asks, coming to stand right in front of the man. He carelessly swings the gun in his hand a couple of times before pointing it straight at his head.

"Who sent you?" he asks again, the barrel of the gun moving slowly across the man's face. "I don't know if they told you, but I'm not a fan of quick deaths. Your friends there," he motions to the fallen men, "had it easy. But you…" He makes a tsk sound. "You either tell me or I'll get the answer out of you." He shrugs, plopping himself on his ass in front of the scared man, as if he couldn't give a fuck if he tried to attack him or not.

More than anything Vlad looks… bored.

"I…" the man stammers, "please don't hurt me," he cries like a little girl and Vlad's smile widens.

"Do tell," he prompts him.

"P... P... Petro Meester," he finally utters the words, and I narrow my eyes, almost sure I'd heard the name before.

"Is that so," Vlad whistles a short tune—in surprise or disappointment, I don't know. "And who told you where I was?" he continues, and my ears perk up.

I watch attentively, curious about the person who sold Vlad out because I know for a fact that very few people had been aware of this location.

"I..." the man keeps on stammering, his eyes wildly looking for an exit where there's none.

More impatient than usual, Vlad grabs his nape, bringing him closer to his face. I push the volume of the sound to the max, wanting to listen to everything that passes between them.

"You tell me that, and I'll give you a quick death. You have my word. If not..." He purses his lips, telling him exactly what he'll do to him, a gruesome experiment meant to keep him alive while his body writhes in pain. The descriptions are so vivid that the man wets himself.

"I don't know... a bald man," he says, his entire body trembling with fear.

Vlad gives a jerky nod, the barrel of the gun at the man's temple before I can even blink, the sound of the bullet going through his brain and immediately killing him almost deafening.

Vlad's expression is grave as he stands up, pensively striding to my location and opening the elevator doors.

"We need to leave," he tells me, "but first, I need to do one last thing."

He takes my hand, leading me to the front of the house before thrusting me behind him.

"Come out, you fucking coward," he yells at the top of his lungs. "Maxiiiiiiim!" His roar would make anyone think twice before showing themselves in front of him.

But Maxim ends up coming out of the house, a resigned look on his face.

I try to peek at Vlad's face and I have to wonder what he's feeling. I know Maxim's been with him for years. To have him betray Vlad like this must be awful. Especially since for so long Maxim's been his only contact to the outside world.

Vlad takes a step forward, only one word crossing his lips.

"Why?"

Maxim has the shame to look down, his legs wobbly as he falls to his knees.

"Moya semya, vo Vladivostoke," he starts, his voice uneven as he talks about his family back in Russia and how Meester had offered him a deal in exchange for their lives.

"Maxim," Vlad says his name, and I can recognize a tinge of anguish underneath.

He's not unaffected. And that breaks my heart.

"You could have asked for help. Ya nekagda ne tebe skazal net. Ti znaesh shto ya vsegda hotel pomogat." He shakes his head, clearly disappointed.

Head hung low, Maxim doesn't even dare look at Vlad. Instead, he takes out a shashka from his coat, handing it to him with both hands.

"Pazhalusta," he whispers.

Vlad's expression falls for a split of a second, before his iciness returns in full force. Grabbing the blade, he doesn't even hesitate as he waves it in the air, the sharp edge cutting Maxim's throat from ear to ear.

He falls to the ground, blood gushing from his body, his eyes wide open as he stares into nothingness.

"Zemlya tebe puhom," Vlad whispers as he stoops low, placing his open palm over Maxim's face and closing his eyes.

Coming toward me, I cannot help but feel his pain as my own. So I do the only thing that I can. I meet him halfway, my arms wrapped around his torso as I pull him into a big hug.

He's frozen still for a moment before he starts reacting, returning the embrace.

"You're safe, Sisi. That's all that matters," he speaks, caressing my hair, his mouth on my temple as he lays a sweet kiss on my skin.

"*We* are safe," I correct him, "I don't want to imagine a world without you," I tell him, my words laced with the agony I'd felt at thinking that something might happen to him.

"Me neither," he responds, his voice hollow. "Me neither."

A quick sweep of the house to get some belongings and then we're both in the car, heading to the airport.

Back to New York.

I don't even want to imagine what awaits us there. From Vlad's enemies to my own disapproving family, I don't think anyone's going to receive us with open arms.

At least we're together. And together we'll brave it all.

24
VLAD

Using a towel to dry my hair, I head back to the main seating area of the plane. With the impromptu attack on the house, I'm thankful that I'd kept the jet in New Orleans. We hadn't lingered too long at the house, grabbing only a few necessities before taking the car to the airport. I hadn't even had the time to wash the blood off, and I'd definitely run a risk driving around drenched in blood.

Still, better being pulled over by some puny cop than risk Sisi's safety even more. They had sent a unit to dispatch me, so there's no doubt that another one would follow when they realize they've lost connection to the first one.

Legs crossed, she's sitting by the window, staring into empty space. Not for the first time, I stop to admire her. Even tired, she's stunning, her beauty unique. She's still dressed in her work out gear, some blood spatters on her skin.

Her blonde hair is lightly stained around the tips. I'd suggested she use the shower first since the plane bathroom is too tiny to fit us both, but she'd insisted that I was in more dire need of it. Of course, she commands and I obey.

She's looking out the window, her expression serene. Too serene considering what she just went through, and that only makes me more in awe of her.

By the time I'd registered that shots were being fired in the house, my Sisi had been dealing with those bastards on her own. I can barely forgive myself for letting her stand up to them by herself. But even as I'm mad at myself for my own failure, I can't help but admire her. She'd bravely faced them and even killed a few on her own.

A smile pulls at my lips.

She truly is one of a kind.

Although she'd handled herself better than I could have ever hoped, I won't *ever* let that happen again. Even if I have to cuff her to me, I will make sure she's never in danger again.

I don't think I could handle it if anything happened to her. Certainly, I don't think the *world* could handle me if anything happened to her. Because one thing is for sure. I exist if she does. That's my only requirement.

She notices me in the doorway, and she gives me a shy smile as she beckons me to her.

"There you are, handsome." Her hand reaches out to touch my face as I sit next to her.

Without even thinking, I tug her out of her seat and onto my lap, holding her tightly. I don't think the sight of those people aiming their guns at her will leave my mind anytime soon.

"I love you," I tell her, nuzzling my face in the crook of

her neck. That she's here and mine is the only thing I need to know to feel at peace.

"I love you too," she says, her soft voice soothing the beast inside of me.

It scares me too to think what I'd be capable of if *anything* were to happen to Sisi. I don't think there are limits to the destruction I'd wreck before joining her.

"I promise I'll never put you in danger again," I tell her, my mind already working on annihilating any potential danger, starting with the people who want me dead. Because if they want to harm me, then they'll surely try to harm Sisi too. And *that* I can't have.

"You can't promise that, Vlad. Even *you* are not omniscient or omnipotent," she chides gently, leaning back to look at me.

"I'll be the very near damned thing if it means making sure you're safe, Sisi."

"Oh, Vlad," she sighs, her eyes clear and fuck, so damned beautiful. "No matter how much I'd like to argue that sometimes things simply happen, I can't. I know what you're feeling because I feel it too." She takes my hand and places it on her chest, right above her heart.

"The thought that those men could get to you while you were incapacitated, or unable to fight them off almost killed me. I would have done *anything* to keep you safe."

"Then you understand. There's this monstrous rage inside of me, ready to be unleashed at the mere suggestion that you'd be in danger. And it's not my berserker rage. No, this is something so much more potent, so much more violent that I fear *no one* would make it out alive."

"I trust you," she immediately says and the words warm

my heart. Just a while ago I'd thought I would never be able to gain her trust back. "And I know I'm safe with you." The corner of her mouth pulls up.

"You're my protector," her smile widens, "my guardian devil," she cheekily adds and I find myself returning the smile. "As long as you're around I know that nothing and no one can harm me."

It humbles me to realize that she truly means those words. She actually trusts me to protect her, and in that moment I vow to never disappoint her.

"But maybe now you can tell me what *that* was all about." She looks at me questioningly, and I release a deep breath.

"I'm not entirely sure. Remember Meester from the club?" I ask, reminding her of the short encounter and that he's been the owner of the fighter who'd lost against Seth. "I don't know why he'd send people after me.

To my knowledge, the only time I offended him was years ago when I refused marriage to his daughter. But he would have had plenty of time to make attempts on my life *before* now," I add pensively.

Things aren't making much sense, and the more I think about it, the more I become suspicious of *everyone*.

"That's odd," she notes and I agree.

"I know I'm currently persona non grata on the East Coast, especially since I killed the leaders of most of the Russian syndicates in the area. Honestly, I would have expected *any* of them to be behind the attack, but Meester?" I shake my head, unable to find a logical connection. "Maybe if he's acting in conjunction with them?"

"Do you think he might be connected to Miles too?" Sisi asks, biting her lip in consternation.

I'd already given her a rundown of the situation with Miles, or at least the new information I'd gathered recently, including the fact that the attack at the warehouse must have had something to do with Miles.

After I'd realized that he had gone to Giovanni Lastra for funding, I'd gotten the idea that he couldn't have been the only one he'd reached out to.

Following the attack, when Vanya had called me out for being too complacent, I'd done a little digging inside the other syndicates' financials. The results had been rather predictable and most of them had been investing with a ghost company for *years*.

The only way I'd managed to connect that to Miles had been by cross-referencing some of the older transactions with those of Lastra, since he'd ended up making some payments to Miles.

As it stands, it's clear that Miles's enterprise isn't just the absurd work of a mad scientist. It's a business. And he's managed to rope some of the most dangerous men from the East Coast into it.

I'm still unsure about what he promised them or what the terms of their agreement were. I have to wonder if he promised them a cut of the business when he succeeded in creating the perfect soldier, or if they'd simply been interested in obtaining those soldiers for their own organizations.

Still, it seems a bit ludicrous that so many people would blindly invest based on mere theories and conjectures. In my memories, and to my knowledge, Miles had never succeeded in creating a perfect soldier.

There must be something I'm missing.

"Possibly," I admit. "I have Seth working in Boston, gathering intel from one of the ruling Bratvas. From what he's been telling me, it's not only money that these people have been funneling into Miles' business, but also people."

Sisi frowns. "You mean they've been scouting potential test subjects?"

"I'm a little unclear on that. Seth's managed to compile a list of missing people, but so far none have had the mutation. There is a chance it wasn't in their records. But with how rare it is," I purse my lips, "I doubt *all* would have had it."

"Then why would Miles need them? More tests? Maybe he's trying something different?"

"That's what we need to find out," I add grimly.

While in New Orleans, I'd tried not to think too much about Miles and the people gunning for me. I wanted to enjoy my time alone with Sisi. Together, in our little bubble, everything had been nothing short of perfect. But it seems I can't neglect this forever.

"One thing is for sure, though. Miles knows I'm looking for him, and he's been trying to take me out for a while," I say, a bleak expression on my face. All my snooping had gotten his attention at last. "But now Meester? If he's also working with Miles, then it might make sense."

"What's the plan?" she asks, "Because you always have a plan." She raises an eyebrow at me, and I chuckle.

"You're right. I've been keeping in touch with Nero and he's been sending me information about his time with Miles and whatever he could remember. Based on that, I put together a couple of places where Miles could have had his headquarters. Of course, I doubt he'd still be there today, but it's a place to start."

"If he's part of such a huge network, then I doubt he'd be so untraceable," Sisi comments.

"And yet he's been eluding me for *years*," I reply absent-mindedly before I still, my eyes widening. "Shit," I mutter.

"What?" Sisi frowns, stepping away from me.

"Let's do a quick recap." I stand up, pacing around the aisle of the plane. "I found out about Project Humanitas from your brother, Valentino, right around the time I realized Vanya had died. So that's about fifteen years ago," I start, feeling a small bubble of excitement build inside of me as I always do when I'm on the brink of a discovery.

"Then Misha's attempted coup happened around ten years ago, when Miles took Katya," I continue and my eyes widen as I remember the events.

"Fuck! Fuck! Fuck!" I curse out, suddenly everything dawning on me.

"What? What is it?" Sisi stands up, coming to my side.

"I got it all wrong, hell girl…" I shake my head. "When Bianca and I were ambushed, there were maybe six people total. If Miles was involved in the planning of it, then he should have known that six people would have never held me back. Let alone the fact that Bianca was with me too."

"You're thinking they weren't sent to kill you?" She narrows her eyes, but I see her features light up slowly as she gets it too. "They were sent to delay you," she finally says and I nod.

"Miles didn't want me dead. He just wanted me away so he could get to Katya. Just like he probably *knew* that Misha stood no chance once I got back."

"He played your brother. But why? All this work *not* to kill you and just take your sister?"

"Miles' mind doesn't work like regular people," I say, gritting my teeth. I should know because I've been emulating his way of thinking for the better part of two decades. "He needed Katya to continue his experiments in-house. But for me," I shake my head, smirking, "he had other plans."

"I don't understand." Sisi frowns.

"Think about it. Valentino found me in an abandoned place, with Vanya dead by my side. There was *no one* else around save for Nero. Now, why would Miles let me go if I were his *miracle*?"

Sisi blinks twice, and I watch as the wheels slowly turn in her head. My little nun may have grown in a convent, but there's no denying her innate intelligence and sage judgement. From the very beginning I've been in awe of the way her mind works, her keen senses of observation almost unparalleled.

Few people I've met have managed to surprise me as much as her, and that's one of the highest praises I could give someone. Of course, also one of the reasons why I love her so much.

"He did it on purpose. He *wanted* you to be found. But why…" Her brows furrow, her head tilted to the side as she ruminates. "God, he wanted to…" Her eyes widen at the realization and I nod.

"Exactly. He wanted to study me in my natural habitat so to speak. This means that I must have passed his tests, and I was ready to be let loose into the world. Nero too, and I wouldn't be surprised if it were Miles who got Nero his new bionic pieces through an intermediary. He's been observing us."

"My God! That's why he's always been a step ahead of you," she whispers, now getting the full picture. "He's been watching you this whole time, hasn't he?"

"That's what I think." I nod.

"Then why would he want you dead now?"

I smirk, suddenly the entire thing looking a little different.

"What if he doesn't exactly want me dead? What if it's just another test?"

"Damn," Sisi mutters, rubbing her arms. "That would make sense."

"But also, it might be that Miles is not personally behind the attacks," I add, offering another angle. "It is a business at its core, and me going after it full force would affect a lot of people."

"That's true too," Sisi sighs. "We have our work cut out for us, don't we?" She makes a feeble attempt at a smile.

"We'll figure it out, hell girl. Now if only I could remember *everything* that happened while I was with Miles… I could at least understand the entire scope of his research."

"Don't force yourself." Her hand reaches for mine, squeezing it in comfort. "The memories will come. When you're ready for them," she says and I grunt.

"There's another thing that's been plaguing me for a while," I tell her. "There was a third person involved with Misha. It's just circumstantial evidence, but based on the circle of connections, it *must* have been another syndicate person. Someone with interests in New York."

"You're right," she agrees, "because who else would have

direct access to both Misha and Miles if not someone who knew them both?"

I'd already gone through all of Misha's connections from New Jersey—most of them dead by now—and I'd come empty-handed. Still, there is one more person...

"I need to look again at all the people Misha had been in contact with," I tell her.

What I don't say is that I'm becoming increasingly sure that this person could be Meester. He knew my father and our family, and he sure as hell knew Misha. Besides, his heated attempt to get me married to his daughter years ago to get some footing in New York does make him suspicious.

But I haven't uncovered any evidence that he's been in contact with Miles—one way or another. That he'd sent an entire squad to finish me off does put him in the running, but I don't want to speak without having any proof to back up my hunch.

"We should do one of those connection boards like they have in detective shows," Sisi suggests, excited. "That way we can keep track of everyone."

"You know what, hell girl? That's not a bad idea at all," I praise her, entrusting her with the task of doing that when we get home.

Home...

Funny how it had never been home before. But one plucky former nun and my entire life's been turned upside down.

"Shit, Sisi. Your brother," I groan as the thought suddenly crosses my mind.

Surprisingly, he hadn't come looking for me in New Orleans. Knowing Marcello, I would have assumed he would send an entire army to rescue his saintly sister from the clutches of the devil—armed with holy water, of course.

But now that we'll be back in the Big Apple, there's no way Marcello won't be alerted to our presence.

"Don't worry. I'll handle that." Sisi puts her hand up, a serious expression on her face. "We'll go to the house and we'll *calmly* explain the circumstances. He's bound to understand, right?"

I don't want to scare her by telling her that there's no way in hell that Marcello's going to understand. But I find myself agreeing with her anyway.

"Exactly, it shouldn't be too bad." I nod, my features strained.

But she is right in one respect. The faster I solve the situation with Marcello, the sooner I'll have time to focus *all* my attention on Miles and his cronies. Though I am sure there *will* be blood spilled.

"There's also Guerra," Sisi bites the inside of her cheek, looking worried. "I don't think they're too pleased either. They'll want some type of retribution to save face."

"I'll deal with Guerra, don't worry." I wave my hand dismissively. They're the least of my concerns right now.

"How?"

"Let's just say I have something they want." The corner of my mouth tugs up. "And they would certainly be put out if I were to offer my services to DeVille instead."

"You're devious." Sisi punches my arm playfully.

"It's the politics of our world." I shrug. "And you're becoming better and better at dealing with them."

"I adapt," she replies, a haunted look on her face. "I always adapt."

Snaking an arm around her, I bring her into me, her front flush against mine. It will never cease to amaze me that despite our different sizes we fit so well, her place right at home in my arms.

"You don't have to adapt anymore, hell girl. From now on, the world will adapt to *you*." I tell her, taking a strand of her hair and pushing it gently behind her ear to get a better look of her lovely face.

She raises her eyes at me, her gaze dazed as she's trying to ascertain the veracity of my words.

"I made a vow to you, Sisi. I'll lay the entire world at your feet. *No one* will ever look down on you again."

I tip her chin up, leaning forward to press a kiss on her lips.

"From now on, everyone will bow *to you*," I continue, watching a small tear make its way down her face.

Pressing my thumb to her skin, I wipe it away.

"You're my goddess," I murmur softly, "my wife, my partner," I lay another kiss on her cheek, tasting fresh tears, "my everything. And that means we rule together."

"Sometimes you're too sweet." She lifts her hand to stroke my jaw, her lips widening in a gorgeous smile.

"Only for you, hell girl. You're my one exception."

"And you're mine," she replies, twinning her arms behind my neck and tugging me toward her, our lips meeting in a heart-stopping kiss.

Truth is, everything I'm doing *is* for her, and will *always* be for her. Including facing my past.

Because I know we'll never be able to live in peace with so many loose threads hanging over our heads.

25
VLAD

he images come unbidden. *My brows twitch as I see
myself going deeper and deeper into a foreign landscape, the
entire scenery unfamiliar and confounding.*

Yet one thing is for sure.

This is me.

*"You have twenty minutes to complete the task," a voice rings out
through a speaker.*

I look around me, establishing my environment.

*The room is the size of a stadium, bleak gray walls surrounding it.
In front of me, there are a few walls that look like obstacles, all of
different sizes, obscuring what lays behind them. There is a big board
close to the ceiling displaying the names of all the participants, each
having a zero next to it—the score for today's game.*

*To my right and left, I see other children, all around my age. They
are in a tense position, their eyes focused as they are waiting for the
signal.*

I don't know how I know that, but I just do.

*In fact, the entire situation feels somehow off. I feel like myself, but
yet my mind feels empty for some reason. There's a steely determination*

to win against all odds. I see it clearly how the only thing that matters is victory.

Aside from that, I can't feel anything.

There's no fear, no worry—nothing. I pat myself down to make sure my weapons are in their designated spots, and at the same time I get the opportunity to check that I am in fact human.

There's a hollowness in my mind that I've never encountered before. Even in my worst moments, I've never been this empty. Like my entire body is just a case housing an absent consciousness.

Still, there's a sharpness to my gaze as I filter and catalogue everything around me. I take note of how many people I'm competing against and I'm making ten simultaneous plans—one for each potential move my enemy might make.

"On your positions," the voice from the speakers announces, and I flex my knees, ready to take off at the designated time.

My hands are wrapped around the hilts of knives secured to my waist, and I know that I will let no one beat me at this.

In fact, my mouth pulls up as I imagine the river of blood that will flow from my hands—the only positive emotion I've felt so far.

The signal is given and everyone starts running.

I don't know much about the obstacles or what lays behind the walls, but I know that nothing can stop me.

I pass the first wall, and I see from the corner of my eyes a small automatic weapon hidden in the floor. It's swift and silent as it opens up and starts shooting toward us.

One boy gets nabbed in the arm, while another gets shot in the face, his entire skull exploding before my eyes, pieces of blood, bone and brain matter scattering across the floor with some landing on me too.

I smirk as I duck and dodge, watching the twitch of the weapon closely and calculating angles.

From the first moment I noticed it, I started observing for patterns, the way the body would slightly tilt to one degree in either direction before loading up to shoot.

A matter of focusing on even the tiniest movement, and I'm able to calculate the place the bullet will land.

While everyone is trying to haphazardly avoid the incoming bullets, I know exactly where they will hit a second before they do.

Luckily, my body is well trained, and there's no delay between my mental command and the execution of the movement. Fluidly moving through the bullets, I'm rushing toward the point of origin, jumping in the air and landing right behind the barrel of the gun.

I know I have a couple of seconds at most before it turns toward me, so I channel all my strength in my arm, grabbing the metal body and wrench it from the floor, throwing it backwards. And because I'm keeping track of the limited time, I don't linger.

The board displaying our names suddenly changes to show the dead, as well as the ones advancing to the next level. I look up to see my name in white with a one hundred score next to it.

The first round.

Somehow, I know that I need to reach one thousand points to be crowned the winner. Ten rounds to be won, ten rounds to show how much I've improved.

There are other people too running around me, all of them having the same intense concentration, keeping their eyes on the prize.

It's still too early in the game to start fighting one another, the trials just beginning. Yet I know that whoever will reach the end with me is already dead, and my eyes filter around the room, studying each person to ponder my competition.

A smile pulls at my lips as I realize that this will be a piece of cake. The harder part is getting across all the obstacles.

With no time to linger, I hurry forward, the next stage of the test starting. Passing by yet another wall that delimitates the trials, I find a pit filled with vipers that takes up all the space in this enclosed area. And in order to advance to the next level, I have to cross it.

Fast.

There's a small rope tied from one end of the pit to the other, crossing right over the vipers. The rope is maybe the size of my palm in thickness. Enough to accommodate one foot at a time.

Considering I've had extensive balance training over time, crossing it would be a piece of cake. The only issue is that the vipers have already been agitated and they reek of violence as they hiss at me.

The moment my foot will hit that rope, I know they will pounce on me. I bet Miles is looking from the sidelines, enjoying the grotesque show we're putting on for him.

And if he wants a show, he will have one.

I still, watching how a couple of girls hurry on the rope, banking on speed to get to the other side. Although their movements are not slow, they are certainly no match for angry vipers.

The snakes attack from all directions, going for their legs and scaring them into falling down into the pit.

Their screams echo inside the room, and I lower my gaze, my lips pulling upwards as I watch tens of vipers coil over their bodies, their venom being injected into their skin.

I let another boy shoot his shot too, and I'm not surprised when he too ends up falling down, the vipers taking him by surprise.

There are more behind me watching with trepidation, probably trying to calculate how to best weather this.

I take a step forward, and with a quick glance toward the pit, I decide my time has come.

Placing my entire body weight on the tips of my toes, I concentrate on regulating my breath and slowing down my heart beats.

When I know I'm close to a catatonic state, or as I like to call it, quiet, I move.

One foot on the rope, my eyes are shrewdly assessing the situation downstairs, my ears perked to hear every sound made by a sudden attack.

I move quickly, and not even three steps later the first viper attack comes. Jumping up, I watch as it skids past the rope before lowering itself back in the pit.

My feet land back on the rope, my balance in check as I lean forward, the arch of my foot making contact with the small surface. I don't waste time as I prop myself on my hands, doing a somersault in the air while avoiding two more incoming vipers.

I thrust my body forward to cover as much distance as I can, my breath slow and calm.

This is key.

I can never let panic take over me. The moment I allow that, it's game over.

And so I continue to do a combination of jumps, high somersaults and hand walking on the rope, twisting around to avoid the snakes, sometimes using my feet to kick them.

Just as I am closer to the other end, I hear a hiss nearing and I realize it's coming from behind me.

From the proximity of the sound, I realize I have no time to duck. So I just turn around, my arm stretched out as my hand catches the head of the viper mid-air, my fingers squeezing its jaw shut so it's unable to bite.

Before I get rid of it, though, I force its sharp teeth into a patch of material from my clothes, pressing forward until the venom starts seeping from its glands. Gathering it tightly, I secure it in a makeshift pouch.

Flinging the viper away from me, I jump on to the firm surface of the other side.

Not wasting another breath, I quickly hurry to the next trial.

A small chamber with a floating target, I pick up a small set of knives. The instructions are pretty simple. The target is touch sensitive, and every time I hit the center, I earn ten points. Ten throws and that's it.

Coincidentally, this is one of my favorite tests, since my aim is pretty darn perfect, if I do say so myself.

Glibly grabbing the knives, I let my eyes follow the target around for a bit, trying to learn its patterns. Since I'm convinced that a computer is controlling the movements, I know there must be a hidden pattern that will allow me to guess the next position.

Surely enough, a few seconds and I note a slight undulation, the target doing two ups before going once down. Then it goes twice down before going once up. The rhythm is repeated, but instead of a straight line, the target is moving in circular motions. Still, the pattern is clear.

I close my eyes, relying on my hearing as I count the positions.

Aim.

The knife embeds itself right in the middle, a loud noise denoting the added points next to my name on the screen.

A smug expression on my face, I just continue to anticipate each position, throwing knives right and left.

In no time, I've accumulated the highest number of points possible, finishing the trial.

Next are a few similar ones involving a combination of weapons and explosives. The first one is still testing our aim, but also our reflexes as we assemble a weapon from zero in order to shoot it at different targets. The second one is a bit trickier, as it asks us to detangle the wires from a complex C4 explosive.

The amount of C4 isn't too much, but it's enough to blast the one person who is messing with the wires. And so it is a life and death situation.

Luckily, I've been paying attention to all the lessons, and I've memorized every single piece of information.

It's gotten to a point where I don't know if my memory is mine or if it's been thrust upon me in one of Miles's crazy experiments.

All I know is that I only need to see something once in order to remember it forever, I'm able to dissect it at atom levels long after I'd seen it.

And so I pass the explosives test too.

Halfway through.

I know enough about Miles' wicked mind to only expect the worst. After all, this is a test to separate the weak from the strong. The ones who will proceed forward and the ones who will not.

Dead.

In the back of my mind, I feel a little pulsation as I think about my sister, the first semblance of feeling in a long time. At least I'd managed to spare her by being Miles' exclusive guinea pig. She's been worsening from all the experiments he'd subjugated her to, and her body is slowly failing her.

I know it. Miles knows it. Everybody knows it. Still, if I can keep her alive, I will.

I'll do anything to ensure her safety.

I barely see her nowadays, though. Miles has me either in training or in testing every single day. The most I manage is to say a few words to her before I go to sleep. Even with my new physical enhancements I'm having some trouble keeping up with some aspects of Miles' program.

The psychological tests have been the hardest, because I could tell that slowly, without even realizing, they were changing me from the inside out.

From the very beginning I've been forced to sit in a dark room with only one screen, nonstop watching atrocity after atrocity until I've become desensitized to everything.

Flesh? Blood? Bone?

I don't think there's anything that can phase me anymore. Certainly not even as I do it myself, the videos are weirdly educational as they taught me how to cut and probe, the entire human anatomy suddenly at my fingertips.

And Miles had been delighted when he'd seen that I could memorize everything after one watch. So he'd started letting me perform some of the experiments.

When you've shut even the last sane part of yourself, there's hardly anything that can make you react. In fact, the more I'd started delving into the secrets of the human body, the more intrigued I'd become, finally starting to share Miles' enthusiasm.

I wouldn't put myself in the same category as him, but at the same time I know I'm not far off.

I barely keep my head in the game anymore. A few more mundane tests and I'm in the lead with a perfect score. I'm… bored.

We should just end this now, since we all know who's going to be the victor. But Miles isn't one to cut corners. Even if he has to sacrifice other potential soldiers in the process, he will see this through, ensuring that only the fittest are allowed to the next level.

Going through the motions, I realize I'm already at the ninth task, and as I see what it is, my mood suddenly improves.

Torture.

The voice from the speakers explains the task. Each contestant that's gotten to this point has to get information from the prisoners—all part of the Mossad.

Known for their thorough training, they are the least likely to break. Especially in the face of a few scrawny children.

My target is in front of me in a chair, hands and feet tied, a bag over his head.

I circle him a couple of times, trying to determine who I'm dealing with.

Another tidbit I'd learned from Miles, but body language can offer a wealth of information. Truth to be told, my only weakness is in recognizing facial emotions. That's why I never focus on the face.

Instead, I look at how the legs twitch slightly, or how the muscles in his arms seem to involuntarily move when he hears me walk around him.

He's studying me just as I am him, and the prospect of finding someone of equal footing has a brand new type of excitement simmering inside of me.

I may be but a child, but my knowledge far surpasses most people. My training too, is nothing to scoff at, and I know that I'll only improve as I grow.

And so to start my session, I remove the bag from his head, letting him see me, watching closely the way his shoulders relax, his entire body at ease as he undoubtedly thinks a child cannot possibly harm him.

Yes, underestimate me. It will be your death.

As much as I'm wont to admit, Miles has given me the best education. Drawing from resources from all over the globe, my mind is rife with every type of knowledge one would need to succeed in this murky torture business.

That coupled with my anatomical experience makes me the perfect candidate to exact the perfect torture.

One look at the countdown and I see I have ten more minutes until the entire test is over. But considering there's another level, I don't want to risk it by spending too much time with this gentleman.

I look down at the note in my hands, the prompt saying I must find out the location of a couple of off-the-books nuclear weapons hidden somewhere along the coast line.

There's a very basic kit of knives and torture tools. Nothing too fancy, just enough to do the job.

He wants us, after all, to improvise on our own. Use our creativity and show him that his lessons have not been in vain.

A sly smile appears on my face as I drag my fingers over the tools, knowing he's watching me closely.

Like me, he's trying to gauge who he's dealing with.

But unlike me, he's already underestimating my abilities.

I pick up the smallest blade, testing its sharpness on my leg. Satisfied with the result, blood trickling down the moment the tip of the blade makes contact with the surface of my skin, I bring it to my lips, licking it clean.

The man is looking at me as if he can't quite believe what he's seeing.

Good. He's starting to become rattled.

Careful with the blade, I bring it to his shirt, the material giving way immediately, his naked chest in sight.

"Any organ you're particularly fond of?" I raise my eyebrows at him in question.

He sputters against his gag, thrashing in his bounds as he's trying to move toward me.

"Tsk, tsk. Now, that's simply rude," I add, plowing the knife right in his thigh, the move calculated, so I don't accidentally nab the femoral artery. Still, it's lodged not far off, ensuring direct blood flow to the artery.

The knife is so deeply embedded in his body, I can feel the bone right under the tip, a scratchy noise ringing out as I push and move it around inside the wound, creating a small socket. The sound is almost *like nails on a chalkboard, the sharpness of the knife ensuring in cutting all muscle and connective tissue.*

He can't even scream out in pain, though he wants to. And I am immensely saddened by that, since it would have been music to my ears. After all, it's all I know.

Opening my small pouch, I take the knife out, watching as the blood shoots out like a small geyser, staining his clothes and falling to the floor.

He's watching me intently as I dip the knife into the pouch, coating the tip in a viscous substance.

He frowns, narrowing his eyes at me.

"Venom," I give him a wide smile, "viper venom," I amend. When I'm done scooping up all the venom, I simply place the knife back inside the wound, watching his face contort in inhumane agony, his skin turning red, his eyes bulging in his head as he's trying to bear through it all.

Ah, but this is just the beginning.

Letting him stew in the venom—literally, I turn my attention back to his chest, quickly making an incising from his clavicle to his navel.

Still having some trace amounts of venom, the moment the toxic substance hits his open flesh, he winces back in pain. It must be like a burning sensation that keeps on gaining depth. And as I cut deeper, his reactions worsen too.

"Let's see," I hum appreciatively as I carefully open up his stomach, flaps of skin on each side. "I believe you can still live with one kidney," I add, my hand hovering over the cozy pair in his side. "I wonder, though, how painful is the removal without anesthetic?" I ask pensively.

He's still not passed out from pain, which in itself is a feat and speaks of his training. Still, the moment he hears about his kidneys, and especially as he can gaze down into his own open belly, his face falls in resignation.

Got him.

Gag off, he's rattling off everything I needed to know.

Eyes on the clock I notice I have five more minutes until the end. Satisfied with his answers, I simply swing the blade under his throat, cutting him up and ensuring a quick death before moving to the final round.

Crossing the final wall, I'm met with a surprising sight.

Miles is casually sitting on a couch, two tables on either side of him.

Even though I'm the first to arrive, there are a few others who also make it.

Immediately, we are motioned at the tables, split in pairs.

I'm coupled with a guy a couple years older than me at one table, while at the other table there is one girl with another boy my age.

In front of us is a spread out Go board game. My lips twitch as I realize what the final trial is.

Strategy.

Miles is a Go aficionado, and he has his own board in his office. He'd even taught me how to play it once, so I have the basics down.

Like chess, one player is assigned the white side while the other the black. But unlike chess, the game pieces are small, round stones. The aim of the game is to gain space on the board.

Like a warring map, the pieces are like flags in areas conquered, the winner being the one with the most pieces on the board.

It's a tiivating game, and certainly one that can give pause to anyone.

Still, it's no wonder that Miles has chosen this, aside from his personal interest in it. The game relies on the strategic placements of the stones to maximize territory. In his eyes, our success on the board should mirror our success in the outside world.

There is just one tricky aspect.

Three minutes.

With three minutes on the clock, it's unlikely that we'll be able to finish a Go game and proclaim a winner. These games can last hours, if not days, so three minutes is really absurd.

Yet as I look at Miles, his insidious smile wide and almost feral, I realize he knows that too.

I shut down my skeptical side and instead focus on the game at hand, victory my only aim. So what if it's nearly impossible? I've been defying the impossible for as long as I remember. This shouldn't be too hard.

The seconds stretch as we start placing our pieces on the board. I'm black while my opponent is white. The moment the game begins, though, my mind hones on anticipating every move he could possibly make.

As long as I manage to calculate his moves in advance, I should be able to also calculate the amount of tries it would take me to win the game.

Our hands move with extreme speed as piece after piece is settled on a square, the territories starting to take shape.

My opponent isn't bad. But he's not great either, which works in my favor.

One minute and thirty-five seconds.

By now half the board is full, my pieces overshadowing his. But there is one tricky aspect to Go. Unless he declares that he's forfeiting, then the game could go on forever.

And so with the seconds trickling by, time ticking, my resolve for victory strengthens. I double down my efforts, picturing all possible outcomes in my mind as I lay a piece down.

I need to corner him so badly that he won't have any other option than forfeiting the game.

Three more moves and I have him where I want. One look at him and his lips are trembling, his entire face sweaty from the mental exertion.

I raise an eyebrow at him, waiting for him to make a move where there's none.

His shoulders slump, and eventually he resigns himself to being the losing party.

There's a resounding bleep in the room, and everyone suddenly stands up.

"Well, well," Miles says, uncrossing his legs and rising from the couch. He's slow as he comes toward me, his hand on my back.

"It seems we have a winner," he declares and a smug expression appears on my face. I don't even stop to think what might be happening to the ones who lost, basking in the praise Miles is offering me and knowing it is limited.

As a mini celebration, Miles takes me to his office, offering me a glass of his precious bourbon and telling me his grand plans.

"We're almost there, Vlad," he sighs happily. "I don't think I've ever seen someone as impressive as you, my boy. You've certainly surpassed my expectations."

I just nod, taking in all the compliments and vowing to do better. Because while I'd been reluctant in the beginning, I now recognize that this isn't just about me.

It's about revolutionizing science and the way humans are seen. It's simply evolution, and I aim to be at the top when these findings are made public.

Certainly, in the beginning I'd thought that Miles' ideas were strange and a little irrational. But soon it had become clear that he was onto something.

After repeated trials, my skin stopped hurting, the pain a slow echo reverberating in my brain, but one I could shut off. My mind too acquired a new focus as clarity started to filter through my old haze of emotions.

He was right. Getting rid of feelings, and especially of fear, was liberating unlike anything. That coupled with the rush of adrenaline when I cut into flesh, dissected organs and played with tissue was almost godly.

I'm smart enough to realize that there seems to be an inverse proportional relationship between my feelings and my hubris. As my emotions became muted, my arrogance grew, my vanity knowing no bounds.

But that arrogance also made me the best, because it made me want to continually strive to be the best.

"And now for your prize," Miles adds, getting up and showing me a poker with a metal circle at the top, the number one hundred etched inside.

Going to his fireplace, he extends the metal into the fire, watching as it becomes hot, the material turning a deep red.

"You've officially completed your one hundredth kill, my little miracle. It's time to celebrate," he drawls, taking the hot poker and motioning me to show him my skin.

I don't even flinch as I tear down my neckline, grabbing onto my shirt and directing him to place it right in the middle of my chest.

With a satisfied smile, he does, his happiness only growing as the smell of burned flesh permeates the air.

As usual, there's a slight echo of pain, but I thrust it aside, focusing on this important day.

It's late when I made it back to the sleeping quarters.

Vanya is on her back, as usual, her stomach wounds still giving her trouble from the last experiment.

Weak.

I can't help it as my mind hones in on those words.

She's weak. Not worthy.

"V." I nod to her when she raises herself on her elbows to peer at me.

"You were gone a long time, brother," she says in that sweet voice of hers and for a moment I feel an unfamiliar—almost forgotten—pang in my chest.

"I won." I shrug, proudly showing her my brand.

She doesn't react as I expect her to. She barely glances at me as she gathers her knees to her chest, placing her cheek on top of them and sighing deeply.

I take a seat too, laying down on my side of the mattress.

"I'm scared, brother," she whispers, her voice barely audible.

Scared. Fear. Weakness.

"Why?" I ask mechanically.

"Change." She takes a deep breath, turning her eyes toward me. "Change is scary," she notes.

"It's not," I answer a little more aggressively than intended. "Being static is scary. Change is good," I point out.

"Until it's not…" she trails off, "Because it doesn't have to be a good change. It can also be a bad change."

"What are you getting at, Vanya?" I snap.

"You, brother. You're changing. And I don't know if I like it," she murmurs, her voice small as she looks away from me.

Without saying another word, she turns with her back to me, promptly ending the conversation.

I stare at the ceiling of our still dirty cell, counting the spots of mold as I listen to Vanya's even breath as she sleeps.

Change…

Maybe she has a point. There are some moments of lucidity where

I ask myself what I'm doing. But then I'm once again embroiled in Miles' fascinating world of science, murder, and morbid curiosities.

And I let myself slip.

26

VLAD

"Vlad?" a voice calls out to me.

My muscles are coiled with tension as I open my eyes, every fiber in my body charged with violence as the memories ring in my mind. Miles had had me wrapped around his little finger.

I'd failed Vanya and I'd failed myself.

One arrogant taste of blood and I'd succumbed, leaving everything behind in exchange for the pursuit of twisted knowledge in gratification of my pseudo-superior intellect.

There's a nothingness inside of me that echoes in my chest, the imprint from the memories too strong, their hold on me even in my waking state too powerful.

I turn to look at the source of the noise, my own mind a derelict place filled with screaming fragments and weeping bells, the ability to recognize reality dim.

Her hair is so light, it looks like a ray of sun aiming to blind me, the urge to shield my eyes increasingly strong. A few strands of hair fall lightly down her forehead, framing a heart-shaped face.

I feel another pang in my chest as I stare at her, a painfully beautiful sight that makes me suffocate, my lungs strained as air becomes trapped inside.

She blinks, her eyes unusually light and quite possibly the most alluring sight I've seen in my life. Leaning forward, she places her hand on my cheek, her voice still ringing in my ears as she keeps on repeating my name.

That small touch activates something inside of me.

My nostrils flare as I take in her scent, a mix of clean soap and something that's inherently *her.* Like flowers on a new spring day, there's a sweetness that inundates my senses, my entire body shuddering as I close my eyes, simply inhaling.

"Vlad," she calls out again, and my eyes snap open, narrowing as they move lower over her body.

She's wearing a skimpy top that leaves nothing to the imagination, her tits full, her nipples pebbled. Moving lower, I note a small expanse of stomach peeking out from tight pants that accentuate shapely hips.

My own pants become painfully tight, my mouth dry as the desert as I swallow uncomfortably.

Need.

There's a mounting need inside of me, and I only know I need her more than I need my next breath. There's something achingly familiar about her, and in a sea of nothingness, she's that small wave that crashes against my being.

I only know that I *need* to own her, to make her so irrevocably mine that she can never escape me.

And so without thinking, I let instinct take over, my body already knowing what it wants even as my mind struggles to keep up.

My arm shoots out, settling against the small of her back and dragging her on top of me. She comes naturally, her legs on either side of mine as she straddles me.

Eyes glazed, I can only watch her in fascination, my nose buried in the crook of her neck as I trail it up and down, wanting to imprint myself with her scent.

Surprisingly, she doesn't put up a fight as I bring her even tighter against me, my senses overwhelmed by her presence as I seek to get my fill of her.

I move my face up her neck, inhaling. Reaching her lips, I let my tongue trace the seam, licking my way to her cheek.

My chest expands with unbearable tension, my cock so hard it could burn a hole through my pants. And she's not helping, squirming ever so slightly and aligning her pelvis right on top of my shaft.

One hand on her nape, my fingers digging in her flesh, I bring her close to me, raising my gaze to let her see the storm brewing inside of me, a savageness waiting to be unleashed—with her the only target.

Her pupils are dilated with desire, her rosy mouth parted as she breathes hard, her ass moving slightly over my erection, her lashes fluttering up and down in a hypnotizingly seductive move.

Holding eye contact, I lower my mouth to her chest, taking one nipple between my teeth, letting my tongue wet the bud through her shirt.

She pushes her tits further into my face, practically begging me to lavish them with attention. A pained, guttural sound escapes me, needing to be closer to her. No, *demanding* to be closer to her.

Her soft whimpers caress my ears, her little movements only serving to make me more unstable.

Using my tongue, I leave a wet trail from the valley of her breasts to her neck and finally to her face. She's at my mercy as she gives me those pouty lips, allowing me to sample everything she has to offer.

Taking her lower lip between my teeth, I nibble at it, all the while watching every play of emotion on her face, attuned to everything that is *her*.

I don't necessarily understand what's happening to me, but I give myself over to this insanity that's threatening to burst out of me.

Holding her closer, I suck her tongue in my mouth, exploring the depths of her mouth and wondering at the way my body responds. My cock swells even more in my pants, and I feel the tip leaking, my balls heavy and almost painful.

Her lips close over mine, deepening the kiss as she lets me swallow her whole, the urgency of the kiss making me sweat with impatience and anticipation. Her tongue plays with mine, letting me take the lead as I chase and she retreats, each stroke sending a bolt of lightning to my cock and making it twitch against my zipper.

Her fingers on my upper arms, her nails are digging into my skin.

I trail my hands down her back until I reach her ass, palming the bountiful globes and enjoying their weight as I knead them, bringing her pussy closer to my crotch and letting her grind on me harder.

But even that is not enough as I feel something overtake

me, an insane animalistic instinct that *demands* that I take her.

Fuck her so hard and deep that she loses sight of life and death, of me and her, or anything else.

My hands on the material of her pants, I grab roughly on to the edge, pulling the seams apart and ripping the fabric.

I don't know what I'm doing. I only know that I need to be inside her.

She gasps, but she doesn't move away, helping me divest of her pants—or what's left of them. Her musky scent of arousal invades my senses and makes me lose my mind. My hand goes between her legs to find her soaked, more moisture dripping from her entrance as I play with her.

"Mmm," her sexy sounds do nothing but increase my urgency as I more or less rip the zipper of my pants in my attempt to get them off.

My dick bounces out, so fucking hard and growing even harder as I know her pussy's waiting for me. Pre-cum leaking from the tip, I swipe my finger over the head, combining our juices, bringing it up to her lips.

Her eyes widen, but she wraps those full lips around my finger, sucking it and swirling her tongue around it.

I groan out loud, that sight is enough to bring me over the edge.

My entire body is strained, and I know I can't waste another second.

My fingers digging into her ass cheeks, I lift her over my erection, impaling her in one thrust.

A low moan escapes her as I push into her body, feeling the way she squeezes the life out of me, her tight little body taking me so deep my balls meet her ass, a loud sound reverberating through the air as flesh meets flesh.

"Fuck," I curse out, clarity and confusion both making their home in my mind.

Like a man possessed, I grip her hips tightly, barreling into her pussy with such an intensity the head of my cock slams against the back of her womb.

Head thrown back she releases a strangled moan as she grips my arms even tighter for support.

"Sisi," I hear my own voice as I say her name, my thrusts increasing in speed.

Deep down I know I'm not being gentle, too much aggression rolling off of me as I maneuver her around.

But even that isn't enough.

I need deeper. Faster. Harder.

"Yes," she cries out as I stand up, taking her with me, her body still sliding up and down my length. She's so fucking wet, her juices are all over my dick and pooling over my balls.

Still holding on to her waist, I settle her on a table, her back hitting the cold surface as I practically tear her top apart.

I watch enthralled as her tits bounce up and down with every thrust, and I can't help myself as my hands close over them, playing with her nipples.

"Fucking hell, Sisi," I grunt, her eyes half closed, her breath hitching every time I hit deep within her womb. "I don't think I've been harder in my life," I tell her, my own breathing ragged.

The marks left by my hands are already showing on her

body, deep, red finger marks that show she's been handled roughly and it only makes me want to brand her further.

"Vlad," she starts, barely able to talk, my thrusts increasing in speed, the table quaking under the assault. Coupled with the fact that we're in air, the sensation is completely mind-blowing. "It's too much," she breathes out, "too good... too..."

She's out of control as her cries intensify, her hands gripping the edge of the table as she tries to ground herself, each violent thrust threatening to send her off the table.

I trail one hand over her stomach and down to her pussy.

Seeing her pretty lips opening up for me and swallowing me whole has me over the edge.

"Feel this, hell girl." I take her hand and bring it to the base of my cock. "Feel how I'm fucking you."

She wraps her small fingers over my thickness, feeling the slippery mess made by her pussy as she moves her hand up and down my length, jerking me off just as the tip moves in circular motions at her entrance, stretching her and stimulating the sensitive area.

"Feel how your pussy's taking me so fucking deep." I grab her hand again, this time pressing it over her lower stomach at the same time as I fully surge inside her, her legs wrapping around my waist as my balls slap against her ass.

I let her feel the contour of my dick through her belly, the head poking slightly every time I thrust into her.

"You're so big..." she whimpers, looking down at her stomach and the way my cock molds to her insides. "God, I feel you in my soul," she sighs, her head hitting the table and thrashing to the side. I make a tsk sound at her, alerting her of her mistake.

"What did I say about God?" I ask her playfully.

I flick my thumb over her clit, teasing it slowly, her back arching on the table, her entire body going slack. Her walls contract around me, gripping me tightly, her sudden release making her scream for mercy.

"Not yet, hell girl. Not yet," I chuckle as I see a flush envelop her entire body, her face red as she breathes hard, incoherent sounds slipping past her lips.

"Now, who's your God?" I continue to pet her little clit, enjoying the way she keeps on spasming, begging me to stop.

"You. Only you," she pants, "you're my God. My everything." She ends on a gasp as another orgasm claims her.

She's so fucking responsive, coming so alive in my arms.

And I have only one goal in life—seeing to her pleasure. And that means I'm *never* going to stop. Not until she's had so many orgasms, she can hardly move. That's the only evidence I need to know I'm doing my job right.

"And you're mine." She turns her hand to wrap it around my own as she looks into my eyes, so much emotion welling in her gaze. "You're all mine," she repeats.

"Yes, hell girl," I give her hand a quick squeeze, "all yours. Body and soul," I tell her, watching the lazy smile that pulls at her lips, her entire face lighting up and making my own frozen heart melt.

She has the power to turn me to dust. And with one smile she has the power to make me indomitable.

Only with her by my side do I feel like I can conquer the world.

It's funny how I've always been a cocky bastard, but it

wasn't until her that I understood what true confidence really meant.

Her love for me gave me hope. And my love for her gave me the confidence I needed to push through.

I'm so focused on her that I barely hear my phone ringing. Mid-thrust, I stop briefly to check the caller ID, realizing it's Nero.

Frowning, I wonder what could possibly be so important since he's never contacted me directly before.

A quick glance at my girl, naked and all spread out on the table, and I know I can't disappoint her.

My lips tug up as I accept the call, setting it on speaker and placing the phone on the table before sheathing myself inside her body again.

27
VLAD

"**V**lad," Nero speaks, his voice loud in the small plane.

Sisi's eyes widen when she sees what I did, and she tries to disentangle herself from me. I don't let her move as I prop one hand in place on her hip, bringing her pussy flush against the base of my cock and ensuring I'm balls deep inside of her before I put my other hand over her mouth, knowing she *can't* keep quiet.

"Yes," I reply, trying to sound unaffected even as I continue to fuck my girl. The only noises in the room are those of skin against skin, the slippery wetness produced by her pussy enhancing the sounds.

Sisi looks embarrassed, but also turned on, her body eagerly seeking mine as she pushes herself into me every time I slow my thrusts.

"I remembered something slightly off about the orphanage my brother and I were in," he says, and my little minx has the gall to bite my finger off.

A smile threatens to form on my face at her audacity. Still

keeping my hand on her mouth, I muffle her sounds as I grab her hip, tugging her closer. Slipping completely out of her, I rub the underside of my cock over her clit, watching the way her eyes seem to flutter closed, her mouth open under my palm.

"Since we were recruited for Project Humanitas right from there, I thought I'd inquire a little to see if they know anything."

"Go on," I prompt him, my voice a little strained.

"The headmistress had changed, of course, but I was able to talk her into showing me their archive," he continues.

"And?"

"There wasn't much, but I found a picture of my brother and me. I've sent it to you just now. It's from one of the Christmas celebrations that the orphanage organized every year in conjunction with some church," he says and I frown.

"Church?"

"I'd mostly forgotten all about it, but there was this lady that always came by to inspect the children. For the longest time I thought she was with the Red Cross because she would also give us physical exams," he explains and I'm intrigued to see where this is going.

At the same time, I feel Sisi smile under my palm, her hand reaching out for my cock, her fingers brushing against the sensitive spot right under the head.

I hiss, shooting her a warning glance, but she doesn't comply.

She pushes me back into her body, clenching her walls at the same time and holding me captive in the tightest place I've ever been.

My body starts sweating profusely as I try my best not to come then and there, the orgasm almost rolling off me.

"Right," I reply, and this time my voice definitely sounds off.

"But now I realize she was from the church. And right after our last physical exam, we were taken from the orphanage and to Miles' facility."

"You think that lady might have had something to do with it?" I ask, my mind tuning in to his words, but my body a slave to Sisi's.

"It might be a lead. I've been trying to track her down since I found the picture, but I thought you'd have more luck," he says and I grunt.

"I'll see what I can do," I reply, quickly thanking him and telling him I'll keep him in the loop.

I quickly end the call, turning my attention to my little minx. Hand off her mouth, she's now grinning at me as she grinds her pelvis, slowly fucking herself on my cock.

"You're wicked," she whispers.

I'm already so close and after holding off my release for so long, there's only one place where I'd like to come.

Pulling out of her, I take a step back.

"On your knees, hell girl," I command her and she dares to bat her eyelashes at me.

"Is that so?" she asks with a soft mew, undulating her body toward me.

"Now, brat," I grit, my voice thick, my balls aching for relief.

Sin incarnate, she moves her body like she's giving me my own personal show. Hopping off the table, she lowers herself to her knees, my cock twitching as she wets her lips with her tongue.

"You don't know how to take orders, do you?" I grip her jaw, gazing down at her.

"Hmm," she hums, leaning into me until her cheek grazes the underside of my cock. She moves slowly, her tongue sneaking out to lick the head before opening wide to take me deep inside.

"Fuck," I mutter as she sucks the tip, her tongue playing with the slit.

One second with her pretty mouth on me and I'm already going crazy. Hand tightly wrapped in her hair, I force myself deeper into her mouth, thrusting until my cock hits the back of her throat.

She gags, spit dribbling down her chin, tears at the corner of her eyes as I fuck her mouth just like I did her pussy.

Like an animal.

Eyes on me, her hands are on my ass as she holds herself still, relaxing her throat to welcome me as deep as she can. Still, her lips are only halfway around my cock.

I feel my balls contract, my release nearing. I pull her head back a little, only the tip remaining in her mouth, more spit accumulating around her mouth and down my cock.

And fuck if I've seen anything hotter.

"Don't swallow," I tell her, her big, tear-streaked eyes looking at me in confusion. She nods, her face achingly innocent and angelic, yet I know what lies beneath the surface.

Sin. My sin.

Her lips wrapped around the head, I fist my cock,

stroking myself until spurts of cum shoot into her waiting mouth.

Like the obedient girl she is—this time—she doesn't swallow.

"Show me how you take my seed, hell girl," I prompt her, stroking her cheek. "Let me see my cum on your tongue."

My dick falls from her lips, and I watch in fascination as she opens her mouth to show me her tongue, cum coating the entire surface with some dripping down the sides of her face.

She looks so thoroughly fucked—and marked—that I can't help the way my heart swells in my chest.

Dropping to my knees next to her, because there's no way I'd ever make her kneel for me if I weren't ready to do the same, I wrap an arm around her waist, bringing her close to my chest.

My hand moves up her neck as I reach her mouth, my thumb gathering the errant cum from around her lips and pushing it back where it belongs.

"Perfect. So fucking perfect," I whisper, searing the image of her like this in my mind.

Her eyes crinkle around the corners as she gives me a saucy smile. Her mouth closing, she sucks her cheeks in as she's churning the cum in her mouth, mixing it with her saliva before parting her lips again, showing me the bubbles on the surface of her tongue, and the way she's playing with it.

"Fuck, hell girl," I rasp, feeling myself growing hard again.

She winks at me, closing her mouth again and swallowing loudly.

"Delicious," she leans in to whisper.

From instinct alone, I grab her by the throat, taking her mouth in a kiss, tasting myself on her lips and loving the way we're always one.

"I can't believe you fucked me on a plane," she giggles, standing up on wobbly feet and going to look into the small bag she'd packed at the house.

"You know killing sprees open my appetite," I joke and she shakes her head at me.

Rummaging through her bag, she pulls out a long sundress, easily slipping it over her head and tying the belt around the waist.

I pull myself together, standing and zipping up my pants. My gaze still strays to her, and I can't help but admire her beauty, the yellow of the dress only serving to accentuate her stunning complexion, the shape showing off her waist and her hourglass figure.

"No." She crosses her arms over her chest. "We're not doing this again. This is the only piece of clothing I have left, and you're not ripping this apart too." She presses her lips together, shaking her head at me.

"Sisi," I groan, though I know she's right. I need to get a hold on myself.

"Don't you have other things to do?" she asks, coming over and picking up my phone. "The photo Nero sent," she explains as she unlocks the phone.

"Shit, I forgot," I mutter, realizing her presence is too intoxicating. She makes me lose track of everything but *her*.

I join her as she opens up the gallery to search for the

picture. Her brows are pinched as she scrolls through *a lot* of pictures of her—sleeping, eating, walking, thinking. I have a snapshot of *everything* she does.

She looks up, raising an eyebrow at me and I shrug, giving her a sheepish smile, unashamed at being caught stalking her.

"I can't help it if you're too damn pretty for your own good," I tell her.

"How come I've never seen you take these?" She continues to scroll through at least another hundred pictures of her—in the garden, in the city, in the bathtub or in bed. I made sure I caught her in *every* state.

There's this sick need inside of me to have her with me every fucking second. I have a hard time standing still even when she uses the bathroom. And she knows this too, since I've prohibited her from *ever* showering alone.

But inevitably there are moments when we can't always be together, and so I quench my thirst for her the only way I can—by staring at her pictures.

Fuck, but I'm gone.

"I wouldn't be me if you saw me take them." I wink at her.

A smile plays on her lips and she doesn't seem in the least offended that I seem to have a shrine dedicated to her on my phone. If anything, she seems to preen under the attention as she scrolls through more pictures.

"Wait…" She frowns as she reaches some older pictures. I groan when I realize which ones she's looking at.

"You were watching me," she whispers.

"I had Seth send me pictures of you up until I went to

Peru since there was no connection there," I explain, and I swear her eyes look glossy with unshed tears.

"Why?" She utters that one question so softly and my heart breaks again for what I put her through.

"I couldn't stay away," I admit. "But I couldn't come close either. I knew that the moment I was within walking distance from you I would throw all caution to the wind and come get you." I sigh as I remember the torment I'd withstood knowing her far away from me.

It had been the worst time in my life, and knowing what I do now about my time with Miles, that's saying a lot.

"Vlad…" She shakes her head, raising her gaze to meet mine and I'm baffled by how much emotion I find in those gorgeous eyes of hers. "I'm here now," she whispers softly, lifting herself up on her tip-toes to lay a chaste kiss on my cheek. "With you."

"You are." I close my eyes, reveling in her nearness. "And that's why I'm never letting you go. There's something wrong with me, Sisi," I admit. "Because I can't *not* be with you. There's a sickness in here." I take her hand and point it to my head, before lowering it to my heart, "And here. It's making me go insane just thinking of a minute without you. It's so extreme sometimes I can barely sleep, needing to make sure you're next to me." I take a deep breath, opening my eyes to see her watching me closely.

"If you're sick then so am I, Vlad." Her melodious voice is the only thing that can soothe the voice inside of me, and as she speaks, her hand caressing my cheek, her eyes full of love, I can't help it as I give myself completely to her. "Because I can't be without you either."

"Fuck, Sisi," I mutter, hugging her, "I'm glad you're not

mad at my collection," I say, trying to add a little levity to the heavy conversation.

"Mad? I'm only mad that I didn't know, because now I want my own of you." She smiles against my chest.

I kiss the top of her head, taking the phone and opening the *received* folder that she hadn't looked at.

"Here," I say as I pull up the photo, frowning a little.

The picture has a grayish tinge to it, making the background of the orphanage seem even more haunted and forlorn. There is an old manor in the back, a few columns at the entrance. On the porch, a woman with two boys is posing for the camera.

The woman is sitting stiffly between the boys while they smile jovially, holding tightly to a small present wrapped in colored paper.

"That…" Sisi trails off, squinting to get a better view of the picture. "That's Mother Superior. I'm sure of it. But how?" She shakes her head. "She's not wearing her habit," she notes and I nod.

I've seen enough fucked up shit in this world that nothing phases me anymore. The fact that Mother Superior might have been some type of scout certainly wasn't something I'd anticipated, but I'm not surprised. More than anything, I'm pissed that I'm only finding out *now*.

"It *is* Mother Superior," I agree grimly. "And that complicates things."

Because if Mother Superior is in any way involved, then this shit has been going on right under my nose.

"But if she's involved." Sisi looks up at me, her brows furrowed as she's working out all the implications.

"If she's involved, then Sacre Coeur is involved. And if

Sacre Coeur is involved," my lips stretch in a thin line, "then the five families are involved."

"We know Miles approached my father, but the others? Did you ever suspect?"

"I did. And I looked through everyone's accounts. The Russians were guilty from the get go and I got the confirmation of their involvement already. But the Italians?" I shake my head, moving to our seats and taking out my laptop.

"I looked through all the accounts I could find, and none had sent any payments to any off-shore I could link with Miles. I've certainly tracked all their other transactions. But Miles?" I shake my head.

"What does that mean, then?" Sisi bites her lip worriedly.

"It means it's much bigger than we thought. And much bigger than *just* those experiments." I purse my lips, endless possibilities stretching before me. "We need to talk to your brother," I add grimly.

"Damn," Sisi mutters.

"Sacre Coeur sponsors another five orphanages." I pull up a document, and Sisi leans in, scrunching up her nose as she reads through the contents.

"So they've been feeding children into Miles' program," she notes before suddenly going still, her eyes widening. "Vlad." Her hand reaches out to grab onto my shirt.

"What? What is it?"

"I just remembered something. And I think you're right. This is much bigger than we anticipated," she says, her lips trembling slightly.

"What is it?"

"It's a very vague memory, but I couldn't have been

more than three, maybe four-years-old. But I remember being taken to the hospital for some tests. I wasn't the only one. All the kids in my class were taken too." She recounts and I have a hard time controlling myself thinking about anyone laying even a finger on *my* Sisi.

"Fuck," I mutter, incensed that something of this magnitude could have escaped me.

"But there's more. I never understood what happened, but kids went missing all the time at Sacre Coeur. I remember just wondering why no one cared about them. After they disappeared, no one even spoke their names again. It was like they didn't even exist," she says, telling me about some who she'd known personally.

Without even thinking, I bring her to my chest, my arms tight around her as I realize how close she'd been to danger.

Fuck!

Sacre Coeur won't get away with this. Especially since I'd already vowed to see the people who hurt my Sisi punished.

"We'll figure it out, hell girl," I speak against her hair.

One glance at my watch and I realize we must be nearing the airport soon, so I tell Sisi to get ready for landing.

But just as I'm about to put my stuff away, the plane suddenly dips, a small explosion sounding from the west wing.

What?

I barely have time to regain my equilibrium as I grab Sisi's hand, making sure she's always by my side.

The plane keeps on teetering, loud noises coming from the engine. Using the intercom, I contact the pilot.

"I think something hit the left engine, Sir," the pilot mumbles.

My hand still wrapped around Sisi, I tug her after me as I look out the window toward the left engine.

"Vlad... that's..." Sisi's eyes widen as she looks at the flames coming from the engine.

"I think we got hit," I say grimly, cursing out. "I didn't realize they'd be in *such* a hurry to get rid of me," I add drily.

"We're going down, aren't we?" she asks, and I turn to her, impressed that she's not freaking out, yelling, or worse, fainting on me.

No, she's just watching the fire coming from the broken engine, her face serene.

"We are," I reply.

Without wasting another minute, I pull open the compartment housing parachutes, quickly making sure everything is in order before putting the vest and everything on me.

"Come here, hell girl," I beckon her, strapping her tightly to my front. "We're going down alright, but we're not dying today," I tell her confidently.

Once the parachute is secure around my back, and Sisi's safely strapped to me, I push the safety door aside, air whooshing in from the high altitude.

The plane is wobbly trying to regain balance, but even so the decrease in altitude is visible, and I know it won't make it without the second engine for too long.

"Ready?" I ask her, and she simply nods, her eyes full of trust.

With no other preliminaries, we just jump.

28

SISI

"I can't believe they tried to shoot down our plane." I shake my head, taking the harness off.

The trip down had actually been exhilarating, and at no point had I been worried about my life, or anything, really. I knew Vlad would get us out of there and that he'd know exactly what to do. My trust is firmly placed in him.

And he hadn't disappointed. No, he'd actually made everything fun. From the moment we'd jumped, he'd tried to distract me from the distance to the ground by keeping my attention on him, offering up silly jokes and trying his best to make me laugh, so I'd forget the situation we're in.

If that's not sweet, then I don't know what is.

But that's just Vlad. My sweet killer.

Throwing the gear to the ground, I turn to look at him, surprised he's not replying.

He has an ominous expression on his face as he watches the plane going down in the distance.

"Vlad?"

"They dared," he starts, a deep rumble that has the hairs

355

on my body stand up, "they fucking dared to endanger your life. Again," he seethes, an aura of danger unlike any other emanating from him. "I'm going to end them," he states, blinking twice before his features are back to normal.

"Yes, you will," I tell him, grabbing his hand in mine, "but first we should get home before we get another attempt on our lives," I add playfully, but he's not smiling.

"We're going straight to your brother's. We need to fix this mess before something worse happens," he says.

"He's going to kill us," I mutter, but Vlad doesn't seem to mind that.

"I'll deal with Marcello. He'll probably throw a few punches and then we'll be able to talk. But since I'm even more of a pariah than before, I'll need his help to figure this out," he sighs, rolling his eyes.

"Really?" I tilt my head to look at him. "Who told you to start this bloody war with the Russians? Should I remind you that *you* provoked them by sending them the heads of their men via mail?"

"I provoked them?" He sounds offended as he mutters something under his breath. "I merely played a little with them, looking to confirm my suspicions about their involvement. Which ended up being true, so it's not like I was wrong." He shrugs.

"But you still started it."

"Did I? Maybe they were going to attack me anyway since they certainly didn't like me being so nosy." He shrugs again, mentioning the warehouse incident where the leaders of all the East Coast Bratvas had banded together to try to kill him.

Alas, he'd just proven to them that he's *not* killable.

Not by a human, anyway.

"Vlad," I purse my lips at him, amusement threatening to spill over. "Just admit that you wanted to kill them in the first place," I say and I watch a small blush envelop his features.

"Maybe." He looks away, and I can't help myself as I raise myself on my tip-toes to kiss his cheek.

Sometimes he's too cute.

Hand in hand, we walk a couple of miles through a never ending field before we reach the main road.

Already tired, I ask him to take a break until I catch my breath, the sun already coming up in the sky which means that cars should start circulating in the area.

"Why do you think Meester keeps on trying to kill us?" I ask.

He's looking in the distance, scanning the horizon for any movement, and for a second I don't think he heard me.

"I have one hunch," he finally says, plopping himself in the grass next to me.

I simply raise my eyebrows, waiting for him to continue.

"He's protecting his interests."

"What do you mean?"

"I've gone over all possibilities in my head, hell girl. I haven't had contact with Petro in years, a decade even. For him to suddenly send people out to kill me? Going as far as to blackmail Maxim into betraying me?"

He purses his lips, tearing the top of the grass straw and placing it in his mouth. "There's only one explanation. And it might be jumping the gun, since I have *no* other evidence for it. But..." He shakes his head.

"Damn it, I hate making baseless conjectures," he curses.

"You think he was the third man involved with Misha and Miles, don't you?" I ask and he nods, his expression grim.

"There's no other reason why he'd be so adamant about wiping me off the face of this Earth. First the house in New Orleans, and now the plane? And something tells me he was behind the warehouse incident too. It's urgent. He's scared about something and he's trying to get rid of me as soon as possible."

"So you think he's just protecting his business interests?"

"Most probably. But that also means that there's something to protect. We need to find out how Sacre Coeur is involved with Miles and after that maybe we can get a clue into the bigger picture."

"This seems awfully complicated," I remark. There are so many connections, and it boggles my mind to try to think how each thread connects to the other.

"If it weren't, it wouldn't have stayed hidden for so long. I have a bad feeling about this, hell girl."

"I'm just surprised that you've never been able to stumble upon it until now."

"Me too. But except for my quest to find Katya and Vanya's killer, I was never in the human trafficking scene. I was never supposed to be in the loop, and it seems that they were watching me carefully to make sure I *never* found out too much."

He shrugs, and I realize he's trying to digest all the information, a small part of him undoubtedly disappointed in himself for failing to see what was right under his nose.

"I told you before, love. Even *you* are not omniscient.

Stop beating yourself up over it." I lay my hand over his, trying to give him some semblance of comfort.

"I just don't understand how I could have missed so many signs. Retrospectively, things are starting to make sense..."

"But that's just the thing. Miles knows you. He knows how your mind works. And by all accounts, his own mind works in a similar fashion. It wouldn't be too farfetched to think that he planned everything to lead you *away* from them. Not toward."

"You're right," he grunts. "No wonder I spent almost ten years looking in all the wrong places. Why, the fact that I found Mr. Petrovic and I got some information out of him was a miracle."

"I think Mr. Petrovic was the glitch in Miles' plan. Remember the goons at the restaurant," I point out and he nods.

"Yes, I don't think he wanted me to find out about him just yet. But that's the thing, Sisi. The more I remember about those years I spent with him, the more I wonder if I truly want to find my sister alive," he says, his voice dripping with vulnerability.

"Vlad," I whisper his name, caressing his hand with my own. "We'll figure it out. We'll find your sister and you'll be able to avenge Vanya too," I tell him, leaning my head on his shoulder. "We'll do everything together. One step at a time."

"Sisi," he takes a deep breath, his head touching mine as he scoots me closer, "I'm so happy you're with me. In all this hell, you're the only thing that's ever brought me joy. True joy." He raises my hand, linking our fingers together. "Even when my judgement gets cloudy, you're there to scare the storm away," he continues, and my heart does a somersault in my chest.

"You know, you can still abandon your life of crime and become a poet," a smile pulls at my lips, "you'd become an instant bestseller," I tell him, trying to lighten the mood.

"Of course," he instantly replies. "You'd be my muse and I'd channel all your loveliness into my words." He turns toward me, and I finally see his lips quirking up in amusement. "But then I'd also have to kill more," he continues, a wicked expression on his face, "since I can't ever share you with the world."

Brushing the hair off my face, his knuckles caress my skin, slowly moving lower until his thumb skims my lips.

"It's already enough that I want to kill every man who's *ever* glanced upon you." His words inflame me even as I realize the precariousness of our situation—stranded in the middle of nowhere with no means of getting home. "But to have the entire world in love with you too?" He shakes his head.

"The entire world in love with me? Aren't you jumping the gun?"

"Nope," he answers immediately, "because there's no way *anyone* would take one look at you and *not* fall in love with you." His voice sends shivers down my back, his words reminding me that Vlad doesn't see me like the rest. In his eyes I'm so precious there's no way others would see me as less.

I raise my gaze toward him, catching his hand in mine as I bring it to my mouth, my lips skirting around his knuckles.

"Thank you," I whisper, "for making me feel so loved."

His regard for me never fails to surprise me, the way his love can be so pure and yet so wicked at the same time.

He treats me better than a queen. Me, the girl who everyone looked down upon—the cursed, unwanted one. Yet when he looks at me with those dark eyes of his, I finally feel like I matter. That all I endured so far was never a misfortune, but rather a test. I had to earn the *fortune* I now have, and frankly, I wouldn't have it any other way.

Because not only did my past shape me into who I am, but it also helped me recognize just how lucky I am to have this unusual man's love.

"You should never thank me, Sisi, for treating you like you deserve. Hell, you deserve so much more than I can give you. Sometimes I worry that you might find someone else. Someone… better."

His voice is low, his forehead slightly creased as he admits this. The vulnerability behind his voice astounds me and I realize that I'm not the only one thinking I'm not worthy.

He is too.

"Vlad," I softly call his name, his dark eyes on mine as I lose myself in those depths. "There's no one better than you. There won't ever be anyone else. Period."

There's a slight twitch in his upper lip as he regards me intently, almost without blinking.

"For me, you are the other half of my soul," I say, and his features relax, a lightness appearing on his face. "You are the one requirement I need to live, just like I know I am yours." I place his hand over my heart, letting him hear how it beats for him. "Don't ever think you're less, Vlad. Because to me you are *everything*."

"Sisi," he releases an anguished sound, "my darling Sisi," he says as he draws me into his arms, holding me so tight we might melt into one. "I can't help myself from wondering what I did to deserve you. You're just..." he trails off, his fingers moving up and down my back in a slow caress.

"Perfection," he finally says, and I snuggle closer in his arms, allowing his heat to seep into my skin, his love into my heart, his adoration into my soul.

And as the sun comes up into the sky, a reddish hue staining the horizon line, we stay like that—wrapped in each other and pretending we are indeed one. That we're not separate bodies, nor separate entities. No, as my cheek rests on his, my body molded to his, we are one being.

"Ya lyublyu tebya," I murmur softly into his hair, telling him I love you in his language, the only reason I'd wanted to learn it.

He stills, shocked.

"Isho," he says, urging me to say it again, "isho."

"Ya ochen lyublyu tebya," I repeat it and he crashes his mouth to mine, prying my lips open and breathing in the words from my mouth.

"Ya tozhe," he rasps. "Ah, milaya, ya tak tebya lyublyu... v etu zhizn mne nuzhna tolka ti odna." His voice breaks as he tells me that I'm the only thing he needs in this life, the sound of his promise of love never sweeter as I know he means it from the bottom of his heart.

I don't know how long we stay like this, but eventually we decide we need to keep on walking until we find a car willing to take us into the city.

Seeing the fatigue on my face, Vlad doesn't even let me try to walk, swinging me over his shoulder and giving me a piggyback ride.

I hold tightly onto his shoulders, letting myself absorb the heat of him.

He keeps on walking, and after some time I start feeling guilty that I'm an added weight on his back. No matter the evidence to the contrary, he's still human.

"You should put me down now. I'm well rested," I tell him, but he simply refuses, stubbornly continuing forward.

"I mean it, Vlad. You can put me down." I tap his shoulder, but he doesn't even reply this time, trudging his way forward.

By chance, I see a car approaching and I start waving my hands in the air, hoping to get their attention.

A couple in their mid-forties stop by us, giving us a one over before inviting us to share the car with them. Luckily, they are also heading upstate, so they can drop us somewhere close to Marcello's house.

Once inside the car, both Vlad and I start relaxing a little. Still, I don't think he knows the meaning of loosening up, and I can see the way his mind is once more at work, most probably working theories and mentally testing future scenarios.

Sighing deeply, I can only hope that the confrontation with Marcello won't be too bad. And before I know it, my eyes drift closed, a deep sleep claiming me.

29
SISI

It's not much later that I feel Vlad slowly shake me awake. I groggily open my eyes just as he gathers me into his arms, thanking the couple for taking us and wishing them a great trip.

"You can put me down," I tell him, my voice husky from sleep. He looks a bit reluctant to do it, but eventually he lowers me to my feet.

I stretch a little, my limbs aching from all the exertion, and I look around us to try to gauge where we are.

"How much longer until Marcello's house?" I raise my head up to gaze at him.

His eyes are focused on me as a slow smile starts creeping on his face.

"What?" I frown.

"You said Marcello's house. Before, you used to call it home," he replies, a little too proud of himself.

"Did I?" I feign ignorance as I keep on walking. Still, I can't wipe the grin off my face as I realize he *is* right. It's been quite some time since I've stopped calling it home. And it's all because my home changed from a place to a person.

"I know you're smiling," he calls out from behind me, clearly amused. "And you're going in the wrong direction," he points out after I'm already quite ahead of him.

I turn sharply, my eyes narrowed at him.

"Just admit I'm your home." His eyes twinkle with mischief as he comes by my side, taking my arm and placing it into the crook of his elbow.

"Maybe." My lips twitch, but that's all I'm willing to give him. His ego is already too inflated.

"I knew it," he whistles, tugging me closer and telling me the house is not too far.

"Are you worried about the meeting?" he eventually asks, his tone serious.

I tilt my head toward him, briefly considering the question.

"I don't know," I answer honestly. Because I really don't. Marcello vehemently prohibited me from having anything to do with Vlad, so I know it won't be a pleasant meeting in the least.

I am, though, a little worried about disappointing him. We might not have known each other long, but I'd learned to respect him and his true care for the family. He may not be an open book most days, but he's always been fair to me and he's given me an opportunity to live with him when he didn't have to. I was, after all, technically an adult when I left Sacre Coeur, and definitely *not* his responsibility.

And so I find myself backed in a corner, since I don't want to lose Marcello's regard, but I will *definitely* not give Vlad up.

"We can just hope for the best, right?" I ask, forcing a smile.

"Marcello isn't an ogre," Vlad jokes, "for all his ogre-ish tendencies. But he can be quite unyielding," Vlad mentions, but upon seeing my eyes slightly widening in worry, he amends, "but I'll take care of it, Sisi. Don't worry about it. In fact, don't worry about anything. I'll handle it all." He peers down at me, his expression so sincere that I can't help but lean slightly into him, placing all my trust in him.

"Okay," I reply softly.

The couple really did us a favor by dropping us close to the house, so we only have to walk a couple of miles to get to the main gates.

Upon seeing us, the guards immediately open the gates for us, welcoming us inside.

I guess they didn't get the memo that Vlad is persona non grata.

There's a long alleyway that leads from the main entry gates to the house, flower beds on both sides of the stone path.

We're halfway down the alleyway when I feel Vlad tense. I don't even have time to ask what's going on as he shoves me behind him, a loud gunshot permeating the air.

Eyes wide, I look up to see my brother and Lina in the doorway. Marcello has a murderous expression on his face as he's pointing a gun straight at us.

"Really, 'cello?" Vlad drawls, taking a step forward. His arm is still stretched out to keep me behind him.

But some type of warning goes off in my mind, and I swat his arm aside, going to his side. I watch in horror as blood pools from his shoulder, the bullet deeply lodged inside. Vlad doesn't seem to even mind it as his gaze is firmly on my brother.

"Are you crazy?" I twirl around, yelling at Marcello. "And you." I turn my head slightly. "You just got shot!" I exclaim, already panicking. I've never seen Vlad hurt before, and the sight of that blood running down his shirt is enough to make me hyperventilate.

It's one thing when he's in a fight and I know there's no one who can best him. But it's quite another thing in this situation, because I'm sure he's not going to engage my brother in any way.

I've seen it before, at my birthday party. There's a part of Vlad that considers Marcello his closest friend, and even though my brother may not share that sentiment, it's clear that Vlad's skewed moral code would never allow him to do something to him. In his own warped way, he cares about Marcello.

Vlad's lips pull up in a twisted smile as he places his hand over the place he'd been shot, feeling for the hole. Fingers drawn together, he sticks them inside the wound, looking for the bullet.

My eyes must be the size of two saucers as I can do nothing but stare at this display of insanity.

His lips twitch as he finds the bullet, more blood dripping from the wound and down his hand. Once he has a good grasp on it, he tugs it out, dropping it to the ground with a thud.

His shirt is a mess, the material shredded around the gun site. But it's the bullet hole that has me worried, so angry looking as it gushes out even more blood.

In all the medical shows I've watched, it's always imperative to *not* remove the foreign object, as it might lead to hemorrhage.

Vlad knows this too. I know he does. So what does he think he'll succeed with this display?

I act out of pure instinct alone, grabbing the hem of my dress and ripping the end of it. I don't waste any time as I hurry to his side and start wrapping the material around his shoulder and across his wound.

"You're crazy," I mutter, a little put off with him for taking his own safety so lightly.

We survive an almost plane crash just for him to bleed out on me from an unnecessary gunshot? No, Sir. I won't have it.

"I'm your crazy," he murmurs softly, his gaze gentle as he looks down at my efforts to reach his shoulder and properly bandage it.

Belatedly, I hear the sounds of steps behind me, and so I do the only thing I can. I spin around and I place my own body in front of Vlad's.

"Enough!" I tell my brother.

He's maybe a few steps away, his gun still pointed at Vlad. Lina is behind him, her gaze filled with worry as she looks between me and Vlad.

"Sisi, get inside the house," Marcello barks the order, his eyes fixed on Vlad.

"I'm not going anywhere," I reply, firmly placing myself in front of his gun. "And you're not shooting anyone either."

"Sisi, go inside." He grits his teeth, and I wonder if this is his boiling point. Still, knowing Vlad's hardheadedness about my brother, I'm not about to leave him alone so he can offer himself up as a sacrifice.

"No." I take a few steps back until my back hits Vlad's front. "I'm not leaving my husband," I state confidently.

"Husband?" Marcello sputters, and Lina's eyes widen as she looks at me intently, probably trying to ascertain the validity of the claim.

I blink twice as I realize a loophole I hadn't thought of before. Leaning into Vlad, I whisper, "The marriage is real, right?"

"Of course it's real," he replies immediately, almost insulted, "I wouldn't fake marry you."

"Good." I nod. "Just wanted to check since the minister seemed a little off. I thought maybe you hired an actor," I admit thoughtfully.

"He was real," Vlad mutters, "I just used a little intimidation on him, nothing more. But the certificate is real and filed. Made sure of it myself." He preens, and somehow I can't take him seriously with a gaping hole in his shoulder that's now bled all over the strap of material I'd wrapped around it.

"Great," I add drily.

"Sisi!" my brother yells at me and I jerk away from Vlad, a little disoriented. "I don't know what he told you to agree to marry him, but you need to back away. I'll take care of him."

"Should I tell him what you threatened to get me to marry you?" I ask him, almost amused.

He immediately shakes his head, the corner of his lip half-turned.

"I don't think it would help the situation we're in," he jokes.

Marcello groans, and from the corner of my eye I see him swinging the gun around recklessly.

"Can you drop the gun and we'll talk after?" I give my brother a smile, hoping to sweeten him somehow.

Lina's quiet by his side, closely observing Vlad and me.

Marcello is about to reply, but then he narrows his eyes on me—specifically my neck.

"You're fucking dead, Vlad. You…" Marcello shakes his head, so much anger rolling off him, "You fucking marked her!" he yells, pointing to the tattoo on my neck.

Before I can even blink, the gun is up and ready to shoot at Vlad again.

"Stop!" I scream at the top of my lungs, fear and worry gnawing at me. "Just stop," I huff out, my voice raw. "I asked him to give me this tattoo," I explain, yet Marcello doesn't seem in the least amendable.

"He didn't force me to do anything," I continue, slowly advancing toward Marcello. "Please, just stop and listen to us, okay? He's not a danger to me." I'm almost in front of him as I keep my eyes on him.

My hand reaches out to wrap around his, trying to stop him from waving the gun around. "He's my husband and I love him. Just give us a chance to explain everything," I add, and for the first time I note a reaction in Marcello.

"You love him?" he asks, incredulity dripping off his voice.

"Yes," I confirm, finally getting him to lower the gun.

He doesn't speak for a moment as his gaze swings from me to Vlad.

"In my office. You have five minutes," he says before

swiftly turning on his heels, grabbing Lina's arm and dragging her into the house.

She's still looking back at me, her features filled with worry. But I'll have time to deal with her later.

After we convince Marcello that our relationship is real.

I hurry to Vlad's side, intent on setting some ground rules before confronting my brother.

"Don't bait him," I start. "I know you will want to. I know you might not be able to help yourself. But *please*, don't bait him."

"You wound me, hell girl," he groans, "now, where would be the fun in that?"

"You're already wounded, Vlad. Will probably be even more if you don't keep your mouth shut. We need his help, not his rage."

"Fine." He lets out a big breath. "For you, I'll make an exception. But I can only promise to tone it down. You know that sometimes I can't stop myself from blurting things out." He sighs, and one look at him has me pursing my lips to stop from chuckling.

"Yes, I have been the target of your errant tongue," I reply, barely containing my laughter as we head inside the house.

Vlad stops, turning his head slightly, his lips curled up in a devious smirk. "Yes, you have," he says before continuing walking.

I frown, and it takes me a second to get the double entendre.

"You're wicked." I elbow him slightly, a smile on my lips.

But as we enter my brother's study, I immediately relax my features, wanting to seem serious.

Marcello and Lina are behind my brother's desk. His gaze has a hawkish quality to it as he hones in on us, watching as we take two seats in front of them.

In the beginning, no one speaks. The silence is deafening as everyone is engaging in some sort of staring contest.

"So." I clear my throat, wanting to get this over as soon as possible, so I can sew Vlad back up. It's a wonder he's kept his calm as he has, since there's a lot of blood coming out of his wound. "Vlad and I are married," I start, and my brother narrows his eyes at me.

"I gathered that," he adds drily.

"'Cello, 'cello, can't you relax a little?" Vlad asks, and my mouth drops open as I watch him lift up his legs and prop them on Marcello's desk.

I turn sharply toward him, my expression clearly telling him to cut it.

He has a wide smile on his face as he lounges in his chair, lifting his arms and placing them behind his head as if he doesn't have a freaking hole in his shoulder.

Not wanting to give Marcello and Lina the impression that we're on less than stellar terms, I lean back in my chair, moving a little closer to him and muttering under my breath, "Behave."

His lips curve up even more, and I resist the urge to roll my eyes at him. He just can't help himself.

"Sisi, I think it's best if we hear from you," Lina finally speaks, addressing me. "What happened? What about Raf?" The questions pour out of her, and I feel a pang of regret. All this time and I'd never once stopped to think how Raf must have felt in this entire debacle.

Granted, the *kidnapping* had been out of my control, but

even after that, between the quarrels with Vlad and our reconciliation, I hadn't for one minute thought about Raf.

Damn!

"There was nothing going on between Raf and I," I start, taking a deep breath. Lina and Marcello are both focused on me as I talk, so I admit to all the lies I told, hoping they won't be too disappointed in me. "He proposed a marriage of convenience when I found out I was pregnant."

"You knew?" Lina gasps, "You knew you were pregnant?"

I nod slowly, shame creeping up my cheeks.

But then I feel Vlad's hand on top of mine as he gives me a quick squeeze and it's all I need to continue.

"Yes," I admit. "I knew."

"Sisi." Lina shakes her head at me. "You knew you could have come to me at any point. Why would you…" she trails off and I can see the disappointment in her gaze.

"I was scared," I whisper, ready to put all the cards on the table. But Marcello interrupts me, his voice thunderous as he practically shoots daggers at Vlad with his eyes.

"You mean Raf wasn't the father, was he?" my brother asks, and I don't know why I feel so embarrassed admitting this, but as I slowly nod I can feel myself growing hotter, my shame making me sweat.

"Fuck, you took advantage of her, didn't you?" he growls, slapping his palm against the table, the noise making me wince.

30
SISI

Vlad is calm even as my brother rages on. His hand on mine, he's the only source of comfort as I find myself in one of the most uncomfortable situations I've ever been in.

"I didn't take advantage of her, Marcello. We're both adults and she can make her own decisions," Vlad drawls lazily, his feet still on the table, his stance relaxed.

And this seems to make my brother even madder, his face red with fury as he looks at Vlad.

"She grew up in a fucking convent, Vlad. What type of adult do you think she is?" he asks, and I frown, not liking the direction he's taking. "Fuck, she probably didn't even know what sex was," my brother continues and at this point my eyes are wide open in shock.

"What did he tell you to convince you to sleep with him?" he continues, directing the question at me. "Did he force you? Did he promise you something? God, I can't believe this," he curses under his breath, seemingly barely in control of himself.

"I'm not a child, Marcello, and I'd prefer if you didn't refer to me as such," I start, the need to stand up to myself eating at me. I may not want to disappoint my brother, but that doesn't mean that I'll let him take all my agency away from me.

"And I'm not an idiot, either. I may have grown up in a convent, but that didn't take my common sense away from me." I almost roll my eyes at him. "I knew exactly what I was getting myself into with Vlad."

"Sisi," he shakes his head at me, "I'm not trying to say you're a child. But you're young and inexperienced. He's ten years older than you, for God's sake. How is that not taking advantage of you?"

"Marcello," I sigh, almost exasperated. "You know him too," I add, sneaking a glance at Vlad and finding him watching me closely, an intense expression on his face. His lower lip slightly curved up, I know he's enjoying the show. But more than anything, I'm glad that he's letting me fight my own battles, since no doubt if he starts talking he'll just put his foot in his mouth, making the situation worse than it already is.

"He has the emotional intelligence of a toddler."

"Hey," Vlad protests from the side, trying very hard to hide a growing smile.

"He didn't even know how to talk with a woman before I came along," I continue, and Vlad groans, the back of his hand to his forehead in a typically dramatic scene.

"Really, hell girl? You have to reveal *all* my secrets?" he asks, an amused grin on his face.

"It's true." I shrug. "You didn't even know how to kiss," I add, winking at him.

"I knew more than you. I, at least, had the theoretical basis down," he retorts.

"Right," I snort, "that's why you were ready to cut your arm open to get me to kiss you again," I raise an eyebrow at him, a little lost in the back and forth.

"You have a thing for blood, admit it," he counters, his eyes darker than black as his pupils overtake his irises.

I feel a need to fan myself, especially as my eyes roam his torso, blood crusted on his shirt and some still flowing freely from his wound. But I move lower and I note that I'm not the only one overly heated by this conversation, a part of him growing right under my gaze.

"Maybe." My voice comes in a breathless tone as I snap my eyes back to his.

"Can you two cut it out?" Marcello's words interrupt us, but the energy is still heavy as I settle back in my seat, taking his hand in mine and reveling in his touch.

He makes me forget myself. Even in situations like this, when I know I must keep my head in the game, he makes everything fade away.

"He didn't coerce me in any way, Marcello. We just…" I turn to Vlad, "Fell in love."

"And when exactly did you *fall in love*? I don't recall you meeting him more than a handful of times. Hell, I don't even know when you two had time to…" he trails off, almost reluctant to say the word *sex* again.

I hide a smile as I realize my own brother might be a bigger prude than me.

"I snuck out," I admit, proceeding to give him a rundown of how we met. "And before you comment again, *I* wanted to see him."

"I'm disappointed in you, Assisi," Marcello states point blank after I tell him about our nightly meetings and how Vlad and I ended up spending time together. "I specifically told you to stay away from him and you disregarded my warning." He shakes his head.

I feel Vlad tense next to me, and I give his hand a gentle squeeze, letting him know he shouldn't intervene.

There's a pause as Lina and Marcello look at each other, something passing between the two of them.

"Fine," Marcello says. "Let's say I understand your history." He waves his hand at us. "What's done is done. I cannot change the past. But that doesn't mean you have to stay married to him," he says dismissively.

"I think you forgot the part where I said I love him," I mutter drily. "I'm not going to leave him."

"Love?" He laughs. "He wouldn't know what love is if it hit him in the face. I'm sorry to burst your bubble, Assisi, but you've been duped," he mentions casually. Lina purses her lips, looking worriedly at her husband.

"Marcello." She lays a gentle hand on his arm, trying to get him to stop talking.

But he doesn't.

"You're right that I know him. That's why I know that there will be a cold day in hell before Vlad displays *any* type of feeling."

"Then it must be freezing," I add ironically under my breath.

Vlad hears me, his eyes twinkling with mischief, and I'm impressed at how calm he is. Maybe he *is* taking my advice to heart.

"Well." He shrugs, taking his feet off the desk and

standing up. "We tried," he says flippantly, taking my hand and tugging me to his feet.

"You're not taking her anywhere." My brother rises to his feet, coming around to stop Vlad. "I don't know what lies you told her, or how you managed to seduce her, but it ends here, Vlad."

Vlad's features change in the blink of an eye. The previous amused expression is gone, replaced with a cold, unfeeling one.

"You might be able to touch me now, Marcello. But you'd better remove your hand before I break it," he coolly states, flinging my brother's arm aside and pushing me behind him. "Out of courtesy for you, I wanted to give Sisi a chance to explain to you how everything went down. But I told you before. The moment you try to take her away from me, all bets are off."

"Really?" My brother gives a cruel laugh. "And where were you when she was in the hospital miscarrying *your* child?" he asks and I gasp, my hand going to my mouth as I can barely believe he'd hit that low.

Vlad's shoulders are quaking with unreleased tension, and for a moment I fear he might snap.

"Enough!" I place myself between them, "That's between me and Vlad, and we've made peace with it," I declare, holding Marcello's gaze.

"Sisi, go get your stuff," Vlad's voice is low and harsh to the ears as he barely contains himself.

"Vlad…"

"Now," he whispers, and that one softly uttered word tells me all I need to know.

With one last glance at Lina and Marcello, I back away from the study, all but dashing upstairs to my room.

Knowing Vlad is likely hanging by a thread, I get a big bag and I stuff some of my most precious stuff inside, thinking I might never get to return here.

I'd anticipated Marcello wouldn't be thrilled about us, but I hadn't thought he'd be this downright tyrannical.

I shake my head as I feel tears burn behind my eyes, disappointment settling deep in my stomach. I really hadn't wanted things to turn out like this. Especially since all I'd ever wanted was to have a family.

A family that didn't shun me.

A sob catches in my throat as I shove some of the dresses I'd gotten with Lina into a bag, the few memories I'd made in this house coming to the surface and making me feel even more forlorn.

"Sisi." I turn sharply toward the door to see Lina tentatively step inside.

"Don't worry, we'll leave quickly," I say, dabbing at my eyes.

Somehow, I don't want her to see how much this is affecting me.

"Sisi," she repeats, coming toward me, her arms cushioning my body as she draws me to her chest. "No one's throwing you out. You don't have to leave." She strokes my hair.

"But I have to." I lean back, looking away. "Marcello clearly won't ever approve of us, and I'm not going anywhere without Vlad," I tell her sincerely.

"You love him that much?" she asks, pressing her lips together in consternation.

"I can't put into words how much I love him," I whisper, blinking away tears.

Why is it that I have to choose between my family and Vlad? Why can't they just accept our relationship? Yes, I know that Vlad doesn't have the best track record, but they could at least give him a chance.

"But you know who he is." She frowns, as if she can't understand how I could possibly love someone like him.

"Yes," I reply, "I know exactly who he is, and that's why I love him. He's never lied to me about who he is, and I've always accepted him wholeheartedly."

"But he's a killer, Sisi. He's a violent, unfeeling killer."

"What about my brother?" I counter, "I know what he did to you, Lina. And you're still here, with him. Can't you understand me at least a little?" My voice thins out, my throat clogged with emotion.

She looks as if I'd slapped her, a red tinge creeping up her cheeks.

"Vlad isn't a saint. I know that. God, I'm aware that he's probably one of the most dangerous men in this world. But he's *mine.*" I point to my chest. "You have no idea how much he loves me, or how cherished he makes me feel. He completes me in a way I'd never thought possible, and I'm not about to give that up. Not even for you," I firmly state and her eyes widen slightly.

"Sisi…" she drifts off as she's trying to read me.

"I understand if you or Marcello can't accept that. It's your choice. Just as it is mine to go with him." I continue to place my stuff in the bag, refusing to succumb to my emotions. "Where are Claudia and Venezia? I want to say goodbye." Another pang hits my chest at realizing I likely won't be able to see either for a long time.

Venezia I'd only just gotten to know, but Claudia? We'd grown up side by side, and sometimes she feels like both my sister and my child.

"They're at the museum with their teacher. Stay, Sisi. Stay and see them. You really don't have to go," Lina continues to plead with me, and the pain in her eyes only serves to renew my own.

"I can't Lina," I whisper, my entire being rebelling at this situation I find myself in. Oh, but how I wish I could have both, my family *and* my love.

But one can't have everything one desires, I think that should be pretty clear by now.

"After the baby…" I trail off, taking a deep breath and wanting to explain to her so that she understands. "I was in a very dark place. So dark I didn't think I'd ever come out of it. Vlad was the only thing that made me feel better, like my old self. He's the one who keeps me sane when the pain threatens to spill over."

She purses her lips, sorrow on her features as she listens to my words. I know it's not fair to her, since I hadn't let *anyone* in about my problems. And it's because I'd held everything in that I'd lost myself to the pain.

"I don't know if it makes sense, if it's anything less than insanity but…" I raise my gaze to hers so she can see the sincerity of my words, "He's my *one* requirement to live."

Just then, the door opens slightly, and Vlad strides in. His lip is busted and I assume Marcello wasn't satisfied with putting a hole through his chest, he had to punch him too.

The bag drops from my hands as I hurry to his side, my fingers tracing the already bruising flesh.

"You didn't even defend yourself, did you?" I ask softly. I'd already expected him to not put up a fight and accept whatever Marcello dished at him. Deep down, I think there's a part of him that believes he deserves it because he betrayed his friend.

Because that's just the type of man Vlad is. *Honorable.* He might be a killer, but he's a principled one, and I respect his honor system, skewed as it is.

"Why would I fight when I know I would win." He shrugs slightly, catching my hand.

"I…" Lina mumbles something, and I realize she's still in the room. "I'll go now," she says, her eyes skirting from Vlad to me before hurrying out of the room.

"I'm sorry," he mutters as I redirect my attention to the luggage. "I didn't think he'd be this unyielding." He sighs deeply.

"At least he didn't kill you," I point out with half a smile.

"At least there's that," he chuckles, walking around the room and helping me pack.

Opening a drawer he stills, his expression strained. I turn to him, my own features drawing up in pain as I see him lift the small ultrasound picture.

"Hell girl," he groans, opening his arms for me to run into. "Fuck, I'm so sorry. Marcello was right. I should have been here. I should have been by your side," he speaks in my hair, holding me close to his chest.

I'd tried all day to be strong, but somehow the sight of that one picture makes me break down, sobs racking my body as I finally let the tears fall.

"Shh," he coos, taking me in his arms and placing me on the bed. "When you hurt, I hurt," he whispers, slowly stroking my back.

31
MARCELLO

Lina gives me a worried look as she hurries out of the study after Sisi. Left alone with the bane of my existence, I close my eyes, breathing deeply.

Before I can help myself, my fist makes contact with his jaw. I already note the way his eyes follow my every movement, or how he just allows my knuckles to bruise his flesh without putting even the smallest effort into defending himself.

He blinks. Slowly. Then a twisted grin appears on his face as he wipes the blood from his mouth, bringing it to his lips.

"Not bad." He shrugs, "But nothing compared to your sister's," he says, and it takes everything in me not to pounce on him again.

He's trying to bait me.

A few breaths later and I have myself under control. I can't fall for his mind games, especially since I know Vlad never does something without a purpose, and the last thing I want is to invite danger into my own home.

Turning my back to him, I take the decanter from the table and I pour myself a strong drink. Already I can feel the hint of a headache emerging when I think about Sisi's claims of love.

I snort out loud, the thought so incredibly absurd I want to laugh. But more than anything I want to know how Vlad managed to brainwash her like this. What is in it for him?

I've never known him to be interested in a woman before, and besides Bianca, I don't think he's interacted with many either. A cynical smile pulls at my lips as I realize that Sisi was right in one respect—Vlad isn't exactly a ladies' man.

Then what's his angle? What is he trying to achieve by going after Sisi?

He's always been a fickle bastard, but even he wouldn't have stooped so low as to embroil an innocent in his games.

"I guess now we can talk openly?" he drawls, plopping himself in the chair again, a languid smile on his face.

It's his usual feigned affability that enrages me further because I know he's not taking this seriously.

"I promised Sisi I wouldn't bait you, but wow is it hard," he chuckles to himself, rubbing his shoulder wound and gazing at his blood stained fingers with an inscrutable expression. But just as it appears, it's gone, and I'm surprised to see he's not already succumbing to one of his episodes.

"Cut to the chase, Vlad. What do you want to leave Sisi alone?" I ask him outright.

He raises his gaze to meet mine, his eyes darkening.

"That's not on the table, Marcello. Not now, not ever. You may not believe me, but I do love your sister." He shrugs casually, "She's the only thing that's keeping me sane. To take her away from me," he pauses, tilting his head to regard me thoughtfully, "would mean inviting war."

"War," I snort.

"And you know how I like my wars." His mouth stretches in a wide smile, teeth glinting in the low lighting of the room, "With no one left standing."

"See, that's exactly the issue, Vlad. You speak so casually of killing everyone, yet you want me to believe you hold my sister in some sort of superior regard." I roll my eyes at him.

"Sisi isn't everyone, Marcello. And that's your first mistake in assuming she's just like everyone else. She's the only reason I haven't killed you for wiping the smile off her face," he says, his voice low, his tone serious.

Standing up, he comes to my side, taking the decanter and pouring himself a glass of whiskey. Instead of drinking it, though, he raises it to his shoulder, dumping the contents all over his open wound.

My eyes are on his face that shows *no* reaction. There's not even the slightest suggestion that he's in pain.

His smile widens as he sees my baffled expression, pouring yet another glass and bringing it to his lips, downing the liquid in one go.

"Why don't we just put this behind us," he starts, "Sisi would be sad if you suddenly stopped being in her life, and that's the last thing I would ever want. So for her good," his lips twitch, "and everyone else's, we should make our peace."

"Are you threatening me, Vlad?" I raise an eyebrow at him.

"Me?" He shakes his head, a chuckle escaping him. "You forget one thing, 'Cello. I don't threaten. I deliver." He places the glass back on the table, a sudden sound that emphasizes the silent tension between us even more.

"So you just want me to forget about everything and welcome you to the family with open arms," I say sarcastically and his face lightens up.

"Exactly," he quickly intones.

"I don't know what world you live in, Vlad, but that's *never* going to happen." I give a dry laugh. "You think to make a whore of my sister and I'll receive you with open arms?"

"Careful Marcello," he hums, his voice strained, his fists clenched, "careful with how you address her," he takes a step forward, his hands suddenly on my shirt.

I see the way his arms are trembling as if he's barely containing himself. He straightens the collar of my shirt, his eyes on my neck.

"Anyone else and they would be at the bottom of a ditch," he mutters under his breath before his lips curl up in a smile again. "But I can't do that now, can I?" he continues, "Not when we're family." He purses his lips, patting my chest before moving back.

Without any warning, he turns around, smashing one of my shelves to pieces. It only takes one contact with his fist for the wood to give way, split into two.

I watch him closely, this display wholly unlike the Vlad I know. Tilting my head to the side, I study the way he breathes harshly, closing his eyes and trying to regain control over himself.

"No one," he grits his teeth, his back to me, "no one insults Sisi." The words are stilted and barely coherent.

"Least of all calling her a *whore*," he spits the word out as if it's the most vile thing.

His knuckles are bruised, the skin peeling off as he continues to assault my shelves until there's nothing left standing.

Still, I don't intervene, waiting for his anger to wear off.

But even as I watch from a distance, I can't help but feel that there *is* something different about Vlad. In the past, he'd have never allowed himself to have an outburst like this unless it was one of his episodes. His mask of civility firmly in place, he likes to present himself as wholly inoffensive to the world.

And now he's doing the opposite.

He turns his side profile to me as his nostrils flare, his teeth bared. Without another word, he's out the door, slamming it in his wake.

I release a deep breath, already tired from the confrontation. At the very least, Sisi hadn't looked any worse for the wear. Save for that monstrous tattoo on her neck, she'd looked unharmed.

I take a seat at my desk, removing my glasses and massaging my forehead.

"Marcello," Lina's voice startles me as she glides across the room, her eyes wide when she takes in the disaster Vlad had left behind.

Stretching my arm toward her, I bring her to my side, my head resting against her belly.

"Are we doing the right thing, Lina?" I ask, unsure of how to approach this. I don't want to alienate Sisi, but at the same time I know Vlad too well to not question his sudden interest in my sister.

"I don't think so," she answers thoughtfully, shocking me.

"What do you mean?" I raise my head to look at her.

Her hand on my head, she threads her fingers through my hair in a soft caress, calming me in the way only she can.

"He went to her room," she tells me, "and I... I stayed behind to eavesdrop," she confesses, a blush on her cheeks. "I don't think he has bad intentions, Marcello. If anything, I think he might be genuine."

"Not you too, Lina," I groan.

"No, listen." She stops me from continuing. "Open your computer and get the feed from the camera across Sisi's room. I left the door ajar, so we should be able to see something," she suggests, and my eyes widen slightly.

"You're devious, aren't you?" A smile pulls at my lips.

"I want to make sure. I'd never forgive myself if I let Sisi leave without making sure..." She shakes her head and I can see how worried she is.

For her, Sisi is like a younger sister. Certainly, she's her best friend and I know how much she cares about her and her safety. Why, since her disappearance at the wedding, I don't think Lina's managed to get a good night's sleep.

Every call I'd get she'd come to my side to ask for any more news about Sisi.

Even when Vlad had called and we'd had confirmation that she was safe, she'd begged me to find her as quickly as possible.

And I'd tried. If it weren't for the fact that Vlad's a crafty bastard, I would have found her location. Instead, Vlad had left no trace of himself, simply vanishing for months.

"Fine," I agree, needing that confirmation, too.

Lina settles nicely on my lap as I fire up the computer. I wound my arms around her, bringing her closer to my chest.

"Have I told you how much I love you today?" I murmur against her cheek. The corner of her lip pulls up.

"Only a hundred times," she whispers, turning briefly to give me a quick kiss, "love you too," she speaks against my lips, and those words alone have the power to restore my mood.

The screen flares to life, and I quickly access the camera feed. Just as Lina had observed, the door to Sisi's room is half open, the camera having a direct view inside.

"Do you think we can get some sound, too?" she asks, and I nod, adjusting the settings.

It's not much, but we can make out some sounds that come out of her room.

The first thing that we see is Vlad carrying Sisi in his arms as he settles on the bed. He's holding her close to his chest, not unlike the position I'm in with Lina.

"Is she… crying?" Lina whispers, straining to hear.

"Yes," I answer almost automatically, unable to believe my eyes.

All my life I thought I'd seen all there was to Vlad. A robotic genius wearing human clothes, his episodes abnormal instances for a usually calm and composed person. In fact, his composure was his winning quality since it allowed him to study the room and make informed decisions.

The outburst from today had been a first, just how the fact that he's touching Sisi so tenderly is a first too.

His hand in her hair, he's stroking it lightly, as if she's the most precious person for him.

"Shh," he seems to say, "When you hurt I hurt," he continues, and both Lina and I stare at each other, unable to believe it's Vlad saying those words.

"He's still a killer, Lina," I feel compelled to add.

"Yes. But he's a killer who sheds tears." She purses her lips, pointing at the screen.

Frowning, I place my glasses back on, squinting to see the so-called tears.

My jaw goes slack, my mouth wide open as I watch stupefied the man who'd been nicknamed Berserker for his murderous rages and how his eyes are indeed shedding tears.

"I've never seen him cry," I add, almost in a trance.

Hell, I'd never seen him do *any* of these things.

He's holding tightly onto Sisi, trying to comfort her. She raises her hands to his face, her thumbs moving gently across his cheeks and swiping the tears away before leaning in to pepper his face with kisses.

I'm suddenly uncomfortable, as if I'm intruding in a private moment meant only for the two of them.

Her hands roam all over his front as she quickly removes his shirt.

"That's it, Lina," I groan, about to close the computer.

"No, wait." She stops my hand. "Look." She frowns.

Sisi gets up to pick up something before taking a seat on the bed again.

"I think she's sewing his wound," Lina whispers, her eyes glued to the screen.

And she's right as I watch my sister painstakingly try to work Vlad's wound, her movements sloppy even from a distance.

"She's never been great at that," Lina jokes, and a small smile plays on my lips.

"I'm surprised she's not squeamish," I comment.

Vlad doesn't even flinch as the needle penetrates his skin, his eyes wholly focused on Sisi.

And that's when I see something in his gaze I would have never associated with Vlad.

Love.

"I think you're right, Lina," I tell her, bringing her hand to my lips for a quick kiss. "Maybe we need to have another chat with them."

32
VLAD

Biting her lower lip, she struggles to cross the needle through my skin. Her brows are drawn together as she concentrates on getting it right, though she's admitted to not being great at arts and crafts.

A smile on my face, I watch her entranced, the mere fact that her two dainty hands are working to put me back together makes my heart swell in my chest.

"Are they still watching, you think?" she asks, lowering her voice.

"I don't know," I whisper, my mouth close to her ear.

As soon as Catalina had left the room I'd noticed that she was lingering a little in the hallway, her hand creeping up to open the door a little better, ensuring the angle gave enough visibility in the room. One look in the hallway and I'd seen a camera pointed right at us.

Although we hadn't acted per se, Sisi's grief still raw, her sadness influencing my own, I had whispered in her ear that her brother might be observing us. So she'd decided the best example of our teamwork would be to patch me back together.

"I still can't believe he shot you." She purses her lips as she pierces the skin. Two fingers are holding together the flaps of flesh as she's sewing them in place. "And you had to dig the bullet out too." She shakes her head and one look into her eyes and I know she'd swat my arm if I weren't the patient.

"It's all about the show, hell girl," I say as I tip her chin up. "I wanted your brother to see that he doesn't intimidate me, no matter how many guns he waves around."

"Were the tears for show too?" she asks quietly.

"Sisi." My voice goes down an octave. "You hurt, I hurt." I bring her hand to my heart, pressing it to my chest, so she can feel that semi-useless organ that beats only for her. "You cry, I cry. We're a team."

A slow smile appears on her face, lighting up her features and making her eyes crinkle around the corners.

"Good," she says and I release a breath, feeling like I just passed the most important test of my life.

"We should head down now." I nod at her to grab her stuff while I put on my shirt.

When she's ready, she shows me her small bag and I feel an ache in my chest at seeing her meager possessions, vowing she'll have anything she desires in the future.

Grabbing her bag, I motion her to go down.

As expected, Marcello is expecting us, a grim expression on his face and I know he doesn't want to admit he was wrong. He looks even more sour as he invites us back into the study.

"So what changed your mind, 'Cello?" I ask, looking

around the room, "Was it my eye for redecoration?" I nod toward the fallen shelves and he groans.

"Behave." Sisi gives me a look and I immediately acquiesce, imitating a zipper over my mouth with two fingers.

"Lina and I have decided to give you a chance." He clears his throat. "We can see how much Sisi loves you, and for that alone we'll accept your relationship," he continues, his back straight, his entire posture screaming high and mighty.

I have to bite my tongue really hard to not reply to him in my usual fashion, since I know this is the longest olive branch he's willing to extend to me.

"Thank you." Sisi is the first to speak, her entire face glowing with happiness. And for that alone I'll keep my damned mouth shut.

"I guess now onto more important business," I change the topic after everyone's had time to be sappy.

"What do you mean?" Marcello turns to me.

"We've discovered some evidence pointing toward Sacre Coeur having dealings with Miles. More specifically Mother Superior." I quickly give them a rundown of everything we'd learned, and I reluctantly tell them about the attacks on the house and the plane too, even though I can already see fire in Marcello's eyes when he hears that I put his precious sister in danger.

"No." Sisi places herself between us when our staring contest becomes too heated. "We're not doing this again. Besides, I handled myself quite well. Vlad's been teaching me how to defend myself," she states proudly, her chin raised high, her features unflinching.

That's my girl!

"We don't need you two at each other's throats," she sighs as she shakes her head, "no matter how much you dislike him being with me." She turns to Marcello.

Fuck, but I love when she's so assertive. It makes me so hard that I have to shift around, so I don't draw unnecessary attention to myself—yet again. I'm sure Marcello wouldn't appreciate me rubbing it into his face that his sister and I are, indeed, having sex. Or the mere fact that her voice, scent, and her fucking presence are enough to give me a raging hard-on—like now.

"Good." She nods, satisfied. "I'm glad we can engage in a civil conversation for once," she comes next to me, grabbing my hand and placing it in her lap.

"I do remember those cases, back in the day," Lina starts, shifting the topic back to Sacre Coeur, "when the twins disappeared. And a few others too. You would always ask me why they weren't looking for them," Lina addresses Sisi, who nods grimly.

"We think there's an entire trafficking ring that may have roots in Sacre Coeur and its orphanages," Sisi says.

"And there's a high possibility the five families are involved," I point out. "We know your father entertained the idea, even if he never fully went through with it." I nod to Marcello, "But I haven't been able to find any evidence that the other families are involved. I've spoken to Enzo, and he has no clue who Miles is, so I'm excluding him."

Catalina's smile grows when I mention that her brother's innocent, and I get the urge to roll my eyes. Enzo is anything but innocent considering the shit he's involved in right now. He may not have wanted Jimenez's empire, but he's stuck with it. And I for one can't wait to see how he's going to deal with that.

"I wouldn't be surprised if the Marchesi are involved, but they've been rather absent from the scene," I start, but Catalina stops me.

"They're dead," she says, and I frown.

Now, that is one piece of news that I had not heard yet.

"Really?" I lean back in my seat, a little surprised.

"Yes, and I don't know who's the next in line to inherit the business. Allegra has a cousin, but I'm not completely sure of the specifics," she mentions, going a little into detail about the Marchesi scheme and how it had gotten them killed.

I keep to myself that I'd already been aware of Enzo's secret, but I have to say I am impressed that she single-handedly killed her entire family.

"Then that leaves Guerra and DeVille, and knowing their enmity, I wouldn't bet any money that *both* would sign up for the same thing," I chuckle.

The Guerra and DeVille dilemma is an old one, going back a few generations. Still, the two families are always at each other's throats, looking for ways to bankrupt and destroy the other. And after Benedicto's eldest daughter, Gianna, had eloped with a DeVille, the tensions became higher than ever.

"Yes," Marcello agrees, looking pensive, "it's one or the other. I've gotten a closer look at Benedicto's financials since we were supposed to merge our families," he adds drily, the animosity directed wholly at me, "and I couldn't see anything suspicious. Again, I was *not* looking for any connection with Miles. But from what I did see, his businesses are *mostly* on the side of legal."

"Then that leaves DeVille." I grimly nod.

The thing with DeVille is that they are quite possibly the most insular family in New York. They play by their own rules, and don't really subscribe to the same principles the others do.

"I'm curious how that would have worked, since by all accounts, Mother Superior was close with Guerra," I throw the theory out there.

"Well, isn't that reason enough?" Marcello smiles wolfishly, "Compete with Guerra for resources. It's all they've ever done. Benedicto was sure that it was DeVille behind Sisi's abduction." He raises an eyebrow at me, and I hear the condemnation in his words.

"Then I'll pay more attention to DeVille. It's certainly bound to be interesting," I reply, ignoring Marcello's jibe.

"You're aware Guerra will be out for blood, aren't you? And I'm not helping you with that," Marcello mutters.

"I can take care of myself, bro-in-law. Don't you worry." I wink at him.

"Might be more difficult now that Raf is missing too," Catalina adds worriedly.

"What do you mean?" Sisi is the first to speak and my hand tightens around hers.

I know she's friends with the boy, but I cannot help the rage that forms inside of me at the thought that had I been one more minute late, she would have been lost to me.

Oh, but how I would have killed the boy myself if it weren't for that stupid promise I made to Sisi. I may be a degenerate, but I am a degenerate who keeps his promises, much to my dismay.

"We don't know the particularities," Marcello answers, "but Benedicto's been in touch, thinking whoever kidnapped Sisi also kidnapped his son. Now, I didn't tell him about your prank, because that would have been akin to declaring war," he says, still eyeing me with hostility.

"Well, that's fine by me," I add, lounging in my seat, a little too happy at the turn of events. I don't even have to move a finger because someone else beat me to it.

"Vlad." Sisi elbows me, and I raise an eyebrow at her. I might be at her beck and call, but that doesn't mean I can't be gleeful because a thorn in my side—a thorn I couldn't myself pull—has suddenly disappeared. So I just shrug, a smile on my face.

"It seems that fortune favors the bold, after all." I lean in, lifting her hand to my lips and kissing her knuckles.

"Or the reckless," she mutters under her breath, and my smile widens.

"I never engage in recklessness, hell girl. I prefer to call it organized chaos," I murmur softly, my gaze trained on hers.

"Only you would take pride in something like that," she snorts.

"But of course." I grin at her, "You know I love my oxymorons."

"Hmm." She narrows her eyes at me, leaning into me slowly until I can feel her breath on my cheek, "Maybe because you're one yourself," she notes, her voice husky and seductive and fuck if it doesn't drive me crazy.

Marcello suddenly coughs, curiously looking between the two of us.

"I believe we were discussing something," he interjects, almost amused.

I'm starting to realize how dangerous it is having Sisi with me at times like this. Not only am I unable to concentrate, but it only takes one word from her for me to lose myself in her voice.

Definitely not conducive to business.

"I have a contingency plan in place, should Guerra decide he wants some type of retribution," I add flippantly. "But the important thing now is to figure out how Sacre Coeur is involved with Miles, and find out what Mother Superior knows."

"I'm not surprised to hear Sacre Coeur would be involved in this," Catalina notes. "Not with all the abuse going on in that place."

Sisi nods, her brows pinched together, and I can only imagine the memories she's reliving.

"We should go in and interrogate Mother Superior." Sisi's face suddenly lights up as the idea pops into her head. "We can go undercover," she adds excitedly.

My lips curve up as I promptly agree, already thinking of the same thing.

"You might be able to get away with that." Marcello nods at Sisi, "But him?" He snorts, "Unless you plan to dress him up as a nun too. Tell me, Lina, did they have any ex-con nuns at Sacre Coeur?"

Catalina can barely hold in her smile as she shakes her head.

"Come on, 'Cello!" I groan, half-amused, half-surprised that Marcello would still have a sense of humor. I'd have thought it all gone by now. "I'd make a wonderful nun.

Why, I even know a prayer." A devious smile curves up my lips.

Everyone is looking at me expectantly.

"Really?" he drawls, a cynical expression on his face.

"But of course. Sisi's been a great teacher," I start and I see her eyes widen as she realizes what type of prayer I know. "I know all about the great coming," I blurt out, unable to help myself. "It's great indeed." I have time to add before Sisi puts her hand over my mouth, shushing me.

"He's not the brightest pupil." She forces a smile, her foot kicking me in the shin at the same time. "I think he mixed up the prayers."

"I don't get why they'd only make a *second* coming. I mean, what about the third, or the forth?" I continue, lowering her hand.

One look in her direction and her eyes are shooting lasers at me. On the other hand, Catalina is laughing, and Marcello doesn't seem far behind. Why, there's a twitch in his upper lip.

"You'll have to forgive him," she adds sweetly, "he's not exactly housebroken. I planned to get him a muzzle, since he's known to bite too, but alas that fell through." She turns to me, raising an eyebrow and daring me to reply.

"I only bite when asked," I speak lowly, only for her ears.

Her mouth parts slightly, her pupils enlarged, and I know I got her. Swiftly, I turn to the conversation, adding.

"Since you don't think I'd fit in as a nun." I sigh, deeply disappointed. "Then a priest should do."

"There are only two priests at Sacre Coeur, and everyone knows them. How do you think you're going to manage that?" Sisi asks.

"We'll just have to off one of them, and I'll be the replacement."

It's quite easy too, since the priests are not always at Sacre Coeur. We just need to choose one, get a copy of his itinerary, kill him and then I'll promptly show up as the replacement.

"It might work," Marcello agrees, "but killing a priest? Really? Isn't that a new low, even for you?"

"I'll weigh their sins and choose the most wicked one." I roll my eyes at him, "If you're so concerned for the state of my immortal soul."

"More like an immoral soul," he mutters dryly. "I'll look into DeVille, maybe I'll be able to get something." I'm surprised he offers to help, but I'm not about to refuse him. Not when I'm public enemy number one—at least in New York.

We go over a few more details, and Marcello promises to keep an eye out for any information that might seem relevant to our quest.

"Well, then we have a plan." I stretch in my chair. "I guess before we leave I should also let you know that I'm a wanted man." I give him a lazy smile, "So if anyone comes looking, say you don't know me."

Taking Sisi's hand, I tug her to her feet, ready to go. "Oh," I turn sharply, "and I need a car."

Marcello looks about to combust as he's undoubtedly digesting my last sentence. He blinks twice, and I groan out loud, knowing what's to come.

"For God's sake, Vlad," his voice thunders, and even Sisi looks surprised at the sudden change in his demeanor. "You're not leaving with my sister. What the hell are you thinking?" he continues to rage on, going on and on about how unsafe it is and how I should be ashamed of myself for putting her in danger.

One foot outside the door, I wait until his soliloquy is done before I reply.

"You should know by now, 'Cello," I tilt my head, my tone serious, "that it's not me, nor Sisi, who is in danger. It's everyone who tries to harm her. You know me, and you know what I'm capable of," I tell him squarely.

"Rest assured that *no one* will make it out alive. Is it an inconvenience? Yes," I shrug, "but Sisi is safest with me, where I can see her, touch her, smell her. If not…" I trail off, turning to look at her and seeing the understanding in her eyes, "Then *no one* is safe."

Marcello continues to sputter, not that I thought he'd relent immediately, but Catalina is quick to pacify him.

Grabbing Sisi's hand, I leave the study, heading straight for his garage and grabbing one of his cars.

"You did better than I expected," she mentions when I'm behind the wheel, revving the engine. "And I'm confident they will come around. Eventually."

"They will," I agree, starting the car and gearing up for a long journey home.

It wouldn't be my preference to return to my place, but it *is* the most secure now. The underground framework is unparalleled and for as much as it was built to keep me in, it will also keep other people out.

Sisi's quiet as she stares out the window, her eyes almost closing.

Intent on letting her get some rest, I focus on the road, mentally going over potential scenarios.

The undercover idea isn't bad, and as soon as we get to my computers I'll do an in-depth analysis of Sacre Coeur and comb through some of the recent footage to learn their patterns.

I already know their security is pretty tough, and while I'd gotten in before with some *persuasion*, the tide's bound to change now that I'm not everyone's favorite person.

No doubt, Mother Superior, too, must have been alerted to my search for Miles, and she's bound to have some safety measures in place if I come calling.

My lip curls up in distaste as I think about that woman who's abused Sisi her entire life. I'd never particularly liked her, but she'd run Sacre Coeur with a tight fist, and I know a lot of the local mafiosi see that as an advantage when it comes to keeping their beloved daughters away from the temptations of the world.

Sisi and Catalina were not the only ones who'd been sent there. In fact, a lot of illegitimate daughters have been raised at Sacre Coeur for decades.

Why, I remember Benedicto Guerra himself has a sister who's taken her vows, with a few others in the same situation.

Still, everyone involved in Miles' scheme is bound to have been notified that I'm out for blood, so I don't expect Sacre Coeur to be any different. In any other scenario, it would have been infinitely easier to bust in, ransack Mother Superior's office and interrogate her and then be gone.

But in this case, Sisi's idea about going undercover has the most merit. And unbeknownst to her, I have another ulterior motive for wanting to infiltrate the convent. At last, her tormentors are going to learn what true hell is, right there in their *holy* place.

"Are we there?" she asks groggily, rubbing her eyes with the back of her hand.

"Almost," I reply and I hear her stomach growling, an embarrassed look crossing her face. "We'll order some food too," I say and she regales me with a smile.

"I can't wait to have a good night of sleep," she yawns, suddenly looking so young and vulnerable.

"We both will, and then we'll tackle everything."

I speed through the city, making it home before it gets dark out.

The compound is completely empty as we make our way inside. We quickly settle inside the bedroom, and Sisi places all her things in my wardrobe before we go pick up the food and head to the kitchen.

"You need to call Sasha," she mentions as she takes a bite of her burger. "I don't think I did a good job with your wound, and I don't want you to have complications because of that."

"It doesn't hurt." I shrug.

"It might not hurt *you*, but who knows what's going on inside your body?" She shakes her head. "I want a *proper* doctor to look at you."

I want to protest and tell her this is nothing compared to some other injuries I'd gotten over the years, but one look at her and I know I can't argue. So I relent, calling Sasha and giving him a rundown of my wounds.

"It's not that deep," he notes when we're in the infirmary. "I'll just disinfect it and close it properly. You're lucky the bullet didn't tear the muscle. That would put you out of commission for a while," he comments and I grunt, noting the way Sisi's assessing everything like a shark, making sure Sasha takes good care of me.

"Done," he says, placing a bandage over my shoulder. "Call me if there's anything else." He nods as he exits the room.

"See, that wasn't too hard." Sisi raises an eyebrow at me, taking my hand and leading me to our room.

We both fall asleep the moment our heads hit the pillow. Holding her close to me, I know that now that I've found my heaven I'm never letting anyone take her away from me.

33
VLAD

"**Y**ou're sure he's dead?" I ask, using my foot to turn the body around.

"Yes," she rolls her eyes. "I hit him pretty hard." She crouches down, two fingers roaming down his neck to find his pulse point.

"You should have waited for me, hell girl," I groan, stooping down to check too.

As I'd promised Marcello, we'd done some research into the new priests at Sacre Coeur, and indeed, out of the two, one had been worse than the other, with a penchant for prostitutes.

After much debate, and arguments from my part, Sisi had managed to convince me to let her handle the priest by approaching him in public and asking him for help. I'd had a wire on her at all times as she'd led the man into a dark alley, and I'd been about to burst out too early a couple of times when his words had been borderline offensive.

I know that Sisi wanted me to trust her with this, but

even as my mind knows she can handle herself, my heart cannot take the thought that she might be in danger.

It had taken everything in me to stay put and let her do her thing, especially as she'd told me how much she wanted to feel she was a part of the operation.

"I don't want to feel helpless, Vlad. Ever again. I like being in control, and while I appreciate your concern, you know I can take care of myself." She'd huffed at me, going in depth and listing all the reasons why she could deal with the priest on her own.

And so I'd stayed put until I couldn't any more. At the first sign that there had been a struggle between them, I'd bolted from my hiding place only to find the priest on the floor, out cold.

"The plan was for you to lure him away, not to kill him in plain sight," I add as I realize there's no pulse.

"Tell him that," she mutters under her breath, getting up and strengthening her clothes. "He was one second from getting too handsy, so I just hit him in his neck, like you taught me. I think I might have hit him too hard," she adds thoughtfully, looking down at the dead man.

"You killed a man with your bare hands. And I don't know whether to be proud of you, or mad that you put yourself in danger." I whistle, the sight of her in that tight skirt giving me a third choice—fuck her for making me both proud and mad.

She bats her lashes, slowly moving toward me as she steps over the corpse.

"Normally I'd ask you what you're going to do about it," she says as she points her finger into my chest, trailing it up my pecs and my neck and letting it rest under my jaw, "but I don't think that would be smart with a dead man at our feet. In plain sight."

"Hell girl." I catch her finger, already uncomfortably hard. "You're not playing fair," I growl as I feel her fitted to my front, my cock against her stomach.

My hand dips low as I drape one leg over my hip, feeling for her naked flesh as I move my fingers up her thigh, tracing the shape of one ass cheek.

"You know you make me hard when you talk corpse to me, hell girl. But when you're actually dropping them at my feet?" I groan, my thumb slipping between her ass cheeks as I move lower.

"I thought you'd enjoy the show." She has the gall to smirk at me, nuzzling her face into the crook of my neck, her tongue peeking out to lick my pulse.

"Sisi," I close my eyes, my fingers already drenched in her arousal. "I'm one second away from taking you against the wall, right in this dirty alley where everyone can see us." My breath ragged, my dick painfully hard, I can barely control myself as I slip a digit inside her, feeling her snug channel strangle the life out of me.

"Would that be so bad?" she asks, her voice low and so fucking alluring I'm about to come in my pants just from the sound of it.

"Fuck, Sisi," I curse, shoving her against the wall. "Does that turn you on? People watching as I thrust into you? Or is it the dead body? You want to come all around my fingers knowing there's a fucking corpse at your feet?" I ask just as I push two fingers inside of her.

Her mouth parts, her breath coming in short spurts. My hand around her neck, I slowly massage the area before I move up, my thumb parting her lips and slipping inside her mouth.

"Tell me, is that what you want?" I thrust harder into her pussy, and her wetness flows down my fingers, coating my entire hand. I feel the way her body's becoming slack in my arms, her eyes wide as they never leave mine, her tongue playing with the tip of my thumb as she releases soft, mewy moans.

"Tell me," I repeat, wanting to hear exactly what she's craving.

No matter how depraved.

"You," she replies softly, her eyes fluttering closed as she pushes herself on my fingers. "You're all I want," she continues, sucking on my thumb as I finger fuck her pussy.

"That's the perfect answer, my sweet little flower," I murmur against her lips, leaning forward and giving her a long lick with my tongue. "Because I'm going to give you a prize for your kill." I continue to thrust in and out of her, my thumb on her clit as I circle the little bud until she's writhing in my arms.

My knee between her legs, I let her place all her weight on me as she starts coming, her orgasm making her gasp against my mouth.

"But I'm not going to fuck you now. Not when *anyone* could see you. I told you before, hell girl. You're for my eyes only. Your sounds." I apply more pressure on her pussy with my entire hand, the back of my palm squeezing her clit while my fingers are buried deep inside her. "Your facial expressions. Everything is for me, and me alone. Understand?"

"Yes." She can barely speak as she crashes against me, her head on my shoulder, her breathing harsh.

"Good." I lift the fingers coated in her essence and I bring them to my mouth, sucking them. "Because I'd have to kill anyone who saw you," I add, my other hand still on her neck as I gently knead her flesh. "I would gouge their eyes out, and turn their brains to mush," I rasp, violence simmering inside me at the thought of another looking at her.

"You'd give them a lobotomy?" she probes, amused.

"I'd obliterate every sensory organ," I continue, and I notice she's getting off on my description. "I'd make it so that there's nothing left of them. Is that what you want, hell girl? You want me to take them apart limb by limb while you watch? You'd like that, wouldn't you? Seeing the river of blood that flows out of their veins…" I trail off, feeling the way her pulse picks up.

"You think I haven't realized that blood turns you on?" She gasps softly, lifting those pretty eyes of hers to look at me, so light and big and fuck me if the way she gazes at me alone doesn't unman me.

"What is it about it that arouses you so? Is it the color? That deep red that mesmerizes and tantalizes the senses? Or is it the consistency? That sticky feeling that reminds you of my cum all over your tight little body?"

Her body starts quivering, my words affecting her just like my touch. Her cheeks are flushed, her pupils so fucking big as if she drowned herself in belladonna. "Or wait," I chuckle softly, moving my mouth over her cheek until I reach her ear, nibbling at the small lobe.

"I think it's the sight of life leaving a body that has you

so hot and bothered. The fact that red is the very essence of life, and when it flows..." I pause as I hear her intake of breath, "You gain control over death."

Her mouth drops open, and the beginning of a moan escapes her lips before I swallow it whole with my mouth, feeling her pleasure as mine. That mere action has me coming on the spot, my cock jerking in my jeans, spurts of cum staining the inside of my pants.

It's minutes later that she gains control of her body, and as she glances up at me, I know that she can feel how fucking hard I came just from pleasuring her.

The corners of her mouth lift up in a mischievous smile.

"You're dangerous," she whispers, her hand trailing down my chest, "but maybe I'm more dangerous," she says as she slips her hand beneath the waistband of my pants, cupping me and giving me a quick stroke, her hand gathering all my cum as she brings it up to her face.

She teases me with her tongue as she licks my seed off her fingers, all the while giving me that innocent look of hers.

"That's it, Sisi. We need to get back," I breathe out, barely able to contain myself. "Now."

She blinks twice as she realizes the urgency of my words and for once she starts behaving, probably knowing that if she pushes me over the brink I *will* fuck her right here, and then I'll have to kill any unlucky passerby.

We quietly load the priest in the back of my car and then we're back at the compound, finalizing the plans.

True to her word, Sisi had designed a board of connections for everyone we'd been able to find information on, with some people still holding question marks—like DeVille and Guerra.

There's a question mark from Meester to Miles as well, but his other connections to my father and brother are becoming clearer.

Dressed in a pair of wide-legged pants and a tight shirt, she's standing in front of the panel, her thumb stroking her jaw as she's considering the information.

"There's something that doesn't sit right with me." She turns to me, frowning. I nod to her to continue, taking a chair and waiting for her to speak.

"See here." She points to all the Russian Syndicates that are confirmed to be involved with Miles. The same ones who are out for *my* blood now. "Some of these are *very* small organizations," she notes, grabbing a file and going through each organization in part.

"Vasiliev has maybe fifty people in total, Semenov has even less. You and Yelchin have the most under you, but even that isn't great."

"Are you criticizing my organization, hell girl?" I drawl but she just rolls her eyes at me.

"With these numbers, why would they be investing in a super soldier experiment? What's in it for them? And an experiment that doesn't have any reliable data either."

My lips curl up and I can't help but look at her in awe.

"You'd be right." I get up from the chair and head to her board, continuing to watch her as she walks me through her reasoning.

"At first, I thought that maybe they'd want these super soldiers for their own organization, and certainly, who wouldn't want someone who doesn't feel pain." She tilts her head at me, "Has no fear and is practically a war machine. But this is an exorbitant amount of money that's been flowing from and into their accounts." She thrusts the papers at me.

I don't even have to look to know what she's talking about, since I have them already memorized.

"Then I thought that *maybe* they were looking to sell them, since they would be a hot commodity to any private or national army," she continues and my lips twitch, pride swelling in my chest as I see where she's going.

She's my match. In absolutely every way.

"But why would they risk *so much* money in something that's not remotely close to a finished product," she asks, her tone serious.

"Are you saying I'm an unfinished product, hell girl?" I fire back, enjoying the way she becomes flustered.

"Vlad!" she exclaims, fuming at me.

"Go on, go on." I lift my hands up to pacify her.

"What I'm trying to say," she takes a deep breath, turning to the board, "is that I don't think Project Humanitas is where they are funneling the money *in* or *out* of," she explains. "Maybe some of it ends up there, since Miles is clearly a fanatic, but how many people do you think would buy the super soldier bullshit? My father certainly didn't and by all accounts he would have been thrilled at the prospect of having killing machines at his beck and call."

"Indeed," I reply, my eyes sparkling with excitement. "Then where do you think the cash flow is coming from?"

She purses her lips, her brows drawing together.

"Human trafficking of some sort. But it must be at an insane scale. Think about it. Children missing. People *without* the mutation are missing. There must be some type of underground ring and *everyone* is involved. The question is, though, what could be so important that all these people were so keen on investing? It's clear everything ties to Miles somehow, but besides his weird, rather personal, plans about the super soldiers, there's no other information on what he could be up to."

"You're right," I agree, my voice full of pride. "My guess is that once Miles realized he couldn't get the investment he needed for his project, he resorted to something else to draw people in. At the same time, he funneled some of that money into his own research. You're right that not everyone would buy into the super soldier crap he had going, even though the results do seem appealing. The research, though, isn't reliable enough for him to be able to push it to the more skeptical people," I add, coming to stand next to her in front of the board.

"And I think that's where Meester comes into play." I point to his photo at the top of the board, tracing his connection to Miles with my fingers. "Ever since my father took him under his wing, he's been extolling the virtues of human trafficking as a source of fast cash. At the time, my father had his own, rather profitable business with drugs, and he wasn't a man prone to change what was already working for him."

"So Meester started his own thing?"

"Yes. You saw the situation at *Papillion*. There's a demand for *everything*. There are just not enough people who can fulfill these demands. Animals, humans, rarities, every one of those is valuable to the right buyer. And Meester certainly capitalized on that."

"And the fights," she notes.

"Yes. His main business is the fighting. He buys slaves from all over the world and trains them to be the next best thing."

"Do you think that might be it? Illegal fighting? But wouldn't that profit from strong, genetically superior fighters?"

"I've thought about that too, and I've managed to pull some data from his past fights. But because everything is so underground, I couldn't find much. The info I do have points toward regular fighters. So if he does have some of those super soldiers Miles might have created, he hasn't shown them to the public yet."

"Then it can't be illegal fighting that everyone is so interested in, right?"

I shake my head.

"No. It's too niche and unpredictable for this many people to be involved in it. I've had a word with Enzo too, since a lot of the stuff that goes on in that sphere is linked to his name. He's been digging into it and he promised to send me an updated file with buyers and suppliers."

"You think Jimenez might have been involved in this?" she asks, frowning.

I'd given her a full rundown of Enzo's businesses and everything that had happened in the past few years when Enzo had struck a deal with Jimenez to sell out his family. But with Jimenez's untimely death he'd become the sole executor of half his fortune.

And since Jimenez was a known sex trafficker in the region, it might make sense that he'd be involved in this shit.

Except he isn't.

I should know since I've been listening in to all of Enzo's conversations for the better part of the year, giving me a good enough idea of what Jimenez left behind and how Enzo's been using those resources.

"Nope," I answer without hesitation. "You could say I'm intimately familiar with the workings of Jimenez's empire since he was the first one I tried to infiltrate in my search for Katya. I know almost every facet of his business and I can assure you he couldn't have been involved. Mostly because he couldn't break into New York until very recently. This." I point toward the board of connections, "Is much older and probably stretches back more than a decade."

"I see." She nods, digesting the information.

"But now, when you figure Sacre Coeur into the equation, I think it's something a bit different," I add, narrowing my eyes.

I have a hunch of what it might be, but I'll reserve judgement for after we get the information from Mother Superior.

"It's definitely something valuable if so many people are willing to bet everything on it."

"We find out what that is, and we find Miles. Because an operation of this magnitude is bound to need a lot of space to manage that flow of people. And most definitely, we're talking about a *lot* of crooked officials that allow this to happen."

"Dear God, but that means levels and levels of corruption," she adds, horrified.

"Yes. And knowing how dangerous going that deep is going to be, I would have ceased this immediately for your safety. But they are already targeting us, so I need to make sure they are wiped off the face of this Earth. Only then will I be at peace," I say, resolute in my decision to end this for good.

As long as anyone aims to hurt my Sisi, then they are as good as dead.

"Vlad," she turns to me, "you know I would never let you do that. Even if it was for my safety. You *need* to find your sister, and even more, you *need* to find out what happened to Vanya. Otherwise you'll never be able to move past this."

She raises her hand, fitting it to my cheek.

"You've seen how unlocking some of your memories has helped you. I believe that once you know for sure what happened to you two there you will be able to move on. And maybe your episodes will disappear too—this time forever," she says softly, her warm gaze full of love.

"You're right." I take a deep breath. "And I do need to get better. For you," I start, leaning into her touch, "and for the family we'll have in the future. I know I wouldn't be able to trust myself with…" I trail off and she knows exactly what I mean as her mouth pulls into a sad smile.

"You're enough for me, Vlad. I just want you to be better for *you*."

"I may be enough now," I trail a finger down her face, tucking a strand behind her ear, "but I won't be enough forever," I tell her sincerely.

I'd known this ever since I'd seen how affected she'd been by the miscarriage. She is so kind and so full of love that any child would be lucky to have her.

"You're going to want children eventually, Sisi, and I *need* to be normal enough to be able to give them to you."

"Vlad…"

"No," I place my finger on her lips, "don't lie to me and don't lie to yourself, Sisi. I know you will want a family someday. And I want that too, because I know what a great mother you'll make. But until that moment comes, I'll do my best to work on myself, so that I'm not a danger to you, or to our children."

"God, Vlad," she whispers, her eyes glossy with tears, "why are you so perfect?" she sighs deeply.

"I'm not. But I aim to be. For you," I lean in to kiss her forehead.

34
VLAD

"We need to focus on her office and her living quarters," I tell Sisi after we'd carefully watched some of the footage from Sacre Coeur, making some notes regarding Mother Superior's patterns.

"She is the type of person who would keep everything on paper," Sisi notes as she dons her habit again.

Unlike the nuns who'd taken their vows, her habit isn't black, but a light-blue.

"I can't believe I have to wear this again," she mutters under her breath as she stuffs her hair into the headpiece. "Well?" she turns toward me, raising an eyebrow.

"What do you want me to say? To me you'd look hot dressed in anything."

"This," she huffs out a breath, taking a hand mirror and examining her birthmark. "That's why I hated these headpieces. This is always so visible." She releases a disappointed sigh.

"Sisi." In two steps I'm behind her, turning her to face me and making her drop the mirror. "This," I brush my hand across her red mark, "only makes you more unique. It gives your beauty character."

I lean in to kiss the spot right above her eyebrow, "The sum of your imperfections is what makes you perfect to me, Sisi."

"There you go again with your honeyed words," she murmurs, blushing to the roots of her hairs.

"Don't put your head down again," I tip her chin up so she can look in my eyes, "I told you hell girl. From now on everyone's going to *bow* to you, not look down on you."

She nods at me.

"You're right. I should stop being ashamed of this," she touches her birthmark with her finger, "it's part of what makes me *me*," she says and I couldn't be prouder of her.

"Yes, I'm glad we're on the same page," I chuckle, giving her a quick kiss on the lips, "now finish dressing so we can go."

"I'm done," she says, appraising me with her eyes, "I can't say the same thing about you, though, Mr. Hot Priest." She motions to my neck.

I'd dressed entirely in black, donning a classical catholic cassock, but I hadn't yet put on the clerical collar.

Taking the white piece off the table, she places it around my neck, making sure it's laid in place and covering my tattoo.

"Now, if you were *my* priest," she starts saucily, suggestively moving her hands all over my chest, "I know I'd be a permanent fixture for confession time."

"Really," I drawl, "and what would your confession be, hell girl?" I ask, curious to see what she'd cook up.

Her lips curl upwards in a feline smile, her lashes fluttering in that maddening fashion of hers, "I'd ask for forgiveness…" she trails off, suddenly imitating a shy schoolgirl as she peers at me bashfully. "For playing with my pussy while thinking about you," she whispers, two red dots staining her cheeks.

Fuck!

"Damn it, Sisi! You can't say things like that and assume I won't be spending the entire time thinking about you in that damned confession booth, playing with yourself while I listen to you moaning your sins," I groan, closing my eyes and willing my body to behave.

We have a plan. A carefully laid out plan that has no room for any mistakes. Or for illicit rendezvous in the confession booth, or me fucking her on the altar table, because damn if that's not all I can think about now, the image of her laid out bare before me, surrounded by holy objects when she's in fact the holiest of them all…

"Fuck, Sisi. You're killing me here, hell girl," I mumble as I reach down to adjust my cock.

"Well, aren't you coming?" I open my eyes to see her already at the door, a satisfied grin on her face.

"You're a goddamn cock tease, aren't you?" I call out as I sheathe my knives before following her.

Her soft laughter is the only reply I get as I try to get back in the zone.

I'm a simple man. I only have two default settings—killing and Sisi. And when the latter is activated, you can damned well bet I'll be useless for anything other than *her*.

The drive to the church takes us over an hour, time in which we go over the plan once more. Since Sisi is familiar with every corner of Sacre Coeur, we aren't going in blind.

Although I'd done my homework by studying the security footage, there are only a few security cameras aimed at the cloisters and the living quarters of the nuns. So I'll rely on her knowledge for that.

As soon as we are somewhere close to the convent, I park the car, doing one last check.

Sisi has an entire artillery strapped to her body under her habit, just like I do. We'd wanted to be as thorough as possible, and since Sacre Coeur's been involved in shady dealings for years, we shouldn't underestimate the place.

"Check your comm," I say as she gets out of the car.

The plan is to have her go inside first, pretending she's returning to the convent after a prolonged visit with her family, and I'd soon join her after going through the validation process at the gates.

She lifts her hand to her ear, clicking the device and prompting me to say something.

"Works," she confirms.

"Good. Give me a signal when you're in," I tell her, almost wont to see her go alone.

"See you in a bit." She gives me a quick kiss before leaving.

While I wait, I listen attentively to everything that's happening around her, my thirst for blood only increasing as I hear some off-handed comments from the guards about her.

"Don't mind them," she whispers as she passes through the security checkpoint, "they probably just heard the rumors about me," she says as if it's no big deal that they just called her an *outcast*.

I clench my fist, my rage mounting as I realize this is just a tiny bit of what she's had to endure over the years.

And ah, but they will definitely wish they'd have kept their mouths shut today. Especially after I'm done with them.

"I'm near the graph," she speaks into the comm, "you should leave in about five."

At her signal, I get out of the car, once more double checking that all my weapons are in place. Since I am a new addition to the convent, they will *definitely* make me go through the metal detector. So I'd had to be a bit clever, and arm myself with obsidian knives. I'd also stacked 3D printed parts of a gun in my cloak, ready to assemble them should the need arise.

All in all, I should be able to pass *any* security check.

Entering through the gates, I meet two guards who look me up and down, immediately treating me ten times better than they had Sisi.

Probably because I'm a man.

Fucking bastards, I scan their faces carefully as they go through all the protocol with me, ensuring that I will know who to kill later on.

There are some papers to be signed, but soon I'm vetted and ready to go.

"Where are you?" I ask Sisi when I make it past them.

They'd been unusually lax with me, not even bothering to make me pass through the metal detector.

"Close to the chapel," she answers.

"Good, I'll meet you there."

I don't even get to finish my words as I hear someone address Sisi.

"Oh, look who's here," a girl says. "Assisi." Her name is uttered with disdain as she continues to insult *my wife.* "What happened, did they realize what a loser you were and they returned you?" She continues, laughing at her.

"They probably had too much bad luck and decided to get rid of her," another one joins in, and they both seem to be laughing at Sisi.

My Sisi.

My feet swiftly carry me in that direction, my vision tunneled as I only see one thing—death.

"Auch." My eyes widen as I hear a voice yelp in pain. "Stop," she continues, and just then I round the corner, having a perfect view of the chapel.

A smile pulls at my lips as I still, crossing my arms over my chest and watching with pride as my girl takes care of those bullies.

Sisi's standing over the two girls, holding one in a choke-hold, while the other is on the ground, her face fitted to the pavement as Sisi pushes her foot in her cheek.

"Please," one continues to beg for mercy.

"Really? What did you do when *I* said please?" Sisi asks, her voice unyielding. "Here, this is what happens when you say please." She smirks before she twists the other nun, pushing her to the ground, her head smashing on the pavement.

There are only gasps of pain as she cannot even stand up anymore, her hands trembling in a poor attempt to move.

"Do you want to say please as well?" Sisi asks the other nun, stooping low to look at her.

She doesn't answer, or can't answer, since Sisi's foot is

still holding her down. Just when I think she might let them go, though, she goes one step further as she lifts her foot, using the momentum to crash it into the girl's face.

There's a small sound through the comm as I'm completely sure that she's shattered her brow ridge.

"Sisi, come here," I tell her, on the one hand extremely proud of her, on the other worried this might draw unwanted attention to us—which I am fine with, but only after we've secured what we're looking for.

She lifts her face up, spotting me in the distance. Her lips curl up and she starts sprinting toward me, a carefree expression on her face that makes me still, staring at her and her magnificent beauty.

Fuck. Me.

I'm pretty sure my mouth is gaping open as I can only watch her run closer, her smile fucking blinding me.

"Did you see," she asks me, excited yet out of breath, "I gave them back what they deserved," she continues, pure delight in her voice.

"I'm proud of you, hell girl," I praise her, gently patting her head.

Somehow her habit makes her seem even smaller and daintier, the top of her head barely reaching the middle of my chest. I'd gotten so used to her around me all of the time that even our size differences had become a moot point.

Though she's tiny compared to me, her personality is a force to be reckoned with, making me completely forget I'm dealing with a bite-sized human.

She's just *my* Sisi.

I'm trying my best to keep a comfortable distance should anyone see us. Still, the sight of her joyful smile as she enthusiastically tells me how she's wanted to do that for the longest time only makes my heart beat faster.

"I've never really resorted to violence before," she sighs, "mostly because they had strength in numbers and I knew that I may have hurt them once, but the next time they would ensure they paid me back in spades. But now…"

She looks up, her lips parting in such a stunning smile, I'm having a hard time not to ask her to let me fucking paint it and immortalize it forever. "That felt so good," she exclaims, jumping up and down in a happy dance.

"Hell girl." I stop suddenly, and she turns to me, tilting her head and looking worried.

"This," I tell her as I place two fingers at the corners of her mouth, tugging them down in a neutral position. "I'll have a hard time concentrating if you keep on smiling, so please, hold it off until we're done," I instruct her, my tone serious.

She starts chuckling at me before shaking herself, a sudden serious expression on her face as she nods.

"Understood," she replies, even though her lips are quivering with unreleased laughter.

The minx.

35
SISI

Vlad can't help his sly smile every time he looks at me, and for all his protests that I shouldn't tempt him further, he sure does a good job of eliciting that response from me.

As we head to the administrative buildings, I realize that the convent is quieter than I'm used to. Especially since it's not quite curfew yet.

There had been the not so welcome meeting with Sofia and Carlotta who just had to spew their venom at me. But for the first time I'd given them what they deserved, even though it was reckless for me to do so.

But when they'd said I was bad luck I'd just snapped, years of being called that to my face made me forget about everything but revenge.

In all honesty, I'd expected Vlad to chastise me slightly for going off plan, but instead he'd just said he was proud of me, his expression full of so much support that I almost melted on the spot.

Still, I can't stray from the plan again until we finish with Mother Superior.

And so as we enter the building that houses her office, Vlad's skills in lock picking have a chance to shine.

"And that's another skill to add to your arsenal," I note, amused.

"You'll see, hell girl. There's few things I'm *not* good at." He winks at me, the door sliding open with a minimal push.

"Show off," I mutter just as he motions me inside, intoning *ladies first.*

The office is very simple, with a desk, a chair, and a few drawers.

"According to what I've observed, she only comes to the office every Tuesday and Thursday, so that means we have plenty of time to search without fear she'll show up," he says as he opens one drawer, taking out the files.

We start sorting through everything in the office, but most of the documents are administrative papers from Sacre Coeur or from one of the orphanages.

"This is mostly donations." I sigh as I finish with one drawer.

"Nothing on my side either," he comments as he shuffles through the papers, his eyes quickly scanning for keywords.

Sometimes I forget I'm dealing with someone who's not quite human. In the time it has taken me to go through one stack, he's gone through three.

"We might have to check her room," I add, disappointed. I'd hoped we'd find everything we were looking for in her office, so we wouldn't have to linger more than necessary.

"Not yet," Vlad says, his eyes still on the papers.

When he finishes his perusal, he drops them on the desk with a thud, looking annoyed.

"You said she *only* kept physical records," he starts, his thumb stroking his jaw.

I nod.

"She was pretty known for her dislike of technology. They even tried to add some more devices to the church and other places around the convent to make it easier for us. But she wouldn't have it. It was a huge scandal a couple years back. She kept saying that technology is the work of the devil and it has no place in the house of God. Unless she's a bigger hypocrite than I gave her credit for, I don't think she'd have any technology."

"You might be right." He goes around the desk, taking out the chair and inspecting the wall. "See? There are no wires for ethernet, or even a socket. On that note, who doesn't use at least a lamp?" He shakes his head, a smile on his lips, "Unless she's reading all these documents at candle light?" he jokes.

But just as I turn my head I spot an empty candle holder, and I show it to him. "Candle light it is," I tell him and he chuckles.

"Why would someone who is clearly not interested in the commodities of modern life be involved in human trafficking? What is she even doing with the money?" He purses his lips, continuing to look around.

"We should go to her room, since there's nothing here." I dust off my habit as I stand up, putting everything back inside the drawers, so it doesn't seem as if someone's been here.

"No, not yet," Vlad mumbles, taking a few steps back and studying the walls.

While the convent is old, the administrative buildings were built more recently, somewhere in the later part of the twentieth century, so everything around is pure concrete.

"If she doesn't trust computers to keep her things safe." He narrows his eyes as he studies the wall behind the desk. "Then she must trust something, right?"

His shrewd gaze moves slowly over every inch of concrete. I frown as I reach his side, trying to see what he's staring at but finding nothing out of the ordinary. Just plain, white walls.

"What is it?" I ask when he takes a step forward, immediately focusing on one spot in particular—the one that's hiding behind the drawers.

He doesn't answer. Instead, he moves the drawers to the middle of the room, heading back to the wall and knocking lightly in the cement. He continues to do this, moving a few inches to the right every time.

Until he stops.

"Hear that," he says, his ear to the wall. When I'm at his side, he knocks again, and my eyes widen as I realize what he means.

"It's hollow."

He nods, his hands moving around the surface of the wall as if he's looking for something. When he reaches a few bumps in the lower half, he flattens his palm against them, pushing them in.

A few tries, and a trap door built inside the wall snaps open.

"I'm guessing this is her trusted place." He smirks, clearly pleased with himself.

Wrenching the fake wall open, we find a very small storage space, all filled with boxes.

"I guess we'll be spending quite some time here," I add drily as we take out the boxes, placing them on the floor. "Or not..." I roll my eyes when I see him already putting down a couple of files, done with them.

"I'm a fast reader." He shrugs.

"No, you're an insanely fast reader. What is that even?" I take a box, removing a few papers and start to go through them.

"I can read almost two thousand words per minute," he says casually, "it helps to sift through lots of information."

"Wow, of course you'd measure yourself," I add playfully, "good stroke for your ego."

He lifts his eyes, looking at me strangely.

"It was Miles who made us test our speed. He wanted us to excel in all areas. And I, of course, was his star pupil," he jokes, and while he tries to seem amused, I can tell he's not unaffected by that memory.

I want to apologize for bringing it up, but I know he wouldn't appreciate that. Vlad likes to pretend he's invincible, especially when it comes to matters of a more emotional nature, since he's not quite used to his feelings.

That doesn't mean he's still not human, with perfectly humane reactions. He just doesn't know how to deal with them.

We continue to look through each paper in part until Vlad finally comes across something interesting.

"What's that?" I ask as he removes a stack of folders from the bottom of the box.

He frowns as he spreads them out.

"Medical files," he says, reading the names of the people they belong to.

"I know those people," I immediately interject. "Everyone is from Sacre Coeur. Wait... does that mean there's one for me too?" I get up, quickly taking a seat next to him.

"Let's see," he shuffles through them until, surely enough, there is one with my name on it.

I grab it out of his hands, too curious to see what's inside.

"This doesn't make sense," I mumble as I go through all the lab results. Vlad leans in to read, his brows furrowing as he points at something.

"Sisi," he starts, and I can tell by his voice alone that it's something bad. "These are all tests that they do for organ compatibility."

"What do you mean?"

"Here." He takes the folder from me, pointing to one page. "This is a confirmation of compatibility for bone marrow." He continues to scan the information, but I'm having a hard time digesting what he just said.

"A bone marrow transplant. For me? But I don't remember being sick," I tell him.

"According to this file, you were three years and seven months old when this happened. And you weren't sick," he says grimly, and there's a hint of violence in his words, "you were the one who *gave* the bone marrow. Fuck, Sisi..." He curses under his breath, quickly going back to the other files.

"This. All this," he says, opening each file and looking at the many lab results, "these are all compatibility results. Fuck." He closes his eyes, his fists clenched.

"Vlad, slow down." I touch his arm, a hint of panic swelling inside of me. "What's happening?"

"Illegal organ transplants. That was the missing piece. That's why everyone would be so willing to get involved, and that's why there are so many levels of corruption. Because what wouldn't people give for a new kidney, or a new lung, when through official channels you wait years for a new organ that may never come."

"Vlad." I take a deep breath, too overwhelmed by this. "Are you saying that they took bone marrow from me to sell to someone? Just like that?"

He nods grimly, the papers in his hand crackling under the pressure of his grip.

"Fuck, Sisi. I'm so sorry," he says, but I can't hear anything more.

I close my eyes, vaguely remembering the hospital visits when all the kids had been given candy after some procedure. I try hard to remember what had happened, but nothing comes to me.

"Who else? Who else donated?" My voice trembles slightly as I turn to Vlad, snatching the folders from his lap. "What did they donate?"

But as we go through each and every file, what we find out is horrifying. There are cases of *every* organ being taken from children.

Children!

And the more we delve into the other boxes, the more names we find from the other orphanages.

"It's an entire ring," I whisper. "And they've been doing this for decades. Decades, Vlad. And no one's found out?"

"But that's just the thing, hell girl. Everyone knew about it. They just protected their own interests because they knew they would, at some point, need these services too."

"So this is what Miles leveraged to get funding for his project. He'd set up the facilities for the transplants, and he'd provide medical personnel, right?"

"Yes. Exactly. And that means that Mother Superior *should* know where his headquarters are, since I bet he's housing all his procedures in the same place."

"I want to know too," I whisper, my eyes on him. "I want to know who took that from me. I want to know who paid for my bone marrow. Hell, Vlad, I…" I trail off, my throat clogging with emotion as I realize just how much this place had exploited me.

Me and all these other children.

"Sisi." He grips my nape, bringing my forehead to his. Closing his eyes, he holds me to him, his breath on my lips, his warmth on my skin. "We'll find out. I promise you. And I'll kill everyone who touched a hair on your body, you get me?"

His hands move slowly to cup my cheeks, urging me to look him in the eyes.

"You get me, Sisi? I'll kill everyone you want me to. You just give me a name, and it's done. Fuck." He releases a ragged breath. "Fuck, Sisi. I can't…" He leans closer, kissing my forehead, my nose, and finally my lips.

"The thought of you, small and defenseless on a fucking hospital bed while some makeshift nurse is sticking a needle into your spine is killing me," he sighs deeply. "It's fucking killing me."

"I don't remember it. I really don't." I press my own hand to his cheek. "Maybe it's better this way, but I still need to find out. I… This can't go on, Vlad. I know the world is a fucked up place, but we're talking about children. Defenseless children with no one to look after them." My breath catches in my throat, because this feels a little too close to home.

I was one of those children, after all.

"They can't get away with it," I continue, almost suffocating from this anguish, a deep chasm opening in my heart as I realize how lucky I'd been to make it out alive.

When others weren't.

"They won't," he's quick to say. "They won't. One word from you, hell girl, and I pull the trigger. That's it. No questions asked." He strokes my hair gently, the emotion in his features almost mirroring my own.

Because we are one.

"I'm *your* killing machine. So use me. Kill everyone you want. You say the word, and their heads drop. It's that easy," he continues, and I can see this is the only way he knows how to comfort me.

"We'll do it. Together," I say, more resolute than ever.

By the time we finish filtering through everything, it's already night. We put everything back, and then we make our way toward the living quarters.

"How are we going to make her talk?" I ask right before we go inside the building.

"Leave that to me, Sisi. I'll make sure she tells us *every-*

thing before I kill her in the most painful way for everything she's done to you."

"No." I stop, my hand on his arm. "Let me." I raise my eyes to his. "I want to be the one to do this. I…"

He places his finger on my lips, not letting me continue.

"I know. I know." He presses his lips in a tight line. "I'll help you with whatever you need. You know I always have your back," he says, his sweet words warming me on the inside.

"I know the whole purpose of this was to find Miles," I tell him before I lose my courage. "But I also feel like I'm finally closing a painful chapter in my life. Past secrets are being revealed, and the people who made my life a living hell are going to be punished."

"I'm glad." He lifts my hand to his mouth. "As long as you're happy, I'm happy," he says and I can't help myself as I quickly jump up to lay a kiss on his cheek.

"Let's do this!"

Except Mother Superior isn't in her apartments. We search everywhere for her, but she's not inside.

"Let me check the cameras quickly." Vlad pulls out his phone, accessing the feed and looking for any sign of her.

"There." He finds her in one frame, leaving her quarters at midnight. Accessing some of the other cameras, we manage to pinpoint her location to somewhere around the church.

Vlad also does one of his tricks and manages to divert all security footage, placing it in a loop, so there will be no trace of us.

"She must be inside the church," I note when we get in front of it.

"A bit too late to pray her sins away, wouldn't you say?" Vlad mutters dryly, aggression already rolling off of him.

He's been like this since we found my medical file. While he hadn't outright said it, I can tell it pains him even more than me, since I don't remember anything. But he has intimate knowledge of what it feels like to be cut and probed, so it must not have been easy to hear that I'd been in a similar situation.

From the beginning I've been able to note the change in the atmosphere around him whenever his moods oscillate, and the tension had become increasingly unbearable as I'd watch him clench and unclench his fists when he thought I was distracted.

In his own way, he doesn't want to bring it up to me in fear that it might trigger a memory, and so I know he's holding back a lot. But after we're done with Mother Superior, I aim to have a conversation with him.

Stopping in front of the church, I take a deep breath, ready to face all my past demons. Nodding to Vlad, I push open the door.

He's behind me, and I feel the way his eyes are studying every inch of our surroundings, so I know that *nothing* can harm me. Having him by my side truly makes me feel invincible, and so I give him one last smile before I school my features.

The reckoning has arrived.

As we walk down the aisle, I see the huddled form of Mother Superior. She's on her knees, her head bent low in front of the altar, a long rosary hanging from her hands. Her head whips back the moment she hears the noise behind her, her eyes having a hard time to discern who it is that's disturbing her private time.

"Don't you know it's curfew time?' she asks, her voice grating on my nerves as I suddenly remember every insult and every mockery uttered by that *very* voice.

I don't answer, stepping further into the church.

My own knight in shining armor is trailing behind, blending in the shadows as he just watches, letting me do what I *need* to do. And his unconditional trust is the only thing that makes me capable to follow through.

The only light inside the church is coming from the altar, where a dozen candles are lit in a small circle, the flicker of light confined to a small area.

And so it's not until I'm mere steps away from her that Mother Superior realizes who I am, her eyes widening, her mouth hanging open in shock.

"Assisi," she sputters, flustered. "What… what are you doing here?"

"Mother Superior," I say somberly, and a wicked thought to play with her crosses my mind, "I've come to give you your dues," I continue, very slowly putting one foot in front of the other.

"How come you're here? You can't be here?" She gets to her feet, looking at me with confusion.

"Isn't that where we all go where we are aimless? To the place we know best? Home?" The word home burns on my lips, and knowing this had been indeed my home for so long does little to quench the need for destruction brewing inside of me.

"What… I don't know what you're talking about," she

immediately counters, although I note a slight twitch in her eye as she looks around for any exit.

"Did you know what they did to me?" I ask, fighting back a smile as she narrows her eyes at me. In spite of her perceived bravado, I can see the slight trembling of her hands, the beads of the rosary moving in a back and forth motion and clinking against each other.

"How they took from my body until there was nothing left? And *you* allowed it," I intone, putting all the strength in my voice and enjoying the way the sound echoes in the church. I lift my finger up and point at her, and finally I receive the reaction I've been waiting on from her.

Her features blank, her mask dropping as she realizes what I mean.

"What…" she whispers, slowly backing away from me. "You're not real." She shakes her head.

Well, well, but I think my ghostly talk seems to be working. And so I push, wanting to see the fear etched on her face.

"It's your fault," I say as I take one more step toward her.

She keeps on shaking her head, closing her eyes and doing the sign of the cross over her body, her lips muttering a quiet prayer.

"Are you scared now? Scared to face your sins?"

My tone is consistent throughout, and I make a conscious effort to not give myself away by bursting out in a scream, demanding to know exactly what she did to me.

And it seems to work as she continues to back away until she trips on the small steps of the altar, falling down on her ass.

Her eyes are wildly looking around for an exit, her hand thrusting that rosary into my face as if it might protect her from me.

Dropping on one knee in front of her, I snatch it out of her hands, flinging it to the ground.

"You," she spews, her brows tightening together, her hand reaching out to touch my arm, "you're not dead," she continues, her voice accusatory.

And therein lies the issue. Why would she think I'm dead if she's not knee deep into this whole thing?

36

SISI

"And how would you know if I died?" I tilt my head to the side, studying her reactions.

"You…" she stammers, and her hands reach out for me once more, probably trying to apply some more of the punishments she'd inflicted on me when I was younger.

There's just one problem.

I'm not a child anymore.

I catch her hands midair, twisting her until my arms around her neck, restricting her airflow.

"I think we have some unresolved issues, Mother Superior," I whisper into her ear. "And I'd like you to cooperate," I continue, grabbing the rosary from the floor and wrapping it around her throat, the beads digging into her flesh.

One glance back, and I motion Vlad to come forward.

He casually saunters up to the altar, immediately immobilizing Mother Superior's limbs to the table.

"And that demon." She spits the word out when she gets a clear view of Vlad. "Of course! I could expect nothing else of you, slumming it with the devil. I told you, didn't I?" She gives a maniacal laugh. "That you'd end up steeped in sin." She sneers at me and before I can help myself, my fist flies down and into her face, knocking her to the side.

Her eyes wide, she looks at me as if she can't believe I just dared to do that.

"Ah, but I'd choose my loyal devil over your facetious God any time of the day," I lean forward. "You who condemn sins, but privately bathes in them. You," my nostrils flare as my anger mounts, "have the audacity to tell *me* I'm steeped in sin? As if every inch of your monstrous flesh," I grab her jaw in my hands, tightly holding her so that she cannot avert her eyes, "isn't rotting away as we speak."

"Why are you here, Assisi?" she asks, her gaze definitely meeting mine, "Still having hang-ups about being abandoned?" She laughs, thinking her words will hurt me.

Ah, but she'll have a different revelation tonight.

Stepping away from her, I simply unfasten my habit, letting it fall to the ground to reveal the artillery underneath.

I'm wearing a black latex suit, completely molded to the body to allow for freedom of movement. On every usable inch, there is a knife or gun strapped to my body.

Mother Superior's eyes widen in horror as she takes in my appearance, while Vlad simply whistles in admiration.

"Go get it, hell girl." He winks at me, and I can't help the blush that creeps up my cheeks.

I'd already had a hard time fending off his advances when we'd been getting ready, but now I'm getting positively warmer under his keen gaze, the thought of revenge and sex —in that order—making my breath pick up in excitement.

"We know about the trafficking ring," I start, taking a seat in front of her and unsheathing one blade. "Now, what I don't understand is why you'd involve yourself in this."

She huffs out a breath, turning her head so she's not looking at me. Maneuvering the blade in my hand, I bring it closer to her cheek, letting the tip slowly mold to her flesh, but still not digging in.

"What do you say, will you answer, or will I cut?"

She whips her gaze around at me and I see a hint of fear in her eyes, even as she pretends to be defiant.

"So be it." I shrug, letting the blade slide down until it reaches the collar of her habit. The knife is so sharp it doesn't take much pressure for it to cut into the material, and I follow a straight line until the entire bodice is wide open. She's wearing a shift underneath, so I cut through that too, baring her naked flesh.

Her entire skin is covered in goosebumps from the cold, and a smile plays at my lips as I continue to trail the blade over the surface, misleading her about the time I'll *actually* cut into her.

"Hmm, what about Miles? How do you know him?" I ask another question, and a slight tremor in her upper lip alerts me that I might have hit a sensitive spot.

Vlad is watching me like a hawk, his gaze intent on everything I'm doing, but he doesn't interfere. If anything, every time I look his way he gives me a nod of approval that spurs me further.

And so when I see the corner of his mouth curl up, I know he's noted her reaction too.

"That demon over there," I motion toward Vlad, "taught me quite a few things," I say just as I push the blade into the upper part of her breast, "all of which include some degree of pain."

She starts moaning low in her throat, the pain getting to her as I use the tip of the blade to dig a tiny hole right over the swell of her left breast.

The moans turn to screams as I proceed to remove a sizable chunk of flesh, a hollow remaining in her breast. There's minimal bleeding, the cut sharp and efficient.

"Mhm, hell girl, now those surgical skills." He brings his fingers to his lips in a kissing sound, approving of my method.

"Let's try again," I say, giving her a small respite from the pain, since I do have some grand plans for her. All of which will include some of the things I'd suffered through over the years. "Tell me about Miles," I repeat.

She directs her malicious gaze toward me, and for a moment I doubt she'll cooperate. But as her body starts slowly shaking—from fear or pain—I know I have her.

"He coordinates the transplants," she mumbles, almost choking on her words. "He provides the facilities and the medical personnel," she continues and I look up to meet Vlad's gaze.

The words are unspoken. It's exactly as we'd theorized.

"And who is in charge of the financial side?" I ask, noting Vlad's small nod of approval at my question.

"I don't know..." She shakes her head. "I swear. I've only been dealing with a few people who are his intermediaries. They are the ones who oversee the logistics, while Miles deals with the actual transplants."

"Who are the intermediaries, then?"

Her eyes skitter around the room before she utters two names.

"Guerra and Lastra," she whispers, and my own eyes widen.

I quickly look up to see Vlad sport the same expression of disbelief, especially after Marcello had assured us that Guerra's financials were in order.

"Maybe Benedicto isn't as transparent as he wants to appear," Vlad comments from the corner.

"Benedicto?" Mother Superior frowns, "No, no. Not Benedicto. Franco Guerra and Nicolo Lastra. Those were the ones who coordinated everything that happened here," she says.

"Now, that," Vlad comes around me, placing his hand on my shoulder, "I believe. But both are dead now, so who are you in contact with?" He raises an eyebrow.

Mother Superior blinks rapidly, surprised she'd been caught in that one loophole.

Her entire body becomes rigid, her lips pursed as she refuses to keep talking.

"Interesting," Vlad notes, silently urging me to continue.

Standing up, I move around the altar, noting the various items placed on the table. A devious smile appears on my face as I have the exact method to make her talk.

Taking an old oil lamp from the table, I disassemble it, seeing there is some oil left inside. Then, picking up a lit candle, I once again plop myself in front of Mother Superior.

The hole in her chest is angry looking, but it's not deep enough to reach the bone.

That will be solved soon.

"Fuck, hell girl, you sure know how to give me a hard-on," he groans from the side, eyeing the items in my hands and anticipating what I have in mind.

Mother Superior just stares at me in horror as she's trying to understand, but only when I start pouring the oil in the wound does she realize what I have planned for her.

"No," she says, her voice barely above a whisper, "I'll tell you," she continues, thrashing against her bonds.

It's a little too late as the moment the oil fills the hole in her chest to the brim, I bring the flame of the candle over it, watching the entire thing ignite.

Screams of pain inundate the church as the fire eats at her flesh. I don't even want to imagine the agony she must be going through as heat spreads through her body, the flame burning through her pain receptors and making her break into a sweat, her breath coming out in short spurts.

"Michele," she heaves, "Michele Guerra," she finally says, and I blow into the fire, putting it out momentarily.

She slumps down, her breathing erratic as she's trying to control herself. Her entire body is convulsing, entirely covered in sweat, her eyes almost rolling to the back of her head.

"Michele is my contact," she breathes out.

"Really," I drawl, not entirely surprised that someone as slimy as Michele would be involved in this.

"Good. See, we can talk civilly." I give her a smile. "And now for the winning question. Where is the transplant center?"

She tries to back further into the table even though her bonds don't allow her much movement. She shakes her head as she looks between Vlad and I, almost pondering if more pain is worth keeping the secret.

"Ellis Island," she eventually replies, her voice barely above a whisper.

I turn to Vlad to see the wheels turn in his head.

"There's an abandoned hospital there, but it's federal ground." He frowns, closing his eyes and exhaling. "This is so much bigger than we realized, hell girl."

"We'll tackle it. One person at a time. At least now we know about Michele too," I add with a sneer.

I'd met the man only once, but it had been enough to firmly put him on my shit list. He's a bigoted cretin who seemed to enjoy making those weaker than him suffer.

"No, you can't..." Mother Superior starts moving, wincing in pain as the rope cuts into her wrists. "You can't harm him," she continues and I frown.

"Why is that?" Vlad stoops low in front of her, snapping his fingers at her when she blanks out.

"He's your brother." She raises her gaze at me, and for the first time I see pure fear there. "You can't kill your own brother," she continues, her voice broken.

"What? That's impossible." I turn to Vlad and he has the same expression of disbelief.

"It's not," her voice trembles as she continues. "Nicolo... he," she audibly gulps down. "When he was younger, Michele had leukemia. Nicolo came to me with an idea, saying that he could get well if we found a match." The moment she utters those words I already know where she's going.

My entire body stiffens, but I can only listen to her as she recounts everything.

"He knew Michele was his son," she gives a dry laugh, "just like Benedicto knew he wasn't his. From the beginning Nicolo had been trying to quietly find a match, and he'd gone through all their relatives with no success. Until he came to me and told me there might be another possibility," she stops, raising her gaze to mine, "you."

"I don't understand."

"Nicolo said there was a possibility you might be his daughter, and by that point you were the last option. Michele was almost dead and getting worse by the day. And so we did the tests," she pauses, her eyes glinting to something akin to... pity? "And they came back positive. Not only were you his sister, but you were a match too," she says, and there's an unusual cadence to her voice, as if she had a personal stake in this.

"So you did the transplant," I continue and she just nods.

Vlad is there to cup my shoulders when I feel myself getting lightheaded.

Nicolo is—was my biological father. Just like Michele is my biological half-brother. My hands start trembling from anger as I realize Nicolo had known all along, and yet he'd been too willing to sacrifice me for Michele.

"Sisi," Vlad whispers in my hair, but I put a hand up.

"Why?' I address Mother Superior. "Why go through all this trouble to help him?"

Her mouth presses in a hard line as she turns her head away.

"Why?" I repeat, taking hold of another candle.

She reacts immediately, thrusting her body backwards.

"He's my nephew," she whispers, "from his mother's

side," she finally admits and for a moment I feel sorry for her, because all she did was for the sake of her family.

But at the same time, how many other people have to suffer for that? Why did *I* have to suffer for it?

I break free from Vlad's embrace, my fingers tightening over the small oil container.

Snatching her jaw open, I pour the entire liquid down her throat, enjoying the gurgling sound when she chokes on it as she tries to spit it out. When all of it has been ingested, I simply grip the hilt of the knife as I plunge it into her stomach, years of pain and humiliation coming to the surface and making me drown in the memories.

I rotate the blade around, making an even bigger hole in her lower abdomen. Her screams of pain don't even phase me at this point, my only goal is to make her death as painful as possible.

For me and for everyone else she's abused.

I dig into her stomach until there's a gaping hole, blood gushing out and spilling on the floor. She screams and chokes on even more blood coming up her mouth and nose, but all her attempts are in vain, because she's held in place by restraints.

Grabbing another candle, I bring the fire over her stomach, holding it close and burning at her insides until the flame meets the flammable oil in her stomach, a spark igniting and quickly extending throughout her open gut.

I take a step back, breathing hard. I can only admire my work as her body lights up like a bonfire, her screams swallowed by small explosions. Her expression is stuck in horror, eyes wide, mouth open. She's already passed out from the pain, and I relish the way revenge never felt sweeter.

For a long while, I just stare at her, letting her death course through me in an attempt to fill the void in my own heart.

But does it really work?

Shaking myself from my musings, though, I look around to find Vlad missing.

"Vlad?" I call out.

I'd been so focused on making Mother Superior pay that I hadn't been paying attention to anything else.

For a moment I'm worried that the sight of blood might have driven him to one of his episodes, and he'd left to get himself together. But as the doors to the church snap open again, Vlad strutting inside and dragging two women by the hair after him, I realize what he'd been doing.

A smile appears on my face as I give him an airy kiss.

"You just know the way to my heart," I gush as he throws Sister Celeste to the ground, accompanied by Sister Matilde, my old teacher.

"I told you everyone who's ever harmed you will be *dead*, hell girl. I might have also paid a visit to those two obnoxious girls from earlier in the afternoon, and safe to say they won't be leaving their beds—ever again."

"You were fast," I praise and he just grins at me, showing white gleaming teeth, his canines long and protruding and making him seem even more the predator he is.

"For you? In the blink of an eye." He winks at me.

Both women stare at me in shock, and their expressions only worsen as they look at the highly flammable Mother Superior who is currently sending sparks all throughout the church.

"Assisi?" Sister Celeste asks, raising her head to look at me.

"What's the meaning of this?" my former teacher asks.

I look down at their pathetic forms and suddenly I can only muster pity for them. Pity for the bitter women that wasted their lives abusing others, and that probably never knew *any* type of happiness.

"Do your thing, Vlad," I tell him. "I want to watch," I say just as I take a seat.

There's an emptiness within me that I hope will be filled by having a front row seat to the spectacle that will be their death.

Vlad doesn't disappoint. Not in the least as he builds a script to hang them off the ceiling, head down.

He's even more impressive as he deftly uses his blades to cut them open from the junction between their legs right up to their jaws. His blades are so sharp, it only takes one good cut for organs to spill on the floor, a more forceful tug and the ribcage is wrenched open too.

I cross my legs, my chin in my palm as I watch their quick disembowelment. When only the carcasses remain, he takes what's left of the oil from the lamp, splattering it around the two bodies before throwing a candle at them.

The flames are quick to engulf them, and just like Mother Superior, they all lose themselves in the fire, smoke gathering in the church, the smell of burned flesh permeating every corner. The entire back part of the church is now ripe with voracious flames looking to swallow everything in their path.

I stand up, ready to leave.

After throwing the last candle, feeding the greedy flames,

Vlad turns toward me, blood staining his face and entire outfit. His eyes are midnight black as his pupils melt into his irises, his mouth tugging around the corners in an arrogant yet dangerous smile.

There's something to be said about the way he looks at me, especially when, keeping eye contact, he opens his mouth, his tongue licking the blood from his lips, his teeth stained with red.

A shiver goes down my back as I instinctively take a step back.

I know this side of him. It's the one that *demands* blood to flow. And yet, it's not just that.

He comes closer, lifting his hand in the air and inspecting the specks of blood. The fire is screeching behind him, the flecks of light illuminating his features and making him seem exactly like Mother Superior had said—a demon.

A demon from the depths of Hell, stepping on hallowed ground and wrecking all kinds of destruction. And there's nothing that can stop him.

His eyes snap to mine, and his smile intensifies. Only one word crosses his lips, and I know I'm in trouble.

"Run," the gentle sound escapes him, but I know what awaits me is anything but gentle.

37
SISI

My feet move back slowly, my eyes on him as I watch his every move.

But so does he. A predator on the prowl, there is nothing escaping him, my every step eliciting a reaction from him.

It's in the way his dimple becomes more emphasized, his smile more forced.

"Run," he repeats and I don't linger, backing away and running at full speed.

Skittering through the main yard, I head toward the cemetery, remembering the mausoleum that had been my true home in this place for years on end.

I feel him on my tail, yet I don't feel threatened—not truly. With his speed, he could have caught up with me already before now. He could have tackled and pinned me down in the mud, his big body on top of mine.

My breath catches, debatable if from running or from the running wetness down the inside of my thighs.

I run along the tombs, jumping over a small cross I

hadn't seen and almost falling. Regaining my balance in a split of a second, I sneak a glance behind, seeing the shape of his form in the night, the way his outline promises my destruction.

I don't stop as I finally make it to the mausoleum, wrenching the door open and entering inside, hoping this will serve as a haven.

But it only takes for that thought to form for me to realize that there's no escaping him. My hands go down my legs as I feel for the knives still sheathed on my body, holding on to the hope that they might save me some time.

I barely take a few steps inside when the door is ripped from its hinges, Vlad's hands on either side of it as he easily throws it to the side.

A low tremor starts from my lips, going down my body and settling deep in my lower belly.

"Vlad." His name on my lips elicits a smug smile from him as he prowls inside, his steps heavy and assured. I keep backing away and he keeps advancing, his eyes dead set on mine, his tongue licking his lips at the promise of blood.

More blood.

One move and he has me by the throat, my body flush to his as he moves his nose up and down my neck, breathing me in.

"Mine," he growls into my ear, his hold on my neck tightening. My arms are flailing around as I try to get him off me, but he doesn't even give me the chance, pushing me backwards until my spine hits the marble coffin that should still house Cressida's remains.

"Vlad," I breathe out, my hands meeting his shoulders as I push with all the strength I can muster. He doesn't even budge. If anything, my struggles seem to only excite him further as he twists me around.

His hand on my nape, he pushes me on the coffin, my back to his front as he grinds his erection into me.

I barely realize what's happening as he grabs one knife, cutting my latex suit from my body. Starting from my neck and down until he reaches my legs, he all but tears it apart, the cold air hitting my bare flesh and making me gasp.

"Vlad, please," I try to reason with him once more, but he doesn't react to my words.

No, there's only his harsh breathing as he trails the knife over my bare skin, placing enough pressure on the blade, so that I feel it denting my skin, but not enough to cut into it.

Knowing the window of time to be limited before he does something even worse, I stop fighting him. I let him believe I've already submitted to him, letting him do whatever he wants to my body.

Then, just as he trails the blade lower, between my ass cheeks, I move, my hand on the hilt of my knife.

Everything happens in slow motion as I jerk around, twisting and turning until the tip of my blade connects with his chest, drawing blood.

I watch horrified as the slash I made seems to get bigger under my eyes, more blood gushing out.

And as I drag my gaze up, I realize he's smirking down at me.

Without any preliminary, the knife is thrown out of my hand, crashing to the marble floor with a thud.

A sliver of fear goes down my spine as I look into his unfeeling eyes and the way his entire demeanor promises nothing but pain and destruction. There's maybe a split of a second in which I try to duck and run past him, but his fingers are back at my throat, pushing me back on to the coffin, this time lifting me up so I'm sitting on it.

I move my legs around, wildly trying to get him to let me go, but if anything, it only makes him more amused as he chuckles at my poor attempts.

One hand holding on to my neck, since he doesn't require much to keep me subdued, he uses the other to tear at his own clothing, ripping the priest cloak until his inked chest is bared to my sight.

His skin gleams in the moonlight, his savagery emphasized by the cruel lighting. Like a barbarian warlord, his rage is his sword, and as my gaze dips lower, I note a very dangerous sword pointed right at me.

"Let's talk about this," I blurt out. Anything to placate him.

But just like last time, he doesn't hear me. His ears perk up at the noise, but he hears nothing I'm saying.

"Vlad," I reach out to him, but he swats my hand aside, placing himself firmly between my open legs. "Please, Vlad," I beseech him again, just as the tip of his cock probes between my folds.

He rubs himself against me, teasing me lightly before surging forward, the onslaught almost making me jump off the coffin.

"V…" I open my mouth to say his name, but nothing comes out. Nothing but a loud moan as he impales me onto his length.

His fingers dig in my hip as he holds me in place, retreating all the way before slamming back into me at full force.

Every and any word I might have tried to get out fails me as I can only feel him ripping me apart, a pain so sweet it makes me whimper, my walls contracting around him, my pussy squeezing him in what I can only describe as a blinding orgasm.

I lose sight of everything. There's no time and space, just his brutal thrusts as he keeps on prolonging the bitter pleasure.

Before I know it, he has me flipped onto my belly, entering me from behind, filling me even more. His thrusts are stronger, more painful, but oh, so infinitely sweeter too as he strokes me so deep, I can't control the unrestricted moans that escape my lips.

"Mine," he grits, his voice low, the bass reverberating in the small enclosure.

His hand still on my neck, he brings me into him, his mouth trailing wet kisses down my shoulder, before biting.

"Vlad," I gasp, his teeth breaking the skin, the pain brief, but searing as he increases the rhythm of his thrusts. His mouth on my shoulder, he alternates between sucking and licking, ensuring that not one drop of blood is wasted.

His hips piston in and out of me at such a terrifying speed that my mind simply can't keep up, another orgasm ripping through me and making me slump down on the coffin, my arms slack on the sides.

Then he suddenly pulls out, his cock still hard as he slaps it against my pussy, coating his entire shaft in my juices before dragging it upwards, between my ass cheeks.

My eyes widen as I realize what he's trying to do, but my body is too limp to put up any fight.

He separates my cheeks, moving his hand around my

entrance as he tests the tight ring of muscles with his thumb. Not unlike the last time, he pushes it inside, using my own arousal to ease the way in. But his thumb is soon out, replaced with the head of his dick.

The head of his massive dick.

"Vlad," I whimper, already scared of having that monster in my ass. Hell, if he'd torn my pussy apart then I'm not sure how much damage it's going to cause my asshole. "Please," I plead, but I don't know exactly what I'm asking him.

His cock firmly in his grip, he guides the head around my tight hole, dipping it low every now and then to gather some wetness from my pussy. But just when I think he's going to push it in, rip me apart in a way that will have me begging for mercy, he doesn't.

Blinking some clarity into my eyes, I move around, tilting my head to the side to see what he's doing.

The blade of a knife glints in the moonlight, the cold steel making me shiver as it touches my skin. Yet it's not my flesh it cuts into.

It's his.

He grips the sides of the blade tightly, dragging it slowly across the skin of his open palm until blood gushes out, dripping increasingly fast down the blade and on to my ass.

It doesn't dawn on me what he wants to do in the beginning. But as he takes his cock in his bleeding hand, smearing the freely flowing blood all over his length, I realize what his plan is. I don't even get to protest as the head of his cock nudges again at my entrance, this time slick and wet and full of blood as my body slowly opens up and starts accepting him.

The head barely slips past my ring of muscles before he brings the blade down his palm again, ensuring more blood flows between my ass cheeks, all gathering in that place where his cock is penetrating my ass. The viscous substance helps his dick slide deeper and deeper inside of me.

All at once I feel so painfully full—a different type of fullness as his thick erection stretches my muscles, pushing them to their limits and showing me a new type of pleasure. The blood keeps on flowing, the slippery warmth coupled with his fat cock digging deep inside, making me become light-headed, too much pleasure building inside of me, my clit burning with unreleased tension.

Slowly, he advances inch by inch until he's fully seated inside, a hoarse groan escaping him as his balls slap against my pussy, my wetness making contact with his sensitive flesh.

"Fuck," I think I hear him hiss as he grips my hips with both hands, pulling his cock out of me before slamming it back in, the blood acting as lubricant to ease his moves.

I gasp at the foreign sensation, but I can't help the way my body simply opens up to his, taking everything he has to offer me. Closing my eyes, I just give myself over to the feeling of being dominated by him. So owned, his brand is seared into my very soul.

Slow at first, his thrusts gain speed as my body relaxes enough to allow the intrusion. There's this wicked feeling of being overpowered, and at the same time I feel like *I'm* the one in power, making him lose all sense the minute he's inside of me.

Snaking his arm over my stomach, he brings me even closer to him, his fingers leaving a trail of fire in their wake as they move lower until they settle on my clit. He presses down on it at the same time as he pushes his cock into me. Fireworks explode before my eyes, and as he continues to stroke my clit, I can only come harder, my release unending.

He's not far behind as he thrusts into me a couple more times before his cock slips completely out of me.

I hear his ragged groans just as I feel his warm seed land on my lower back, and I can't help the way my heart squeezes tightly in my chest.

He's mine. This savage man is all mine.

I'm still slumped on the coffin when he helps me down, gathering me in his arms and wrapping me in the strips of cloth from his cassock.

"Did I hurt you?" he asks, stroking my hair, the warmth in his gaze unmistakable.

"No, not at all," I sigh in pleasure, nestling closer to him.

"I think there's something wrong with me," I admit softly.

When we'd hashed a short plan, right before confronting Mother Superior, I'd been the one to suggest doing a simulation of last time when he'd lost himself to the blood. But this time, he'd be in control.

I know he always gets in the mood to fuck after a gruesome kill, so I'd asked him to chase me down and take me like a beast. I wanted to be dominated by him. At his mercy as he pounds like a savage into me.

He'd been a little reluctant in the beginning, but as I'd assured him that if he *did* hurt me I'd call out a safe word, he'd been open to try it.

There's something to be said about being stripped of control, being at the mercy of pure animalistic lust as he overpowers me.

And just because it's *him* I can let go.

My cheeks go red as I realize just how much I enjoyed the feeling of being his prey, the adrenaline rushing through my veins as it mixed with the serotonin of his claiming. Just the feel of his hands on my throat as he'd ruthlessly thrust into me had made me come harder than ever.

He rutted me like a beast, a claiming that went far beyond anything we'd tried before.

And I know that he loves it too—craves it more than he'd like to admit. But he's been denying himself, because he can't bear the thought of hurting me.

"There's nothing wrong with you, Sisi." He leans down to lay a kiss on my brow, tenderly caressing my face.

"I don't know," I release a breath, "maybe I should be more traumatized after what happened," I say and he blinks slowly, pain evident in his eyes. "But there's something about relinquishing all control *to* you." I raise my hand to cup his face. "I think that turned me on from the first time we met."

"Don't," he places a finger on my lips, "don't let anyone tell you what you should feel or shouldn't feel. Fuck knows, I've been fighting myself from the beginning, trying to be gentle with you like you deserve, when all I wanted was to throw you up against a wall and have my way with you." He smiles wolfishly, "Violently," he whispers, "ruthlessly," he traces my lip slowly, "like an animal in heat. Mark you up in ways you could not erase from your Goddamn soul."

He takes a deep breath, his eyes infinite pools of fire and ah, but drowning never seemed so hot before.

"You know there's this violence in me," he brings my palm to his chest, right over his heart, "it's dark and turbulent and barely contained, and it wants nothing more than to swallow you whole. That you embrace *every* part of me, even the savage, uncivilized one..." he trails off, and I can see the conflict inside.

"I know you're not much of a believer, Vlad," my lips draw up, "but our meeting was meant to be. *Inevitable*. That's what I would call our relationship. No right or wrong... just us."

"Inevitable," he nods thoughtfully, " I like that."

"I love you," I say, leaning toward him, my tongue sneaking out to lick the shallow knife wound I'd given him.

"Fuck, Sisi," he hisses in pleasure. "I love you too, hell girl." He breathes hard, his eyes closed. "So damn much."

It's a little trickier to get cleaned up after our little adventure, but we manage to slip unnoticed out of Sacre Coeur when everyone is freaking out over the fire at the church. Police and firefighters are both at the scene, and the sheer incompetence is astounding as Vlad gets away with killing the security guards too.

"They offended you." He shrugs as we make it back to the car.

I shake my head at him, although his regard never fails to warm me up.

Once we get back to the compound, we start planning.

38
VLAD

"I've got eyes on it," I call out.

Since Ellis Island isn't exactly the most welcoming place for outsiders, and the security cameras that are around have a restricted area of coverage, I'd had to switch to a Plan B. I'd sent drones to get some footage.

I know it's a risky avenue, but I'm also not about to barge inside unprepared. I need to at least have an idea of the layout of the hospital, and the surrounding terrain.

"Already?" Sisi gets out from her chair, coming to my side to look at the screen.

"Three of the drones made it inside. Two were shot down," I explain, "we have to hope these are going to get enough footage before they're found too."

It's very likely that they are already looking for them, since the previous ones should have alerted them to the potential presence of others. Still, I'm hoping we can get *something*.

"Won't this put them on their guard?"

"It's a risk I have to take," I reply grimly. "It's not ideal, but I would never go in blindly."

She nods, continuing to watch the screen.

The remaining drones provide us with an additional hour of footage before they are also shot down. But that hour is our only insight into what goes on inside the hospital, so Sisi and I start carefully analyzing each frame, making a scheme of the building and what to expect inside.

From what we can see, though, the hospital is anything but *abandoned*, with shiny new equipment on all levels. Since we'd sent the drones at night, there hadn't been many people wandering the halls, but the few we'd caught on camera we'd been able to identify.

"These are all immigrants," I note as I compile a list of the faces we'd spotted. "Immigrant doctors and nurses," I continue as I sift through the data. "It makes sense, since some wouldn't be able to get their qualifications recognized to work in an official hospital. Although it's a little ironic, since the hospital itself used to be an immigrant building," I chuckle.

"Do you think they know what's happening?"

I purse my lips, nodding.

"Yes. But this is likely the only type of work they could find that doesn't ask them for their certifications," I say as I show her where some of these people are coming from. "It's smart. Get personnel from war-torn countries so they have *no* way to provide documentation."

"Isn't this another form of trafficking?" she asks thoughtfully, and a smile pulls at my lips.

"Only if they are taken from their countries. If they were hired when they've already settled here, then no."

"Interesting," she notes, biting the end of her pen. "What do you think, then? Are they sourcing them from *here*, or are they trafficking them?"

Pushing the files we'd printed on the personnel we'd identified toward her, I point to some of the dates.

"These people have been missing for *years* in their respective countries. And there's no record of them *ever* being in the US. My guess is that they were brought over with the incentive of starting a new life, but then they were roped into the business."

"I don't feel sorry for them." She shrugs. "They've known about the stuff Miles' been doing on children and they've never thought to speak out?"

"I don't think we should judge them outrightly. If someone ever thought to speak out, they wouldn't be alive anymore. This is too deep. Even if someone were to compile evidence and show it to the authorities, how would they know *who* to show it to? There are too many people involved in all chains of command. The system is simply rotten to the core."

"But isn't this like fighting with windmills then? We end Miles' reign, but who's to say there won't be another Miles just taking his place?"

"That's what you get when you reach the belly of the beast. You cut one head, another grows in its place. It's *never* truly over. Especially when it comes to something as profitable as this. Where there is demand, there will be supply."

"I get that," she sighs, "but it makes me feel helpless, and I don't like it."

"I wish I could shield you from all the horrors of the world, Sisi," I turn to her, tucking a strand of hair behind her ear, "but I can't. The only thing I *can* do is vanquish any danger that might threaten you," I pause, "and make sure you're strong enough for when I'm not there."

Her hand reaches out for mine as she gives me one of her stunning smiles.

"I'm strong *because* you're with me," she says quietly, "I don't want to think of a time that you won't be with me, Vlad. Because that's out of the question."

I grunt, because I could not fathom a moment without her either. But no matter how much I'd like to be with her *forever*, the truth is that this lifestyle might take me out eventually.

Even I am not invincible.

Hell, the fact that I've made it this far it's astounding. But while the odds might not always be in my favor, for Sisi I'm willing to go through hell and back to ensure that she'll never have to shed a tear for me.

We continue to watch the footage in silence, until Sisi points to the screen, stopping the video.

"I think there's something underground," she notes, her finger on a small vent at the bottom of the building.

I zoom in, noting the bars and the fact that there seems to be something there.

"Might be where he houses his project, if he keeps the hospital strictly for transplants."

"What are we going to do, then? We can't just barge in." She bites her lip, looking at me worried.

"No. We're going to need help," she frowns and I clarify, "backup. I've already spoken with your brother and he's willing to help. Enzo and Nero are in too, so our combined forces should be enough."

"But it's still federal ground. How are you going to get around that?"

My lips twitch.

"I'll be jumping the gun a little," I add, amused, when I see my phone blink with a confirmation message from Nero.

"I'll be using Meester," I tell her, and her eyes widen.

"How come this is the first time I'm hearing this?" She raises an eyebrow, almost offended.

"Because I've been trying to finalize the plans with Nero and your brother and make sure it's a viable alternative."

"Explain." She leans back, her arms crossed over her chest.

"The island is clearly well protected and they will see us coming immediately. We need a trump card to get in there undetected."

"And how will you convince Meester to get you on to the island when he's been trying to kill you for the last few weeks?" she asks skeptically.

"Nero's got it covered," I chuckle. "He has his precious daughter currently in his possession. In fact, we'll be doing a video conference with Meester once we get to your brother's house, and I'm sure it's bound to be very convincing."

"Damn," she whistles, "that's not a bad idea."

But then she frowns.

"How old is his daughter?"

"She's probably in her mid-twenties." I shrug. "But don't worry about her too much. She's not innocent either."

"What do you mean?"

"In restricted circles they call her the black widow. She's been married three or four times, and all her husbands ended up dead under mysterious circumstances. All within a short while of the marriage, too. I hear Meester's been trying to find her another husband for a long time, but no one is brave enough to marry her."

"She sounds interesting." Sisi grins. "I want to meet her."

"And you will. We're heading to your brother's tomorrow morning."

With a rough understanding of the island and the hospital, we call it a day.

~

"I DIDN'T REALIZE THE BASEMENT HAD A DIFFERENT entrance," Sisi says, her arm tightening on mine.

We'd compiled all the information we could find about the hospital, so now the only outstanding issue is planning the attack.

I'd spoken with Nero on the phone last night, and while he'd had some minor issues with Meester's daughter, he'd assured me he'd be here today and we'd be able to jumpstart the plan.

"I think Marcello sealed the entrance from the house," I reply, telling her about the rather dissolute history of the basement. "He probably didn't want Claudia or Venezia to venture there by accident."

Heading to the back of the house where a trap door leads to the basement, I feel the hairs on my body stand up, my head whipping around in the direction of the roof.

One step and I have Sisi thrusted behind me just as a bullet hits me straight in the forehead.

A paint bullet.

My mouth opens, but no sound comes out. Not when

Sisi swats my hand aside, plopping herself in front of me and laughing to her heart's content.

"You're all blue," she can barely speak as she bends over, holding onto her stomach, tears at the corner of her eyes from too much laughter.

As if this wasn't enough, the basement door opens to reveal Marcello and Catalina followed by Adrian, all chuckling at my expense.

But if Adrian is here…

I look up just in time to see Bianca jump from the windowsill of the first floor, landing on her feet and smirking at me.

"You." I grit my teeth, unable to even muster any type of retort, since who's going to take a blue man seriously?

The paint is smeared all over my face and dripping down my suit, making me an official honorary smurf.

"Well," she starts, an amused expression on her face, "you got your wish." She shrugs, casually strutting back to her husband. Or is it her former husband?

"When did I ask to be painted blue?" I mutter dryly, raising my hand and wiping some of the goo from my eyes.

Sisi is still laughing by my side, but when she sees that I'm not exactly amused, she quickly takes out a napkin, helping me get some of this shit off my face.

"Oh, I don't know," Bianca rolls her eyes dramatically, "maybe when you called me sobbing and asking me to kill you stealthily, so that you wouldn't see it coming?"

I frown.

"I did that?"

"You're a moron," she immediately replies, whipping out her phone and playing a recording.

*Just put me out of my misery, B! Before I do something worse…
Like go after her.*

I swallow, embarrassed to be put on the spot like that, since that is clearly my voice. And though I have no recollection of that particular incident, I can wager a guess as to when it could have happened.

"I was under the weather," I mutter, but she has to take it a step further and play another recording.

One where I'm actually crying.

I can't live without her…

Heat creeps up my cheeks as I realize I wasn't just crying. I was fucking sobbing.

"Motherfucker," I mutter under my breath.

"Sounds familiar?" She quirks a brow, knowing she got me.

"When was that?" Sisi frowns, looking at me questioningly.

"When I sent you away," I mumble, "I might have experimented with some narcotics," *a lot of narcotics* "but I don't remember it very well."

"And you were criticizing me," Bianca chimes in, and I'm getting increasingly pissed at her.

Did she really have to embarrass me so thoroughly in front of Sisi?

But I don't have time for that now. Not when I need to make it clear to Sisi that I'm not a drug addict.

"It was one moment of weakness." I turn to Sisi, grabbing her hands in mine and urging her to look me in the eye. "And it was a one time thing. I swear," I tell her, needing her to know I'm not secretly shooting up.

She purses her lips, narrowing her eyes at me.

The others are talking in hushed voices, or at least

that's what it sounds like, because all of my attention is focused on Sisi and her reaction. I don't want her to think I have a drug problem on top of *all* the other problems I have.

"That doesn't sound like one time," she replies skeptically, and I curse out.

"Okay, maybe it was a few days. One week tops," I amend, cringing at my own explanation. "But I haven't touched it in months, hell girl. I swear to you." I give her my pinkie so she can see I'm in earnest.

She doesn't look convinced, but she does lace her pinkie with mine.

"Fine. You're off the hook," she says and I breathe out, relieved. "But only because you sound so damn cute crying about me," she leans in to whisper.

"Sisi," I groan. "How many times do I have to tell you? I'm *not* cute." Because how can any self-respecting man be cute? "You can call me anything else. Like sexy, handsome…" I pause to think, "Fierce?"

"Of course," she readily agrees. Almost *too* readily. "You're fiercely cute," she continues, thereby ending me.

But as she raises herself on her tip-toes, brushing her lips against my earlobe, I can't help the way I become hypnotized by her.

"Don't forget that blue is my favorite color," she whispers, her voice husky and sexy and doing weird things to my heart.

"Cut it out, love birds," Marcello's voice ruins the moment as he all but snatches Sisi from my side. "I may accept that you're together," he motions between us, almost in disgust, "but that doesn't mean that you get to rub it in my face," he says before promptly placing himself between the two of us.

A smile threatens to pull at my lips and I look at Sisi to see the same reaction.

"Damn, 'Cello, but you're taking the overprotective brother to a whole different level," I drawl, sneaking my hand behind his back and grabbing Sisi's pinkie once more. She can barely contain her amusement as she looks up at her brother.

"That's right, Marcello," she nods, "I thought we'd agreed I'm an adult and I can decide for myself. Besides, we're already married."

I feel a surge of satisfaction in my chest as I hear her defend our relationship, and as I catch her eye, I can't help but wink at her.

"Look at you being all sappy," Bianca interjects as she comes forward, hand in hand with Adrian.

As if she should talk. She forgets how much sappiness I've had to endure from her for years.

"I have to say I'd never thought I'd see this day, Kuznetsov," Adrian chuckles. "*You*, hitched?" He shakes his head, as if it's the most preposterous thing. "Gotta say, for a long time I thought you were in the closet." He shrugs, lazily looking at Bianca with an adoring look.

I roll my eyes at them. Since when has my sexual orientation become such a hot topic? But I don't reply, because it wouldn't be fair to call myself straight either. Not when the *only* object of my attention is *her*. If anything, I'm *assisied*. And if that's not a term, then I'm making it one.

Circumventing Marcello's rather unyielding form, I

swoop Sisi up in my arms, a little tired of this little game he has going.

I know he has a lot of misplaced guilt because he was the one who gave her away to Sacre Coeur, but that doesn't mean we'll forever have to mind his tender sensibilities.

"Okay, that's enough," I address everyone, my tone serious. "I think we can move past the animosities, Marcello. Sisi is my wife, and that's not going to change whether you like it or not. Instead of commenting on my love life, we should be discussing other important businesses." I nod at them.

They all stare at me as if I've grown a second head. Even Sisi is gazing up at me, her eyes wide, her mouth slightly parted.

"Now it's not fun anymore," Bianca sighs, and the others seem to join her, all looking rather disappointed. Instead of arguing, they turn their backs to me, returning to the basement. Even Marcello looks suddenly disinterested and doesn't even blink twice at Sisi and I being so close to each other.

"What's happening?" I ask Sisi, a little confused about what just happened.

"They were taunting you because you're so easily riled up," she confides, a sheepish smile on her face. "Especially when it comes to me."

"Goddamn," I mutter, already tired of this.

And they wonder why I don't like to socialize.

Heading inside the basement, we go to the meeting room where a round table occupies the center of the space, with chairs strewn around in disarray. There are a couple of computers to the side and a big projector illuminating the other side of the room.

"This hasn't changed much in the last ten years," I add, shooting a glance at Marcello. I'd been a fixture in his house due to our parents' friendship, and I'd been here more times than I could count.

"At least you dusted it off before you called us here," I swipe my hand on the table, noting it's clean.

"Vlad," Sisi pokes my arm, "stop antagonizing people," she mumbles, shaking her head.

Shrugging, I just take a seat at the table, watching attentively as Sisi does so as well, so I can pull her chair *right* next to mine.

As the others take their seats as well, I turn to Bianca.

"How come you're here? Isn't your contract expiring in a few months?" I raise an eyebrow.

I'd gone through a lot of trouble to get her a job with some connections in Russia and I hope she's not slacking, since that would reflect badly on me. And with my reputation already in tatters around the country, I don't need that abroad too.

"We're here to help, you idiot." She rolls her eyes at me, her hand going to her belly, and stroking what I realize is a rather large bump.

My eyes widen.

Now that's something I would have never expected of Bianca.

"She's four months pregnant," Adrian explains, "so she's taking it easy with the assignments. But when Marcello called to tell us about your situation, she insisted on coming here," he adds dryly.

Adrian and I had never gotten along, mostly because

he's always been jealous of my friendship with his wife. I don't know why he would be, though, since I've made it clear to him that Bianca's never been on my radar as a woman, or anything really except my partner in arms.

But somehow he got it into his head that I was a threat, and he's never stopped being a pain in the ass about it.

"Why, Hastings, I must say I am impressed," I jibe, "already," I glance at my watch, "thirty minutes and you haven't insulted me. We might become best friends yet."

"As if," he snorts, "you have a better chance of becoming a canonized saint," he mutters under his breath.

"Wouldn't be too hard," I shrug when I note Sisi's small smile. "I'd just make sure to become mummified after death. You'd do that for me, wouldn't you, hell girl?" I murmur softly, leaning into her and inhaling her fresh scent.

She turns so that only her profile is visible.

"Only if I get to join you," she answers saucily, "we'd be two mummies," her voice is breathy as fuck and damn if my cock doesn't jump in my pants at that sexy sound, "wrapped in each other and ready for the afterlife."

"Fuck, Sisi," I groan.

"Ew," Bianca's voice puts a damper on my growing erection. "I see now why you're with her," she says before she points at Sisi, "or why *you're* with him." She shakes her head, disgusted.

"Can we drop the odd morbidities," Marcello says, massaging his temples with his fingers and looking completely done with us. Catalina, on the other hand, seems a bit more receptive to our relationship as she sends a comforting smile to Sisi.

That alone puts her in my good books.

Even Marcello, for all his sputter and protests, managed to surprise me by inviting Bianca and Adrian. It might not be much, but there's always strength in numbers, especially when they happen to be an assassin and a trained fighter.

Just then, Enzo and his wife stride through the door too. My eyebrows shoot up as I realize Marcello's really gone big with this.

"Nero should be here soon." Is the first thing Enzo says as he takes a seat around the table.

"You," Bianca spits out, launching herself at Allegra. Her eyes widen, and she barely evades Bianca's attack, Enzo quickly placing himself between the two of them and shielding his wife.

"I guess no one told B about the new developments," I joke, but no one seems to be laughing.

A short explanation from Enzo and Bianca finally retreats with a huff, plopping herself back on her chair where Adrian promptly tries to comfort her.

"It's nice to meet everyone," Allegra says after a complete rounds of introductions. Her accent is thick— thicker than Enzo's—and probably the best way to tell it's not her sister, since Chiara had developed a flawless English accent from all her years of travel.

Safe to say that Chiara hadn't been *anyone*'s favorite, least of all Bianca's, since she'd had an affair with her father, while also trying to come on to her husband.

While we wait for Nero to show up with the highlight of today's meeting, I quickly catch everyone up with what we'd found out at Sacre Coeur.

"Sisi," Catalina gasps, horrified when she hears that Sisi had been the target of such a transplant. Marcello's fists are clenched as he undoubtedly blames himself again for what happened to her.

"But that's not the most important thing," Sisi interjects, and I can tell she's trying to move the conversation away from her, since she doesn't like to be seen as a victim. "There was something else that Mother Superior said." She gives me a worried look, but as I nod, she turns toward Marcello.

"Nicolo was my biological father," she explains with a sigh.

Marcello is trying his best to stay still, but I can tell how much this is affecting him, especially in light of his own conflict with Nicolo. He'd been so obsessed with Marcello's mother that he must have assaulted her at some point, resulting in Sisi's birth.

"But the most unexpected twist," I add, "is that Nicolo fathered another," I pause and everyone looks expectantly. "Michele Guerra."

"You're joking," Marcello is the first to interject, and I just shake my head.

"I wish I were," I reply, telling him all about Michele's leukemia diagnosis and the fact that Sisi had been a match.

"It makes sense why he would prefer Raf for the succession," Catalina notes and I nod.

Michele was already hated for his attempted assault on Catalina, but as everyone hears about his current involvement with the clandestine transplants, it's safe to say he's now most reviled.

"That bastard," Enzo curses out, vowing to kill Michele himself.

"Children," I put my hands up, "we're getting ahead of ourselves. Right now the most important thing is to break down the organization, and then we can pick them apart one by one."

"Good, because Michele is mine." Marcello grits his teeth.

"Do you want to call dibs too?" I ask Sisi, since she has *very* good reasons to hold a grudge against him.

"Not really," she shrugs, "he's such a shit human being that he'll end up dead one way or another. I'm not particularly keen on being the one who kills him."

"I'll do it for you," I eagerly propose the alternative.

"No." She puts her hand on top of mine. "Let him flounder. Once Miles' operation ends, he won't have any more resources. I want to watch him drown like a fish on dry land," she says, her eyes full of fire as she turns them toward me.

I can't help myself as I grab her nape, bringing her into me for a quick kiss.

"And there he goes again," Marcello mutters.

"You know, Kuznetsov, for someone who proclaimed he'd never exchange bodily fluids with *anyone*, you're exchanging quite a bit." Adrian chuckles.

"And there goes our truce, Hastings," I groan, still keeping Sisi next to me. "But she's not just *anyone*," I grumble, almost offended he'd lump Sisi in the same category as all other ordinary people.

"She's the *only* one who makes exchanging bodily fluids madly appealing," I speak as I look down at her red stained cheeks. There's also some blue residue from the paint on my face, but I'm not about to point that out.

Instead, I caress her face softly as I remove all traces of

the paint. I wouldn't want her getting mad at me for getting her dirty, too.

"Can we *stop* talking about exchanging bodily fluids," Marcello interferes in a loud voice, "especially since *that* is my sister. And I really don't want to imagine…" he trails off, a loud sigh escaping him.

"I'll end up putting a bullet through his brain," Marcello mutters, with Catalina by his side trying to calm him.

"What can I say, 'Cello. I have that effect on people," I add smugly.

At this point, getting people to want to kill me seems to be a skill.

39
VLAD

We spend some more time catching up with what everyone's been up to, and since Sisi is asking me nicely, I make a marked effort not to get on anyone's nerves—again. It's not as easy as it seems, because I have to bite my tongue from blurting out anything that might be misconstrued as offensive. After all, we might be all gathered together here, but I know most don't have any lost love for me.

If anything, I'm just a necessary evil.

My hand on hers, since I need to have her near to function, I just put on my most charming smile as I try to *play along*.

A while later, the door bursts open and Nero barges in, his face devoid of any expression. Draped over his shoulder is who I expect to be Meester's daughter, her entire body tied in a potato sack. There are muffled noises coming from inside, but he doesn't seem to mind it.

With a glance at the room, he gives a quick nod before

he settles his prisoner on a chair, making quick work of removing the sack, while preserving her bounds.

"Salome Meester." He nods to her as he pulls the cloth from her head.

Salome Meester isn't a bad looking woman, at least I guess so. My senses are skewed when it comes to that sort of thing, because I only have one golden standard, and she's sitting next to me.

Black hair and pale skin, Salome has dark-blue eyes framed by dark lashes. Together, they give her an almost doll-like appearance, and definitely inoffensive. You wouldn't think that someone looking that innocent would have gone through at least three husbands by now.

But as she turns her eyes to Nero, her stare deadly, I can see that there is some fire under that innocuous appearance.

"Remove?" he asks, pointing at her gag. When everyone agrees, he does so, lowering it down her face.

"You fucking bastard. I'm going to fucking kill you! I'm going to strap you in my menagerie and have my wild animals feed on you!" she spits at him, thrusting her body forward as she continues to curse Nero out.

"Or not." He belatedly nods, firmly placing the gag back in place.

His hand lingers a little too long on her face, her eyes widening slightly.

Interesting.

"I guess we can finally call Meester?" Marcello asks, and I can see he cannot wait for us all to leave his house.

Why, he shouldn't have been the host if he's going to be so grouchy about it.

"I'll do the honors," I rise from my chair, slowly heading to where Nero and Salome are.

"You…" Salome mumbles behind her gag. She narrows her eyes at me and I can see a hint of recognition.

"It's been what? Eight years?" I ask, amused.

She'd been underage when Meester had to ask me to marry her, and when I'd refused, he'd promptly married her off to someone else. I'm not even sure she was legal when that happened.

"Why am I here?" She asks when I finally decide to let her speak.

"I'm sure Nero must have told you why," I add and her eyes skitters to Nero.

"Him?" she asks, "until a while ago I was pretty sure he was a mute." She smirks at him but he doesn't react at all. A bored expression on his face, he just stares at her. When she sees her taunt doesn't work, she huffs, turning to me.

"Why am I here? You heard I'm back on the marriage mart?" She flutters her lashes suggestively.

I already feel someone drilling a hole into my back, and I don't have to turn to know Sisi's probably one step away from lashing out.

"Carry her to the torture room," I instruct Nero, not wanting to touch her and get in trouble with my wife.

Nero does as told, placing the gag back in place and taking her out of the room.

"I hope you don't plan to torture her yourself," Sisi says as she comes to my side.

"Nope," I reply, "didn't even touch her," I continue, putting my hands in the air.

"Good." She nods, satisfied. "I can do it."

"You?" I ask, surprised.

"Of course. This is primarily *our* business, so if you can't do it then it befalls to me," she states matter of factly, raising her hands and gathering her hair into a tight bun at her nape.

"Right," I answer, once again in awe of her. "But we only need to roughen her up a little so that Meester will take us seriously."

"No worries," she immediately replies, folding the cuffs of her shirt and following after Nero.

"That's my sister?" Marcello asks almost in disbelief, his eyes on Sisi's retreating figure.

"No. That's my wife," I say proudly, "and she's a force to be reckoned with." I clap him on the back, before I follow after her.

We make quick work of the torture room, decorating it to show we're not playing, and installing a camera right in front of Salome.

Sisi hadn't been kidding when she'd said she had it covered, as Salome is now sporting a busted lip and an already bruised eye.

Still, the most astonishing thing was the fact that even in her beat up state, she was chatting with Sisi as if they were long-lost pals.

"I'm not your father's biggest fan," Sisi mentions, "since he's tried to kill Vlad and me at least twice now. But since you're not on his side, I guess we can be friends," she smiles, "after he's dead."

"You guys plan on killing him?" Salome raises her gaze around as she asks the question.

Nero grunts, still by her side.

In fact, he hasn't left, even while Sisi was rearranging her face.

Allegra is at the end of the room with Enzo and Adrian, while Marcello is arranging the camera in place. Catalina had taken Bianca upstairs to feed her, since she'd gotten some pregnancy cravings.

"Yes," I answer honestly. "He's as good as dead."

"Damn," she mutters under her breath. "Can you make sure I'm his official heir before you kill him though? I really don't want to wake up and find that he's given *all* his money to some charity or something. Not that my father is very charitable, but he'd do it just to spite me." She sighs deeply.

"Why would he do that?" Sisi asks.

"We fucking hate each other. The only reason I haven't killed him myself is because I kept hoping he'd change his will," Salome says, disappointed.

Sisi turns sharply toward me.

"Will it work then? If he hates her?"

"Oh, he hates me all right, but he still needs me for a male heir," Salome interjects. "That's the only thing I'm good for apparently." She rolls her eyes.

"Good, that works then," I nod, going back to the camera to ensure everything is fine.

I tell everyone to step aside, ready to record Salome begging her father to save her, but I'm a little surprised to see that Nero seems reluctant to leave her side.

"Nero?" I ask, my voice sharp.

His gaze meets mine and he nods, stepping aside.

"Put your best act on, Salome. I might even forge his will for you if you're successful," I promise.

Her eyes grow wide, her pupils sparkling with excitement.

"Deal," she agrees.

I start the countdown, and then I tell her to begin.

The camera zooms in on Salome's face, her bloody lip and her purple eye as she's trembling, sniffling.

"It's all your fucking fault, old man! Why couldn't you just let me be?" she cries out, cursing her father and calling him all types of names.

Well, if this is her way of sounding convincing, then so be it.

"Do you know what they threatened to do?" she continues to yell, her face red from the exertion. "A hysterectomy. Say bye-bye to your heirs, Papi dear. I know I won't miss them." She smirks at the camera.

I bring my hand to my forehead, unable to believe how *that* message is going to get Meester to cooperate.

"I'M SURPRISED THE VIDEO WORKED," SISI COMMENTS AS SHE joins me on the deck of the boat.

Everyone is completely geared up for whatever we'll find on the island, and while I would have liked for Sisi to stay behind, since it *will* be dangerous, I couldn't stop her from coming.

I know she would have followed me anyway, because if there's one thing I've learned about her, it's that there's a stubbornness to her that infuses strength into any decision she takes.

She never backs down, regardless of the dangers

involved, and the attack in New Orleans had shown me that just as I'd go to any extent to protect her, so would she for me.

She twines her fingers with mine, her head resting on my shoulder as we watch the boat leave the harbor.

"Meester is just as mercenary as I'd pegged him," I tell her, sneaking a glance to where Meester is sitting on deck, restrained and currently being interrogated by Enzo.

The negotiations with Meester had gone according to plan. Although Salome's message hadn't been a traditional one, it had honed in on Meester's interests.

When I'd spoken to him it had taken a while to convince him that we actually have his daughter, but after seeing the recording, all traces of doubt had evaporated and he'd agreed to help us get to the island. He'd given away his trump card too, as he'd asked at least a dozen times to make sure his daughter—specifically her womb—would be safe.

It had also confirmed, without a sliver of doubt, that Meester has been involved with Miles all along, including all those years ago when they'd roped Misha into their plans and attacked my house. For that alone, I'm reserving the right to send him to his grave after everything is over.

"We're so close, Vlad," Sisi whispers.

"Indeed," I reply stiffly.

Now that the moment of reckoning is so near, I don't know how to feel about everything. I am especially wary about hoping to find Katya alive. Because she is, she might be just a shell of a human.

After we'd gotten Meester to cooperate, we'd put together a plan of attack, and both Enzo and Marcello had volunteered some of their best men. I'd given them a rundown of Miles' experiment, especially the tests he'd put us through as children.

Anyone reared on those terms is bound to become a deadly motherfucker—if they are lucky enough to reach maturity. And so we'd chosen the men with the most experience in hand-to-hand combat and shooting.

The plan is rather simple.

Taking Meester's boat to reach the island, we've stashed some of the best soldiers on board. The minute we get to the island, the first task is to take out the coast guard and ensure that the port is clear. Then, a few other boats will come in to help with the evacuation.

From what I'd seen on the drone footage, the entire hospital is occupied, so we'll need enough space to take everyone to safety.

Then, after everyone's been evacuated from the premises, we'll raid the basement.

Sisi had brought up a good idea that the evacuation should be organic and not hostile, because the moment we start moving that many people out of the hospital and enforcements are sent from the basement, everyone will be caught in the crossfire.

Instead, she'd suggested that the two of us go inside disguised as hospital personnel and sound the fire alarm, guiding everyone toward an exit where Enzo's men will pick them up and lead them toward the port.

Then we'd have the freedom to move around as we tackle the basement situation.

"There's something eating at you," she shrewdly notes, leaning back to study me.

I take a deep breath. Nothing ever escapes her.

"After so many years, revenge is so close I can almost taste it. But what about after?"

In my original plans, I'm ashamed to admit that I hadn't planned on living much longer after fulfilling my promises. It had all been a matter of keeping my word to my sisters and then…

I'd never had anything to look forward to, and with my lonely existence, there wasn't much to keep my attention.

Now, thinking of being free from my vow, and with everything behind me… I feel lost.

"We'll deal with it when the time comes," she replies, taking my face in her hands and urging me to look her in the eyes. "But I'm here. I'll always be here. And together we'll get through everything."

"You're right." I bring her knuckles to my lips, laying a kiss on each one. "We'll take it a day at a time."

Her lips stretch into a blinding smile, the type that always has the power to leave me breathless. Especially as she's dressed in one of those black latex suits she'd had custom made, weapons sheathed all around her body.

I curl my fingers through the hoops that hold her belt in place, dragging her into me.

"Did you see the way Marcello's eyes were shooting daggers at me when he saw what you were wearing?"

"He thinks you've brainwashed me somehow," she chuckles, "he even took me aside to ask me if we're on any drugs."

"Damn Bianca and her big mouth," I groan. "Now I don't *only* seem like a dysfunctional killer. But a doped up dysfunctional killer. Just what I needed," I mutter under my breath.

"Don't worry," she smirks conspiratorially, "I told him that you've given me a strong cocktail of serotonin, oxytocin and dopamine. He shut up."

I blink twice and before I know it a smile spreads on my face.

"Hell girl," I drawl, pride swelling in my chest. "That's the best thing I've ever heard. I think I'm in love," I whistle, winking at her.

It seems that my sense of humor has been rubbing off on her.

"He might have been on to something, though," she raises an eyebrow, "since we *are* getting high," she leans in to whisper, "on each other."

"Sisi." I place my hands on her shoulders, lifting her off the ground and firmly placing her away from me. "We're going to war, yet when you speak to me in that husky voice of yours all I can see is you, me, and a bed."

"I thought a bed wasn't necessary," she retorts, and I close my eyes.

My nostrils flared, I'm having the worst time controlling myself as I look at her enticing curves and the way every sinuous move is a fucking work of art. Even as she lifts a finger to tug a stray strand of hair back in her updo, I can't help the way my cock twitches.

Or the way my heart beats loudly in my chest, my veins throbbing with unreleased pressure.

Goddamn.

This woman is going to be the death of me.

The hidden smile on her face tells me that she knows *exactly* how she affects me, and she's capitalizing on it full force. If it weren't for the circumstances we currently find ourselves in, I wouldn't waste a second to show her that a bed *isn't* at all necessary—the deck would do just fine.

But as the island comes into view, the moment we've been waiting for fast approaching, she quickly sobers up.

Meeting with everyone on deck, we quickly go over the plan again, delegating tasks. Enzo and his wife are in charge of getting everyone off the island, while Bianca, Adrian and Marcello are our back-up for after we evacuate the hospital.

Their men are also on standby awaiting orders.

After we do another check of the equipment, making sure all communication devices are working, we are ready to go.

As the boat moors into the port, Enzo releases Meester from his restraints, going to talk to the coast guard.

We all wait in the back until we get the signal to proceed.

As soon as we are on solid ground, a small fight ensues. There are maybe five coast guards in total, and it takes me and another man just as many minutes to dispatch them before they can ring the alarm.

Phase one done.

A few men take the clothes off the coast guards and resume their spots at the control station, ready to receive the other boats coming to the island.

Before we leave though, I make sure I give Meester his due. One cut across his stomach and I order everyone to let him bleed out before dumping him in the water. It's what traitors deserve after all. And I don't think Meester has *ever* been loyal to anyone in his life.

Live as a traitor, die as a traitor.

Besides, he's outlived his use. And while he does deserve

a more drawn-out death for everything he's tried against me and Sisi, there's no time to dwell on particularities at the moment.

I have one purpose.

Get to Miles.

The way clear, Sisi and I head to the hospital, the others following quietly behind and waiting for further instructions.

"From afar this looks abandoned," Sisi mentions as we reach the service entrance. Avoiding any security camera, I take out some tools from my pocket, working on the lock.

"It's the smartest location to do this unbothered," I tell her, placing the tension wrench inside the lock. "No civilians would trespass, and no one would think anything amiss is taking place because it's federal ground."

The door gives way with a click, and Sisi gives me a dreamy smile, walking inside with me following after her.

We enter the laundry area, and turning to me, Sisi assures me she's got this. A smile playing on my lips, I nod to her, urging her to go on.

Although there isn't a moment that I don't worry about her safety, I also trust her skills and know she can take care of herself. And I know that by smothering her with my over-protectiveness, I would just be stifling her potential.

I'd meant what I told her before. I want her to be strong on her own and not depend on anyone. Because I fear there may come a time when she'll have to be strong for me too.

While I wait in one of the rooms, she goes out, catching the eye of one of the nurses.

"What are you doing here? You're not allowed to be here," the woman calls out to Sisi, her foreign accent unmistakable.

One loud noise and the door opens with Sisi dragging the woman inside.

"You're getting awfully good at knocking people out," I note, amused, while she's taking the nurse's clothes and putting them on.

"It's fun." She shrugs, winking at me.

Once her outfit is in place, she goes out again, this time luring one of the doctors to the laundry room.

In no time, I'm dressed as a doctor and we are both out in the hallways of the hospital.

There are multiple levels to the building, but as we pass by open rooms, all full of people, the picture starts to become grimmer.

"Dear Lord," Sisi whispers as she stops in the doorway of one room. Turning my head to see what she's looking at, I realize the room can't be more than a hundred square feet, but it has around six children, crowded in bunk beds, all hooked to IVs.

"How are we going to evacuate them?" she asks, pointing to their conditions, "I don't think they are fit to walk, let alone run if there's a fire alarm."

My lips stretch in a thin line as I consider the possibilities. Raising a finger to my comm, I contact Enzo, letting him know the plan might not go as smoothly.

"We'll send people in to get the ones who can't move freely," he replies, and we hash out a new plan.

Instead of ringing the alarm right away, Sisi and I do some rounds on all levels, cataloguing who might need assistance and who can move on their own.

What we're seeing is dire, though, and Sisi is getting increasingly more affected as she sees more and more children on their little beds, barely able to move, because they might bust their stitches.

"God, Vlad," she whispers, "that could have been me. That could have been any of us."

My hand on her shoulder, I give her a quick squeeze.

"There's nothing we can do now except get them away from here," I tell her.

"I know," she sighs, writing down the last of the room numbers that might need assistance.

With that done, we ring the fire alarm, watching as people start running around, a chaotic mess quickly forming in the hospital.

"We can't linger," I tug her to me as she continues to look at the sick children with sadness in her eyes.

"I know," she eventually acquiesces, but I can see the change in her demeanor.

"I wish I could make them suffer so bad." Her voice is barely above a whisper, her hands balled into fists. There's a new conviction in her eyes, and the fact that this upset her has me seeing red.

"Oh, but I will, hell girl." I take her hand, unfurling her fist and massaging it slowly. "I'll make sure they rue the day they were born. And you," I lift her fingers to my lips, "will have a front row to witness their agony."

40
VLAD

"**E**veryone should be out by now," I mention as I kick open a door leading to the basement.

As we'd looked through the building, I'd also found an old blueprint of it. While I can assume that the underground level's been built much later than the building plan, I'd found a door that leads directly there.

"Shouldn't we wait for the others?" she asks as she takes off her nurse's outfit, dumping it on the ground. I do the same with my white doctor's coat, the extra clothing only impeding our movements. And we'll need all the freedom to move.

"They'll come. Eventually," I add dryly.

There's this anxiousness building inside of me, every step I take making me imagine the moment I'll finally confront Miles for everything he's done to us.

Vanya.

Not for the first time, I wish she were still here. I wish she could see me making Miles pay for what he did to her, and for all the suffering he put us both through.

More than anything, I wish she could see me keep my promise.

I won't fail you, V.

Decades of preparation, and it was all for this moment.

Holding tightly onto Sisi, I lead us down a windy path to a cellar-like space. Cobwebs everywhere, it's clear this particular entrance has not been used in a long time.

"The others are in the building." Sisi nods at me just as we reach a long corridor.

"Stay close to me," I tell her, my eyes already scouting the area.

Taking a deep breath, I let myself scan my surroundings, all my senses ready to pick up any signal.

There's an eerie silence, the only noise, our steps as we carefully move forward.

Sisi scrunches her nose in disgust when we reach a particular area where the stench of the old cellar is too much.

I tighten my hand on hers, letting her know she should be on guard. According to the plans we'd looked at, this tunnel *should* lead somewhere. But the destination hadn't been recorded on the blueprint, likely because it was built much later. I could wager a guess, though, as to where this leads.

I still, placing my hand up for Sisi to stop too. Raising a finger to my lips, I motion for her to be silent and listen to the noise.

It's very faint, but as I close my eyes and hone in on it, I can almost make out the sound of footsteps.

One. Two. Five.

My hand up, I use my fingers to indicate how many

people are heading our way. She nods at me, a grim expression on her face that slowly gives way to excitement.

I should know, since it emulates my own very well.

I guess that until our reinforcements arrive we'll have time for one tiny play.

Stretching my arm out to her as if I'm inviting her to waltz, I wink at her, and she knows exactly what to do.

She fakes a curtsey as she lowers her hands to her feet, getting her shoes ready for fighting. Her entire outfit's been custom made for one purpose: to suit our style.

And we'd had enough time practicing to develop a very particular style. Especially as my stretched out hand tightens over hers, tugging her into me with a whirl.

"Ready for the showdown, hell girl?" I ask, amused.

I don't know how prepared the men coming our way are going to be, but I have no doubt that they are no match for us together.

Her lips curl around the corners as she bats her lashes at me, her arm coming to rest around my shoulder.

"You don't have to ask twice," she purrs slowly.

I may have taught her how to fight and hold her own, but we'd also trained so we could complement each other in a battle. Inspired by the first time we'd faced those men in the restaurant, we'd practiced for hours until our bodies became in sync—not that they weren't already.

There's something about the way we communicate. Half the time words are obsolete as one glance says everything.

The sounds of boots hitting the floor becomes louder and louder until the five men I'd counted appear in sight, weapons raised and aiming at us.

"You know it might hurt, right?" I drawl as I trail my

hand down her back, where her latex suit is covering bullet-proof equipment.

"You can kiss it better later," she murmurs.

My lips are already on hers, the corner of my eye studying the movements of the men as they charge and…

I spin her around to a silent tune, the only noise the bullets whizzing past us as we move in sync, avoiding most incoming shots, while closing the distance between us and the men.

It's a waltz of death as Sisi and I glide on the floor, every step taking us closer to our targets.

And just as I see that we're in the right spot, I spread my hands over her waist, raising her up in the air.

The men seem completely baffled by our display, and they're not even trying to aim at us any more, bullets fly haphazardly in all directions as one barks some orders at the others to focus.

It's in vain, though, as their eyes are stuck on Sisi's sinful shape as she twirls in the air. Almost mesmerized, they don't even see the knives as they shoot out of her hands and land in their chests.

The leader of the unit screams some commands as two men go down, the others immediately entering a different formation as they surround us.

"Ready?" I ask, smirking.

"Let's do this," she says, her hands firmly on my shoulders as I swoop her in the air, her legs stretched out, the blades at the tip of her shoes extended. Spinning her around, I give her enough momentum to coordinate the attack, her blades nipping two men right at their jugulars, blood immediately gushing out.

"One more behind me, hell girl," I whisper, lifting her high before lowering her to the ground and pushing her backwards. She glides on the ground between my legs, and bracing herself on her elbows, she sends her foot right in the last man's face, the blade making contact with the area under his chin.

Finger on the trigger, he manages one last shot before he drops dead.

"Well." I dust my suit, opening up my shirt to remove the bullet stuck in my bulletproof vest. "I'd say that went well."

She's smiling widely at me.

"That was rather easy," she replies when I help her up.

"And sexy as fuck." I whistle, my eyes roving appreciatively over her figure.

Even if the men hadn't aimed their guns at us or meant to kill us, they would have still ended up dead, because they'd been a little too generous with their gazes.

Taking back our weapons from the fallen men, we're ready to move on.

"I have to say, those were *not* what I expected," she notes as we continued walking. "We didn't even have to try. And *I*'m a beginner," she adds, almost outraged by their performance.

"I'm guessing someone's simply playing with us," I say as I narrow my eyes at the exit of the tunnel.

And so it seems, because as soon as we're out of the old tunnels, we find ourselves in the middle of some weird intermediary chamber, two men and one woman waiting at the exit.

"What is this, *The Hunger Games*?" I groan as I realize it's just a game. Likely Miles is watching us even now, having fun at our expense.

"I'll get the girl, you get the guys." Sisi nods at me, her fight stance in place as her attention is focused on the girl.

Wielding a long chain, Sisi's opponent doesn't look to be older than eighteen. But what immediately strikes me is her gaze—it's blank.

"Sisi," I call out, my voice tense. "Please be careful. She's not normal."

I quickly scan my own opponents, noting the same glazed eyes—emotionless.

I need to finish with them as quickly as possible, because if these are part of the experiment, then chances are that they are anything but ordinary.

And Sisi doesn't stand a chance.

One eye perpetually fixed on Sisi, I take a step forward toward my own opponents. Both are holding battle axes, and as they look at me a smirk appears on their lips.

Ah, the taste of war.

It's something I'm intimately familiar with, as I'd had a hard time adjusting to the real world after I'd returned home. Every interaction I'd had with someone would start with the thought of killing them, this thirst for blood so deep within me it had taken me years to learn how to subdue.

And I know exactly how they feel. There's excitement in war, in fight, in the taste of the kill. There's an intoxicating high that comes only when you have power over death, and for more than half my life I'd been a slave to it. To this beast inside of me that's *never* satisfied for anything less than destruction—total annihilation.

They move forward, their smiles widening, and in their arrogant minds they can already taste victory.

Unluckily for them, they were sent after the wrong person. Now the question is rather simple. Weapons or no weapons. But as they charge forward, I don't get to make that decision. They make it for me.

My lip curling upwards, I just duck and dodge, avoiding every strike of their axes, one eye still on Sisi.

One kunai in each hand, she's holding tightly on to the hilt as she parries the strikes of the other girl's chain.

The air whooshes past my face as the blade of the axe glides one inch away from my skin.

Realizing I'd let them have their easy fun, I decide to end the game. My hands shoot out, both wrapping around the shaft of their axes just as they swing them toward me.

Oh, they're strong.

But not as strong as I am.

One foot forward, I push against them, letting my hand become slack for one moment as bait before holding tightly and wrenching the axes from their hands.

The force of my push sends them backwards, and for a moment they look disoriented as they realize their weapon is missing.

There's something odd about their reactions.

Besides the dead eyes, because been there, done that, there's something else, their focus a little off.

And as they continue to charge me, using their fists now, I immediately note what's wrong.

Robotic.

It's like their entire purpose is to end me, but without the conscious action behind it.

Fuck!

It seems Miles may have changed his plans. Certainly for them to reach this age in the experiment, they would have had to be almost as strong as me. For them to still live…

I duck again, spreading my arms out and gathering momentum before letting them come at me full force, bending my knees and falling to the ground just as I strike, each axe blade heading for their guts.

Their grunts of pain are the only thing I hear as the axe cuts into them, opening them up for a river of blood and organs as I continue to dig the blade inside, making sure the damage is debilitating and permanent.

When there's a gaping hole inside, I just give them another shove, the blade hitting the back of the spine in what I can only call a lovely melody.

Ah, the symphony of death.

They fall to the ground, their moans of pain quickly forgotten as I turn my full attention to Sisi.

She's breathing hard, but she's still holding her own against the girl. One wrong move, though, and she lands on her back, the chain ready to strike at her.

I move faster than I've moved in my entire life, crouching in front of her and bearing the entire brunt of the chain as it makes contact with my back in a deafening sound. It's the only thing that makes me aware I've been hit, since there's absolutely no pain.

Sisi's eyes widen as they look at me, but I'm not done.

I turn ever so slightly, my ears perking up as I listen to the girl wielding the weapon. The air swirls around me as she takes the chain back, pulling it toward her before sending it flying toward me once more.

This time, attuned to the situation, I raise my hand, moving to the left and catching the chain just as it's about to hit me. I grip the end of the metal tightly, yanking it and the girl toward me.

She's off balance as she falls forward, and not quick enough as I rip the chain from her hands, throwing it aside. My hand on her throat, I only get one glimpse of clouded eyes as I apply a little pressure, her neck snapping, her head bending to the side.

Throwing her body to the side, I turn to Sisi, helping her to her feet.

"I don't think I'll ever get used to seeing you in action," she breathes out, her chest rising and falling, her breasts emphasized by the tightness of her suit.

Her palms come up resting on my chest as she feels me, her touch igniting my already adrenaline fueled body.

"What are your muscles made of? Pure iron?" she asks, her pupils engulfing her irises, and I realize I might not be the only one who thinks the two f's go together. Not when she raises herself on her tip-toes, her tongue out as she licks my cheek.

"Hmm," she purrs softly, her warm breath touching my skin in a sweet caress, "even your sweat turns me on," she continues, her fingers trailing up until she's tracing the outline of my neck tattoo.

Then, before I can even react, she's off me, her gaze behind me.

"Careful," she warns, and I swiftly turn around, ready to deal with whatever failed experiment Miles' decided to send my way.

But I only get to take one step toward the newcomer

before a bullet lodges itself in his forehead and he simply drops dead to the ground.

"You couldn't wait for us, could you?" I hear Bianca's voice, and I look back to see her strut into the room, her husband on her trail, joined by Marcello who has a grim expression on his face.

"Really, Vlad? You could have gotten Sisi killed," he all but yells at me, his features drawn up in anger.

"*Really*, 'Cello, that little trust you have in me?" I drawl, resisting the urge to roll my eyes at him.

"I'm fine, Marcello." Sisi turns to him, and *she's* rolling her eyes at him.

Fuck, how I love this woman.

I don't give in and grab her for a high five, knowing that if grumpy Marcello's made an appearance it's not long before growly Marcello will follow suit. And I know that then I won't hear the end of it.

"I told you I've been training with him. I'm not helpless." She pushes her chin up, standing up to him defiantly.

"These people are trained killers, Sisi. It doesn't matter how much training you have. And you're a girl too," he continues, and I almost groan, knowing he just dug himself a grave.

"What?" Sisi blinks as the words set in. "I'm a girl," she speaks slowly. "So that means I can't fight? That I can't defend myself?" She places her arms over her chest and I know we're in *serious* territory.

For someone like Sisi, who enjoys having control over her own life above all, being reminded that her gender might hold her back is akin to the worst insult.

Thing is, she might be a girl, but she's a damn kick ass

girl and anyone should feel fucking lucky to have her by their side.

Knowing how heated she must be, I join her, draping an arm over her shoulder.

"Aren't you the same person who told us that our gender shouldn't hold us back?" She narrows her eyes at Marcello.

"Yes, but it's not the same," he replies. "You can choose whatever profession you want, but that doesn't mean you should dive head first in front of danger. And this," he waves at the bodies on the ground, "is even worse than normal danger."

"'Cello, calm down. As long as Sisi's with me there's nothing to worry about. Besides," I say as I look down into her gorgeous face, "she *can* kick ass," I praise her and I'm rewarded with a radiant smile.

"You?" He all but yells. *Again.* "You're the most unstable man I've ever encountered, Vlad. Yeah sure, you're guarding her from danger because you're the worst danger," he mutters, annoyed.

"Are we doing this again?" I raise an eyebrow. "I told you Sisi is in good hands. I'd never willingly let *anything* happen to her."

"What about unwillingly? Everyone here knows about your episodes. It's not a secret that you're *not* normal. Who's to say that instead of protecting her, next time you'll kill her yourself?"

I close my eyes, taking a deep breath.

But I can't control my own body's reaction as I leave Sisi's side, and in two seconds I have Marcello by the throat, backing him into the wall.

"What are you insinuating, bro-in-law?" I can barely

contain the raw anger radiating from me. It's in every pore as it seeks to be let out.

"This!" He looks at me in the eye, not even blinking as I lift his entire body's mass off the floor, my fingers tightening around his pulse. "This is exactly what I mean. You're unpredictable."

I grit my teeth and instead of proving to him that I *am* indeed *that* dangerous, I let him go, fighting against myself and trying to regulate my breaths.

As if through a haze, I feel Sisi's small hand reach for mine, cradling it to her chest as she looks worriedly at me.

"He's doing better, Marcello," she says loudly, her eyes only on me. "He's been working on himself and he's doing much better. He hasn't had an episode since New Orleans, and I'm proud of him."

Fuck, but is there any way I could love this woman more? In her eyes, I see everything I've been craving my entire life.

Love. Tenderness. Acceptance.

She knows my deepest secrets, and she's never once turned away from me. Not only that, but she's publicly stood up for me, time and time again, even against her family.

I don't think there's any universe in which I wouldn't adore her.

"Sisi..." Marcello starts, but one sharp look from Sisi is all it takes to promptly shut him up.

"You *don't* understand, do you?" she asks, her voice grave. "There's *nothing* you could tell me about him that would make me love him any less. I know who he is and what he's done. I know *everything.* And I'm still here." She takes a deep breath, and I can tell she's trying very hard to keep her temper in check.

"All my life I've been told how to be, and how *not* to be. Yet no one's ever asked me what *I* want. No one but him." She points her finger at me. "If I told him I wanted to fight, he taught me how to fight. If I told him I wanted a tattoo, he gave me a tattoo. If I told him I wanted to kill someone, he gave me the opportunity to do so. He never once doubted me, never once told me I shouldn't *do something* because I am a girl."

She's breathing hard, her fists clenched by her side as she looks up at Marcello, unflinching at his harsh gaze.

"You may disagree about our relationship, but to me, he's the only one who's given me wings to soar, instead of dragging me down and chaining me to the ground. And *this,* my brother, is the last time we're going to have this discussion."

She narrows her eyes at Marcello, before doing something that completely floors me. Taking a step forward, she lifts her fist, banging it against her chest. "He. Is. Mine," she says, emphasizing every word. "The end."

She twirls around, not even waiting for Marcello's reply, and raises an eyebrow at Bianca and Adrian, who've been silently watching the whole thing.

"Don't look at me." B shrugs. "I like you. And I think you're good for him." She motions toward me. "Besides," she continues, "it takes a whole different type of person to deal with his surly ass, so for that alone you have my respect."

"I'm neutral," Adrian is quick to point out and I give him an appreciative nod. At least he knows when to shut up.

"Good." I open my arms, a wide smile on my face since I'm now fully in control of myself. "Now we can leave the family drama behind and go kill some bad guys?"

Sisi twines her arm through mine as we go first, ignoring the groans behind us.

Leaving the dead bodies behind, we continue down another small corridor that finally gives way to a wide tunnel.

"So this is where the action is," I add dryly as I note cages on each side of the tunnel.

Hell, the underground compound seems to take up the entire surface of the island.

The first few cages are empty, but as we advance, we start seeing young children as well as teenagers on both sides.

"Fuck," Marcello curses out when he sees the extent of Miles' depravity.

Bianca too, for all her emotionless demeanor, seems shaken up when she sees the condition they are all held in.

Dirty clothes, dirty, festering wounds, the smell of rotting flesh is ripe in the air.

"What the fuck," Adrian's voice rings out when we stop by one cage where a little boy is sitting on the floor, face down, flies gathered over the entire surface of his body. The smell coming from him confirms that he's been dead a while, and his cellmate, another boy his age, has had to withstand this all along.

Even worse, as I look closer at the boy huddled at the other end of the cell, I realize he's not far behind.

There's a gaping hole in his stomach, leaking yellow and

green puss, his mouth bruised, his entire body almost purple.

He sees us stop next to his cage, but he doesn't react—he can't react. Only his eyes move around and indicate that he's still alive.

"Lord," Sisi whispers, her hand tightening on my arm, "this is even worse than upstairs."

I grunt, my lips pursed. Somehow, I doubt this is going to be the worst that we'll see in here.

In true fashion, the images only get grimmer as we move on, and considering the size of the enclosure, we'll have plenty to see.

Raising a finger to my comm, I give Enzo a quick rundown of what to expect here, and to make sure he keeps some of the doctors from the hospital to take care of whoever will survive from here. After letting me know he'll do his best to bring people down here to take the children, I close the connection.

"These are the failures," I say, cringing at my own words.

But the more I look at their dilapidated cages, the rotting flesh and the infected wounds, the more my mind seems to be pushing something at me. Like a memory of sorts, it's there, yet I can't fully grasp it.

"Are you okay?" Sisi asks, her tone worried as she looks up at me. My hand on my temple, I squeeze my eyes shut and give her a firm nod.

"Must be bringing back memories," I mutter, even though nothing I'd remembered so far had been this dire.

Sure, Vanya and I had been living in a tiny mold infested room, but it hadn't been *this* bad.

She nods slowly, even though her eyes tell me she doesn't fully believe me.

41
VLAD

"This must be the place they are sent to die." I change the subject, pointing to another cage housing yet another dead person.

But the more we advance, the more putrid the stench becomes.

Everyone brings their sleeves to their nose, unable to withstand the fumes.

We're about halfway through the tunnel, and at this point *all* the cells are filled with dead people.

"Fucking hell," Bianca curses, using her hand to swat some flies aside.

But it's not just flies.

Rats, maggots and other insects are all strewn around the area, the ground teeming with them as they chase their next meal.

Even I'm becoming disgusted by what I'm seeing—and I don't remember the last time I got disgusted. Especially as the little bugs are crawling on the floor, scattering away any time we make a step forward.

Unable to help myself, I grab Sisi and I make her get on my back. I don't want her anywhere near *that*.

"You shouldn't have come, Bianca," I hear Marcello tell her as she's heaving by the side. "It can't be good for your pregnancy," he continues as Adrian pats her back, trying to help her.

"I'm fine," she wheezzes, "I don't think Diana likes dead people smell," she jokes as she wipes her mouth with the back of her hand.

"I don't think anyone does," I add dryly as Adrian takes her in his arms too, cradling her to his chest.

"This is an infestation. I can't believe this." Marcello shakes his head as he steps on a few bugs, the sound of their carcasses snapping reverberating in the air.

"But why would they keep them here? Some of them are long dead," Adrian adds, pointing to one cell where a body's half eaten by the various insects and scavengers.

"Because it's a punishment," I answer.

"A punishment? For whom? They're already dead!" he exclaims.

"For the ones who are still alive." I point to a few cells that are cleaner, where there are no traces of corpses. "It must be another brainwashing trick. Imagine spending even an hour in this place, surrounded by death and things that consume death."

"Damn." Bianca's features draw up in disgust. "This is another level of fucked up."

"It is," I agree. "And it's not even the worst," I say and I feel Sisi's arms tightening around my neck.

"I'm sorry," she whispers into my ear, her voice only for me to hear. "This can't be easy for you."

"Don't worry about me, hell girl. We're one step closer to Miles, and that's all that matters."

The tunnel finally ends, and it's like we can finally take a deep breath of not so rotten air.

"What the fuck," Bianca curses as she breathes out, her chest rising and falling rapidly, "I've never been a fan of putrefied flesh," she adds dryly, her lips curled in disgust. "That is simply too much."

"It's smart, though," Sisi says as I put her down to her feet. "Another type of behavioral therapy. Especially for a child, that would be sure to traumatize them."

"Exactly," I agree. "It's a form of control. Deep down, on a psychological level, because you're just scared into submission, but also because it simply desensitizes you. You saw those people's blank gazes."

"And I thought I'd seen the worst there is to see of humanity," Marcello mutters, rubbing his eyes. "This might just trump it all."

"How big is this underground compound? We've already been walking for what feels like forever," Bianca complains, one hand on her stomach as she coos some shit to her baby.

Gotta say, I never thought I'd see Bianca as a mother. And now she's pregnant? I'm surprised Adrian let her come, but then again, it's Bianca we're talking about. She would have gotten her way whether he wanted or not.

Still, I note the way his eyes never stray from her, always ready to intervene if necessary. Not unlike my situation with Sisi, he lets Bianca do what she wants while being ready to protect her at any moment.

It's funny how things are suddenly put into perspective. A year ago I would have never imagined empathizing with

Hastings, or Bianca, since her obsession with him had never made sense.

Now? I want to laugh out loud at the irony, because if anything, I'm worse than Bianca's *ever* been.

I sneak a glance at Sisi, marveling at the strength reflected in her features, and I know that what I feel for her goes beyond mere obsession. She's under my skin, in my blood, in my Goddamn heart. There's no place left that she hasn't touched or left her mark on.

She owns me—every fucking atom of my body is hers.

A sudden noise snaps me back to reality, my eyes narrowed, my attention focused on whatever's coming from the other end of the tunnel.

"Down!" I yell, just as the others tune in to the noise.

I bring Sisi down with me, pleased that everyone's listened to me and is currently on the floor.

One more second and a projectile flies from the other end of the tunnel, hitting the back, a small explosion ensuing.

"Damn," I curse out. "He brought out the big guns."

"Won't the structure collapse?" Marcello asks.

I shake my head.

"The main walls are steel dressed in concrete and that was a small range projectile. Unlikely to cause any damage to the structure. Us, however..." I trail off just as another projectile flies at us.

"We won't be able to continue forward if they keep on hitting us. I can't even see the other end," Bianca complains.

My lips stretch in a thin line as I analyze our options.

There's some sort of smoke or mist at the end of the tunnel, likely on purpose so we can't detect whoever is shooting at us. And the moment we get up to walk, we'll be hit.

"B, give me your gun," I tell her, an idea forming in my head.

"My gun?" she asks, scandalized.

"You can't see, so you can't shoot," I point out.

"Well, you can't see either."

Fucking B and her obsession with her guns. She's never let anyone handle her precious babies, and while I can respect that, in this particular case, it's just dumb.

"Yes, but I can hear."

She knows me well enough to realize that it's the only advantage we have in this particular scenario.

"Fineee," she groans, pushing her gun to me on the floor.

"What are you going to do?" Sisi whispers in my ear, her body close to mine.

"I'm going to listen for his location."

She frowns. "You can do that?"

"I hope so," I answer grimly.

The truth is that this, too, had been part of Miles' training. I'd had extensive sessions of fighting blindfolded and relying on my other senses to gauge an attack and to make sense of my adversary. And after, I'd just continued to foster those skills, my profession benefiting greatly from them.

"Everyone quiet," I say as I assume my position.

On my belly, I place one elbow on the ground for support, my other hand on the gun as I wrap one finger around the trigger.

Closing my eyes, I breathe in once before stopping my

breathing all together and slowing the beats of my heart, so I can have no interference.

As soon as silence greets me, I turn my attention forward to the foreign presence. My ears open up and that's when I hear it. The sound of boots balancing on the ground, of clammy hands moving around the weapon and of anxious breaths as he's undoubtedly trying to scout us.

More than anything, I hear the small moves he makes, the cold ground almost crackling under his steps.

He's advancing.

So if we're not going to him, he's slowly coming toward us.

A smile pulls at my lips and I continue to listen to his small steps as he marches forward. There's a slight hesitation to the way he's moving, as if his very life depends on this assignment.

And in a way, it does.

Because the moment when I'm sure of his position comes, the gun in my hand ready and angled up, my finger gently squeezing the trigger.

And then I listen.

There's a short pause before two breaths come out in short spurts, the sound of knees crashing to the ground letting me know I'd hit him. His body falls further, the metal of his gun hitting the cement. I document each sound, making sure he's out.

Yet even as I know him to be dead, I still listen, just in case there are more people.

"Clear," I say when I'm sure the danger's past.

We all get up, moving forward until we encounter the fallen body of a teenage boy.

"Damn, your aim was sweet," Bianca notes when she sees the bullet ripping through the boy's neck, a clean exit mark on the other side.

"He's testing me," I add tensely. "This is all a test."

"So he *is* watching," Sisi comments, looking around the tunnel for any cameras.

"Yes, and I bet he's enjoying himself immensely."

Exiting the main tunnel, the road bifurcates—one toward the right and the other to the left.

"We should split up," Adrian suggests.

"We'll go this way," I nod to the right, taking Sisi's hand in mine, "we'll call if anything."

"I'm coming with," Marcello is quick to interject, the same grumpy expression on his face.

"Fine." I wave my hand dismissively, since I am not in the mood for another argument.

As soon as we establish some ground rules, we split up.

Holding on to Sisi, I can't help but be amused at Marcello trailing closely behind, his attention wholly on us.

"Relax, 'Cello, I'm not going to ravish your sister in a dirty hallway." I give him a bored look, although the idea has merit—at a future time.

Marcello presses his lips together, not answering my taunt. Instead, he continues walking, almost grumbling something under his breath.

"I'm not as helpless as you imagine," Sisi addresses him. "I'm really not, Marcello."

"I just worry about you, okay?" He reluctantly admits. "I know I haven't been present in your life and that my behavior can seem a little… overwhelming. But I have your best intentions at heart, Sisi."

Sisi is quiet for a minute, her teeth nibbling on her lower lip.

"Thank you. It means a lot that you care," she starts as she gives him a tremulous smile, "but I've got this. Please trust that I know what I'm doing."

"Alright," he relents, even though he doesn't seem any happier about it.

"Good, I'm glad that we've ended this family *un*happiness chapter. Now we can focus on the more important stuff…" I trail off as we come to a standstill.

The entire atmosphere is different here, and as we stop before the glass door, I realize that we've just leveled up.

The door has biometric protection, so that confirms that it's not just an ordinary space. Bringing my smart watch into view, I try to tap into the framework, a little bummed when I realize it's a closed network and I can't access it as easily.

Not one to despair, I simply pull the panel from the door, quickly inspecting the wires. I have to admit that my engineering skills are rudimentary at best, but I've been known to hot-wire a few things in my life. And so a few minutes of trial and error and the door is broken—I mean open.

As soon as we enter inside, however, the difference is stark.

This room is sterile, the smell of bleach permeating the air. It almost looks lab-like in its immaculate condition.

White walls, white floors, and four electric doors.

"Dead end," I comment as I realize the doors are likely cages of some kind, each one of them having a tiny opening to allow for food.

"This looks like a mental ward," Marcello notes as he walks around.

Out of nowhere, there is a bang against one of the doors, followed by a few other bangs in each of the others.

"There's someone inside." Marcello goes to one door, returning the knock to let them know we are there.

"We need to figure out how to open these doors," I say as I study each one in part, noting they are opened by ID cards plus biometrics.

"I guess we'll have to do a repeat of the other door," I mutter dryly when I see there's no other way to open them without breaking them down. And so I quietly get to work on the first door, taking out the electrical panel and playing with the wires. Once I have a winning combination, it's all a matter of repeating it for the other doors.

"You never fail to amaze me," Sisi whispers as she raises herself on her tip-toes to kiss my cheek.

"You need to lay low with the skinship, hell girl. You know my mind can only juggle so many things at once," I murmur softly.

Truth is, when it comes to her, my mind can't take anything else *but* her.

"Vlad," I hear Bianca's voice in the comm. "I think we found the main area. There's a huge arena here," she continues, describing an arena the size of a football field, full with multiple levels for spectators.

"Damn," I mutter, realizing exactly what that's for.

Suddenly memories of the trials we'd been put through resurface in my mind. How Miles had pitted us against each other.

The winner takes it all.

And I'd become so addicted to getting his approval that I'd done everything to win those trials. I'd killed, maimed, and tortured. No one had been spared from my singular purpose.

Become the best.

Remembering the things I'd done just to gain his acceptance makes my skin crawl. Because I might loathe him with all my being now. But at one point I didn't. I looked up to him.

"We'll meet you there after we check something here," I tell her, briefly explaining what we'd found.

"Vlad," Marcello calls out, his brows pinched together as he looks from door to door. "We opened the doors, yet *no one* tried to come out," he points out and I frown.

"You're right."

Without any preamble, I yank the first door open, surprised to see a girl who couldn't be older than ten or eleven sitting at the end of the room, her back against the wall, her eyes wide as she looks at us in fear.

"What…" Sisi whispers as she gets a better view of the girl.

Surprisingly, she looks healthy. In fact, even her clothes are clean, which is *not* something I would have expected given what I know about how Miles conducts his experiments.

Curious to see who else is in the other rooms, I open the next one, and the next, until I'm at the last one.

All of them house prepubescent girls.

All but the last.

My eyes widen as I note a couple huddled together next to a bed. The male is obstructing my view of the girl as he places himself in front of her in a protective stance.

"Nero?" The name slips from my mouth, but even then I know that this *isn't* Nero.

Their faces are identical. Short black hair and blue eyes. But this man is bigger. His body is that of a professional body-builder, his muscular built dwarfing that of the girl behind him.

"You're Nero's brother," I state.

The one who supposedly died twenty years ago.

"Nero?" His voice differs completely from Nero too. There's a hoarseness to it as if he'd stretched his vocal cords to the extreme. "Nero…" he repeats, his features clouding as if he's trying to remember something long forgotten.

"I'll be damned," Marcello mutters when he sees the man, he too noticing that he's almost identical to Nero.

"It's his twin brother," I add grimly. "Sisi, please stay back." I stretch my hand to keep her out, recognizing the protective stance he has over his female and knowing he might be dangerous if he thinks we're a threat.

"It's okay," I start, giving him a quick outline of who we are and that we're going to get them to safety.

"Brother?" he asks, frowning. "My brother?"

"Yes, Nero is your brother. He thought you'd died years ago," I explain.

But then a small voice calls out from behind him.

"We're free? We can leave?" the girl asks, peeking slowly over his shoulder.

"Shh," Nero's brother turns to her, "I don't know if we can trust them, *Bia mia*. You know I'd never put you at risk."

His voice is completely different as he addresses her. Softer, warmer.

Full of love.

"Nothing will happen to you. I vow to you. We are currently evacuating the entire compound," I feel compelled to explain.

"Please, T," she continues, and I see her hand reach out to caress his shoulder, that one touch rendering him incapable of refusing her.

"If you think to cheat us, you will die by my fists." He turns to me, his gaze grave.

"Agreed." I shrug.

I'm already getting restless as I think of the imminent meeting with Miles, my temples throbbing as I imagine just how I'm going to drain the life out of him—slow and painfully.

The man helps the girl sit up, and the first thing I notice is the slight bump she's cradling with her hands, her stance protective as she takes a wary step toward us.

When the light hits her face I freeze.

Dark hair that flows down her back and reaching to her knees, pale skin that almost looks translucent in the stark neon light, and dark eyes that I see every time I look in the mirror.

"Katya?" My voice trembles as I utter that word. "Katyusha?"

She blinks slowly, her eyes focusing on me as if she doesn't recognize who I am.

Still, the features are identical to the Katya I used to know. The Katya from ten years ago.

Her lips quiver, her eyes glossy as she takes a step forward.

The man, noting the change in her, instinctively reaches forward to place himself between us.

"No, T. I know him," she utters softly. "I know him…" she continues, her voice breaking in a sob. "He's my brother."

"Brother?" the giant asks, turning to me and assessing me carefully for the first time. "Vlad?" he asks and I nod, surprised to hear my name coming from his lips.

"Vlad," Katya's voice rings out as she continues forward. Slowly—ever so slowly she steps into my waiting arms as I stiffly embrace her.

Katya. My sister is alive.

"How…" I find myself speechless for the first time as I look at her.

She doesn't look bad. Certainly not how I would have imagined her to look if I ever found her.

But there's this bleakness in her eyes that's replaced the youthful vibe from before.

She looks worn, and jaded, and entirely too old for her twenty-six years.

"You're here to get us out," she breathes, a hint of hope sparkling in her eyes. "T," she turns to the man, "we're really going to be free," she says before she goes back to him, sobs racking her body as she closes her arms around his massive frame. "We made it."

"Ah, *Bia mia*," he gently strokes her hair, "we did," he whispers as he continues to hold her.

A soft hand slips into mine, startling me from the sweet scene in front of me.

Sisi lays her head on my shoulder, her fingers tightening over mine.

"You did it, Vlad," her voice is so full of emotion, and one look at her face tells me she's on the brink of tears, "you found her." She gives me a smile that could rival the sun in its intensity.

And for the first time I feel my chest expand, relief flooding every cell of my body.

"I did," I reply, "*we* did," I amend, because she's been with me every step of the way.

Not wishing to risk their safety more than necessary, I call Enzo to send a team to evacuate them, telling him to take special care with them because they are family.

Once the men make it to our location, I hand them over with the promise that we'll catch up later, and that everything will work out.

Alone once more, we head to the arena.

<h1 style="text-align:center">42</h1>
SISI

My soul hurts for Vlad as I see his expression filled with confusion. The way I'm sure he's beyond happy to have found his sister, but unable to show the sentiment.

A myriad of emotions cross his face, as if he doesn't know which one to settle on, the feeling wholly unfamiliar.

My hand in his, I do my best to comfort him, let him know I'm there for him with my presence.

Everything we've seen so far has been gut-wrenching, but there is light at the end of the tunnel, and as I look at Katya, her features so like Vlad, I know that we'll get through this. She might be the last piece to heal his fractured soul.

After the people we'd found are handed over to Enzo and his team, we silently continue to the arena where Bianca and Adrian are waiting for us.

I don't even know what to expect anymore. Not after what I've witnessed since stepping off that boat, the torture and suffering housed in here beyond anything I could have *ever* imagine. The images of those dead children being covered in flies and devoured by maggots had remained stamped on my retina, and I don't think I'm likely to forget them anytime soon.

For that reason alone, I hope that Vlad gives Miles what he deserves.

The worst death possible.

Taking advantage of the fact that my brother is ahead of us, I quickly lean into Vlad to whisper.

"You did great," I praise gently, knowing he hadn't exactly known how to react, the hug he'd shared with his sister was stiff and uncomfortable.

"She didn't look bad," he replies, almost mechanically. "She looked way better than I expected to find her."

I nod in agreement. I, too, had been surprised to see her looking so healthy.

"She's pregnant," I comment. "Do you think that man is the father?"

It hadn't been hard to guess that there was something between the giant and Katya, not with the way he was ready to defend her with his life. But the entire premise of captivity seems antithetic with a budding romance.

"I'm not sure," Vlad replies. "I don't know for sure what the purpose of that area was, especially since the other prisoners were all under twelve. But I do have an inkling," he adds grimly.

"You think he was breeding them," I say what he'd already theorized months before. Because while Katya didn't have Vlad's condition, she might have been a carrier for it.

"Yes. And it's much more plausible if Nero's brother was used as a sperm donor, since he *has* the condition."

"But that would mean..." I trail off, the thought horrifying.

"Yes. That would mean this isn't her first pregnancy."

It's been almost ten years. I don't even want to imagine what she's been through and how many children she's lost because of that monster. Having gone through something similar myself, I know how much of a hole the loss of a child produces in one's soul. But there's a world of difference in comparing our situations, and my heart weeps for what she must have been through.

Going over potential theories, it's getting increasingly clear why Miles would resort to carriers of the gene for his human incubators instead of people who actually had the mutation.

"Because they are so rare, Miles wouldn't waste their potential like that. Not when he already had a shortage of people to include in his experiments to begin with," Vlad explains.

Miles would keep the girls with the mutation for his experiments and breed the ones with the carrier gene. It would also explain the differences in how the former were treated versus the latter. Because for all the trauma Katya nonetheless had endured, the conditions in which she was living could be considered luxurious compared with the others.

This should be a crime against humanity.

I can't help but shudder the more I think of the horrors these walls have seen, and all the suffering they've absorbed from all the innocent children who've lived and died here.

It doesn't take us long to reach Bianca and Adrian, both of them waiting outside a door.

"You didn't go inside?" Vlad asks.

She shakes her head.

"We didn't know what to expect since it's a huge open area," she grimaces. "I threw in a mini mobile camera to get some footage, though."

She removes a small tablet from her bag, showing us the video feed from inside.

"There are cameras everywhere," I point out with my finger, surprised to see it's not just CCTV. No, these are big, professional cameras fully equipped with ring lights and speakers.

There are stairs on each side of the room, leading down to the main field. All around, I see a seating area for spectators, and I realize that this is exactly like a stadium.

"He's broadcasting the events," Vlad comments. "Smart." He smirks in spite of himself. "Since these are life and death trials, never mind the fact that it's mostly children competing against each other, a lot of people on the dark web would pay good money to see it."

"How are we going to go inside, though? Bianca is right that it's too open. They could hit us from all sides," Marcello asks, pursing his lips.

"Leave that to me."

Vlad doesn't even wait for us to reply as he pushes the door open, almost flying down the stairs and striding inside the stadium until he's in the middle of the field.

"Long time no see, Miles," he shouts.

I don't even think as I follow after him, my brother and the rest are hot on my trail.

And just as we reach Vlad's side, the entire stadium comes to life. The big lights we'd seen earlier flash, light infusing every corner of the stadium.

"Welcome, welcome," a chuckle resounds from the speakers.

Vlad turns his face toward a big booth on the right, a twisted smile playing at his lips.

"I'm guessing you know why I'm here," Vlad challenges, his chin raised high, his eyes two slits as he focuses on that particular spot.

"I would have preferred for this meeting to happen under different terms," Miles' voice booms, "but I'm nothing if not adaptable."

"You might find it hard to adapt to my fists," Vlad mutters dryly.

"Ah, but how I've missed that wicked sense of humor, Vlad. I've been anticipating this meeting for years. You've turned out to be just like I predicted. *Invincible*," he proudly quips.

"Not quite." Vlad smirks. "You did whatever you could to take away every bit of humanity I had. Sadly, it didn't quite work out. I am here after all."

"It took you long enough though," Miles remarks through the speakers.

Vlad's fists are clenched by his side, and I know Miles struck a chord in him.

"I'll refer to my initial assessment, Vlad. Your specs are impressive, but there's always been one thing keeping you back from achieving perfection," Miles continues, "your puny attachments. I thought your sister was the key to breaking that, and for a while I really saw my success in you. But you had to continue on the path of no return," he tsks.

It's odd, but his manner of speaking reminds me a lot of Vlad. And I'm not the only one to notice, as the others regard Vlad with an odd look on their faces.

"*Vanya*," Vlad stresses the name of his sister, his jaw locked tight with tension. "What did you do to her?"

More laughter.

"What I did to her?" Miles chuckles. "Wouldn't you want to find out? Who knows…" he trails off, amusement clear in his voice. "I might even have the video."

"Vlad." I feel compelled to go to his side.

Because I know how to read him better than anyone. I can see behind his polished facade and into his tortured soul. And I know that right at this moment, there are turbulent seas behind his dark eyes, his control threatening to snap.

"Breathe," I urge him, my voice soft as I lay a hand on his arm. "Breathe," I repeat when it doesn't seem he's heard me.

But slowly—ever so slowly—his breathing does regulate, the tension gradually relieved as he brings the world into focus again.

"Thank you," he whispers low, his gaze still stuck on the illuminated booth.

"I have a deal for you," Miles bursts out, and a screen flares to life behind us.

Turning, I gasp when I see the image on the screen.

Vlad and Vanya.

They're both huddled in a small, dirty cell, their eyes defiantly looking at the camera.

"What do you want?" Vlad grits his teeth.

"Simple. I want to watch you fight my best soldier. One last trial." There's a sick amusement in his voice. "If you win, the video is yours. If you don't… Well, you don't."

Vlad frowns.

"That's it?"

"But…" Miles trails off, a mischievous quality to his voice. "No weapons for you. No bulletproof equipment either," he continues and I still.

No weapons? Nothing?

"You have a deal." Vlad is quick to reply, already working the buttons of his shirt before throwing it to the ground. He does the same with the bulletproof vest. He's effectively taking everything off but his boxer briefs.

"No weapons." He raises his arms to signal.

"Vlad." I take his hand in mine. "It's too dangerous. You don't even know who you're fighting against," I try to plead with him.

Because one thing is clear. This is another one of Miles' tests. And I fear that it may be too much.

"Don't worry about me, hell girl. You know there's no one out there who can beat me."

"No weapons, Vlad. For you. That means he can have weapons. How is that fair?"

"Miles is anything but fair. Trust me that I'll be fine," he says, taking my hand off his.

"Take care of her." He nods to Marcello before striding away.

I can only watch stupefied as he openly courts death. And for what? A video to open his wounds raw again?

"Vlad. Sisi is right. This is madness. Do you really need

that video? You know he killed her. It should be enough," Marcello tries to argue.

A lopsided smile appears on Vlad's mouth, half his face obscured by the play of shadows.

The white of his teeth gleams, his canines even more emphasized by the skewed lighting. The change is immediate.

The predator is back.

"I *need* to know," Vlad answers curtly, the danger reflected in his eyes unmistakable.

And just like that, I know.

"Let's go." I motion them to the bleachers, my eyes still on Vlad's almost naked body. "Trust him," I tell them when I see them hesitate.

"Sisi…" my brother groans, but I quickly shake my head.

"Think about this." I try to be as rational as possible. "Your men are coming here. In fact, as we speak they are on their way. If anything were to happen." I pause, because I can't fathom anything happening to Vlad. Now or ever. "They will have our backs."

"Fine…" he reluctantly agrees, and we all head to the seating area of the arena.

My hands in my lap, I'm trying my best *not* to show just how much I'm worried about this upcoming fight. Because while my trust is fully placed in Vlad and his abilities, this is Miles we're talking about. The same Miles who's been eluding Vlad for the past ten years.

He's bound to have something under his sleeve, and I know he's going to play dirty.

Alone in the middle of the field, Vlad looks like a barbarian warrior with his inked body and rippling muscles.

"I didn't know he packed *that* under his clothes," Adrian remarks, admiration in his eyes.

Truth is that Vlad's body *is* a work of art. Not one ounce of fat, every muscle is defined, some better emphasized by the presence of the jet black ink against his pale skin. The tattoos make him look even more dangerous if one pays attention to the details—the war scenes beautifully depicted on his flesh, the demons fighting to get out of him and lay siege to the world.

And as I watch him take his stance, I know he's ready to unleash them on whoever Miles will send.

"He's going to win," I state confidently.

"Of course he's going to win," Bianca snorts. "The guy's a war machine. I don't think there's anyone who can best him…" She abruptly stops as the doors in the arena open to reveal Vlad's opponent.

"I think I misspoke," she amends, blinking in surprise at the newcomer.

As he steps further into the arena, I get a good look at him.

He's massive.

That's my first thought as I take in his monstrous frame. Whereas Vlad's built is muscular but lean, his opponent looks like he's had his muscles pumped with air.

But it's not the way he looks that has me freaking out. It's what he's wearing.

His entire chest area is covered in some sort of armor with spikes protruding from within. It seems that the armor covers every weak spot in his body, thereby making him *really* indestructible.

He's holding a battle axe in each hand, wielding them around as if they're an extended part of his body.

"Dear God." The words slip from my lips.

He looks anything but human as he advances forward. And as I get a better look at him, I realize he has the same blank gaze as the soldiers we'd fought earlier.

"How can he get past that armor?" Bianca shakes her head, echoing my own thoughts.

There are very few open spots in the armor where the pieces meet each other. But other than that, there's absolutely no place Vlad could hit without hurting himself first.

The warrior smirks at Vlad, and that's when I realize he's holding something else under his armpit.

A helmet.

"My god." I can't help the way my body starts to shake, anxiety clinging to me like a second skin as I look between Vlad, all but naked, and the newcomer, all but armored.

He puts his helmet on, and just like his armor, it has spikes all over the top surface.

"I don't think I've ever seen an armor like that," Adrian notes, frowning at the metal piece.

"It must be heavy, right?" I ask, my eyes glued to the arena. When they agree, I continue. "Then Vlad has the speed advantage. I'm sure he can work something out. You know him," I half-turn, a feeble smile on my lips, "he's unbeatable."

"I wish I could share your enthusiasm, Sisi," my brother comments, his features grim.

The moment they are both within a few feet of each other, the battle's already begun.

I try my best to make out Vlad's expression, curious how he feels about his opponent. But then I remember.

He doesn't know fear.

And so my anxiety sparks up, because I don't want him to have reckless confidence. Not in the face of *that.*

They circle around each other, and Vlad seems to be assessing him, his eyes roving over the armor in what I can only guess is an attempt to find a weak spot.

"How do you even fight something like that..." Bianca mutters, getting closer to her husband.

"I don't think you do," he answers grimly.

His words worry me since he has years of experience as an underground fighter. So if anyone could gauge the odds of the match it would be him.

Yet the more he speaks, the more agitated I get.

Calm down.

Closing my eyes, I take a deep breath.

This is Vlad we're talking about. He's not only physically unbeatable, but he's also a genius. And if someone can beat the armored guy weaponless, then certainly it's him.

The giant charges him first, thrusting his armor-clad body into him and hoping to penetrate him with the spikes. Vlad is indeed faster as he ducks, rolling down on the floor toward the man's feet.

Gripping his ankles, one of the only areas not covered by spikes, he flexes his muscles to throw the man forward.

Vlad's entire face turns red from the exertion, and as much as the giant struggles to get out of his grasp, he can't.

Instead, I watch dazed as Vlad uses his unnatural strength to lift him off the floor enough to catapult him forward.

The giant loses his equilibrium, the momentum causing him to fall face forward, his helmet slapping his face from the inside. No doubt, at the contact with the ground, the spikes also reverberate through his whole body. He reels back in pain, sluggishly trying to get up.

"No way," Bianca curses.

"How much do you think that man weighs?" I ask, still shocked by what I'd just witnessed.

"At least four hundred pounds. More with the armor," Marcello mutters an answer, his eyes fixed on the fight, his expression showing the same type of wonder I'm feeling.

"It's the angle that baffles me," Adrian comments, "that was one hell of a throw."

"I told you he can do this," I repeat, my confidence now stronger than before.

He can do it.

Just as the man tries to scramble up, Vlad quickly jumps up, managing to snatch one of the battle axes from the giant.

"Now they're a little more evenly matched," Bianca says, her eyes glued to the middle of the arena.

This time, it's Vlad who tackles his opponent, barging into him with his axe raised. The other man parries the blow, trying to land one of his own on Vlad's body.

Their movements are in sync as one hits and the other deflects, axe hitting on axe. Still, I can see that the other man is trying to get Vlad closer to him, so he can get crushed by his armor.

But as they continue to duel, it's pretty clear that their skills are on a similar level in that area.

"You can do it," I whisper a prayer to help him win.

43
SISI

The battle continues with Vlad keeping a comfortable distance, but still striking at him with his axe. Yet one wrong move and the giant's axe passes right by Vlad's arm, the blade skirting the skin just close enough to scratch him and draw blood.

My heart in my throat, I can't help it as I stand up, my hands held together in a prayer.

A cruel smile appears on Vlad's face as his fingers brush against the blood on his shoulder and he brings it to his lips.

The giant cocks his head as if he's trying to understand what he's doing. And right in that moment Vlad strikes.

He's so fast it's almost unreal as he swings the axe right at the base of the man's neck. But instead of trying to breach the armor, he does something else. He lodges the blade right where the helmet meets the chest armor, and wiggling it around, he applies enough force to lift the helmet up a little.

He retreats, removing the blade and twirling in a

blinding move that even his opponent has a hard time following.

Switching hands, he places the axe in his left hand, distracting the man with his right as he repeats the blow. This time, the momentum serves to help him send the helmet flying in the air.

The man releases a battle cry, his eyes wide and crazed as he simply charges Vlad.

I watch Vlad's expression's attentively, and I notice the way his lips curl up, his eyes crinkling with amusement.

He's enjoying this.

The man is on him just as Vlad throws the axe aside, the force propelling it somewhere in the bleachers. Then, using his hand, he spreads his open palms on the giant's shoulders even as the spikes seek to burn holes through his skin.

A gasp escapes me at the sight.

But he knows what he's doing.

Hands on his shoulders, he lifts himself in the air. One moment he's doing a handstand on the man's shoulders, the spikes entering his hands, blood slowly pouring out of the wounds, the next he's behind him, doing a spin in the air and landing back to back with the man.

But this time, he manages to grab the giant's neck in the space between his armpit and his elbow, putting pressure right at the unprotected area of the neck.

Their heights are similar, but as Vlad increases the pressure on the man's neck, he starts bending backwards, following Vlad's movements.

I note the slight curl of the corner of his mouth, the way he starts slowly walking, dragging the giant's body with him.

It's all a game.

It was all a game. I'm almost sure he *let* himself get hit to make the other man think he was going down and then gain an opening over him.

The giant continues to struggle, Vlad's grip on his neck is too strong to allow for any movement.

He drags his flailing body in a circle all around the stadium in a slow *fuck you* to Miles. Heading back to the middle, he looks up at the booth as he simply squeezes tightly, the neck snapping, the man's movements stopping.

Instead of letting the body fall to the floor, though, he takes the axe the man had dropped and grabbing him by the hair; he proceeds to cut the head off the body.

Three hits—that's all it takes for the head to become detached from the neck, blood flowing to the floor.

"Ew." Bianca scrunches up her nose in disgust.

Rotating his arm backwards, Vlad leans back before throwing the head with all the strength he can muster toward the booth where Miles is. The glass crashes as the head breaks through.

"Vlad," I call out, but he doesn't hear me.

Instead, he's walking slowly, yet intently toward the booth. His entire body is strung high, adrenaline coursing through his veins and making him even more unpredictable than his reputation.

I want to go to him, but Marcello holds me back, shaking his head and telling me to let him deal with it.

And as I turn my head back in Vlad's direction, I see him climb up the wall, using different wires to hold his balance until he reaches the booth.

Using his fist, he smashes more of the glass until he can fit inside. But he doesn't go in. No, he reaches inside the booth, his hand taking hold of a piece of material before he throws a body out.

"What…" My mouth is hanging open as I stare at what just happened.

There's a man on the floor of the arena. A small, old man who has the most twisted smile I've ever seen. Even as he struggles to get off the ground, blood already pouring out of a head wound, he's arrogantly smirking at Vlad.

Jumping from the booth, Vlad's eyes are completely glazed as he heads toward whom I presume is Miles.

"I was right," the man starts, "you *are* my little miracle."

"Tell me," Vlad growls as he keeps his pace, slowly advancing, his eyes completely focused on Miles. "Tell me," he repeats in a deadly voice that should make people shudder.

Instead, it only makes Miles laugh more, looking at Vlad with a mix of awe and satisfaction.

"You are my greatest achievement," he says, his eyes sparkling with delusion.

"And you'll be my greatest kill," Vlad sneers, his nostrils flared as he takes one more step, his arms riled up with tension, the veins protruding, his muscles strained.

"Really?" Miles arches an eyebrow. "Without finding out what happened to your sister?" he chuckles, and that sick sound is already grating on my nerves.

I want to get there myself and kill him for everything he's put Vlad through. He deserves nothing but the worst torture imaginable for everything he's done.

My own blood is boiling as I cannot wait to see how he meets his end.

"You killed her," Vlad spits the words out, and I feel his rage as my own.

"No, Sisi," Marcello tightens his grip on my arm as I try to go to him again, "let him see this through." He nods at me.

But just as I'm about to say something, Miles' maniacal laugh resounds in the entire arena, the echo reverberating through every nook and corner.

"Me? Think again." His mouth twists up in arrogance, just as he lifts his hand, a small remote control in his hands.

The doors of the arena open again, this time five soldiers coming through. My eyes widen as I realize that Miles never intended to tell Vlad anything. He merely wanted to test his strengths.

"You're dead," Vlad threatens when he sees the other people come into the stadium.

"I wonder…" Miles quips as he presses a button on the remote control.

The screen flares to life once more, the picture from before now a video.

We all turn to look at the screen as the events start playing. What was before two children comforting each other in the darkness soon turns into the most gruesome scene I've ever witnessed.

Tears make their way down my cheeks as I see Vanya fall to the ground, her body beaten and battered, a huge hole in her chest leaking blood.

But my heart hurts even more for the boy next to her. The one who's holding her still beating heart, crushing it in his grip—all the blood draining to the floor.

His eyes are completely blank as he stares at her corpse,

as he simply lifts the heart to his lips, his mouth closing over the organ as he bites into it.

"What the fuck," I hear Marcello's voice behind me.

Bianca and Adrian are both saying something, but I can only stare at the events playing on the screen.

"No… No…" Vlad's voice reaches my ears as he too stares at the screen, his eyes wide, his mouth hanging open in shock. "It can't be…"

"It's fake. It has to be fake," I whisper, even though I know it to be real.

"Oh, Vanya, what happened?" My voice breaks as I realize that this might very well be the end.

Vlad falls to his knees, his entire body trembling, a loud howling sound escaping his lips.

"Let me go, Marcello. I need to be with him."

I have to be with him.

Because I feel his pain as my own, and my entire being is quaking with anguish.

His features are drawn back in so much pain, torturous sounds escaping his lips as he brings his fists to his chest, banging them loudly against his ribcage.

I know what he's doing. He's trying to punish himself.

I can't let him.

"Let me go, please. You don't understand." I try to wrench myself away from my brother, knowing that every second matters.

There's an urgency inside of me, an instinctual reaction because I *know* this can only end one way.

"No, Sisi. It's too dangerous. *He* is too dangerous."

I shake my head, my limbs trembling.

He hurts, I hurt.

"No, Marcello. I need to get to him. I need to get to him before…" The words die on my lips as I see the sudden change. The change I knew was going to come.

No.

"No," I whisper, my entire heart breaking as I see him give in to this sorrow and embrace the darkness. "No, Vlad, please don't," I continue, even knowing it's already in vain.

There's nothing left behind his eyes.

Nothing.

He's gone.

A gasp escapes me as I realize the immensity of just what happened—of what will continue to happen. He'll just retreat into himself until he loses himself completely.

"Let go!" I cry out, desperation clawing at me as I see him slowly stand up, the predator in him awake and ready for blood.

And it only takes a few steps for him to reach Miles, wrapping one hand around his neck while the other is holding on to his head.

Even Miles' gaze is now full of horror as he realizes what he's unleashed.

A little pressure from his fingers and his neck bends sideways, his eyes dead to the world. Just like him. But Vlad doesn't stop. No, that's not right. *This* Vlad doesn't stop.

He continues to turn the head around until the vertebrae are all broken, a flap of skin the only thing holding the head attached to the rest of the body.

Bracing his knee on his shoulders, though, he pulls at the head until even the skin gives way, blood gushing out and splattering all over Vlad's naked body.

"What the..." Adrian is flabbergasted as he and Bianca stare at this display of savagery.

Except it doesn't end.

He takes Miles' head and crushes it against the ground until the brain is scattered all over the floor, the skull shattered in a million pieces.

He's sheer force and brutality.

No humanity left.

I feel like I can't breathe as I look at him like this.

Sweat and blood cling to his skin, his eyes dark and unyielding, and somewhere in my heart I know.

I lost him.

My entire world collapses as I grasp the full implications, and once more I try to get free.

Vlad's already turned his attention to the newcomers, a brutal grin on his bloody face as he saunters toward them.

They attack full force—all at once. But no one stands a chance. Not when he moves twice as fast, his thirst for blood the only impetus for him to continue.

He grabs the head of one girl, banging it repeatedly against the wall until her face is an unrecognizable mess. Someone tries to tackle him from behind, but even in this haze that covers his mind, his senses are sharp as he easily moves aside, dodging the attack.

Letting the girl's body drop to the ground, he starts pummeling into the man who dared disturb him.

It goes on and on, this bloodbath.

It won't ever stop.

Spurred by pure desperation coated in a desolation that tugs at my heartstrings, I give a last push, throwing all my strength in wrenching my arm free. I don't wait for Marcello to react as I race toward him.

Wait for me.

Where he goes I go. *If* he goes, I go.

I run toward him at full force, but even that is not enough as arms surround me, holding me back.

Suddenly Bianca and Adrian are at my side too, and Vlad, seeing that there are no more victims for his taking, directs his crazed gaze toward us.

"We need to take him out." Bianca shakes her head, her gun up and ready to fire.

"Please don't!" I manage to yell, but it's all in vain.

Vlad is already wrenching the gun from her grasp, throwing it away, his hands on her throat as he lifts her in the air.

"Vlad, no!" I plead with him, though I know he can't hear me.

Adrian is immediately on him, barely managing to get him off Bianca, taking her in his arms and away from him. A shot resounds in the air, and I don't know who hit whom.

I don't care.

It might make me a horrible person, but I don't. I only care about one thing.

Him.

"Let me go to him. I can talk to him." I turn my tear-streaked eyes to Marcello, trying to get him to see reason.

"He's out of control, Sisi. Too dangerous. He'll kill you." His voice is grave as he answers, his gaze on Vlad as he's surveying his moves, slowly backing us away from him.

"He won't." I vigorously shake my head. "He really won't."

"He's not the Vlad you know anymore, Sisi. He's… gone."

"Don't," I gasp, my stomach rebelling, my entire being shattered at those words. "Don't."

He can't be gone.

I don't know what's happening, but I can't breathe. The entire room starts spinning as I gasp for air that won't come. My lungs feel full and empty at the same time, but no matter how much I try, I can't get a hold of myself.

I'm trembling from head to toe and even words fail me as I try to gain some control over myself.

My eyes misted, I feel my brother drag me back to the bleachers. He barks some orders, the words almost foreign. But as I look to the side, I see it.

Men. Soldiers. All armed.

And all pointing at Vlad.

"Marcello…" The words barely make it past my lips. "Wh-what's happening?"

"I'm sorry, Sisi. But he wouldn't want to put you in danger," he says grimly.

"Tell me it's not what I think it is," I whisper. "Tell me."

"I'm sorry, Sisi. He's gone. There's nothing we can do." He continues just as Vlad tackles some of the soldiers, ripping into them like a savage animal.

There's no conscience left. I know that. But he's still Vlad.

He's still my Vlad.

"Let me try. Please, don't do something you'll regret!" I beg him, trying to get my wrists free.

I just need to reach Vlad and everything will be fine. I know it.

Marcello's holding tightly onto me, all the while dragging me back and trying to put more distance between us and Vlad.

"Please, Marcello." I continue to beseech him, all the while trying to escape his grasp.

Looking down at me, he gives me a sad smile and a small shake of his head.

"Now," he yells.

Immediately, shots ring out. I jerk back, turning and watching in horror how Vlad falls to the ground, holes in his naked chest, blood pouring out.

"No, no, no," I mutter incoherently, and for the first time in my life I don't care about anything.

One brief moment of lucidity reminds me of the knives in my boots. Lifting one foot, I prop it on my other leg as I unsheathe the knife from the front of the boot. I don't think as I slash, stabbing my brother and startling him into loosening his hold on me.

Then I just dash.

It's a storm of bullets as I run toward him.

Toward the only thing that matters.

I feel every hit, every bullet that hits my body. And as I fall to my knees in front of him, I can only cover his body with mine. Shield him like he's done to me so many times before.

There's a cacophony of sounds as Marcello orders them to cease fire, my name on his lips ringing into the arena as he yells at me. A voice so near, yet so far away.

Blood is everywhere.

My body. His body.

I lift a trembling hand to his face, urging him to look at

me, seeking for some confirmation that there's still life in his eyes.

"I'm here," I whisper, knowing he can't hear me. Knowing deep down that he's gone.

"Where you go, I go." I gently caress his cheek, his hollow gaze staring down at me.

He's gone.

And so am I.

44

VLAD

PAST

"**Y**ou're not listening," Vanya's voice grates on my nerves as she keeps on tugging on my arm.

"What do you want, Vanya?" I roll my eyes at her.

Since when has she become so needy? Doesn't she understand that I have other things to do?

I train daily, from dawn until noon, and then I study and help Miles with his experiments. There's very little time that I have off, and when I do it's for Vanya to blow my ears with her incessant chattering.

She doesn't seem to understand that what I'm doing is going to revolutionize science *and* warfare. She doesn't seem to understand *anything*.

No matter how much I try to explain to her that Miles' discoveries will change the world, she doesn't get it.

All she knows is to nag at me every day.

She's always hungry or scared, or in pain.

Weak.

The thoughts come unbidden, and while I know she is my sister, I can't help but feel ashamed of her. I've been trying to make excuses about her to Miles for a long time now, telling him it's just a matter of time before she comes around and realizes the importance of what we're doing. That she's finally going to put in some effort into completing the trials and experiments.

But the more time passes, the more I see her for what she really is.

Weak.

Weak-bodied and weak-minded, she can only drag me down.

"We have a test today," I remind her instead of admitting I have no idea what she'd been talking about. "You should get yourself together. We can't afford another failure," I tell her gravely.

After all, her failure also reflects badly on me.

"Vlad…" I turn to look at her, purple circles under her eyes, gashes all over her skin. "Can't I skip it?" she asks in a small voice.

"Vanya," I start, my tone serious, "you forget what I'm doing for you," I remind her, "this," I trace the small laceration on her skin that's mostly healed, "is a blessing."

She knows what I mean too, because anyone else with her poor endurance would have died a long time ago. Instead, I'd always assigned her tests that I knew she could handle, and when the opportunity arose to help her I did. But doing that is risky for me.

I've just gained Miles' trust. If I mess this up now, then

I'll lose everything. Vanya too, since she would *never* be able to survive under normal conditions.

"You know what happens to others." I raise an eyebrow at her, lifting my own shirt to show her the myriad of scars that run along my torso.

But my case is different.

I've become so inured to pain, so used to being cut open and put back again, that nothing fazes me anymore.

Nothing hurts. Nothing shocks.

I'm… empty.

It's interesting when you put it like that, since in the time I've been with Miles I've only become smarter, stronger, faster. But while my brain has soaked in all available knowledge, my soul has slowly faded away.

Empty.

Even the sight of Vanya battered and in pain fails to rouse any sympathy out of me. The only reaction I get is a rational anger that she can't do better.

Cold rationality.

Every type of warmth that I might've possessed at some point is gone. Sometimes, I don't even remember what it was like to… feel.

"I can't do this again, Vlad," she complains, shaking her head slowly. "I…"

Her eyes are bloodshot, her lips chapped. "I don't know how long I can continue like this," she whispers, and I see what she's doing.

She's done it before. Trying to get me to pity her. And maybe before it would have worked, but my patience's run thin.

"You have to, Vanya," I tell her, exasperated. "You'll become stronger. You'll see." I nod at her, leaving her in her tiny corner while I stand up, righting myself and preparing for today's tests.

Miles and I had developed another system—a new area of immunology that could aid us in improving our model for the perfect soldier.

The body can be strong and can resist however it wants in the face of pain, but it's all in vain if the immunity is compromised.

And so we'd started theorizing and putting together a list that could affect immunity and how we could stop it.

Everyone's already been vaccinated against most known diseases, but there are other things out there that can prove just as deadly.

Like poison. Or venom.

We'd already gone through the poison stage, and we've been ingesting small dosages of ground leaves from poisonous plants like belladonna, aconite, datura and many others.

Of course, we lost a lot of people until we got the dosages right, but ever since then I've noticed an increase in alertness, my body responding better to my commands, and thus proving our experiment was well on its way to success.

After a lengthy trial, Miles had slipped a larger dosage of aconite in my food without telling me. It had all been to eliminate bias or the placebo effect from the findings of the study, and seeing that I survived, I'd say the experiment worked.

Vanya, however, hasn't fared so well. She's been sluggish since her last dosage of belladonna, her focus impacted as well as her appetite.

She's getting weaker.

I don't want to admit this to myself, but I don't know how much long she's going to last like this. And I don't know how that makes me feel.

She follows slowly behind me as we go to the lab area, dragging her feet on the floor and trying to get my attention with her petty tricks.

"It's not going to work, Vanya," I sigh, grabbing her hand.

Her head is hung low as she continues to walk with me.

"There you are," Miles greets us, his white lab coat, and his manufactured smile on. "I've already prepared the specimens, and I'll randomly select one for each." He flutters his fingers over a couple of syringes as if he's debating which one to choose first.

"So?" He turns, arching a brow, the syringe with the venom in his hand. "Who goes first?"

I give Vanya a small push, my eyes on her as I try to tell her with my expression that this is her chance to show Miles she's improving.

Her lashes flutter as she blinks rapidly, her eyes on me as if she's seeking my opinion.

I just give her a quick nod, pushing her slightly toward Miles.

"Little Vanya," he exclaims, "wonderful."

She's quickly placed on the reclining bed, her arm, already riddled with needle marks, stretched out and waiting for the shot.

Her eyes are set on me, her gaze blank.

No, that's not right. Her gaze is filled with something, yet I have a hard time understanding what it is. Her eyes are down-turned, but clear. It's not happiness, nor is it sadness. It's…

I don't know.

I can differentiate a few expressions, and I've taught myself what to look for in happiness and in sadness. But her expression? It's neither.

I frown as I continue to watch Miles inject the venom into her skin.

She squeezes her eyes shut at the invasion, the place of injection already swollen and red.

"Aren't you curious how this will go?" Miles asks me as he prompts Vanya to hop off the chair for me to take her place.

"I know it will go well," I reply confidently as I take a seat, folding my sleeve and presenting him with my mangled arm.

For all the needle marks that Vanya has on her skin, her arm looks pristine when compared to mine.

Long, jagged scars run all along the length of my forearm and go well into my upper arm. The result of surgery on top of surgery, of having my arm opened up to test my pain or to study its anatomical structure, I'd endured everything.

Even now, Miles has a hard time finding a vein to inject me into, the scar tissue prominent and gnarly. He purses his lips as he turns my arm around until he finds a good site to dump the venom into my skin.

"You each have a different venom. We'll see how you react to it." He smirks.

Vanya looks between the two of us, a sigh escaping her

when she realizes we've started talking about the merits of the experiment and what the next stage is if it's successful.

And as we go back to our sleeping quarters she doesn't even bother to talk to me anymore.

After that, it only gets worse. She no longer asks me to help her or spare her, coming with me to every appointment and getting injected with the venom as expected. She doesn't even complain about the pain, or the swollen skin.

In fact, she just doesn't interact with me at all.

In the beginning I'm ecstatic, thinking that she's finally come around and that she's accepted why we are here and our importance in the grand scheme of things.

But more time passes and I can't help but note that for all her quiet demeanor, there is something strange about her.

I can't put my finger on it. But something is niggling in my mind.

Something isn't right.

And it only dawns on me when she starts feeling off, her pale skin changing color, more bruised and swollen than usual. She's barely moving, sleeping in all her spare time.

When I bring up the issue to Miles, he tells me that it's probably the venom slowly working on her body. While I'd reluctantly nodded at his explanation, I still can't help but feel that something isn't right.

The following day, Miles calls both Vanya and I to his surgery room.

The situation's already become too dire, and one of Vanya's eyes is so bloodshot and swollen, I feel it's going to burst out at any point.

"Don't worry," Miles smiles down at me. "This is an

opportunity to learn," he says as he instructs Vanya to get on the bed.

She looks at me, her eyes almost sparkling with undefined feelings. But she doesn't protest as she sits down.

She doesn't even make a sound as Miles makes an incision around her eye, cutting dead tissue that had been rotting in her socket.

I'm on the sidelines, watching as her eye is semi-detached, hanging out of her socket, tiny movements denoting she is aware and she is watching me even through that limp eye.

Though I show no reaction, there's a small prickle down my spine as I watch the blood pool down her face.

"This shouldn't be here," Miles tsks as he removes a rather large maggot larva from behind her eye. "I wonder how it got here," he muses.

Taking out the larva from behind her retina, he drops it into a small glass.

Then he just struggles to put her eye back.

For all his brilliance, I know he's not an eye surgeon. So the prospect of him working so in depth around Vanya's eye has me feeling a little off. I can't exactly put my finger on it, but it's not a pleasant feeling.

"Done," he exclaims, telling her to get off and instructing us to go back to our room after he administers one more shot of venom in each of our arms.

"How's the eye?" I ask Vanya as she goes to her small corner. Miles had slapped a small bandage on it and called it a day.

She shrugs, her features blank as if she doesn't care.

"V, how's the eye?" I ask again, something bursting to the surface at seeing her so indifferent.

"It's okay," she replies, her voice soft but there's something lacking.

Unable to help myself, since something keeps bothering me and I'm not one to back down in the face of a challenge, I go to the small supply I'd taken from the lab, taking out some disinfectant.

"Show me." I take a seat next to her, my hand going to her bandage.

I know Miles didn't use any anesthetic, or disinfectant— he never does. So she needs to get the area cleaned, at least to the best of my abilities.

But as I peel back the gauze, her eye immediately drops, falling about an inch off her eye socket.

Not wanting to scare her more than necessary, I pour some disinfectant and I dab it around her eye.

She looks at me blankly, examining my features in detail. I don't question her sudden interest in my face, happy that she has something to distract her from her eye. When I'm finished, I gently push the eye back, plastering some new gauze on top of it.

As I make to move, though, something happens. Her hand reaches out, touching my arm.

"You called me V," she utters the words so softly I barely hear her. "You never call me V anymore," she notes, tightening her fingers over my arm.

I shrug. "It depends on the moment," I tell her, not wanting to examine the meaning behind her words, or the fact that I had, indeed, stopped calling her V a long time ago.

"I like it." Her lips pull up in a small smile. "It reminds me of old times."

I grunt.

"When we were a team," she continues, looking at me expectantly.

"We still are, V. But you need to pull your weight too," I retort. "You know I'm doing this for *both* of us," I continue, shaking my head at her.

Her smile immediately drops, her good eye unblinking as it takes me in.

"I see..." she says, and I don't understand what she's seeing.

"Good." I nod, getting up and preparing for my next bout of training.

The next days are even worse as Vanya struggles to get out of bed. Her limbs are swollen, her skin a yellowish tinge and hot to the touch.

And just when I start to get a little worried, Miles calls me up to his office.

"Your sister hasn't been doing well." Is the first thing he says as I enter the room.

I don't answer as I take a seat, waiting for whatever it is he wants to tell me.

"You know I have no need for weaklings here," he continues, looking at me with a raised eyebrow, as if gauging how I'm reacting to his words.

"Yes, Sir." I nod.

"I'm glad we're in agreement, because I have an assignment for you."

I frown. An assignment?

"Of course," I readily agree, since it's not my place to disagree.

"The final test if you will. And then you'll be the first graduate of the program." He chuckles, pouring himself a glass of alcohol.

"Final test? What do you mean?" I ask, confused.

It's the first time he's said anything about graduation, or a final test. I thought it was all supposed to be continuous learning. Trial and error as we map the way to scientific revolution.

"What was the first rule I taught you, Vlad?" he asks, the corner of his mouth curling up as he regards me attentively.

"Remove all attachments," I immediately reply, the scene in which I'd killed Lulu flashing briefly in my mind.

"Indeed. Do you think you still have any attachments?"

"No, Sir."

"What about your sister, then?" he inquires, amused.

"She's nothing." I don't even think as the words slip past my lips.

"Is that so…" He walks around the room, swirling the liquid in his glass in a pensive manner.

I cock my head, studying him and trying to understand what's happening.

"Then it won't be too hard for you to kill her." He suddenly stops, turning to me, his eyes shrewdly assessing my reaction.

"Of course not."

"Wonderful. I trust it will be done then?"

I nod slowly, a small frown appearing on my face as it dawns on me what he's asking me to do.

"But here's the catch, Vlad. I don't want a clean death. I

don't want a mercy killing." He smirks. "Give me a show," he opens his arms in a dramatic gesture, "show me how you put to use everything I've taught you!

Going to his desk, he opens a drawer and throws me a set of knives.

"Entertain me, Vlad!" He tips his glass toward me before downing it in one go.

As I walk back to the room a heaviness settles on me. I don't know why my chest feels stiff, my *self* trapped in my body, a cage that stifles me and holds me so tightly I can barely breathe.

A small war brews inside me. Do I kill her? She is my sister. But Miles is right that in attachments only make you weak. And *weak* is something I never want to be.

Not when I've worked so hard to cleanse myself of any weakness I may have.

And so as I continue to rationalize the decision, the answer is clear.

I need to be strong.

Vanya will only drag me down—with this frail attachment I still have to her, and with her inherent weakness.

I will be strong.

By the time I reach our room, the decision is made. And somehow, Vanya knows it too.

She watches me closely as I step inside the room, the knife set hidden behind my back. As she looks at my face, she closes her eye, taking a deep breath. When she opens it again, a peace seems to settle over her features.

Slowly, ever so slowly, she gets up. Her steps are wobbly, her movements awkward as she can barely control her own body.

"Vlad," she says my name in that melodic voice of hers, and for a moment my heart beats painfully in my chest, the beats loud and aggressive against my ribcage.

And even as I rationalize the improbability of *that* I know something is wrong.

I'm wrong.

But I don't dwell on that. Not when the final test is within my grasp. Who knows, Miles might take me up as his full time assistant.

She's in front of me, tilting her head to the side and gazing up at me as if it's the last time she's seeing me. As if she *knows*.

"I never told you," she starts, suddenly looking away, "but I know what you did for me."

I blink twice, frowning.

"What do you mean?"

"I know you tried to save me, and in the process you lost yourself. And because I know that… it's my fault too," she takes a deep breath, "I don't blame you. I don't blame you at all."

"Vanya… V," I call her name, a sad smile on her face when she hears it.

"If it hadn't been for me…" she trails off, and I note a tear in her good eye. "Maybe you would have still been you."

"I don't understand," I say. And I don't. How could I have lost myself when I finally found my calling?

"I know you don't." She shakes her head.

Seeing her so close, I realize I need to take advantage of her proximity. Opening up the knife set, I take the biggest blade out, ready to fulfill my mission.

But as I raise it in front of her, she doesn't move. She doesn't react at all.

She just looks into my eyes, a small nod as she waits for me to kill her.

And in *that* moment, for all my conviction that I need to do this, for all my rationalizing that I should kill my own sister—my twin—I find that I can't.

"I can't." The words slip out of my mouth, my voice barely above a whisper.

My chest is uncomfortably stiff, a tension throbbing in my temples as I look at my sister. The way her once beautiful hair is now a mess of dirt and blood. Or how her pale skin that once gleamed is now yellow streaked with purple bruises. Or how her eyes, once radiant, are now…

My breath catches in my throat as memories come rushing down, the pain slowly increasing, my limbs paralyzed with fear as I just look at her.

"I can't, V," I whisper.

"Yes, you can," she replies, and before I know it, she grabs the hand holding the knife, pointing the tip of the blade right under her sternum before pushing with all her might, angling it up toward her heart.

There's a loud gasp.

I don't know if it's from me or from her. Her lips parted, she keeps on pushing the knife into her flesh.

"Finish it," she gently urges me. "Let me be at peace, Vlad. I don't want to hurt anymore."

Those words break something inside of me as I push the knife deeper, reality lagging behind in my mind.

I push and push until I know I've punctured her heart.

And just as I withdraw the knife, blood rushing down and draining from that vital organ, something else happens.

A sob catches in my throat, my cheeks damp as my eyes leak some sort of liquid—tears. I watch the blood slowly leave her body, her good eye stuck in the same position, her body flailing around before it falls, and I feel the worst pain I've ever felt in my life.

I'm not supposed to feel pain.

I'm not supposed to feel.

And yet I do. I feel it to the core of my being. It shatters every corner of what I deem to be the self, until I find myself stripped of what essentially makes me human.

Was I ever?

My eyes hone in on that blood—her life's essence—as it keeps pouring out. Leaking and leaking until there's no more.

"No," I snap. "No." I shake my head, the knife dropping from my hand as I kneel before her, my hands grasping at the blood and trying to put it back inside of her.

"You can't," I mutter incoherently, "you can't leave me, V... No."

There's a craziness inside of me that seems to be unleashed that very moment, my sanity spilling over the normal bounds and flooding every cell in my body with *in*sanity. Because there's no other explanation for what I'm doing.

Not as I'm trying to stuff the blood into my already dead sister. Not as a pain filled battle cry escapes my lips, my fingers settling on the knife as I hit it against her chest, opening her up and grabbing that organ from her body, cradling it in my hand and trying to get it to work again.

"Please, V," I say as I pump the heart.

Me, who prized logic over everything.

Meet the illogic.

I lose track of everything as I simply push my rational mind as far away as I can, locking it away and throwing the key. I give myself to everything that is irrational, savage, and emotional.

Everything is hazy as I see myself smash her body to pieces in a blood fueled rage.

Blood is everywhere.

My blood. Her blood. Our blood.

It bathes my body as I take comfort in knowing her life's force is on me.

In me.

And as nothing else works, I just bring her heart to my mouth, biting into it, feeling the way her blood fills me.

We're one.

Because she can't be gone. She can *never* be gone.

Red is everywhere. A brilliant red that beckons me. A vivid red that promises to fulfill all of my wishes. A lively red that's her. My Vanya. My twin.

But she's gone.

And I just lose myself.

PRESENT

It's all foggy as I can no longer differentiate between what's real and what's not; what's past and what present. There's a pounding in my ears as everything becomes static noise. My pulse is elevated, blood thumping in my veins and clouding my judgement.

I only feel a deep hole in my chest—the size of the hole I put in my sister's as I'd ruthlessly killed her.

Years. So many years I spent searching for her killer when I could have just looked in the mirror.

Vanya…

What's left of my heart breaks even more as I remember her words.

I don't want to hurt anymore.

Whose fault was it that she hurt?

Mine.

Because I'd spiraled out of control, my ego the size of a skyscraper as I thought I had all the answers. A kid of barely eight taking on the entire world and revolutionizing science.

Laughter bubbles in my throat as I realize how much I'd allowed Miles to play with my head. He'd turned me into a robot ready to do his bidding.

And I killed her.

Everything comes rushing in. All the events from twenty years ago are suddenly crystal clear in my mind as I see myself engaging in all sorts of experiments, being the lab rat and the lab coat.

Vanya…

I can't help it as I fall to my knees, my teeth bared as a howl escapes me, all the pain I'm feeling threatening to over-power me.

Vanya…

My kind sister who never hurt anyone. My twin.

Once my everything.

I can't do it. I can't come to terms that these two hands that I'm staring at were the cause of her death. I used these fingers to wrap them around the hilt of a knife, stabbing her heart until all the blood poured out.

I can't.

My body starts trembling, the pressure building inside of me reaching a boiling point.

And I snap.

I barely realize how I move or when I move. Adrenaline is coursing through my veins, my entire body pumped up and ready for destruction.

I only feel the wind caress my skin as I glide on the floor, my fists ready to wreak havoc, my only purpose to raise hell.

I need chaos. I feed off of it. Because only in chaos can I silence that voice that tells me I'm my sister's killer.

I *need* the chaos to survive.

And they *need* to die.

Moving forward, I grasp on to Miles' feeble body, all rational thought leaving me, and only one purpose remaining.

Blood.

I want to see his blood flooding the room. I want to see his life leaving his body.

Death. I want to see death.

I grab on to his neck, twisting until he's moving no more, and yet I keep on pulling, knowing it will give way eventually, unleashing a violent storm as rivulets of blood wash over me.

And when his neck pops, blood and bone finally spurting out, I don't stop. I just take his head and I smash it to the ground until his skull becomes pieces smaller than fine sand. Until there's no more.

But I need more.

More blood.

I feel myself wading through people.

Hitting, smashing, destroying.

Only the sticky feel of blood as it coats my body makes me feel a little more at peace. Everything that comes into my path is doomed.

I hear bones breaking, skin tearing, blood spurting.

A pleasure unlike any other overtakes me as I simply give in. I succumb to this animalistic rage, hoping to lose myself. Lose every part of me that still remembers, every part of me that *knows* about Vanya.

Because the alternative is too painful.

And so I continue.

I kill and kill and kill. It's the only thing that feeds the beast.

Until I can't anymore.

I don't feel the pain of the bullet that hits my side. I only feel the blood as it gushes out of me, the force of the hit propelling me back and making me lose my balance.

Unwittingly, I fall down, my breathing labored, and my lids heavy.

In the back of my mind, I know something's wrong. That I've been critically injured. But I can't react.

"I'm here," I think I hear a voice.

A very familiar voice.

"Where you go I go," she continues, the sound so melodic it makes my dead heart weep.

And as I feel a small hand cup my cheek, dragging my gaze down, I blink some clarity into my eyes.

The haze is slowly lifting to reveal a blonde goddess

looking at me, her eyes red from crying, her features contorted in pain.

I open my mouth, wanting to speak, but no sound comes out except a hoarse grunt.

She frowns, never taking her hand off of my skin, her body cushioning mine even as more blood falls between us.

"Si... Si..." I manage to get the syllables out, the effort seemingly taking everything out of me.

"Yes," she whispers fervently. "Yes." She brings both hands to my cheeks as she pulls me toward her, her lips on mine as I taste blood and tears. "Yes," she speaks against me, and I inhale the words just as I inhale her.

"Hell girl," I groan, my mind gaining some alertness.

"Vlad, my Vlad," she continues to speak in short, pained sounds that make me hurt for her.

You hurt, I hurt.

Everything comes rushing in, the memories, the pain.

The love.

"My Sisi," I croak, my arms reaching around her small body to tug her to me. And as I feel around her back, I find pieces of metal embedded in her clothes.

"What..." I start, but she silences me with yet another kiss.

"I'm fine. We're fine." She drags her lips across my cheek. "Everything will be fine."

I don't know why those words simply break me. And I do something I should have done a long time ago.

I let myself feel.

45
SISI

"What are you doing out and about?" My hands on my hips, I glower at him, my expression showing him I'm not joking.

"I'm fine, hell girl. Besides, who's going to help with the renovations?" He gives me that charming smile of his in hopes it will melt my anger away.

Melt me it might, but not my anger. Not when he's just gotten out of bed, his stitches not completely healed.

"Not someone who was shot four times in the chest, Vlad." I roll my eyes at him. "Certainly not someone who was *just* at death's door. Drop the shovel and come with me," I beckon him toward me, an eyebrow raised as I wait for him to argue.

He doesn't, because he knows he won't win with me. Not when I've stayed day and night by his side, nursing both his body and his mind.

Something had happened to him that day at Miles' compound. Gaining all of his memories back had shifted something in him, and he'd changed—utterly and irrevocably.

For days after he'd been mortally wounded, he'd languished in bed, fighting between life and death, and I don't think I've ever felt greater anguish than thinking he might just… die.

Still, I'd had to be strong for both of us. I hadn't left his side for a minute. Even as my own bruised flesh had been paining me, my back riddled with small wounds from the impact of the bullets against the bulletproof vest.

I'd put everything aside, because in that moment, I had one purpose—him.

But when he'd come to, the change had been obvious in his features, in the way he held himself. More than anything, I could see a new lightness in his eyes.

He hadn't talked at first, staring into empty space.

But slowly, he started opening up, telling me everything that happened.

How Vanya died.

Though rationally he realizes it wasn't his fault, he can't help but hold himself accountable for everything that happened to his sister.

"You're so hot when you're bossy," he drawls when he comes to my side, his arm snaking around my waist.

I catch it, swatting it aside as I turn to him, a thunderous expression on my face.

"You don't get to play the charming rogue when you're barely on your feet, mister. If you think about getting out of bed again, I'll bury you myself, since it's clear you have a fervent death wish."

"Hell girl," he murmurs as he comes closer, his mouth

skimming my cheek, "you know I love it when you threaten me." His breath on my skin, I can't help the involuntary shiver that goes down my body.

"I'll let you bury me," he starts, and I note the amusement in his tone, "only if I get conjugal visits," he whispers, and my lips twitch.

"Vlad," I exclaim, scandalized.

I can't believe he's still in the mood to joke.

"Fine, fine," he finally acquiesces, "I'll go back to bed. But you're coming with me."

I can't find it in me to refuse him, so I end up going to bed with him.

"You should forgive your brother," he suddenly says as he holds me to him. "You know he meant well."

"He would have killed you," I whisper, still unable to remove that scene from my mind. "One more bullet and you would have been *dead*, Vlad." My voice trembles as I look up at him, his dark eyes watching me intently.

"You saved me when I didn't deserve it, Sisi." His hand comes to rest on my head before he slowly moves his fingers down my hair. "But I *was* out of control. I could have…" A breath catches in his throat, and I recognize the agony behind his expression.

"But you didn't. You're here, with me. We're both alive. As for Marcello… I will, eventually. Not yet though," I sigh.

I understand why he'd done that, but at the same time my heart cannot bear to think of the alternative, of what might have happened if I were a second too late.

He would have killed him.

And for that, I don't think I can forgive Marcello anytime soon. I cannot even bear the thought of being in the same room as him, the urge to do harm too over-whelming.

"You haven't had any episodes so far." I change the topic as I jump out of bed to get the medical kit and change his bandages.

He pulls himself into a sitting position as he awaits for me to come tend to him, his expression pensive.

"I don't think I'll have more in the future," he mentions, and I frown.

"Why?"

Bringing the kit to the bed, I start to carefully take off his bandages before inspecting the condition of his wounds.

"These look good." I smile as I clean the areas, happy to see there's no infection and everything seems to be healing great.

He grunts, staring above my head as I continue to change the bandages. I'm focused on my task when I hear him speak again.

"The episodes," he starts, his voice far away. "I think they were my way of dealing with Vanya's death and the guilt I had over it. Blood..." He takes a deep breath, and I still, knowing this is an important moment for him.

"Blood reminded me of what I'd done. Of *her* blood on my hands. And every time I saw it, it made me go a little crazy."

It's clear he's been thinking about this a lot and I cannot help but worry for him. Ever since the day he found out that he'd killed his own sister he's changed. I don't know if it's a conscious change, but I do think that the last episode freed something inside of him.

"Vlad." I raise my gaze to him, searching for his expression. "Vanya wouldn't have blamed you. You know that."

He purses his lips in a sad smile.

"I do. I do, Sisi. But that doesn't take away the fact that I feel an emptiness." He brings his fist to his chest. "Here."

"It's normal." I cover his fist with my hands, bringing it to my mouth and lightly brushing my lips across his knuckles.

"It's normal to feel like that. It's *human*. And though disputable," my lips curl up, "you *are* human. Give yourself time. To grieve. To mourn. To forgive yourself."

Besides his physical injury, his psyche had been the most affected by what happened. He's slowly starting to open up about his thoughts and feelings and I appreciate anything he chooses to share with me. No matter how long it takes, I'll be there for him, and I'll offer him my love and support—unconditionally.

At the end of the day, it can't be easy for a man who's never allowed himself to feel *anything* his entire life, to suddenly be flooded with all of these strange emotions. Sometimes I see him struggle to make sense of what's happening inside his mind, and it hurts my heart that there's nothing I can do to take away his pain.

He nods thoughtfully at my words, though his gaze is distant.

"Time…" he repeats.

"We have all the time now. And maybe getting closer to Katya might help you." I throw the idea out and he immediately grimaces.

Daunted by facing the outside world and still getting used to freedom, Katya and Tiberius have been living at

Vlad's underground compound for the past month. In the meantime, we'd been staying at Vlad's childhood home as I'd thought that fresh air and some open space would do him good.

Although I'm still not on speaking terms with my brother, Lina's assistance had been a blessing as she'd helped Katya and Tiberius accommodate to their new reality, while I'd been nursing Vlad back to health.

I'd visited them a few times, and they'd come down here often too. Vlad, though, has not been too open with his sister, barely exchanging any words, their meetings stiff and awkward.

I can't exactly blame him, though, as I know he harbors some type of guilt for what happened to her, but he can't continue like this forever.

"I'll try," he grumbles, the words barely audible.

"You better." I slap him playfully on the arm.

"Auch! Convalescent here, hell girl." He feigns a moan of pain.

"As if." I snort. "You weren't convalescent when you were trying to dig a hole in the garden. Couldn't you have asked someone to do it if it was so urgent?" I roll my eyes at him.

His reaction to pain is still the same—nonexistent. Although that makes me happy in this particular scenario as I can't imagine how much four bullets through the chest would hurt.

Truth is, Vlad's always been a very physically active person, and I can't imagine what being stuck on bed rest must be doing to him. Even so, I'm not about to endanger his health just because he's pouting at me.

"We need to get started soon, though," he complains.

After he'd come to, we'd had lengthy talks about our future and what we wanted to do next. We'd also had extremely difficult conversations about what we'd found at Miles' compound and how we were going to deal with that. But together, we'd decided to help the children we'd rescued from Miles' laboratories, and give them a new purpose in life.

"An academy?" I'd been surprised when Vlad had suggested the idea.

"They are all different. Be it by birth, or because of what was done to them. They don't know how to fit into society, and most of them have no one to turn to," he'd explained, managing to shock me with his thoughtfulness.

"We'd teach them how to adapt to the world, and we'd give them a purpose." His smile had widened, and I'd known it had to be something insane.

"An assassin academy," he'd proudly declared, making me blink in confusion.

"Think about it. They are already primed for killing. But this way, we can teach them a more ethical way of killing," he'd paused, probably realizing that doesn't exactly apply to him, "or at least some sort of honor system, so they don't become too dangerous. So they don't become *me*."

"That's not a bad idea," I'd replied. And the more I mulled over it, the more I realized the merits of the project.

"Instead of foisting some impossible standards on them like Miles had been doing, we'll foster their natural talents and make them the best damn assassins the world has ever seen."

The more he talked, the more I realized how enthusiastic he was at the prospect. And with his mental state so fragile, I knew this was the perfect thing to help him get out of his slump.

He'd have a goal, a mission. And so he wouldn't let himself succumb to the pain that is the truth of Vanya's death.

But while I'm actively supporting his new endeavor, that doesn't mean he can strain his barely healed body. He has plenty of people to work on that.

Another side effect of toppling down Miles' and Meester's business had been recruiting a lot of new people under Vlad's leadership. Most had also sought him out after news got out that he'd been the one to dispatch all the syndicate leaders, and many men had declared they wanted to work for the strongest, not the weakest.

It had been rather fortuitous, as we've recently put together the plans for the academy, and we'll need *a lot* of people to make Vlad's vision happen.

"I want things to go back to normal. I feel useless like this..." he groans, lifting his fingers to his temples and massaging them.

"I know," I sigh. "But I *need* you to be healthy, Vlad. I can't have another scare like that one."

I still have nightmares of him being shot, blood pouring out of him...

I shake myself, knowing it's never helpful to dwell on that.

"You won't. I promise you." He takes my hand, tugging me toward him. "You're my one reason to get well, hell girl. So I will," he murmurs softly, his lips on my forehead as he trails small kisses all over my face. "Everything for you."

"Good," I whisper, leaning into him and feeling his warmth on my skin. "I love you," I tell him, my lips parted as I give myself over to a breathless kiss.

"I love you too. Always."

A FEW MONTHS LATER

"You know you don't have to do this, Sisi," my brother tells me from behind.

Fixing my hair, I turn to face him.

"Are we doing this again, Marcello? I thought we moved past that." I shake my head at him when I see the slight smile on his face.

"I had to try." He shrugs, giving me his arm.

As we head out of the house and toward the garden, he suddenly stops, laying a kiss on my forehead.

"I'm sorry," he apologizes, and I note that he really means it. "I've known Vlad my entire life, and I thought I knew everything there was about him. But I guess I never tried to look deeper. Not like you did." He gives me a brief smile.

"I may never be completely comfortable knowing you're with him, because I've seen him at his worst, and… well, you know his worst too." He chuckles. "But I can see how happy he makes you. I've also seen how happy you make him. Even as I'm reluctant to admit it, there's something about you two when you're together. Almost as if you're always in your own little world."

My lips tug up into a smile at his words, because he *is*

right. There can be a thousand people around, but if Vlad is next to me, then it's always going to be just the two of us.

"I recognize you have something special, and you have my promise that I won't try to interfere again."

"Thank you. That means a lot to me," I tell him, going on my tip-toes to give him a kiss on his cheek. "And thank you for welcoming me to the family."

"Sisi. I'll always be your family." He pulls me into a hug. "No matter what," he continues, and my heart warms at his words.

"Good," I sniffle, already the urge to cry overwhelming. "We should go before I burst into tears," I joke, grabbing his arm and starting again toward the garden.

A small gazebo is at the end of the walking path. Vlad had built it with his own hands when he'd gotten the green light that he could finally do physical work. And he'd dedicated it to his sister's memory. A V insignia sits at the top of the roof, the shiny marble glinting in the sunlight.

There are two rows of seats on each side of the windy path, all full of friends and family. Lina, Claudia, Venezia and Katya are on one side, all wearing dainty light-blue dresses, each holding a small flower bouquet.

Their faces light up when they see us approach, and I send them an airy kiss and a wink as we continue to walk.

On the other side, Seth, Adrian and Tiberius are standing behind Vlad, their black suits dashingly elegant even though they must be sweating in this heat.

And then there's him.

My Vlad.

He looks nervous as he paces around, his head whipping in our direction as we near the gazebo.

And when he sees me, his eyes grow wide, his smile blinding as he looks upon me, his gaze smoldering with love and... I grow hot just as I feel his attention on me, a blush going up my cheeks.

I suddenly feel breathless as I step next to him, Marcello handing him my hand—with no funny retort either.

"Ready?" he whispers, tugging me close.

I raise my head, moistening my lips to reply to him, but as I note the wicked gleam in his eyes, my mouth parts of its own accord, no sound coming out.

The corner of his mouth lifts in a lopsided smile as he smirks at me, that sinful arrogance that always drips from him and makes me want to both kill him and love him at the same time.

Still, there's no mistaking the rapt adoration in his eyes as he peruses my face, moving over every inch of exposed skin and leaving a trail of goosebumps in his wake. He doesn't have to touch me or do anything.

Just the way he looks at me, as if he'd shred my wedding dress off of my body before prompting me to run so he could hunt me has me sweating under layers of tulle.

I know what he's thinking.

His teeth skim the surface of his lower lip as his attention is fixated on my neck, right where his initial is branded against my skin.

"Are you pleased with how everything looks?" he purrs, never once taking his eyes off me.

"Yes," I breathe out, the sudden nearness getting to my head and making me dizzy with want.

Damn it.

Even now, of all days, I can't seem to control myself

around him, so lost in his aura, his energy enveloping me and swallowing me whole.

"It's exactly like I wanted it," I tell him, which earns me a grin from him.

The idea of a formal wedding celebration had come to me after I'd found the perfect wedding dress online. I was simply browsing the internet when I'd come across this stunning off white gown with a tight bodice and a flaring skirt reminiscent of a Victorian ballgown. I'd been so struck by it, that one day I found myself blurting out to Vlad that I wanted a real wedding.

He'd been surprised at first, since I hadn't mentioned that before, but he'd quickly adapted, calling everyone and putting things in motion for me to have my perfect wedding.

He's been so sweet, taking care of absolutely everything, making sure everything had my approval before the big day.

Now, I find myself wearing my dream dress, at my dream wedding, with my dream man. And I can't help the giddiness that forms inside of me.

"Shall we then?"

"We shall." I smile.

The ceremony is short but sweet, and compared to my first attempt at a wedding, I actually listen to all the words.

My hand in his, the warmth that seeps from his skin is the only comfort I need to know that we are in this not only till death do us apart—but beyond.

The ceremony nears its end as the minister urges us to exchange rings.

"I knew I missed something the first time," Vlad mutters amused as he slides a gorgeous silver band over my finger.

"I was so mad at you I didn't even realize it," I admit, as I take my turn at placing the ring on his finger.

We'd had them custom made, and we'd engraved two phrases very dear to our hearts on the inside of the bands. The same phrases that we utter now, when we are pronounced husband and wife.

"There's no Vlad without Sisi," he's the first to say, bringing my fingers to his mouth for a sensual kiss.

"And no Sisi without Vlad," I complete the phrase, my pulse speeding up the more he lingers with his lips on my flesh.

In this moment, no matter how much I'd wanted a fully organized wedding with everyone in attendance, I only want him—to ravish me, mark me, sear himself in my soul.

But alas, we cannot have that.

Not when we're suddenly interrupted by everyone as they come to congratulate us on the nuptials.

"Congratulations, Aunt Sisi," Claudia gives me a big hug.

"Thank you, love." I kiss her cheeks, happy to know we're now welcomed in Marcello's home and I can see her any time I want.

Everyone comes to me for kisses and a hug. One look to the right and I notice Vlad in a similar situation as men come to shake hands with him, congratulating him for the wedding and for finally getting himself a woman.

I almost blush as I hear some of the conversations they are having, but the girls are quick to take me aside, the gossip and chatter going strong.

We'd turned the entire back garden into a venue for the

wedding, and with its front view toward the ocean, it really is the dream wedding.

"I always wanted to ask you." Bianca comes to my side, a glass of nonalcoholic champagne in her hand. "How did you tame him?"

"Tame him?" I raise an eyebrow.

"I've known him for more than a decade. I *know* him. And yet, I don't think I do, do I?" she asks, her gaze turning toward where Vlad is deep in conversation with Adrian and Marcello.

"I didn't tame him. I don't think someone like him *can* be tamed," I answer honestly.

Even without his episodes, there's still a savagery to Vlad that defies every logic. He's a wild beast in an expensive suit, and he knows it. Oh, he definitely knows it as he gives me that wicked grin of his, arching an eyebrow in a quiet dare.

"I just…" I pause, trying to find the words. "I saw him. I saw who he was behind the mask."

"You're probably the first and the last," she mumbles, downing her glass. "I'm going to grab some of that cake," she suddenly changes the topic, her palms over her huge belly, "this kid will be the death of me." She shakes her head, heading to the cake stand.

I mingle a little more with the guests, taking the time to talk a little with everyone in part.

"How are you doing, Katya?" Grabbing a plate of cake, I take a seat next to her.

She's not as far along as Bianca, but her pregnancy has had some complications, so she's not allowed to move a lot.

"Good." She smiles. "Great. This is… wonderful. I'm so

happy for you two," she tells me, her words imbued with warmth as she takes my hands in hers.

Tiberius is next to her, looking out of his element among so many people, his gaze fluttering from side to side as if he expects danger at any moment. His hand is placed protectively over Katya's shoulder and he hasn't moved from her side for a moment.

We still don't know exactly the extent of what happened to them in captivity, and both are currently seeing a therapist to help them deal with the residual trauma. Katya's mentioned in passing, though, that she's had a few other pregnancies before this, but I hadn't probed about what happened to those babies, since it must be a tough subject for her.

"I don't think I could have ever imagined that it would be Vlad who saved me—us," Katya continues, her gaze on her brother. "I always thought there was more to him than what people were saying." She turns toward me. "I'm happy he has you."

"Thank you." I squeeze her hand. "I know it's been hard to get closer to him. But don't give up. He's not the best when it comes to emotions."

"Really?" she asks, amused, pointing to the crowd that's gathered at the back of the garden.

I frown as I see Vlad wheeling in a grill and setting it up, calling out everyone's attention.

"Thank you everyone for coming to celebrate our wedding." He lifts a glass up. "I think I'm supposed to do a speech?" He frowns. "Maybe... or maybe not," he smiles roguishly, "but I'll do one anyway."

Taking off his tux blazer, he drapes it on a chair, slowly folding the sleeves of his shirt.

"The first time I saw Sisi, I knew I could never live without her," he starts and red creeps up my cheeks as I realize what he's doing.

Everyone claps at his words.

"She took one look at me and then ignored me. If that's not love at first sight, then I don't know what is," he continues, everyone chuckling at his joke.

He quickly sobers up though.

"I could stand here and extol her virtues forever, since even her imperfections are perfect to me," he winks at me, "but more than anything I want to thank her."

My eyebrows shoot up, curious at what he has to say. Everyone is listening attentively too, and I think for many this is the first time they are seeing Vlad being anything other than his jokester self.

"Thank you for trying to save me when everyone thought I was doomed. Thank you for *saving* me when everyone gave up on me. And thank you for saving me when *I* thought I was beyond saving." He pauses, an unyielding intensity in his eyes as he looks at me. "That I am here, right now, is all because of you, hell girl. And that's why," he smirks, "moving forward I will live *only* for you."

Everyone claps again, with some people whispering that this can't be the same Vlad they knew.

But as I look at him, so dashing in his plain white shirt and black pants, I can only feel immensely flattered, my heart beating loudly in my chest at his declaration.

"I'd also like to give you a gift," he says, and now I'm

even more curious as I watch him work around the grill before taking off his shirt and sitting down on a chair.

Sasha gets up and goes around him, a small pouch in his hand as he takes out a scalpel.

My mouth parts in surprise as it dawns on me what he's doing.

I'm not the only one completely flabbergasted by this display, gasps erupting around me as the scalpel cuts into Vlad's back, removing a small square of flesh and placing it on the grill.

"I know it's customary for the newlyweds to share cake, but I want to share myself with you, Sisi. If you'll have me."

I stand up on shaky legs, slowly going toward him, my mind in a thousand different places as I realize just how special this is.

"Yes," I answer as I reach his side. Going around his back, I place my hands on his shoulders as I lean in to lick the bits of blood pouring from the cut, closing my lips over his skin. "This is the most wonderful surprise, Vlad," I tell him sincerely.

"But first, I want Sasha to take a piece from me too."

The words are barely out of my mouth as he turns toward me, his eyes wild.

"Hell girl," he groans and I think he's going to refuse. He places his forehead on my shoulder, breathing harshly. "Having a part of you…" he trails off. "I wouldn't dare ask for that."

"You don't have to. It's freely given." I caress his cheek, placing a quick kiss on it before sitting down.

The process is fast and not as painful as I would have imagined.

Vlad's piece is done, while mine is quickly cooking on the hot grill. When we have both a piece of each other in our hands, we look into each other's eyes, slowly bringing the morsel to our mouths.

I watch as his lips close over a piece of me just as I bring the piece of flesh to my mouth.

The burst of flavor is immediate, and it takes everything in me not to moan at the taste. Or even worse, jump on him and tear at his clothes.

He seems to have a similar reaction, and his gaze doesn't stray from me as he slowly chews on the piece of meat.

"You're part of me now, hell girl. Just like I'm part of you," he drawls, his dangerous smile engulfing me whole.

"Yes, we're finally one."

The moment stretches between us, and it's like everything fades away. There's no noise, no people around—just us.

We gaze at each other and I know that what we have is stronger than *anything* in this world. There's nothing that could tear us apart.

Not even death.

Because where one goes, the other follows.

At some point, the guests leave, and we're finally alone. The entire house, though, is a mess and will probably need a thorough cleaning.

"You were such a gentleman today," I praise him, playing with the collar of his shirt and teasing the small expanse of flesh visible.

"Is that so?" he asks, and my eyes zone in on his lips, licking my own in response.

There's just something magnetic the way he pulls me

toward him without even trying. My body just reacts to his, and like a moth drawn to a flame, I can't possibly resist. I want him to consume me.

"Make no mistake, Sisi," he starts, his hands going down my dress until he grips the tulle of my skirt firmly in his fist. "I am still a beast. But now I'm a lucid beast." That dangerous grin again, and in no time, he has the material ripped from my body, shreds falling to the ground as a look of pure satisfaction appears on his face.

"Run, my little nun. Run."

He smiles wolfishly at me, his muscles rippling with withheld tension. His eyes are attuned to my every move, and I know he's ready to pounce.

And what do you do when you have a predator hot on your trail?

You run.

And hope he catches you.

46
VLAD

TWO YEARS LATER

"Are you ready, hell girl?" I move to grab her hand, but she's not next to me.

Turning around, I spot her still struggling to lock her gear in place.

"Sisi," I groan, especially when I see her little frown of concentration and the way she's biting her lip…

Not good for my self-control.

"Just a second," she says, placing a finger up.

Not only does she have a *fuck me now* expression on her face, but she's also drenched in blood, and the combination couldn't be more lethal to my senses.

"Done," she breathes out, relieved. "No matter how many times I do this, I never get it right," she mutters before taking her place next to me, slipping her hand into mine.

"We're already late." I purse my lips, looking at my watch. "The party started thirty minutes ago."

"We'll get there." She pats me on the shoulder, winking at me.

"Let's do this," I say as I open the plane's trap door, the air pressure immediately hitting me in the face.

One look at Sisi and I'm ready to go. Still holding each other's hands, we jump.

Somewhere on the way down we both release our parachutes, safely landing on solid ground.

"How do I look?" she asks as she divests herself of her gear, patting her dress down as if it were the most elegant thing.

"Good," I grimace as the words fly out of my mouth.

She does look good—to me. I'm not sure people will appreciate us showing up drenched in blood from head to toe.

"We look terrible, don't we?" She sighs deeply, her shoulders squared.

"If Bianca wants us to be present, she'll have to receive us like this too." I attempt to cheer her up.

She shakes her head, proceeding to walk in front of me. I don't hesitate as I catch her hand, bringing her into me and swooping her in my arms.

"I think tradition dictates I carry you in my arms." I run my nose around her face, inhaling her scent.

"And who am I to argue with tradition?"

"Good," I chuckle. "I thought you'd have objections. Besides, it's been approximately five hours since I last had you in my arms. I need to catch up."

She mumbles something incoherently, but she eventually smiles at me, not putting up a fight as I carry her toward Bianca and Adrian's house.

Today it's Bianca's birthday, and she's always very anal about everyone attending. And since Sisi and I depend on her expertise at the academy, we can't risk upsetting her.

Soon after Bianca had given birth, her contract in Russia had ended and she'd been in search of a new job. While she's not completely done with private assassinations, she accepted to become an instructor at our academy, V Academy—named so in homage of my sister.

The first year had been a little difficult as things were just taking off, the kids were a little skittish around us as they were getting used to everything.

From the people we'd rescued from Miles' compound, thirteen of them had decided to stay with us, their ages ranging from six all the way to fifteen. All of them had come with different traumas from being Miles' lab rats for so long.

The only thing I'm thankful of is that, from what I gathered, the sexual abuse stopped with the new generation. The guards' interactions with the children were monitored more strictly and no outside interferences were allowed in Miles' plan. Of course, that doesn't exclude Miles' own sick depravities, but the kids haven't been too forthcoming on that front yet.

Because every student was dealing with different traumas, we'd had to make allowances for each one, and that meant designing a standard curriculum, but also targeting each age group separately while also carefully cultivating everyone's personal strengths.

Safe to say, it hasn't been easy organizing everything.

Sisi and I had also started to teach them by example, and sometimes when we go on a mission we would choose a student to accompany us depending on the skills required for that particular mission.

The academy has been a success so far, with the oldest already embarking on missions on his own.

We've also decided recently to expand, and to look for new recruits.

Sisi had come up with a plan to look for people like Seth, who'd been forced into a life of perpetual fighting for a living and who have no skills other than their fists. We would be ensuring their freedom as well as a job if they decide to remain with us.

Just now we'd returned from a mission in Vermont, since some sources had been talking about a child slavery ring in the area. Unfortunately, it had been a bust.

"At least we got to kill some bad guys," Sisi comments, echoing my own thoughts.

"True. If nothing else, we got a little blood shower." I smirk at her.

Considering the state of our clothing, it looks like we had a full on blood bath, not just a shower.

But since today's company isn't likely to be offended by our appearance, then we're not in a hurry to change.

"Hmm," I murmur in her hair. "You look so delectable right now I know what I'd like to do..." I trail off suggestively.

"Party first. Other things..." She bats her lashes at me. "Later."

"You're killing me, hell girl," I complain.

Although my episodes had ceased after I'd found out the truth about Vanya's death, I haven't suddenly become normal.

The thirst for blood is still there—I just have full control over myself now.

And Sisi knows too well just how much I love to see *her* in blood. A turn on for both of us, we'd continued our tradition with the blood baths at least once a month.

It was rather simple. We'd randomly choose some targets from a wanted list, and then we'd kill them until the bath water was fully red. Then, we'd just give in to our animalistic urges in a mating that usually leaves us both out of commission for at least a day.

And looking at her cheeks, so prettily flushed, her mouth slightly parted, I know she wants it—yearns for it.

Luckily, before my thoughts can take a rather dark turn, we arrive at Bianca's place.

"Took you long enough," Bianca says as soon as she sees us standing on her doorstep. But one closer look and she scrunches her nose at us. "For fuck's sake, couldn't you have taken a shower?" She shakes her head, urging us inside and toward the bathroom.

"There are children around." She narrows her eyes at us, as if we've committed the worst offense. "Take these clothes and come out when you're clean. *No blood!*" she exclaims, thrusting some clothes into our arms.

She doesn't wait for a reply as she turns on her heels, returning to the main area of the house.

I guess motherhood only made her more irascible.

The party is in full swing, music blasting in the house.

And as I look down at Sisi, her baffled expression mirroring my own, we both start laughing.

"We forgot to tell her happy birthday."

"I don't think she would have appreciated it in our

current states," I add dryly, opening the door to the bathroom and putting the clean clothes on a rack.

"For an assassin she's very sensitive when it comes to blood."

"She's always been like that. She prefers neat kills." I roll my eyes, because where's the fun in that?

"Her loss." Sisi shrugs, slowly unbuttoning her dress and shimming out of it.

"But do you know what this means?" I ask as my eyes become fixed on her sinful body. She knows what she's doing as she's seductively removing her underwear until her naked flesh is all on display.

And all mine.

In two steps I'm behind her, my front fitted to her back as I slowly move my fingers down her shoulders.

"We have time for a quickie," I whisper in her ear.

Her breath hitches, her pulse picking up as I continue to languidly caress her skin.

"Fuck," she mutters, the sound of her husky voice going straight to my cock. "I've been waiting for this all day," she says, quickly turning around to face me.

"Hell girl," I rasp when I feel her hand moving down my chest before she cups me through my pants. "I've been walking around with a raging hard-on ever since you pulled the knife from that man's throat," I breathe out, the image forming in my mind again. "The blood gushing out and bathing you in red… Hades in the ninth circle of hell but I would have fucked you right there on top of his corpse if the police hadn't showed up."

She purrs at my words, her nose leaning into me and

breathing me in, her hands grabbing the hem of my shirt and pulling it over my head.

"And I would have loved that," she replies just as her lips close over my neck, sucking and licking her way up.

"Fuck," I curse out, too impatient to wait.

Grabbing her by the nape, I bring her forcefully into me, all the pent-up desire exploding in one kiss. I open my mouth on top of hers, devouring her very essence as I feel her curves mold to my body, my erection nestled against her stomach.

Her fingers go lower as she fumbles with my zipper, pulling my pants down and wrapping her hand around me.

"Sisi," I groan at the feeling. "I need you now," I tell her, my hands going to her ass as I lift her up, impaling her on my cock in one swift thrust. She's already soaked, her pussy easily taking me inside, her tight heat wrapped around me and welcoming me home.

She moans deep in her throat, and I push her up against the wall, her back hitting the cold tiles as I start pumping in and out of her.

My hands splayed on her ribcage, her legs wrapped around my waist, I continue to viciously kiss her just as I aggressively thrust into her, letting her feel just how much she affects me—how much she owns me.

"I can't believe I lasted until now," I tell her in between harsh breaths.

"Me neither," she whimpers. "I kept clenching my thighs on the plane," she pauses on a moan, "hoping you'd notice and…" she cries out when I hit a spot deep inside her, "And take me. Fuck, Vlad, harder," she commands me and I can only obey.

Her eyes are half-closed, her rosy mouth parted as she mewls every time I advance and retreat.

"Oh, I noticed alright." I bring my mouth down her neck, my teeth nibbling at the sensitive skin. "But I knew once I started I couldn't have stopped until I had you on your knees and begging for mercy. We would have never made it here."

She knows this too. If I'd gotten even one hand under her dress, then it would have been game over.

"Even this is torture," I continue, sucking hard on her skin and leaving my mark. "Since it's just an appetizer."

"Tonight," she moans, "I need more," she prolongs the sound as her pussy clenches around me, her legs tightening around my body as she comes.

"Tonight," I repeat, my hand trailing up her body until I close my fingers over her neck, "I'll have time to destroy you."

Her eyes roll in the back of her head as she gives herself over to the pleasure, and that alone is enough to send me over the edge too, my cock swelling inside even more as I come deep in her pussy.

"It's a promise," she says as I lower her down.

My cum is running down the inside of her thigh, and I swipe it up with a finger, bringing it to her mouth. Her eyes on me, she opens up, sucking my finger in.

"I want you all marked, hell girl. I want everyone to see, smell and hear who you belong to," I whisper as I lean into her, leaving another love bite on her neck, just in case the first one wasn't visible enough.

"Yes," she breathes out, barely holding her balance as she teeters toward me.

"I wonder if our host would prefer cum instead of blood." I tenderly caress her face. "I'd have you draped in it…" My fingers brush her nipples and she gasps, her pupils so fucking dilated they engulf her irises. "Cum dripping from every inch of your skin…"

"Tonight," she says in that breathy tone of hers and I'm already hard again.

But we still have to emerge from the bathroom and mingle with the guests, so we quickly shower, after which I can't help myself from fucking her again, this time making sure my seed stays inside of her, so that she feels me every time she takes a step.

"I didn't realize it takes you hours to shower." Bianca arches an eyebrow when we finally emerge from the bathroom.

"There was a lot of blood," Sisi shrugs, her expression so genuine you wouldn't think to contradict her.

"Whatever." B shrugs, her eyes suddenly narrowing behind us. "Diana, no! Not the knife," she yells before running toward her daughter.

"Happy Birthday, B," I call out from behind, wanting to ensure we don't forget the reason we're here.

She doesn't seem to hear, and while she oversees the children, we start mingling with the other guests.

We end up bumping into Allegra and Catalina, both currently very pregnant and in the middle of a discussion on child rearing.

"Did you guys plan on giving birth at the same time?" Sisi asks, leaning into me.

"No, but somehow it happened," Allegra chuckles. "At least they will have someone close in age to play with."

"I can't believe you're not going crazy with so many children."

"You get used to it," Lina says before scrunching her nose, "eventually."

"Any plans for you, Sisi?" Allegra asks suggestively, and I note the slight blush on Sisi's cheeks.

"At some point. We're still in the honeymoon phase." She winks, gazing up at me for confirmation.

"What Sisi wants, she gets," I reply, squeezing her hand.

We'd had lengthy discussions on the topic, and we'd both agreed that if we do have children, it's going to be later.

I'd told her that I'm ready to have one whenever she desires, but she'd replied that she wants to have more time to ourselves. Deep down, I think she's scared of having another miscarriage like last time, and I know it was one of the darkest periods in her life. If that's the case, then I can only be there for her and support her decision when the time comes.

Fuck knows, I love having her all to myself, *all* of the time. But maybe a little Sisi running around the house wouldn't be so bad.

At some point.

"For now, he's enough," she says softly, raising on her tiptoes to give me a kiss.

"When you do, you'll have us to help. I'm sure we know all the tricks by now," Lina mentions, amused.

"Oh, especially when it comes to raising them." Allegra purses her lips, shaking her head. "They're all cute little monsters until they grow up. That's when the real nightmare begins."

"Tell me about it," Lina sighs, "Claudia is going through puberty and I don't think we've ever had worse disagreements than now."

"Come on, Lina. She's a great kid."

"I think she's been learning from Venezia and her teenage rebellion. Now that's another issue Marcello and I have been dealing with," she sighs. "She's gotten it into her head that she wants to finish high school at a public school."

"Would it be so bad? She needs some sort of normality, Lina. You know she's never had any outside friends," Sisi comments.

"I don't know… That's what I'm afraid of. She's young and too naïve to let her go out in the world by herself."

"She needs to experience the world at some point. Think of this as easing her into it."

I can tell that Sisi's a little peeved about their reluctance with Venezia.

Since we'd redone the house in Brighton Beach, Venezia had become a permanent fixture, visiting almost weekly. She and Sisi had developed a very close bond and Sisi's been trying to convince Lina and Marcello to give her a little freedom for a while now. Even with no danger looming in the horizon, Marcello hadn't been too enthusiastic about sending his baby sister to a public school.

"Why don't you let her try it for a semester at least? Who knows, she might not like it. But at least let her experience it on her own," Sisi continues.

"We'll think about it," Lina replies, the most she's probably willing to acquiesce. "That's right, did you hear about Raf?" She quickly changes the topic.

My hand immediately tightens on Sisi's shoulder at his name, mostly because I'm still bitter that she almost married him.

"No." She frowns. "Did they find him? What happened?"

"He was spotted running with some cartel people. Marcello got an account about him but... He doesn't seem like the same Raf you knew, Sisi."

"What do you mean?"

"He's the right hand man of the boss. It's an obscure cartel, only recently appeared on the map."

"Fenix," I add grimly.

"You know about it?" Sisi turns to me.

"Not exactly. I know about its existence, but since it doesn't interfere with my business, I've never looked deeper into it." I shrug.

"But how could he have ended up with them? Why not come back and take his rightful place?"

Not long after Rafaelo's mysterious disappearance, Benedicto had suspiciously up and died, leaving Michele in control of everything within the famiglia.

"Michele put a price on his head. He can't step anywhere on the East Coast without every assassin in the area hunting for him," I answer grimly.

Sisi turns her sharp gaze toward me, and I know what she's thinking. Why did I never tell her about that?

But how could I when I go mad with jealousy just thinking about him? When I want to go on a killing spree when anyone mentions his name? He may be *only* her friend, but to me he is a reminder that I could have lost her.

And I can't stomach that thought.

The girls continue chatting while I stay stiffly by Sisi's side, trying to think of ways I can redeem myself with her.

And when she drags me in a darker corner of the house where the music isn't so loud, I know I only have a small window of time to plead my case.

"Before you say anything, hell girl. Yes, I knew about the bounty on his head, but I had no idea he'd been sighted. That cartel is mostly active in New Mexico, so I had no reason to dig deeper."

"But why wouldn't you tell me? We share *everything*," she replies and I feel the slight disappointment in her voice.

"I don't like it when you talk about him," I admit in a low voice. "It takes everything in me not to go into a murderous rage when he's mentioned."

"Vlad," she sighs, "he's my friend. He's never been *anything* but my friend."

"I know. But I can't help it, hell girl. The mere thought that you could have married him haunts me even now. I *can't* not be jealous, even when I know I shouldn't be."

"You silly beast." She shakes her head, a small smile playing on her lips as she punches me playfully. "You know you're the only one for me," she murmurs softly.

"I do. I do," I whisper against her hair as I hug her to me. "But that doesn't mean I'll stop being jealous. *Ever*."

Not when I know what a prize she is and what a lucky bastard I am for her to even look in my direction.

"Well..." she trails off, "you're lucky sometimes I like it when you're jealous," she continues as she trails her finger over my chest, "when you revert to a caveman state and have your wicked way with me."

"Fuck, Sisi." I grab her hand, my breathing ragged as I

struggle for an ounce of self-control. "You're driving me crazy."

"Not now," she retorts saucily. "Tonight."

"Tonight," I repeat bleakly, already counting down the seconds.

<h1 style="text-align:center">SISI</h1>

ONE YEAR LATER

When we decided to try for a baby, I expected to be slightly anxious considering what happened in the past. But what I did *not* expect was for Vlad to be the one who was *most* anxious.

From the time we took the first positive pregnancy test, he's been by my side twenty-four seven. And by that I mean that even when I go to the bathroom, he waits by the door and he asks question after question to ensure I'm all right.

At first, it was sweet. But as time went on, he became more and more overbearing. To the point that he's enrolled us in three different expecting parents courses, because in his own words: *we have to be ready for any eventuality.*

I'm six months along now, and I desperately wish to be done with this pregnancy. Not only because I can't wait to meet our little one, but also because I need to go back to having a modicum of privacy.

Not that before the pregnancy I had much, but I could at least go to the bathroom by myself, or make myself a sandwich without a shadow hanging over my shoulder.

Vlad, being Vlad, will not let me eat anything until he reads off the label to make sure there isn't any type of toxic substance inside the food item. He's become so bad with his 'food safety' rules that he now will not let me eat anything that's overly processed.

Next thing I know, he might as well open a bakery, a butcher's shop or even an entire chicken farm just to make sure the products come from a safe environment.

"Hell Girl!" He calls my name as he thuds down the hallway. I'm propped up on a chair watching TV when he comes inside the room with a huge grin on his face.

"What is it?" I raise a brow, expecting something outlandish.

"I have great news!"

I narrow my eyes. Lately, our definitions of 'great news' haven't aligned as much.

"Do tell," I add drily.

"I finally closed the deal on that business."

I tilt my head to the side.

"What business?" I don't remember him mentioning anything about a certain *business*. Then again, with pregnancy brain, I've filtered out most information about business—he does have a *lot* of those. Sometimes I don't even know how he has time for it. He's always *here*. And yet, he always has time to run an insane amount of business and *not* run them into the ground.

I've always found that fascinating about him, my clever boy.

"It's the beef jerky you like," he says, pride emanating from his voice.

"Say what?" I take my legs off the chair and get into a seating position as I glare at him.

"The one you always order online? I told you I wasn't exactly sure how organic they were but you loved it so much that I didn't want you to stop on my account."

I blink. "So you did what?"

"I made them an offer they couldn't refuse. Now I have access to all their accounts and certifications and I am happy to say they *are* organic." He smiles to himself.

I'm still in shock. While I jokingly thought he might do something like this, I did not expect him to…actually go through with it.

"You bought off the company?"

"On the bright side, now you can have all the beef jerky you want! And they also own another side business, it's a monthly subscription box of the top cuts of beef. So that's an added perk."

"Yes, the monthly subscription I have," I mention drily.

"And now you can have it for free! How cool is that? And I can vouch the beef is top quality. You know, you can never trust labels these days. At least now you can eat in peace knowing it's the best of the best."

"Vlad… I was already eating it in peace."

"Well…" He scratches the back of his head. "Now *I* can watch you eat in peace."

I close my eyes and massage my temples.

"Since this is out in the open, tell me, what else have you done that I might not have any knowledge of?"

"W-why do you think I might have done something?" He stammers, eyes wide like a deer caught in headlights.

"Spill it."

Panic enters his features.

"I—"

"The truth, Vlad. I want the entire truth."

"Well…" he clears his throat and straightens his back. "Not *that* much."

I let out a long sigh—it *is* that much.

Tapping my foot on the floor, I wait for him to continue.

"The supplements you've been taking. Supplements are never FDA approved, and I saw they had this little thing called *proprietary blend*, and you *never* know what a company might put in that and not disclose it."

"So you bought it off?"

"Not entirely, just enough stocks so I could have access to the information. I'll have you know I attended a board meeting and demanded they add more transparency to their labels. I've also visited their labs and they seem to be safe. The formula, too, is good—I consulted with a doctor on it, I'll have you know."

"What else?"

"Uhm…"

"Vlad, it's the moment of truth."

"Let's see. I really did not do *that* much, all right? It's just that I was worried about some products you used."

"What products?"

"Your shampoo and body wash," he blurts out. "Any small amount of toxins might be bad for the baby."

"So you bought it off too?"

"Just enough stocks so I could ensure their testing is rigorous enough for pregnant women."

Good Lord! This is getting out of hand. And I don't even think we've scratched the surface.

"Fine, what else?"

"A chicken farm!"

My lashes flutter in disbelief. Perhaps I have a knack for clairvoyance because damn… I was on point.

"You eat eggs daily. I couldn't let you eat some *random* eggs. Who knows how some people take care of their chicken?"

"So you bought a chicken farm to what? Spoil the chicken?"

"Well, yes. But this was right around the time you got pregnant. Haven't you noticed how much better the eggs are? The flavor alone is much more potent."

"Good God, Vlad. What else?"

"Why are you looking at me like that? I did what I thought best." He says with a pout and he reminds me of a cute puppy. I shake my head at him. He won't win me over with his cuteness today—not until I get all the information out of him.

"Vlad, tell me."

He takes a brief moment to speak. And that's how I know we have barely scratched the surface.

"You also eat a lot of cheese…" he adds sheepishly.

"All right, got it, you bought a cheesemaker."

"Actually, I invested in an Amish-run farm and that gets us all the best cheese and milk—most natural too. No preservatives."

Another sigh.

"Continue."

"I bought stocks in a few other companies, but nothing over the top, just baby toys and other baby products—I *have* to make sure they don't have any toxic substances in them," he adds vehemently.

"Oh, Vlad…"

"Are you mad at me? Please say you're not mad."

He comes over to my side and drops to his knees in front of me. Placing a quick kiss to my bump, he lays his head on my stomach as he wraps his arms around me.

"I'm not mad. But you've gone overboard with this."

"I know, but I need to make sure anything you consume is good for you and the baby."

"I appreciate everything you do," I murmur as I thread my fingers through his thick locks. "You'll be the best dad."

He lifts his head up, his eyes wide and hopeful.

"You think so?"

"I *know* it."

XANTHIYA KUZNETSOVA CAME WAILING INTO THE WORLD AND into the waiting arms of her father. Classic Vlad, he would not let anyone else help with the birth—no, he got a midwife certificate to do it all himself.

Poor girl, she might have to wait until she's seventy to date with such an overbearing father.

But one thing is for sure: she will be so loved, she will never have to wonder what love feels like.

THE END

Curious about Marcello and Lina? Read Monster in Disguise. For more on Rafaelo and Michele, read the War of Sins Series.